“Geoff Hazel has given the world a [illegible]sight into his work as an Australian in his role as United Nations Police Officer — who have the courage to stand up for democracy — and to call out those who shoot and maim in a cowardly way, those little people in Indonesia who are fighting for their right to live as they please in a democratic society. The work of the UN was essential then and will continue to be as long as individual freedom is threatened.”
— Elizabeth Jess, author of *John Jess, Seeker of Justice*

“With the twentieth anniversary of the independence referendum in East Timor just passed, many younger Australians are asking what it was all about and how Australians came to be involved, not just in supervising and securing the referendum but in the dramatic events that followed. Geoff Hazel answers many of those questions. He served as a deployed member of the Australian Federal Police in the mountainous region of Ermera during the referendum, and his book, Picture a Dry Riverbed, is an important contribution to the joint history of East Timor and Australia. Written almost exclusively in a narrative style, it is a well-written and fast paced book that tells an interesting and exciting story of those turbulent times. It is a book that would be of equal interest to those with similar experiences or for the history novice or curious readers more broadly. The author is able to call on his significant experience serving in Vietnam, and later with the United Nations in Cyprus and Mozambique to provide a useful context for the reader on a number of levels. The text is nicely accompanied by a series of high-quality and relevant photographs which enhance the story-telling and provide depth to the narrative. The inclusion of italicised versions of reports written contemporaneously adds authenticity and drama

to the narrative. There is occasional deviation from the overall narrative with the inclusion of useful dialogue and perhaps more of this might have enhanced the appeal to a wider audience. Nevertheless, this book is a key contribution to the history of East Timor more generally and most particularly one of the most important events in their history; the 1999 referendum, which later lead to the establishment of the new nation of Timor Leste. Those with an interest in this subject will not be disappointed."
—Reviewed by Mick Pert, author of *The Kissing House*

"Until now I have known very little about the work that the United Nations does and so I found Geoff Hazel's book to be a very powerful, informative & humanised insight into the sensitive & dangerous tasks assigned to the UN. Certainly an eye opener into the complex interrelationships between politicians, police, militia, UN personnel, volunteers, students and the differing ethics & needs of local community groups. From a historical perspective, I now have a much better understanding of the issues facing East Timor & Indonesia.

I very much enjoyed Geoff's first person writing style, the respectful way he managed his own personnel & his professional, cooperative approach to the many numerous "incidents".

I had difficulty putting this book to one side. I wanted to know more. All this despite having to navigate the numerous acronyms, all of which are entirely necessary. For me the Glossary was an essential tool. The images were a bonus & enhanced my understanding of the people & the environment."
— Kate Clements, *A Flight Against All Odds: Scotland to Australia in 1968*

"What a fascinating story of the Australian Federal Police involvement in the East Timor self-determination struggle. Told in fine

detail by one who was not only on the ground, but was right in the middle of the action. This campaign is, to a large extent, unfortunately overlooked by history. Mr Hazel has done a fine job of bringing it all to very vivid life. Top Read!"
— Ian Dolby, author of the *Firebird* series

"Geoff Hazel has given us a fascinating insight into the life of the Peacekeeping Company during the vote for independence in East Timor in 1999: With very basic creature comforts and certainly no instruction book, and with a backdrop of gun shots and villagers with machetes, they were tasked with creating order out of chaos, so that the voting might go ahead. They showed extraordinary courage. This story deserves to be told and Geoff has made us understand the human side of such an event. Great reading, anyone who enjoys history and politics will find this story of the utmost interest. Glad you found your voice Geoff and congratulations to you and your team on a job well done. What a momentous event to be a part of !"
— Alison Lewis, author of *Seasons of Life* & *Missing*

"A great read, well written and factually interesting. It took me back 20yrs!! Refreshingly accurate account of what apparently happened in Ermera!

One comment: that incident at Ermera on Polling Day with the truckload of Militia that were blocking the intersection that Crazy had to pass through on his way back to Gleno, was in my recollection, a little more 'up close and personal' than me standing on a table in the Polling centre. I recall that I was having quite a 'long chat' with the Militia head at the time with the barrel of his automatic inches from my face and attempting to persuade Polri to do their job!! I was also having a 3way conversation on the radio with Crazy, Jim France and Sandra whilst trying to

resolve the impasse. It was finally resolved and the rest is history. Cant wait till its published. You write very well. Proud to have served with you and all 'The Turtles' mate. Will never forget that 3 months in '99."
— Don Barnby, ex Army SAS, served in Vietnam, became a police officer and served on three Peacekeeping missions

"I have really enjoyed every page so far. (I have flicked back & forth between different chapters & now I need to start at the beginning & read it properly)

I dread to think how many hours you have invested in this Geoff.

I'm not just trying to being polite here Geoff — But I really like the style of writing as well as the content.

There are so many things / people you mention, that I had forgotten about. (Plus some things which I never knew about)."
— Rob Walker, UK CivPol

Picture a Dry Riverbed

Dangerous days:
a personal story of
unarmed Aussie coppers
in East Timor in 1999.

GEOFF HAZEL

Published in Australia by Sid Harta Publishers Pty Ltd,
ABN: 34 632 585 203
17 Coleman Parade, GLEN WAVERLEY VIC 3150 Australia
Telephone: +61 3 9560 9920, Facsimile: +61 3 9545 1742
E-mail: author@sidharta.com.au

First published in Australia 2019
This edition published 2019

Cover design, typesetting: WorkingType (www.workingtype.com.au)

Hazel, Geoff
Picture a Dry Riverbed
ISBN: 978-1-921030-89-5
pp348

ABOUT THE AUTHOR

The author was born in 1948 and grew up in and around Army camps in Victoria and New South Wales. His final schooling was at Granville Boys High School where he was a member of the schools debating and basketball teams. He was also the Senior Under Officer in the schools Army Cadet unit.

On his 17th birthday he entered the Defence Recruiting Centre in Sydney. Sixty eight days later he was enlisted into the Australian Regular Army. After recruit and infantry training he was posted to 3rd Battalion the Royal Australian Regiment which was then based in Woodside, South Australia. A few months later (he can tell you the exact dates) he met is future wife, Margaret, on a blind date. They were married the following year only months before his deployment with the battalion for his first tour of duty in South Vietnam. During that tour, amongst other scraps, he was involved in the Tet Offensive 1968 and the Battle of Coral/Balmoral, the Battalion was later awarded the Unit Citation for Gallantry for this action. On return to Australia he was posted as a recruit training instructor and his son, Leigh, was born in Wagga Wagga 12 months later.

In late 1969 he was invited to become a member of the Australian Army Training Team Vietnam and he went on to serve in that unit as an adviser to South Vietnamese forces during 1970-71. He proudly wears the two citations, USA and South Vietnam, awarded to that unit.

After this tour he received some career advice from a former company commander and resigned from the army on 8 September 1972 and was sworn into the Australian Capital

Territory Police on 11 September 1972. In 1979 the ACT Police became a founding part of the new Australian Federal Police. He undertook many roles and rose through the ranks becoming a commissioned officer in 1990.

Early 1992 was his first deployment as a UN peacekeeper, this time in Cyprus. In 1994 he was the contingent commander for the 2nd AFP contingent to the UN mission in Mozambique. 1999 saw him deployed as the UN Civilian Police commander in the district of Ermera, East Timor where the contingent was awarded the Australian Group Bravery Citation. In 2001 he was the senior peacekeeper, all facets, on Malaita Island as part of the International Peace Monitoring Team, Solomon Islands. In 2003 he returned to Cyprus this time as the AFP contingent commander and the commander for all UN police on that mission. From here he accepted an invite to spend a short period of time with the Department of Peace Keeping Operations, New York.

In 2004 he retired and undertook some consultancy work and become a volunteer with Red Cross in their Emergency Services area. Medical issues eventually led to him withdrawing from the Red Cross but he still volunteers with Legacy.

Dedicated to our heroes, the families who stayed at home in the past, now and who will in the future.

ACKNOWLEDGEMENTS

All my rolls of film remained in the vehicle when I was evacuated from Dili, fortunately others who served with me were more than willing to send me photos they had taken to make sure I had at least a reasonable photo record of the times. Shortly after our final evacuation and at my request many of them also provided documents on their experiences. We have remained in contact and recently they have all given approval for their documents or photographs to be included in this book. Without them it would not be the same story.

In order of when they arrived in Gleno my thanks goes to the following police officers — Paul Morris (Aust), Don Barnby (Aust), Rob Mills (NZ), Wayne Corbett (NZ), Phillip Hunter (Aust), Brett Swan (Aust), Max Knoth (Aust), John Tanti (Aust), David Savage (Aust), Tom Kinsella(USA), Randy Martinak (USA), Peter Watt (Aust) and Rob Walker (UK).

In addition, I need to thank Associate Professor Bob Breen OAM, Deakin University, and Tammy Pemper, author of Scorched Earth, for their constructive evaluations.

With special thanks to the late Right Honourable Tim Fischer, former Deputy Prime Minister of Australia, when launching his book *Ballot and Bullets — Seven Days in East Timor* his first four words were "Picture a Dry Riverbed.".

GLOSSARY OF TERMS

AEC Australian Electoral Commission.

AFP Australian Federal Police.

Brimob *Brigade Mobil* or *Brimob* (mobile brigade) A special branch of *Polri* (see below) with a paramilitary role to conduct security stabilization operations and providing security protection for VIP or vital facilities.

Bupati The Major or Regent (Indonesian: *Bupati*) of a Regency (District) which is the level of local government smaller than a province. *Bupati's* are elected by popular vote in the Regency for a 5 years term.

Cemat Local dialect for village chief.

CivPol (also UNCivPol) Term for United Nations Civilian Police that came into effect in 1964. In 1999 the United Nations was in the process of changing the term to UNPol — United Nations Police.

CNRT East Timorese political party.

DEO District Electoral Officer; in UNAMET a volunteer for UN service.

Ex-pat an abbreviated form of expatriate. A person temporarily or permanently residing in a country and culture other than that of the person's upbringing or legal residence.

Falantil Falantil (or FALANTIL) originally began as the military wing of Fretilin (see below) in response to conflicting political interests with the other parties. The name FALANTIL is an acronym of its full name in Portuguese, *Forças Armadas da Libertação Nacional de Timor-Leste.* This translates as 'The Armed Forces for the National Liberation of East Timor'.

FRETILIN a socialist political party established in East Timor on 20 August 1975.

Hercules (Herc) The Lockheed C-130 Hercules is a four-engine turboprop military transport aircraft. It is the main tactical airlifter for many military forces worldwide.

IDP Internally Displaced Person, sometimes incorrectly referred to as refugees.

INTERFET The International Force for East Timor (INTERFET) was a multinational peacekeeping taskforce, mandated by the UN to address the humanitarian and security crisis that occurred immediately after the results of Popular Consultation ballot were announced.

JOC UN Joint Operations Centre based in Dili. Included representatives from all operational components of UNAMET (see below). Senior CivPol officers were rostered as Duty Officers in the JOC 24 hours a day.

KaPolda Indonesian police, Commanding Officer of a Province.

KaPolres Indonesian police, Commanding Officer of a District.

Kopassus	abbreviation for *KomandoPasukanKhusus* (Army Special Force Command) is an Indonesian Army special forces group that conducts special operations missions for the Indonesian government.
Kiwi	Nickname for person from New Zealand.
LO	Liaison Officer.
LZ	Landing Zone — also known as Helipad. Designated place for helicopters to land.
MLO	Military Liaison Officer.
NCO	Non-commissioned officer.
ONUMOZ	Organisation Nations United, Mozambique 1993-1994.
POLRI	The Indonesian National Police (*Kepolisian Negara Republik Indonesia*) is the official police force. Prior to 1999 a part of TNI (see below).
Polda	Indonesian police headquarters for a Province.
Polres	Indonesian police headquarters for a District.
RAAF	Royal Australian Air Force.
Satphone	Satellite telephone.
SRSG	Special Representative of the Secretary General of the United Nations. The leader of UNAMET and the most senior UN person present in the mission.
TNI	*Tentara Nasional Indonesia*. The Armed Forces of Indonesia. Formerly *Angkatan Bersenjata Republik Indonesia* which was known by the acronym ABRI) and in those times *Polri* was under direct ABRI command. TNI includes the Indonesian Army (TNI-AD).
UN	United Nations.
UNAMET	United Nations Assistance Mission East Timor.
UNCivPol	(UNPol) See CivPol.

PREFACE

The last sound I remember hearing was a barrage of automatic weapon fire and Max Knoth near me saying, 'You can relax boss, you got us here safely and we're alive. Someone else is making all the decisions now,' before everything went fuzzy.

I blacked out.

I had the feeling my eyes were open. Had minutes, hours passed? I could hear the unmistakable rumble of the four powerful turboprop engines. I was no longer in the UN headquarters in Dili. That's where I had been. I had to work out where I was now. I forced the fuzziness from my head, blinking back white spots. Through a strange haze in which the world around me was swirling I could slowly make out the curved metal above me covered with the wires and cables providing the controlling mechanisms for the aircraft. My brain acknowledged that from previous flights, I was obviously in a C130 Hercules transport aircraft.

Instead of sitting down in the same way I'd arrived in Timor a couple of months earlier, I was lying flat on my back. From what I could see I knew I was on a stretcher. They were evacuating me from Timor. If I could will my muscles to move, I'd fight the evacuation. But my body wasn't responding. Not from pain. I felt no pain.

As I gritted my teeth and heaved myself into a sitting position, I saw the Loadmaster standing at the end of the stretcher.

I said, 'How did I get here?'

He patted me on the leg and replied, 'Lay down mate, you're ten minutes from Darwin.'

That's not how I wanted to leave Timor, not like this. Where were my men and women? Where were those who served with me? I wanted to get up. Nothing. My mind and muscles rebelled. I felt the hand on my leg again. My eyes closed and the now familiar darkness rushed in and took over.

My eyes flicked open. Across the room I could see a youthful, winsome apparition in a nurse's uniform. I saw her put my backpack into a wardrobe and she was in the process of shutting the door. I had to stop her. Attempting to speak seemed to be one of the most difficult things I had ever done. My throat and mouth had never felt so dry. I heard a tired, croaky voice. It didn't sound like me, but I could feel my mouth moving and I'm sure my brain sent the instructions.

I distinctly heard, 'That bag has to stay within arm's reach.' I guessed the words came from my throat.

She turned towards me and smiled. 'It's good to see you awake.'

She came over to the side of the bed; checked the drip-feeding liquid into my right arm and started taking observations. You know, pulse, blood pressure and all the things they do regularly in hospital. While she was doing this, I used the communications skills I could muster to convince her that I really had to have the backpack within arm's reach. I must have been a little convincing because straight after the observations she got it from the wardrobe and put it right beside the bed.

I could reach out and touch it, and immediately I felt safer. I leaned back and sighed. For eight days that bag had held my life in it. Each of the men and women under my command carried one. Food, clothing, water, first aid kit, spare clothes, malaria pills and letters from home. Everything I — we — needed for survival.

Our safety had always been under threat but in those last days the threat to our safety, in fact our lives, multiplied which meant we had to be constantly ready for an immediate evacuation. So, the bag was always kept close. In the end all other options vanished, and we evacuated.

I remember asking a lot of questions. Where was I? Plus, all those supplementary questions a police officer always wants to know. What, When, Why and How? She told me I had been medically evacuated and was now in Darwin Hospital.

Then the nurse turned to the other bed in the room. I glanced at the patient to see if by some off chance I would recognise him. The first thing I noticed was that the tall, heavyset man had a large bandage across his abdomen, which the nurse was checking. Later, when we were both feeling better, he introduced himself as Earl Chandler, an American Police Officer. He'd arrived in Timor a little after me and had been deployed to Liquicia District.

After the UN had announced the results of the referendum in Timor, 'Big Earl' had been shot in the gut by a high-powered military rifle during the evacuation from the UN compound in Liquicia. How long ago was that? Three days, maybe a little more, I guessed. I heard the front entrance to his compound had come under direct attack by a large, well-armed group. To survive, Earl and his team of unarmed UN personnel surprised their attackers by doing the unexpected. They jumped into their vehicles and drove out through the wall at the rear of their compound. Though this enabled them to escape from the main group of attackers, they came under small arms fire from several other locations. This was when Earl was hit. All of their vehicles took hits from the gunfire and most of the other UN people had bullets slice past them. Now Earl was lying there wearing only boxer shorts and a bandage around his middle.

The nurse walked to his bed; Earl's words caught both of us

completely by surprise 'I bet you're just dying to see me naked.' Although the 'naked' was pronounced in an American drawl, 'neckid'.

I still did not know exactly what was wrong with me. I recall very little of those first few days except a fuzziness. I think more often asleep than awake but then the awake bits felt a little like I was still asleep. The support and care from the nursing staff has stuck in my mind. They were the greatest. Much as I wanted to, I couldn't find a way, nor ever could, to adequately express my appreciation. During my waking moments they even took me and my intravenous fluid bottle onto the balcony where, especially in the early days, they always had a cigarette or two for me. Gradually my weary body, and brain, recovered. I was told it was complete physical and mental exhaustion and, dehydration.

So now the story of how I got here and the group who worked with me and gave themselves the name, 'Ermera Turtles'.

CHAPTER 1

Initiation of the Mission

The Situation

This story of East Timor's journey to independence started many years ago but for my purpose I'm starting this story in early 1999. After years of guerrilla resistance to Indonesian rule, the President of Indonesia offered the East Timorese people a vote on their political future. At first the options were — become an autonomous region or remain a normal province within Indonesia. For many reasons the options changed to a question of whether the East Timorese people wanted their end of the island of Timor to become an autonomous region within Indonesia or be an independent micro-state. The Indonesian armed forces, custodians of a unified Indonesia, were opposed to their President's offer of independence for East Timor. The province they had invaded in the 1970s was likely to vote for independence. Years of fighting and bloodshed to suppress an independence movement would have been for nothing.

As a result of international negotiations, and with the approval of the UN Security Council, an agreement was reached for the United Nations to prepare for and conduct what was called the Popular Consultation. In an amazingly short order, plans, negotiation, organisation and training where implemented for the formation and deployment of an international mission into East Timor. Included in this process was the deployment of police personnel from 29 nations as United Nations Civilian Police

(CivPol) officers. The mission mandate had two tasks for this group: protect the ballot boxes; and to advise the Indonesian Police.

They both would prove to be difficult and dangerous. Playing my part in the successful completion of this mission would require me to call on every bit of training and experience from my previous 35 years of service in the Army, Australian Federal Police (AFP) and on secondment as a UN CivPol to other UN missions. I was assigned to lead the CivPol in the Ermera District. The individuals working with me would be from all around the world and the working environment in Ermera, as was to be the case for all districts, would prove to be intimidating, violent and ultimately life threatening.

LOCATION MAP: EAST TIMOR

Districts of East Timor

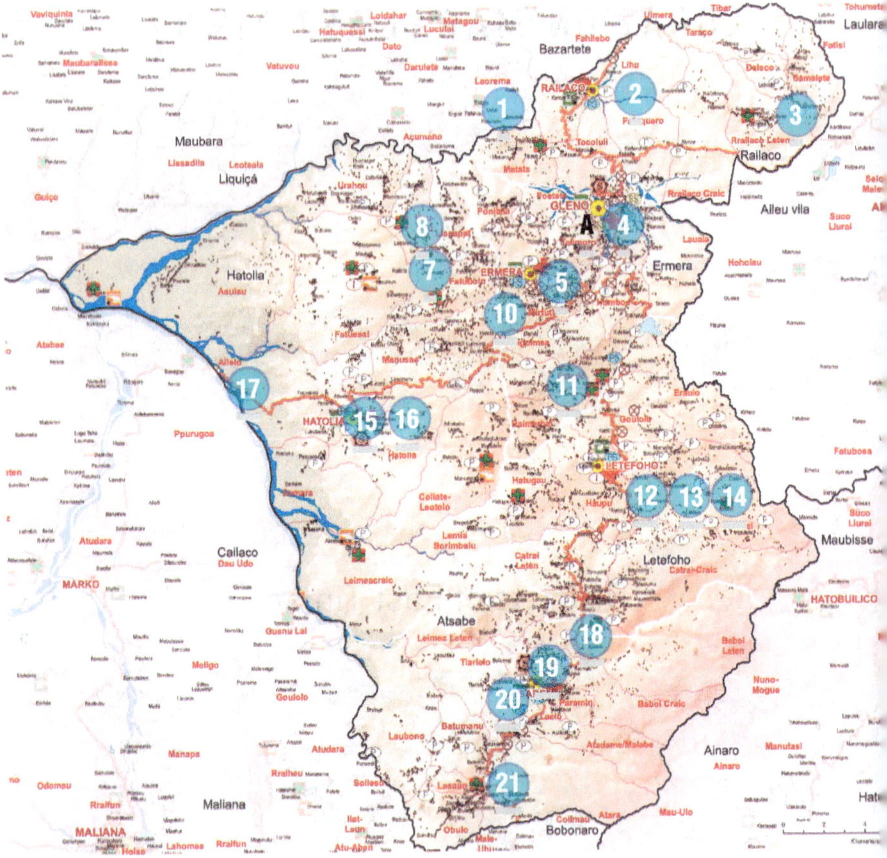
Bazartete
RAILACO
Railaco
Laulara
Maubara
Liquiçá
Lissadila
Leoteala
Vatuvou
Leorema
Aculmano
Tocoluli
GLENO
Ermera
ERMERA
Aileu vila
Hatolia
HATOLIA
Fatubolo
Manusae
Ppurugoa
Cailaco
Dau Udo
MARKO
Atsabe
Leimea Leten
LETEFOHO
Letefoho
Maubisse
HATOBUILICO
Ainaro
Maliana
MALIANA
Bobonaro
Lahomea
Odomau
Atudara
Goulolo
Meligo
Manapa
Laubono
Batumanu
Babol Craic
Atadame/Malabe
Mau-Ulo
Manutasi
Atara
Lasaun
Hohotau
Fatuboea
Suco Liurai
Hatugau
Coilate-Leotelo
Lemia Sorimbalu
Catrai Leten
Catrai-Craic
Leimeacraic
Guanu Lai
Railaco Leten
Railaco Craic
Taraço
Tibar
Ulmera
Fahilebo
Lihu
Deleco
Samalete
Fatisi
Tohumeta
Atabae
Guiço
Maubaralissa
Veviquinia
Loidahar
Hatuquessi
Lucutai
Dato
Darulete
Metagou
Urahou
Ponilala
Matata
Ramboe
Estado
Paramin
Tiarlelo
Leimea Leten
Eraulo
Goulolo
Hatolia
Atudara
Rraifun
Holsa
Nuno-Mogue
Babol Leten
Sollesu
Rralheu
Lauala
Ilat-Laun
Atu-Aben
Obulo
Colmau
Lacio
A
1
2
3
4
5
7
8
10
11
12
13
14
15
16
17
18
19
20
21

1.	Leorema	Morris
2.	Railaco	Mills then Robert
3.	Railaco Leten	Nitaya
4.	Gleno	Pena and Watt
5.	Ermera Village	Barnby
6.	Potete	Corbett
7.	Fatubesse	Ruslan
8.	Fatubolo	Ali
9.	Homboe	Cubell
10.	Mirtutu	Martinak
11.	Estado	Amorin then Diouf
12, 13, 14	Letfoho	Delmer, Robin and Ashraf
15, 16	Hatolia	Swann and Tanti
17	Sare	Kinsella
18	Launa	Hunter
19	Bobo Leten	Natsakon
20	Atsabe	Somchai (Sam)
21	Lasaun	Knoth
A	Headquarters	Hazel, France and Mills

CHAPTER 2

Last Night in Darwin

Thursday 1 July 1999 was my last night in Darwin. It was spent as a sardine. I slept in one fifth part of a converted steel sea container set in one of four seemingly endless rows dropped into place as temporary housing for UNAMET personnel transiting to East Timor. Each container was divided into five 'bedrooms'. Each bedroom was for two persons and just wide enough at the entrance for the fitted window and door. Inside were narrow bunk beds against one of the metal walls, a small metal table, a very narrow wardrobe, and no chair. Room between the bed and wall was so tight walking sideways with your toes under the bed was the most efficient way to move about. At the back of each room there was a second window, fifty per cent of which was filled with an ancient air conditioning unit. When turned on the resulting rattles and shakes were loud, and the din vibrated off the metal walls. But without that infernal machine the heat would have been unbearable.

When we arrived in Darwin a few days before the senior Non Commissioned Officers (NCOs) of the detachment had managed to persuade the senior Australian Air Force (RAAF) NCO, also known as 'The MAN', in charge of allocating accommodation that me, as 'the boss' and a senior AFP member should, at the very least, get a room by himself. I considered this very thoughtful of them. In fact, their mission had a more practical objective. Shortly after I moved in, detachment members arrived and piled their excess baggage and the contingent equipment on the top bunk. Fortunately, I had already decided to sleep in the bottom bunk! Even with their practical reasoning I heard whispers of another reason. No one wanted to sleep in the same room as a boss who snored like a lumberjack. For whatever their reason, I appreciated their effort.

As of right now there was no more time or possibility, even though in the back of the mind there was a desire, for a last-minute dash to the food stores of Darwin. It was too late to get additional non-perishable food and then overcome the impracticality of squeezing more into the two allowed bags, one a large backpack and the second a canvas carryall. Prior to departing Canberra these bags were already packed to the limit. Tightly packed in were uniforms, issue equipment, first aid kits, personal items, a little bit of civilian clothing, every bit of non-perishable food they were capable of containing and toilet paper. Experience from previous deployments taught me it was not possible to have enough of the final item on the list. Further space was non-existent. Of course, not everyone had the same priorities. One member had substituted 120 kilograms of personal training weights in lieu of food items! Personal choices can be quirky.

A miracle had happened on the flights to Darwin. The contents of the bags compressed so shopping expeditions, the plural is correct, to town resulted in the purchase of an additional $250 worth of food which was manipulated into every corner of the bags. Why did I do this? Because food is an essential and I had heard about difficulties in this area. We already had a nickname for East Timor, 'Jenny Craig Island'. Known and expected issues dictated the food purchases be non-perishable, tinned stuff, condensed milk, powdered potato and spices were the most desirable. Not to forget the soft toilet paper.

With anticipation I closed the zipper for the final time, and it held. It was all in, including some vegemite. The bags were delivered to the RAAF.

With the bags gone it had been time for the last evening meal at the RAAF Other Ranks Mess. It was a barn of a building more the size of an aircraft hangar than a dining room, but it was the only eating area on base big enough to manage the feeding of all the police, military, UN employees and volunteers who had arrived from around the world.

After dinner I did the short walk to the beer garden of the Sergeants Mess for what would be my last drink before departure. For most this was a cold beer. But I had a different need. I had little doubt, if I really wanted it, I would be able to get beer of some sort where we were going. On the other hand, I had no doubt a reasonable Aussie red wine would probably be unattainable. I would miss it with dinner. So, it was a bottle of Penfold's red for me with two extra glasses, for I knew others would join me. Even this was not the same as home, because in Darwin to keep wine for even the shortest period it is stored in the refrigerator. So, the bottle came cold and the wine too cool to start with.

The blood red rays of the setting sun cast a reflected ruby glow as we sat beneath the palm trees of the RAAF Sergeants Mess beer garden. From the deep shadow of the covered bar the television picture was bright and crystal clear.

The 7 o'clock news started. The first video clip had an immediate impact. Throughout the bar area the chatter in a dozen or more languages ceased. On screen were two UN personnel, one of whom was Australian CivPol Craig MANN. They were providing First Aid to bloodied East Timorese villagers. Cowering in a corner behind them were women and children, fear so great even on the small TV screen it could be seen in their eyes. The background sounds were clear and unmistakable; gunfire;

screams of terror; and, every now and then, the ominous thud of a large, solid object striking the side of the building.

Over this the reporter's fervent tones told the story. The location was the town of Maliana, East Timor. The UN had been holding an educational session on the forthcoming Popular Consultation. Two unarmed UN Police officers were acting as security for a UN Volunteer, who was informing local people about the program for registration and voting in the upcoming ballot.

Pro Indonesian armed Militia attacked this group. People were shot, slashed with machetes, and struck with large rocks and anything else that could be used as a bludgeoning weapon. The two unarmed UN Police officers stayed on site and were providing as much First Aid as they could from their personal kits. The UN Volunteer went to the local Indonesian Police (Polri) to get assistance. But, according to the news report, the assistance took a very long time to arrive.

After the news item there was silence. In living colour, we had seen and heard what tomorrow would probably bring. My mind was running through the emotions. There was moisture in my eyes, it must have been from airborne dust for I was too tough for tears, shock and surprise that such a brazen attack would be carried out in the presence of UN personnel and the international media. I felt apprehension, if I was honest, and guilt, guilt because I was still in Darwin.

Seconds later the silence broke with the babble of multiple languages. The sound was almost palpable. If the attack was intended to strike such fear in our minds so we would decline to serve, it failed. Fear was there but it was held in check by an increased determination now not only fuelled by professionalism, but also by that bit of guilt and a whole lot of anger. It had already become personal.

Nobody stayed late that night. After sharing the bottle of

red with a number of old and new friends I headed off to my bottom bunk. Training was over, administration complete, we were inbound, as a fully-fledged part of UNAMET, the United Nations Assistance Mission East Timor.

CHAPTER 3

Arrival 2 July 1999

4.45 a.m. What an ungodly hour to get out of bed. It had been hard to sleep. Troubled thoughts. Many uncertainties. The news last night coupled with the nervous energy and anticipation had kept my mind whirling. Add the rattling air conditioner and it is amazing I got any sleep at all. But I did get a little, just before the pounding on the door announced it was time to get up and get moving.

At 7.05 a.m. we were all on board the white over grey C130 Hercules transport aircraft with a big black UN painted on the sides. We were a very mixed international group; males and females; Police (CivPol), Military Liaison Officers (MLOs), UN permanent staff and United Nations Volunteers (UNVs) from the full variety of occupations vital to create the components necessary for a successful mission.

Hercules aircraft, known as Hercs, are not comfortable. Passengers on these aircraft are generally in the non-paying category, therefore, creature comforts have never been considered essential. There is no sound insulation, so ear protection is highly recommended. The RAAF supply disposable ear plugs that do an acceptable job. The interior is one of pure working aircraft; wires, cables and other unfashionable pieces; no wasted cosmetic internal covering, just working bits capable of rapid re-arrangement to accommodate a wide variety of uses.

In our case the front half of the cargo area had been fitted with rows of narrow seats that bore a vague resemblance to those found on a civilian passenger plane. But the rows were much closer together and the seats did not recline. Access was by one central aisle with about 8 narrow seats on either side. There was a small space between the outside seats and the curved fuselage. Seat belts were fitted but knee space was at a premium. At the rear was cargo, including our personal bags, strapped down on pallets. There was one toilet at the rear of the cargo bay, fitted just above floor level, in front of the ramp on the starboard (left) side. It was in clear view of anyone who cared to turn their head. The only augmentation for privacy was a pull-around curtain. No one was seen to use this facility during our 90-minute flight.

Opportunities to look out the few small windows were limited, but as we came in to land the aircraft banked and I had a brief glimpse of a large town to the left. The rest of the view was ocean or sky to the right and jungle covered mountains to the left.

The landing was uneventful. As the pilot taxied the aircraft to the terminal the rear ramp was already being lowered. Tropical heat and humidity immediately flooded the entire cargo bay. Smells penetrated, combinations of diesel fumes, rotting vegetation, exotic foodstuffs and, well, whatever! Within 24 hours, these aromas would be just part of daily life. But that initial burst had an impact on my olfactory sense. Once the aircraft stopped it did not take long to disembark. I felt that tinge of excitement and expectation which always comes at the start of something completely new. This time it came with just a little tinge of anxiety.

In front of us was a strip of mown grass about 60 metres long, just wide enough for one vehicle, leading between two stands of head high tropical grass to a low, unimpressive red-brown building. This building was the international airport terminal. The dense sound of motorised transport, predominantly diesel and two-stroke, could be heard but not seen. Turning through a full 360 degrees revealed the blackness of the tarred runway and aircraft parking area and green; the blue green of mountains in the distance; the grey green of long tropical grasses; and, the yellow green of banana, palm and other tropical trees. Without the noise and the runway, I could have been miles from civilisation.

An old forklift with smoke pouring from the exhaust bounced its way down the mown path and dropped a pallet of baggage. It was up to us to unpack and only moments into it I knew not all of our bags had arrived. I queried one of the local staff. He responded by shrugging his shoulders and indicating no more pallets would be brought to the passengers.

One of our more language-gifted passengers elicited the rest would be going through customs as freight. In Darwin we had heard about freight. Freight took days, if not weeks, to clear customs. There was no way my precious food stocks were going to be put through as FREIGHT! I decided it was time to walk onto the tarmac and look at the other pallets, which I could now see being dumped by the decrepit forklift. I knew they held our personal luggage and therefore felt completely justified. For a blink of an eye there was just a hint that a very young, armed and uniformed Indonesian Police (Polri) officer would resist my going onto the tarmac, but the purposeful look on my face seems to have satisfied him he was facing an obviously senior officer, whose battered blue beret and ribbon bars indicated experience and knowledge which gave him the authority to do what he wanted. Only a little bluff, but I was very glad it worked.

Two of the pallets held a mixture of personnel bags, including trunks for the New Zealand contingent, known as Kiwis, and UN computer equipment. Now the computer equipment was freight, the rest was not. With a few brief orders I organised the group, who were as keen as me to get hold of their bags. The pallets were unpacked, and the personal items passed down a human chain to the terminal building. The computer equipment was then repacked onto one pallet. I never did find out, or care, if the arrival of an empty pallet created any problems. I, and all the others, now had all our personal belongings.

After the bright sunshine on the tarmac the inside of the terminal building was dark. It was also very hot and so humid it was uncomfortably sticky. The electrical equipment, such as lights and air conditioning, weren't working. They could have been switched 'Off' but I doubted they worked at all. One small area had working electricity and was well lit. From there enough light spilled over to allow us to move around while avoiding the obstacles scattered throughout. In the glare of the well-lit area we could see a number of persons in uniform; some were Polri, others in uniforms I presumed were customs or immigration. I could also see machines bearing at least a resemblance to baggage X-ray equipment and metal detection archways.

Sweating and uncomfortable, we were directed towards those machines. The sooner we got out of that building the better. Again, I got the chain passing system into action. Not only was this the best way of moving our stuff, it also made it a little more difficult for the officials to identify pieces of luggage with a particular individual. Surprisingly there was no resistance to this from the authorities. In Darwin we had been told horror stories of officious and obstructionist authorities, but they just put it all through the machine without comment. At the same time, we all walked through the metal detector. Was the metal detector working? I don't know but as a simple observation lot of us where in uniforms with metal accoutrements and it did not 'bleep' for anyone. This would indicate some issue. Perhaps the setting was very generous, it was not switched on, or, it did not work at all. Perhaps it was just there to impress us.

Once on the far side we waited as the bags went through the

X-ray and were thrown into a pile. Nothing was allowed to be touched.

Then, once all bags were through, 'Okay you can go'.

That was it. We had completed the whole process in a matter of minutes. The chain was re-established, and the bags and trunks moved through the land side door and onto the waiting UN transport. We were out of the building and into the more comfortable warmth of direct sunlight. We were in East Timor.

Me, Dave Savage and John Tanti part of the chain passing to the UN vehicles.

If the terminal building had been hot and muggy, the UN bus I caught was even worse. A good number of us, no one really knew how many but definitely more than the 23-seat capacity of the bus, were jammed on board. It had no working air conditioner and a motor that whistled and wheezed and emitted the most horrendous fumes. Fortunately for me an American police officer saved a seat in the back row, second in from the door. Even though we were packed in like sardines propping open the back door allowed a breeze to funnel in, evaporating most of the sweat and providing a slim cooling effect. It also blew away those exhaust fumes.

The views we experienced on our drive through Dili, the capital of East Timor, were typical of towns in most troubled developing nations. Dust was everywhere; low level buildings were in obvious need of maintenance; in any open space there was long grass with banana and palm trees; no sealed footpaths, nor gutters for the rain; children playing with makeshift toys in the streets; scraggly dogs and chickens by the dozens; small stands and shops selling cigarettes and 'cool' drinks along the roadside; the occasional take away food stand; DVD and CD shops, were they selling pirate copies; and the smell of diesel fumes.

'Does it look much like Vietnam?' asked someone.

It didn't take me long to consider memories of my two 12-month tours of duty in the Vietnam War and the much later peacekeeping missions in Cyprus and Mozambique.

'Except for differences in the people it looks and smells exactly like Vietnam,' I quickly replied.

This part of our journey ended at the Hotel Dili. In its time it was probably up market. Now it just looked run down and the high outside wall needed a fresh coat of paint. Immediately inside was a large courtyard where it was difficult to see the paving through the layer of grime and dust. Leaning against the inside of the front wall were a number of small structures serving as a kitchen, a shop and an eating area. Scattered throughout the courtyard were small round tables with pink plastic chairs and large grass umbrellas. At the far end of the courtyard was a wide sweeping stairway that went up the one level to what had been a grand entrance. The balustrades and stairs were crumbling at the edges. It just looked tired, but I could see that it had been magnificent.

UN administrative personnel, known as Field Service Administrators (FSAs), were waiting for us. They told us this was where new people were brought while they waited for deployment to the districts. Those assigned to Dili would have to use their UN allowances to find their own accommodation but, in the meantime, you could pay for a temporary accommodation right here. While I did not get to see the individual rooms in the hotel, I did go into what had once been the grand entrance foyer. This was now jammed with UN-issue mosquito nets spread over single beds all with luggage piled at one end. Privacy was non-existent. I never found out if individual rooms even existed, but I presumed they were there and had been allocated to the females. Or perhaps they just went to those prepared to pay more.

We were now sorted into groups according to the districts in which we would be serving. I would be deployed to the district of Ermera with AFP Officers Phil Hunter, Brett Swan, John 'Turbo' Tanti and Max Knoth. I was told a small group of UN volunteers, who had arrived a couple of days earlier, would also be travelling with us to Ermera.

CHAPTER 4

The Role

The UN Police Commissioner, retired Australian AFP officer on contract Alan Mills, arrived shortly after. He had given general briefings during the training phase in Darwin. Today he told me I was being deployed as the CivPol Commander in the District of Ermera. Our conversation included a short personal briefing for me on the little information on Ermera he had. It was still very early days in the mission and knowledge was at a premium. Everyone was still on a 'steep learning curve' trying to get 'situational awareness' — what was going on and what did that mean for getting the job done? His final words in the briefing were there are a number of relatively large South American contingents yet to arrive and to ensure equality across the different nationalities, combined with the relative ranks and experience the contingent commanders should have, there was a high probability that he would have to replace me as the district commander with one of them.

For reasons both professional and personal, I requested a change in the allocation of personnel. I would like Dave Savage to be reassigned to Ermera. Dave had served with me in Mozambique and I knew he was an exceptionally capable worker in uncertain environments, and, of more immediate importance, he was a great cook. In fact, a lot of the foodstuffs in my bags had been purchased at Dave's direction to complement items he had purchased and packed. The Commissioner told me my high professional regard was exactly why Dave was being sent to Maliana. He had the necessary experience to provide support vital to another AFP member who was on his first mission.

Then he added, 'if I had known about his culinary skills, I would have been tempted to keep him at headquarters.'

'I put Knoth and Tanti with you because I am a bit concerned about them. I know you can manage them but I'm uncertain of interaction between them and senior officers from other nations', the Commissioner said.

Although sorry not to have Dave, I saw having both John and Max in a distinctly positive light. They both stood tall, over 190cms, 6 foot with a good plus in the old measurement and were relatively young and very fit. I was also just over 6-foot-tall but they had a few centimetres on me. I had no trouble visualising them standing on either side of me whenever serious troubles arose. It was a very comforting picture in a land of males of modest stature. We were unarmed so a strong physical presence was likely to be helpful.

Those staying in Dili headed off to find accommodation. For the remainder of us it was supposed to be only a short wait until the convoys arrived to take us to our districts. Three convoys of six vehicles, each vehicle with a locally employed driver, were due to arrive at the hotel. In the UN plans sometimes go astray, today was one of those days. Two convoys of six convoys arrived and with them were two vehicles of the third convoy. As luck would have it, the convoy missing four vehicles was the one allocated to Ermera. Through interpreters I questioned some of the drivers and it slowly came to light the other four vehicles had driven out of the transport yard and turned right instead of left. No one had seen them since. Past experience convinced me this was the last we would see of those four vehicles. I didn't know it at the time, but this would become my first lesson in East Timor. First impressions can never be relied on, never make assumptions.

The vehicles themselves were a bit of a surprise. They were brand new Land Rover Discovery's, full four-wheel drive (4WD) vehicles. I later found out they had been in a warehouse in Japan for two years while the Rover company unsuccessfully attempted to break into the Japanese 4WD market, the home of Toyota Land Cruisers and many others. When the UN had an urgent need for 4WD vehicles the company saw an excellent opportunity and the UN got them for a very good price. While new the long storage was to be the cause of some early troubles as tyres tended to brittleness and batteries had a bad habit of going flat. The bonnets of the early vehicles had been unprofessionally hand-painted white and affixed with a large black UN sticker. A white UN sticker had been placed on each of the front doors.

The other convoys loaded up and departed. The Ermera crew just had to hang around while attempts were made to locate our missing vehicles. So, with nothing much else to do we decided to try the food at the hotel café, or was it a shop or restaurant, it was very hard to tell. From the blackboard menu hamburgers appeared to be the safest choice, even though the price was a little rich. When I finally got mine, I knew the price had been very rich. The buns looked like hamburger buns, but only about one third the size. The bread was so dry it was probably a week old. Then there was the meat, well, whatever the thin bit of grey material was that should have been meat. It tasted like, really it didn't taste at all. Finally, the salad, one thin slice of what looked like a small tomato. When I added the exorbitant price of the 'cold' drink I could have had a very good meal in a Darwin café.

My lack of appreciation of this situation became even worse when I found out the operator of the whole business was an ex-pat Australian. Even though a few spoke to him there was no chance he was going to do the right thing and look after his countrymen. Apparently on arrival of the UN he had immediately altered his prices, UP! In coming months some justice would be served as other premises opened and the Hotel Dili became the venue of last resort for all internationals.

After four hours of waiting I managed to get agreement for us to load up the two Land Rovers and, with the assistance of a headquarters Hyundai van and its driver, travel to Ermera via the UN warehouse, where we were to pick up supplies. The Hyundai would then return to Dili with the escort.

CHAPTER 5

The Trip to Gleno

We piled on board with our bags and headed for the UN warehouse. There I met JJ, the head storeman. Now JJ was a short thin man with a broad northern English accent and very poor dress sense. When he smiled you could see it had been a long time since a dentist had seen the inside of his mouth. He was a most unusual storeman. He had a policy for stores to be issued as quickly as possible to the people in the field. He did not believe in holding on to them for judicious counting and reporting. In Australian service organisations such storemen are a very rare commodity.

When I told him who I was, he told me we were too late, the Ermera supplies had already been picked up. Between us we came up with a best guess that the missing four vehicles of our convoy had also made off with the supplies. We had no trouble agreeing that both vehicles, rations, water and equipment were long gone. Given this assumption, he agreed to provide whatever he could as a replacement and directed contingent members to the equipment and supplies they could load. JJ and I then sat and chatted, exchanging stories about our previous missions and further discussing the likelihood of ever seeing those four vehicles and the equipment again. While he was thus occupied everyone else loaded vehicles with everything they had been pointed to and everything else it was possible to fit in, especially ration packs and bottled water. JJ did not ask for a signature for anything.

With the vehicles loaded it was time to depart. Prior to leaving

I needed to empty the bladder. JJ just directed to any wall inside the warehouse as the building had no actual toilet, inside or out. This turned out to be one of the luckiest toilet breaks I have ever taken. Walking down the warehouse I saw a pallet with stretchers on it that looked remarkably like the ones purchased by the AFP for the contingent. They should have been issued to individuals while they were in Darwin but somehow, before we arrived, they had all been shipped to Dili as freight. When I asked JJ, he told me they were the Australian stretchers and he would be most happy if I took them off his hands. Room was found, they were loaded on board, and we drove off. Later that night we would be very glad I had needed to go to the toilet at just that time and location.

From there it was a short drive through Dili's twisting streets to Polri Headquarters. We had been told to go there to seek approval for travel and, for our safety, to get a Polri escort. I must admit for the whole day I was continually geographically embarrassed by the seemingly endless number of twists and turns we made in our brief travels around Dili. It would take a couple of visits before I was comfortable in quickly locating everything I needed to do in the city.

As we drove west along the divided 4-lane highway I noticed the Polri Headquarters sign ahead. The surrounding wall and main gate of the complex was freshly painted and in very good repair. Inside the compound all the buildings looked well maintained. The walkways, grounds and building surrounds were all clean and tidy. It gave an impression of a disciplined, efficient organisation.

We stopped near the Headquarters building and as I got out of the vehicle Polri personnel standing or sitting nearby reacted immediately. They stood to attention and the senior NCO saluted, showing respect to my rank. From the propaganda we had heard in Australia this was the opposite to the reaction I expected. Another NCO approached and in good English offered to escort me to the Operations Centre. We walked to the nearby building, the largest I could see in the compound, and entered after crossing the wide covered verandah.

The majority of this building was taken up with a large central room. On the verandah side, which faced the east, was the main door and full-length windows, now fully open with a slight breeze being dragged in by the ceiling fans. Inside were high ceilings and the windows on all other sides were smaller and set up high. Large ceiling fans slowly circulated giving an impression of coolness. On the wall opposite were various maps of East Timor and its districts. In the centre was a large table. When I entered the outer area, I saw two senior UN Police officers from Dili in deep discussion at the central table with two senior Polri officers.

A relatively young officer wearing a 'Liaison Officer' brassard on his right arm approached. I explained why I was there and that I hoped to get an escort to Ermera. I included an apology for arriving at a far later time than expected. In excellent English he informed me I should wait until the senior duty officer was free from the other meeting and politely showed me to a set of lounge chairs by the large windows.

We sat and chatted, over two cups of coffee each, for about 20 minutes. Primarily he was seeking to ascertain the meaning of each service ribbon on my uniform. The discussion at the main table continued. For most of the time I was not able to clearly hear or understand what was said, however, there were occasions when the volume increased from one or both sides; heat was regularly entering into their discussion. As best as I could work out neither party had any intent or willingness to compromise and the discussions were going nowhere. After a particularly loud session the Dili UN officers left. My Liaison Officer (LO) immediately went over to speak with his superiors.

In a matter of moments, the two officers, both majors, came over and joined me. One was the Polri Headquarters duty officer and the other was the Officer in Charge of all Brimob in East Timor (Korps Brigade Mobil- Mobile Brigade Corps, abbreviated Brimob is the special operations and paramilitary unit within the Indonesian National Police (Polri). It is also known as one of the oldest existing units within Polri having been established in 1945 to assist in disarming Japanese soldiers. Some of its main duties are counter terrorism, riot control and high-risk law enforcement where the use of firearms may be needed.) Polri and Brimob had all been members of the Indonesian Armed Forces until 1 April 1999 when a government reform was implemented to create police forces separate to the Indonesian Army. In both manner and demeanour members of Polri and Brimob were similar to army personnel.

We commenced our discussion with coffee, my third cup, and brief personal introductions. Once we got down to business, I realised the LO had properly briefed his superiors because they quickly explained to me the convoy for Ermera, with its escort, had left some hours ago. I apologised for our late arrival and explained our missing vehicle problem. This generated a good laugh from everyone present and they agreed with me the UN was unlikely to see those vehicles again. They offered to try to locate them for me when I provided further descriptive information.

As I was still hoping to get to Ermera I asked them, as a complete newcomer, what procedure I needed to follow to get an escort for the following day. At the same time, I indicated I would appreciate advice on where to find a place to feed and accommodate my contingent and myself for the night. There was a short conversation between the two of them and then the Brimob Major, through the LO, informed me accommodation would not be necessary as he would personally escort me and my convoy to Gleno, which was the administrative centre of the Ermera District, and we would leave almost immediately.

While hoping for an offer of this kind I have to admit I had not expected success. I quickly seized the opportunity by promptly agreeing and sincerely thanking him. Apart from an intense desire to begin work, I had the ulterior motive of getting as far from the Dili UN Headquarters as soon as possible. In most work situations my level of contentment can be inversely calculated according to the distance between me and the headquarters above me.

The Major went off to make his arrangements and I went outside to inform the contingent of our good fortune. I found the four police officers had been split up and each was standing with separate group of Polri. They appeared to be in enjoyable and good-natured conversations and by listening for a short time I realised the Polri were just as curious about us as we were about them.

I hopped into the Hyundai and we left first. Fuel requirements dictated a stop had to be made for the Hyundai at the service station just down the highway. While the driver was filling the vehicle, the convoy drove past. A Brimob vehicle in front, the two UN vehicles and a Polri vehicle at the rear. They were not travelling fast, and I expected no trouble to catch up.

The van filled, the bill paid, and we drove out of the station.

As we hit the highway the driver asked me, 'Do you think this car is petrol or diesel?'

I had seen the diesel sticker on the dashboard, 'It's a diesel.'

Before he had time to answer, the engine cut out and we drifted to a halt. He had filled it with petrol. Now we were sitting 600 metres from the service station on the edge of a two lane 'highway' in a vehicle that was going nowhere, no radio, farmlands on both sides, in a foreign country going through a form of civil war; and night was closing in.

Was I apprehensive? Was I ever! Was it warranted? I do not know. Fortunately for us my new Brimob friend realised we had not caught up and had returned. The van was going nowhere and there was no room in the other UN vehicles for me or the equipment. The Brimob Major offered to put the equipment in his vehicles and indicated I could travel with him. Before we left, he arranged for the UN to get the location of the van and its driver. I felt a little concern at leaving him there by himself, but I was informed he would be perfectly safe and back in Dili long before we got to Gleno.

That was the start of an interesting two-hour trip to Gleno. While I had been geographically out of sorts inside the city, now I knew where I was as I had studied maps in Darwin. We were heading west along the coastline. On our right were rock formations, dark coloured sand and the sea. On our left were the foothills of a mountain range.

At the first fork in the road we went left, the general direction was south, and we were going inland. The sign to the right said Liquicia. Straight after the intersection we commenced climbing the first of the foothills that began our journey into the mountains. It was a hill I would from then on refer to as the best part of Dili. The first hill out of town. The temperature and humidity started dropping almost as soon as the front wheels commenced the climb. Of course, it may also have had something to do with the distance increasing between me and HQ.

Inquisitive conversation was the order of the day. Considerable help was provided by the young constable who sat in the back with me; he had an excellent command of English. The small incident with the mistake about fuel turned out to be an excellent conversation 'ice breaker'. Through the young constable the Major and I talked about past experiences, it was obvious he was assessing my experience, skills and attitude to the mission at hand. Of benefit to me he explained a bit more on the recent separation of Polri from the Indonesian military. As part of this he stated, at least at officer level, service in the military was seen as more important than service in the police. From his perspective most military officers regarded the police as a second-rate organisation that should still be under the control of the military. When they had been one organisation military units had always had priority over police for personnel and resources. Since the split Polri, including Brimob, still felt TNI tried to deny them the resources they needed.

The young constable doing the translating provided some extra information when he told me Polri were trying very hard to establish themselves as equal to the TNI and from his perspective the officer level members were almost desperate in their attempt to gain respect. Respect from the people, respect within the international law enforcement community and, most importantly to them, respect from the TNI officer corps. He was a very perceptive young constable.

Apparently, the way I requested assistance caught them a bit by surprise. From everything they had been told before the UN arrived, they expected nothing but arrogance from Australian police and that had been their experience up until that time.

From my perspective it was a very worthwhile trip. I had learnt a lot on the best way to relate to Polri officers. In reality it would be similar, but not quite the same, to my deployment as part of the Australian Army Training Team Vietnam so many years ago. Knowledge and experience from that deployment had played its part in my approach earlier that day.

As we slowly climbed into the mountains, I had the opportunity to look around and begin to develop an understanding of the topography. The road twisted and turned its way around the walls of the ridges with steep drops into ravines and valleys on the other side. At the same time, it was a seemingly endless climb. The very narrow road was sealed; well most of it was sealed. There were some broken up sections that had not been repaired, as yet, I hoped! It was a very narrow road. On most of it two vehicles travelling in opposite directions could just pass each other. However, there were parts where if one of the vehicles was a truck or a bus someone had to stop and get off to the side of the road, occasionally one would have to reverse to a wider spot. With the Brimob vehicle in front it was never us who got off to the side of the road or did the reversing. There were even a couple of spots where it looked like a giant had stood in the valley below and taken a great bite out of the road. In those places I wondered how far the undermining went below what was left. No guard rail existed on the roads and looking over the edge was an unpleasant experience.

I am sure I have never been on such a winding road in all my life. In later days, after driving further inland from Gleno, I would change my mind and consider this road to be 'straight'. While looking at mountainous terrain, the steep valleys and the thick undergrowth I understood how it had assisted the Australian Commandos to be so effective in their fight with the greater number of Japanese soldiers during World War II. Falantil, the East Timorese insurgents fighting for independence, had gained the same advantage in their campaign against the Indonesian forces. This topography when combined with support of the local population was ideal for a guerrilla fighting.

By the time we reached the highest point the blackness of a moonless night had fallen. As we crossed the final ridgeline, I could see the lights of a good-sized town in front of us.

'Gleno' the Major informed me.

From the apparent distance of the lights I expected we would arrive in five minutes. But it took a further 15 minutes of winding our way down and around the valley wall till we reached the edge of town. On a solidly constructed concrete bridge we crossed the 60-metre wide dry riverbed. Once across this I was in the outskirts of Gleno. Immediately on the left was the camp of the locally based battalion of Indonesian troops. Then the town itself. In the dark of the early evening it was difficult to make out. But I got a general perception of decay.

After what seemed like another dozen turns, we had gone past the local Polri HQ and were pulling into a semi-circular dirt driveway. There was enough light to see a low, sad, green coloured building. Out front flew the blue and white UN flag. This was UN District Headquarters, Ermera. We had arrived.

UN HQ in Gleno, now in a distinctive UN blue that Nicolai painted in one day.

CHAPTER 6

The First 15 Hours in Ermera

After an enthusiastic and good-hearted farewell our Polri escort headed off back to Dili. I turned and walked the few steps to the low stone wall in front of the headquarters building, down three steps and across the 4-metre strip of flat, dusty ground before climbing the three wooden steps to the narrow front verandah. Entering the front doors, I was immediately welcomed by the few people were there. All were volunteers from the electoral teams who were writing letters, reading or preparing for the following day.

From one of the offices Samulcia Brownie, the UN Security Officer for Ermera and a former government minister in Liberia, came over to introduce himself.

As the Security Officer he had a few questions. 'Who are you?' 'Why are you here?'

Initially he had trouble accepting my answers because he was not expecting further CivPol for at least 3 to 4 days. But, after a telephone call to someone in Dili, he was convinced we were where we belonged, and he wholeheartedly joined the welcome. This quickly became a deluge of information exchange from all sides as we sought information on Ermera and they wanted updates on the outside world. Others arrived and joined in. I am not sure how much I assumed in that first hectic hour, but I am sure it was only a small part of the total information given.

Samulcia apologised for the absence of the Regional Coordinator (head of the electoral component of UNAMET in Ermera) telling me he had already finished for the day. He was sure we could catch up early tomorrow as there were plans to insert two electoral teams into the Hatolia sub-district in the morning. Before our arrival the plan was to put just the electoral workers in, but now I should allocate two of my new CivPol to these teams and they could travel on the same convoy. By now the crowd gathered to meet us included the UN volunteers going to Hatolia. They quickly made it known they were much happier knowing CivPol would be with them. To them CivPol meant safety and security.

It was not the job of CivPol to protect international personnel or locally employed East Timorese electoral staff, but it was to become obvious all CivPol had to accept this role and meet the challenge in the constant intimidating environment. The quality of UN staff was uneven. There were experienced UN Field Staff at one end of the spectrum and enthusiastic but inexperienced UN Volunteers on the other end of the spectrum. The UN had deployed hundreds of UNV to make up the numbers of electoral officials required to educate the population on a secret voting process and then conduct the ballot on the day. For a number of these people English was a second, or even third, language. A potential problem that was overcome by the enthusiasm of all involved.

The majority of the locally employed East Timorese had little, if any, experience in the roles they would be fulfilling. Training had to be conducted on everything and communicating with those whose English was rudimentary made this a bit more difficult. One of the criteria for employing local staff was to have some understanding of English, the official language of the mission. In their favour was an immense desire to do well.

Samulcia had a task for me. He told me I had to contact Polri to arrange travel approval and an escort for the next day's team placement. It seemed a reasonable task, but I couldn't remember my way back to the local police station, even though it had been pointed out as we drove past. So, I thought it might require bit of effort to get this job done. Then my immediate thought was, work has started already, no settling in time on this mission. From now I would have to find ways and means to achieve what was obviously not impossible, just complex or difficult. Settling in was something that would just have to fit in around the work.

From this relatively brief meeting I now knew that assumptions made in Australia about the working environment in East Timor were irrelevant. The people in each of the eight UN districts would not be based centrally. Travel times between villages dictated that Ermera, and every other district, would have to distribute small groups of electoral officials to sub-district locations. It was either that or allow travelling time to consume too much working time. The challenge for me was to adapt to these new circumstances, gather information about the sub districts and develop plans to meet the new requirements in Ermera. East Timor had depended on the Indonesians to conduct elections, now it was the UN's job to do so without meaningful Indonesian support. Though to me at this time the provision of escorts had been cooperative and good-natured.

In his early planning the Ermera Electoral Coordinator had decided there would be three subdistricts with three to five electoral teams based in each. The remaining teams would operate out of Gleno. Sub districts were to be set up as the people, equipment and vehicles became available. The very next day would show us that even this break up was insufficient to ensure complete coverage of the entire District. A fourth sub-district would be required.

From a range of discussions, I gathered the intention was for each electoral team to consist of two District Electoral Officers

(DEOs), in all cases they were UNVs; a CivPol Officer, allocated by me; and two or more locally-employed East Timorese staff, one as a driver and the other/s as general hands. Each team would have a Land Rover Discovery vehicle. Driving was a role most of the CivPol members felt more comfortable doing themselves so few of the East Timorese drivers were required for that task. This did not prevent them being an effective working part in the teams, there was more than enough work for everyone.

Language was another challenge. It would be impossible to communicate and prepare the population for the ballot without local interpreters. The intention was to have an interpreter working with each electoral team. There was never a time when we were even close to having enough interpreters to do this. The Co-ordinator's alternative plan was to put one with each sub-district and have three at headquarters. In the end we had only four qualified interpreters attached to the district. Later arrival of Malay CivPol and a few of the UNVs helped a little in this area, but generally needs had to be prioritised in allocating tasks to these four hard working locals.

As the day was coming to an end, I got my first complete surprise and my first important lesson about East Timor and the dedication of East Timorese. The four vehicles that had turned right when leaving the transport compound had all arrived in Gleno. Not only had they arrived but they brought with them the full stock of supplies they collected from the warehouse. The Security Officer, and others in Gleno, had assumed the other two vehicles were the ones that would never be seen again. So, we all learnt a lesson that day. East Timorese were basically a very honest people. This is something they would demonstrate time and time again.

I took the time to talk with Brett Swan, Phil Hunter, John Tanti and Max Knoth about who could or would be deployed to what location. Partly they had the answer for me. At Polri

Headquarters, and on the trip up to Gleno, they had worked out they would probably be working in pairs and had already decided their preferences, as long as I was happy with their choice. Brett and John would work together as would Phil and Max. I saw no reason to change this arrangement and now it was just a matter of who would be heading out the next morning. Both groups stated a preference to be first. The same basic reasons; they wanted to get on with the job; no one saw any advantage in settling down in Gleno just to move a few days later; and, although unstated, they wanted to get away from their headquarters and run their own show. I fully understood all their reasons and in short order made the decision for Brett and John to join the Hatolia teams.

Brett and Phil.

Having been warmly welcomed by an ever-increasing number of UNV there was the issue of dinner and where to sleep that night. After a little while we were able to contact the CivPol already deployed who arrived and took us to their home. The house was only a short drive up a hill, followed by a turn down a narrow track with a final sharp right-hand turn and descent to the gates at the side of the house.

At 7 p.m. East Timor time, fifteen hours and 45 minutes after the start of our day, we heard the words: 'Welcome to Bad Manor'.

In the dark the house looked rather impressive. Solidly constructed of concrete and rather larger than I expected to be available for rent in a remote mission area. When we walked around to the front, we came across a set of steps that looked in far better condition than those of the Dili Hotel. These led to a wide covered front verandah and the main entrance. It did not take long to catch up with the two Australians, Paul 'Morro' Morris and Don 'Barney' Barnby and for the introductions to their housemates; two Spanish police officers — Antonio Cubel, the contingent commander of the Spanish police, and Jose Pena; and two Kiwi's — Rob 'Fingers' Mills and Wayne 'Crazy' Corbett.

The boys were just about ready to start their evening meal and, with a bit of extra salad added, we were invited to join. The conversation was fairly hectic as us newcomers sought more police specific information on the local area and the 'old hands' had similar desire as the UN electoral officers for news from the 'outside'. If there is one common point in all mission areas, it is the difficulty in obtaining news about the outside world. I handed over the mail I had collected from home to the two Aussies.

After dinner we had a quick tour of the house. It had a very large dining room, 11 of us had fitted easily, a good size lounge area, satellite television with limited channels, five bedrooms and a bathroom with a European style toilet. However, the water only ran a few hours each day, well most days, and during those times containers had to be filled so that water would be available for cooking, washing, showering, and flushing. Pipe water should not be used for drinking or cleaning teeth. The UN had been providing bottled water and the power supply was not all that reliable. Care had to be taken with the number of appliances turned on at any one time, one too many and you had another blown fuse, and there were times of total power shutdown for the village. There was also an outside area for showering with a second, two-footprint squat toilet. Because of the small diameter of the internal pipes, with the accompanying threat of a blockage, this was where you were expected to go for 'Number Twos'.

Antonio invited me to set my stretcher up in his bedroom, it was the only one that had sufficient room for another bed, and the four others set up along one wall of the dining room. Without those stretchers from the UN warehouse one of us could have slept on the lounge but the rest would have been on hard concrete floors.

Gleno from Bad Manor

Once settled we wandered out and joined the others on the verandah and took our first real look over the township of Gleno. The 'Bad Manor' was situated on the side of the hill and had an excellent view over almost the whole town. Now it was time for my first taste of Bintang, Indonesian beer. I told you I knew that it would be possible to get a beer wherever we were going. What I did not expect was that an excellent diuretic would be provided at the same time, from the same bottle. Just in case it was the strain of the day that had the diuretic effect for that night, I did try consumption on a few later occasions, each time confirming it was the Bintang!

While we were chatting on the verandah, I realised Paul Morris was a little put out by my arrival. He had been leading the CivPol team since his arrival as the senior CivPol with prior UN mission experience. Naturally being replaced had a negative impact. This was something I understood and would have to work on to maintain team cohesion. As far as professionalism goes, I could not fault him. He provided me with a comprehensive briefing covering all aspects of his time in Ermera. He included that he had already obtained approval and arranged a Polri escort for the trip to Hatolia. There was one job he had no trouble handing over, in fact his voice was almost joyous when he told me that I would now have to attend the daily 8 a.m. meeting with all other UN component leaders.

Our six housemates told us stories about their work with the electoral teams. Four had already developed good working relationships with particular teams. Antonio had a location but was awaiting the arrival of UNVs to finalise the team. Paul, because he had been more tied up with management, had yet to be allocated. There were still insufficient people and equipment to establish all the planned teams. On top of this I had a personal hope for sufficient CivPol to enable me to create a small dedicated command cell and an investigation team. For the electoral processes I would leave things as they stood. For other things further allocation of duties would have to wait a little longer.

Paul told me of his belief the local Indonesian police commander, Lieutenant Colonel Gultom, was not a genuine member of the Polri and the others supported him in this. The basis for their suspicion was that Gultom did not wear service ribbons on his uniform, in fact he was the only Polri commissioned officer they had seen who did not to have them. They found it highly unlikely an individual could have achieved his rank in Polri without earning a series of service medals and thus have the ribbons on his uniform. Their suspicion was that Gultom was actually from the Indonesian Army, and probably from Kopassus, the Indonesian Special Forces.

Later I came up with a different possibility. As previously stated, until 1999 the Indonesian military and police and been one organisation, ABRI. Within the previous twelve months ABRI had been divided into two organisations, the military became TNI and the police became Polri with Brimob as a sub-unit. I could well imagine Indonesian authorities selecting legally qualified people from outside the former organisation to become leaders of the police. Gultom did have a doctorate and it was definitely not in medicine. I could also see the benefit of having individuals qualified in the law to be present in East Timor to negotiate with the UN, which can be a very legalistic.

By 9.30p.m. us newcomers were a little weary, so we headed off to the relative comfort of our stretchers. I pulled out that extra bit of comfort from my bags; my mission pillow. One of the original pillows purchased by my wife and I a number of years ago and now just kept for UN missions. At home the pillow had long since been replaced. But, even with the odd sweat stain or two, it was still more comfortable than anything I had found in any mission area. Therefore, like all previous missions, I had packed it, with a pair of single cotton sheets.

Roosters at 4 a.m. What a cacophony of noise. Each one of them doing its utmost to out crow the others. How anyone could sleep through that noise amazed me. So, I went and stood on the verandah and looked over the township. The low-lying areas were now shrouded in fog, just one more thing I had not expected in a tropical location. Not only was there a fog, but a definite chill in the air. My mind started on additional alterations to my expectations and added further preparations I should undertake.

I heard a noise at the side of the house and wandered around to check. There I met Vanda, the local lady employed by the boys as housekeeper and cook. She had arrived at her usual time to prepare breakfast and start on the washing. I don't think she was very happy finding four others sleeping in the dining room, and then to find a fifth wandering around was no help at all. No point holding her up, so I unsuccessfully tried for a little more sleep. Finally, I gave that up and went for my first shower, well, I filled the bowl with water and used a ladle to wet myself before soaping up and then used the ladle to rinse with cold water. That cold water was a bit of a setback, but it was also a simple problem I was sure I could, and would, remedy.

By the time I finished showering and shaving the rest were starting to stir. Breakfast was on the table. Breakfast! In the centre of the dining table there was a large plate overflowing with what looked like orange potato wedges. In fact, they were wedges made from sweet potato. Vanda had cut them and boiled them up when she first arrived. Now they were sitting there, cold, waiting to be eaten. Coffee was on the table to go with the wedges. That was breakfast. Later Crazy told me, jokingly I think, he was sure that Vanda had been sent by the local Militia to attempt to poison them.

While the others could take their time, Paul and I had a meeting to attend. It was only a few minutes' drive to headquarters because Gleno really is a small town. Once there Paul showed me the CivPol office. This 4-metre by 3-metre room was my office; the CivPol interview room; the district radio room; and, because it had the one computer allocated to CivPol, the typing room. With just a little imagination we would make it work.

The meeting started slightly late, which apparently was

normal. Paul introduced me to the Regional Coordinator, and head of Electoral Component, Allessandro Righetti from Italy; the Senior Military Liaison Officer (MLO) Lieutenant Colonel Baldev Singh from Malaysia, Samulcai Brownie, the Security Officer(SO) who I had already met; the UN Field Service Administrator (FSA), he who had control of logistics and supplies; and Allessandro's personal assistant, Ingeborg from Norway, who was taking the minutes.

For the majority of the meeting I kept my mouth shut, concentrating on studying people and processes. Primarily the meeting was reports from the previous day and setting the individual tasks for that day. It was a productive meeting, but the timing was wrong. By the time it finished, and tasks were allocated to the teams nearly three working hours had gone. Considerable time was being unnecessarily wasted. At the end I suggested we make a change and hold the meeting at the end of each day so a much earlier start could be made each morning. Without discussion, the suggestion was immediately agreed to by all. Allessandro stated we would have our first evening meeting at 5 p.m. that day.

Success breeds boldness so I immediately put forward another request to have one of the new vehicles allocated to me. My request was granted. With the meeting over it was time for me to join up with the convoy taking the teams to Hatolia.

CHAPTER 7

First Patrol

After the meeting Alessandro and I chatted over coffee in his office while the convoy prepared. Polri would be escorting four UN vehicles, Alessandro's Toyota Land Cruiser, the two Land Rovers allocated to the teams and a third to assist in transporting of their equipment and personal effects. It took far longer than I expected to get the convoy together with even the Polri escort showing signs of impatience. Brett and John provided the driving force that finally overcame the inertia of a few. Two hours later we were underway. I was learning about the different perspective individuals had on punctuality and personal organisation.

As we reached the edge of town Alessandro's driver pointed out barricades and a lean to on the side of the road.

'The Militia set up a road block every night,' he said.

I made a mental note that I would have to call in and visit one night. I was surprised how quickly we were off the flat land and again climbing along the side of a steep ravine. To our left the jungle wall appeared almost vertical and was near impossible for me to penetrate visually. From above the vehicle and out of the depths of the jungle I heard for the first time 'Hello Mister'.

This greeting was constantly used by children throughout East Timor for everyone in the UN, whether they were male or female. On this hillside the vegetation was so thick it took me another seven or eight minutes of hearing 'Hello Mister' before I finally managed to see a child. I was surprised to see the child was carrying a large machete in his hand. Another lesson learnt, once outside the main town almost every male and the majority of children carried a machete when they were outside their village. The machetes were just part of daily working life.

Then there were the other road users, primarily microlite buses, motor bikes, pedestrians and coffee trucks. The coffee trucks were the largest vehicles. All were painted the same muddy yellow colour. At this time of the year they were people movers, you could even say makeshift buses. Every now and then we saw an Indonesian military vehicle and on a very rare occasion a private car.

The trip proved the ideal way for Alessandro and I to get to know each other. He was experienced in the conduct of elections with a good grasp of implementation methods. However, he acknowledged he had little experience in leading or planning activities for an organisation like the multi-national group now assembled in Ermera. We both realised and accepted our close cooperation would be key to conducting the Popular Consultation efficiently and effectively. Alessandro and his driver passed on information about the local area. For example, where the town of Gleno stood there had once been rice paddies and vegetable gardens. The few houses that had been there, such as Bad Manor, were on the ridge lines and belonged to the wealthy. When we got back if I looked across the riverbed from our headquarters, I would see the village of Ermera, the former district centre, high on the opposite ridge line. A direct walk would take 20 minutes of hard slogging; to drive it was a minimum of half an hour on the only road. My immediate thoughts were for security at this location. If, as was distinctly possible, the Militia attacked a team in Ermera Village then an alternative escape route was essential. I would have to either find or create at least one alternative route; one way in and out was not safe or acceptable.

Even though there would be times when we disagreed, the rapport Allessandro and I established on that trip stayed with us for the remainder of the mission. When the time came, I was able to put forward my ideas on employing CivPol officers effectively.

It was on this trip that I first floated my interpretations of the CivPol mandate. On the first task, 'protecting the ballot boxes', I explained how I could, if asked, justify extrapolating the spirit of this task to become 'protecting the ballot process'. In part this was because if the ballot process fell apart then there would be no ballot boxes to protect. On the second task, 'advising the Indonesian police' I realised there were significant challenges. Nothing had been set down on what 'providing advice' might or might not include. However, Polri had accepted responsibility for the physical security of all UN personnel. This was an obvious area where advice could be provided, and collaboration would be essential. Advising Polri on protecting the ballot process was another area for advice and collaboration. I also explained my intention to have CivPol investigate incidents whenever possible. While taking action was something they could not do, my reasoning was advice could only be offered if I had relevant information.

For me there were parallels between what I needed to do in 1999 and how I had operated in the Vietnam War advising South Vietnamese Army Units. For different reasons, both the South Vietnamese Army and Polri did not want advisers telling them what to do, let alone actually following advice. Anyone with the audacity to advise without solid information and knowledge was doomed to fail. My priorities would be to prepare and conduct an active patrol plan and initiate investigations. With good information, and a very diplomatic approach, it might just be possible to create an effective working relationship with my counterpart, Lieutenant Colonel Gultom.

Allessandro accepted my interpretations.

Local knowledge would be important. Gleno had been built by the Indonesians as the new district administrative centre because there was a shortage of available land in the village of Ermera and, given the ridge-side location, definitely no flat land. The site chosen was the nearest significant area of flatland in the area. According to the locals, no account had been taken of this being their prime farmland and obviously this created dissatisfaction in the local community. The majority of current residents in Gleno were from other Indonesian provinces. This was a divided town with enduring animosities.

I also learnt that the dense vegetation on the mountain sides was directly connected with the growing of coffee beans. The tall trees were an integral part of the process as they provided the essential shade necessary for the dense, lower-growing coffee plants. On good stretches of this road, and most other roads, patches of raw coffee beans were spread for up to five metres in length and over the full width of the road. The driver informed me the coffee growers wanted vehicles to drive over the beans as this was the most efficient means available to crack the hard outer-shells. My immediate presumption was to make sure I checked my next cup of coffee for a rubbery taste.

Suddenly in front of the vehicle I saw something that brought my heart to my mouth. If the bites out of yesterday's road had been taken by giants, the one now in front of me had been done by a Titan! There was just enough room for the Land Cruiser to fit between the edge of the bite, with its immediate drop into a green nothingness, and the now vertical side of the ravine. I opened my eyes and saw we were on solid ground again. It was an inauspicious start to my first trip into the real mountains.

After fifteen minutes we turned off the sealed road. The rest of the trip would be completed on narrow, winding unsealed roads which saw us climbing and descending over two major ridge lines as well as a number of smaller ones. Over the whole journey there was only one section where the road was straight for more than 80 metres. What became known as THE straight was high in the mountains and on the south side of a very steep slope. Even in the dry season there was constant moisture which adversely impacted on the road surface. At one spot in the middle of this straight the edge had dropped away so much planks had been laid to support the ravine side wheels of passing vehicles. On later trips even I accelerated across the planks. There were also places where during heavy rain, prevalent in the monsoon season, torrents of water would come down the gullies and leap across the road. Driving on this road during the wet season was likely to be impossible. Later as I travelled around the district, I found this road was typical of all others.

The road to Hatolia.

Other roads in Ermera.

The Hatolia road had another unique feature. There was a particularly narrow valley, almost a canyon, almost vertical up on one side and a perilously steep drop into the ravine on the other. There were a couple of places where a good 'long jumper', if there had been room for a run up, could have cleared the gap between the roads on either side. But only if he/she did not think about the 60 or so metre drop in the middle. Near the end was an old stone bridge, just wide enough for the Land Cruiser. As we exited the bridge on the Hatolia side there was a little trouble. The Land Cruiser was too wide for the road. To keep the outside wheels on the road and prevent the vehicle falling into the ravine, the mountain side of the vehicle had to be scraped along the vertical rock wall. Sitting there I could hear the sound of damage being caused. My immediate thought was at least I'm not the driver who has to put in the accident report. The UN is very particular about damage being caused to its vehicles. After we arrived in Hatolia, Brett and John told me from their vehicles they could see one inch of the outside wheels of the Toyota hanging over the edge, in thin air. The Land Rovers, being narrower, had no difficulty at this location.

Finally, we crossed the last ridge line. The view over the wide river valley below us was spectacular. In the foreground the village of Hatolia sat picturesquely on a low hill that lay between us and the riverbed. A riverbed which was so wide and so dry I had trouble not only imagining it full, but also imagining the torrents of rain that would be required to fill it.

Our trip had covered a total distance of 32 kilometres in just over 2 hours. Already I knew that the first task I would give Brett and John was to find alternate routes out of Hatolia. Apart from not being happy with anywhere with only one way in and out, if trouble did occur here then the route we had just travelled could, and probably would, be easily cut off.

After the initial warm welcome, the villagers took us to the house they had prepared for the incoming teams. It had been thoroughly cleaned and a new concrete floor had been laid. The team was never asked to pay rent for this house. While being much smaller than Bad Manor, there was just enough room for all members of the two teams. Power and water were available, but only when the village generator was turned on. The toilet, well there were the two footprints to mark the squatting position over a porcelain bordered hole into the sewerage pipe. There was a small water cistern and ladle beside the toilet to wash one's contribution down the hole.

Communications could be a challenge as the village had no telephone line. An unsuccessful attempt to contact Gleno by radio concerned me. Brett was not deterred, sending John off to find a place where he could get direct radio contact. It did not take him long to establish radio contact after a short drive up the hill. For the time being I accepted this situation but made a mental note I would have to get on to UN technical staff to guarantee radio communications between Hatolia and Gleno.

After a tour of the area we were invited to lunch at the local 'café'. Youngsters, who lithely clambered up the nearest trees, cut down a selection of coconuts and then sliced them open with the same type of machetes I had seen being carried by just about every male. I had my first taste of fresh coconut milk; not bad. The accompanying dish of locally-made donuts did not seem to fit the occasion or the locality. But I was to find donuts were readily available throughout East Timor. You could almost consider them a local dish. I never did think to ask when or how they were introduced. Donuts were followed by the coconut flesh as the final course.

After lunch local leaders led us up the hill to the church which was their recommended site for registration and the ballot. While Allessandro and the teams were inspecting the area, I spoke with other locals about how additional teams, planned to be based in Hatolia, would get to and from their working locations. The observations I made during the drive had given me doubts about the ability of at least two of the proposed teams being able to get anywhere near where they were supposed to work. Discussion with locals confirmed my fears. I would have further talks with Alessandro with a view to making necessary changes to his plan. I now realised in East Timor plans could not be made purely from a map, physical reconnaissance was essential.

After a while one of our Polri escort politely asked me if it was time to return to Gleno. He gave the impression they wanted to be back, and finish work well before dark. I had a short discussion with Alessandro. He agreed. We said a fond au revoir to the teams and the village. By the time we left I am sure we had shaken the hand of every person in the village.

It was a good feeling to have successfully placed our first two teams in the field. The drive back was just as slow as the drive out, and 'Yes' this time the opposite side of the Land Cruiser was damaged at the rock wall. After we returned to Gleno I completed the accident investigation report for Allessandro and then suggested if he visited Hatolia again he should use a Land Rover. In the coming months he made two more trips to Hatolia, both times in the Toyota. However, he did make one change on those two trips, each time he came home via Liquicia. A longer trip, but damage to only one side of the vehicle.

On arrival back at base we found more UNV had arrived. I had met some of them in Darwin and they were happy to see a familiar face.

'I feel like I have been here a week already,' I told them.

Ermera Sub Districts

CHAPTER 8

Getting Started

With Paul's assistance I put together my first UN report. Headquarters in Dili required each district to report daily. For the first weeks I phoned reports through on the telephone conscious it was an easily tapped 'party line'. I considered it probable Indonesian intelligence personnel monitored all calls we made from the two telephones in our headquarters. It was also likely the three telephones in private houses occupied by UN personnel were also being monitored. As well as the verbal report, either before or after making the telephone call, the information was put into a written report which was sent to Dili by the first available person travelling there. In the early days this could be two or three days after the report was completed.

Around this time, I met Helen, an Australian employed by the UN as a Political Affairs Officer (PAO). She was fixated on the past, blatantly pro-independence and anti-Indonesian. In a situation where professional impartiality was absolutely essential, not only for facilitating the ballot but also for personal safety, Helen was the 'loose cannon' who could increase the danger for us all. She was in East Timor under an assumed name because she and her husband, who was a journalist, were banned from entering Indonesia because they were well known for anti-Indonesian media reports. While I understood her dedication, in my view the UN had made a mistake employing her in this sensitive role.

The first evening meeting was uneventful and concluded just before 7 p.m. The decisions included –

a. Two teams would have to deploy into the north-west area of the district. This was an area originally planned to be covered by additional teams in Hatolia. However, during our trip to Hatolia we identified a lack of navigable roads between the two areas which created a requirement to identify an alternative base for those teams. We considered keeping them in Gleno, but the additional travel time precluded this option. The priority was identifying a location or locations for the registration centre/polling site, team housing and sub-district base. At the same time, they would have to start preparing the voters with information on where, when and how to vote.
b. Two teams would be conducting information sessions in Gleno and the Ermera village; and
c. We had to prepare an induction program for arriving UNV before they were allocated to teams and deployed to sub-district locations.

After the meeting I took my car and drove up to the Bad Manor. It was the only vehicle in our fleet painted red; at that time all others were painted green. I had decided I would make myself as visible as possible to all stakeholders; UN personnel, local population, the Militia and the Indonesian authorities and security forces. I expected significant personal physical presence by me would have a positive impact on confidence in the UN staff and the local population. At the same time, I hoped to imprint a tinge of doubt on the Militia, who had been formed by Indonesian authorities out of their paramilitary civil defence auxiliary known as WANRA. I wanted everyone to know I was 'out and about', the eyes and ears of the UN.

Fortunately for me my arrival at the Bad Manor coincided with the serving of the evening meal. Over dinner that night the usual exchange of information included tasks for the following day. After a convivial dinner and long discussions into the night I had a brief night's sleep before the 4 a.m. rooster alarm went off. Murder was definitely on my mind. Calmness prevailed, however, and I rolled over and went back to sleep until 6 a.m. when I rose for the obligatory cold ablutions and the boiled, but now cold, sweet potato breakfast. Something really would have to be done about breakfast.

Then it was straight down to headquarters for I was concerned about the Hatolia teams and wanted to try and contact them. Even though I knew the radios would not work until they drove up the hill, I could not get past the need to assure myself they were alright. They did not answer my call. Half an hour later Brett called in. Before I could check how the night had gone, he got in with a complaint. Their planned patrol to a location reported to be the gathering place for a large number of Internally Displaced Persons (IDPs) had been cancelled. Polri officers could not provide a security escort because, although the local Polri station had plenty of officers, they did not have any vehicles. Therefore, no escort, no patrol. I could sense the frustration in his voice. Brett had an alternate plan for the day but sought my advice on two other points —

- was it necessary to have security with them every time they went anywhere; and
- if so, could they take them in the UN vehicles when nothing else was available?

Okay, so now I had a problem to solve. This was an important policy to develop for both security and practical reasons. I contacted UN Headquarters in Dili. Technically the UNAMET agreement with Indonesia stated that Polri would provide security for UN personnel. But there had been no time to work out how this would be achieved. In far off UN Headquarters in New York no one had considered Polri may not have sufficient vehicles.

All those I spoke with were in general agreement we should not travel without an escort. However, I was told I could approve vehicle movement without an escort, but any adverse result from my decision would be completely my responsibility.

The UN Headquarters was firm about whether Polri officers could travel in UN vehicles- NO! Armed personnel should not be seen in UN vehicles; and, conveying Indonesian personnel might be seen by some as supporting the Indonesian side of the vote. UN personnel had to be neutral and impartial. This was reinforcing that truism, professional impartiality is essential! More administratively, the insurance arrangements made by the UN for their vehicles precluded carrying passengers who were not working directly for the UN. Therefore, only UN personnel were to travel in UN vehicles.

Between telephone conversations with HQ staff in Dili, I tasked Paul Morris to get in touch with Polri to arrange a meeting for me as soon as possible. About the time I had finished with Dili, Paul came into the office with the local Polri LO, Captain Ari. Ari had served as a UN CivPol in Kosovo and spoke excellent English. We spoke at length about the security issue. Essentially Polri only had four vehicles for the entire district. One was the Commander's vehicle, another was for the local Brimob unit; and the last two were based at Polres (the district Polri HQ) and were for use anywhere in the district. I already understood the driving difficulties of the district and quickly surmised those vehicles were highly unlikely to ever be available for the sub districts. Captain Ari informed me the only vehicles likely to be in village Polri stations were a few privately owned motorbikes.

I was still wondering why we needed security escorts at all, so I asked Captain Ari.

Ari's answer, 'To protect you from Falantil attack.'

Falantil were the military arm of the independence movement.

This was a deceptive response because Falantil welcomed the UN presence, confident the ballot would give them what they wanted, independence. I had already realised it was not prudent to raise this inconsistency with Polri Officers as the Indonesian military and police had been fighting Falantil for many years. Personally, my security concerns were directed more to the potential of attack from the Militia groups established by Indonesian authorities. But you could not expect Ari, or anyone from Polri, to acknowledge that. This was something I would have to discuss at a higher level.

Ari appeared eager to get away, but I managed to keep him a little longer to discuss some other points. By the time he left I had an undertaking he would meet me, at my office, every afternoon. From those meetings he would take issues I raised back to his commander and attempt to have them resolved. He would try to have answers for each of my questions at our next meeting. At my request he provided me with a telephone number to contact him in emergencies. Later we would have our own radio link. It took more pressure to get him to promise he would try and arrange an early meeting with his boss.

It was almost impossible to believe these conversations took up the entire morning. With no firm outside answer I was already formulating my own opinion. There were ways and means around mandatory requirement for Polri escorts. After I gathered a little more information, I would put my ideas into a plan. It would then be a matter of selling it to Allessandro, UNV and CivPol. At that time, I had not thought about the need to sell it to Polri. They clearly had an agenda around escorts which, at this early stage, I began to realise was about our supervision and control rather than our security.

The early part of the afternoon was spent house hunting. There were a few options I considered before deciding to take one of the smaller places. It had two main advantages. It was the only one with any furniture, a single bed, no mattress, a large desk, and three pink plastic chairs, and, it was in a group of four houses, the others being occupied by Alessandro, Baldev and Samulcia. That made overall security much easier and gave me reasonable access to telephones, one each in the homes of Allessandro and Samulcai.

The house had two bedrooms. The kitchen had just a built-in bench, nothing else. The bathroom had a one metre by one metre by one metre water cistern with a pipe, no tap, just above it, a two-footprint toilet and an area in front of both where one could wash. The bathroom did have a door. I signed for the place the next day. No point in denying reality.

Water supply was an issue. The pipes laid for the town water supply were very porous. If the water was left to continually run the supply would be exhausted in a very short time. So, for about an hour each day the water was turned on. But it wasn't always the same hour each day. So, the pipes over the house water storage cisterns either had no tap or the tap was always in the open position. On top of this was the occasional period when the water was not turned on for an extended period, usually two or three days. The longest I experienced was five days.

Two bathrooms, one upmarket because it has tiles.

A few minutes before 7 p.m., just as the daily management meeting was finishing, there was an urgent radio call from Helen. She had been at a pro-independence rally and there was trouble with a group of Militias. She was right in the middle of it. Fortunately, Ari was outside waiting for our evening meeting. Now was my first opportunity to test the level of cooperation I would get from Polri. As soon as he understood the problem Ari was on his radio to his headquarters. I was on the radio calming Helen and trying to stop her escalating tensions. Ari did get the local village Polri to move reasonably quickly. They arrived at Helen's location without too much delay and stepped between the UN personnel and the Militia. A Brimob squad sent from Gleno arrived at 7.20 p.m., calmed the Militia and persuaded them to depart. The Brimob squad escorted Helen back to Gleno. It was comforting to know Polri had been instructed to keep UNAMET international staff safe, even if the UN persons had created the situation that led to the potential for violence.

The Militia complained to Ari that Helen had actively advised villagers to vote for independence. I tracked her down and spoke with her about this accusation that violated UNAMET's neutrality.

She did not deny the accusation stating, 'You know what the Indonesians have done in this country.'

I understood her feelings, and probably shared them. But in our current roles we could not openly express them. I tried reasoning with her and explaining the need for professional impartiality. Her unwillingness to accept anything I said was extremely frustrating. There was no change in her attitude. For now, I made a mental note to keep a closer eye on her, for her safety as well as ours. Once again, my thoughts were that she was the loose cannon who could get us all killed.

By now it was well past the usual time to head to Bad Manor for the evening meal. When I arrived, I found the place full. The boys had invited a number of the UNV up for dinner. Even with the added crowd there was plenty of food left for me.

After eating I was chatting with Don Barnby and telling him about the house I had arranged. We were overheard by two of the new volunteer arrivals from Australia, Diana and Saku, so they joined in. That afternoon they had been allocated to a Gleno-based team and were looking for a place to live. Moving in with me seemed to be the perfect answer to them. I gave them an honest description and staked my claim to the only bed. They were still happy and quite prepared to use the UN-issued stretchers. So now I had two 30-year-old Australian females as my house mates. The first thought that raced through my mind was I wouldn't need Dave Savage's cooking skills. Time would reveal it was not a very accurate expectation.

Diana was a university graduate who had recently worked, in reality served, as a volunteer on the UN mission in Chechnya. Everything I heard about that mission indicated it was one of the toughest. Atrocious weather conditions, living conditions worse than the poorest in East Timor and constant danger from both sides. For months she had survived everything they threw at her and, even after all that, put her hand up once again as a volunteer, this time in East Timor. A lady with a lot of guts.

Being so experienced she travelled very lightly with everything having a practical use in a mission environment. Work-wise she quickly established herself as one of the most capable workers in the Electoral Component. Originally, she and Saku were the UNV on one team. Diana could also prepare meals, although they tasted much the same as mine. I don't think they were at the standard I may have had with Dave Savage. As the time progressed, she formed a relationship with Allessandro that later blossomed into marriage. They both returned to Timor after UNAMET as full time UN employees. They were part of the UN support to the subsequent international military intervention, INTERFET. The last I heard they were together and working for the UN on the mission in Nepal.

Diana formed a strong friendship with our other housemate, Saku, even though they were very different people. Saku was a highly qualified legal professional who had taken leave from the Human Rights Commission of New South Wales to take on the role of a UNV in East Timor. She was definitely a big city woman who was not as well prepared, due to a lack of experience and information, for living in a remote locality. She had far more overall luggage than Diana with much of it unnecessary and almost unusable in the local environment. To her credit, she got through those difficulties and never let them interfere with her work performance, although she was used to being in control and at times would make decisions on others without consultation.

Like Diana she was extremely capable, and her strengths allowed Allessandro to withdraw Diana to Headquarters and leave Saku as a one UNV member team. I know he would have liked to have put a second person there, but he needed the help at Headquarters and was one person short. Diana being in Headquarters also helped me as she quickly became a capable base radio operator and was willing and able to help out on the many times she was needed.

After discussions with Antonio, the Spanish contingent Commander, I put him in the team with Saku. The two of them bonded and became a very proficient team with a very good working relationship. During the registration phase they would complete the work in their village quicker than anyone else. They were so efficient Allessandro was later able to re-direct Saku to the village of Sare for the final days.

Later, after I purchased an iron, there was one area where Saku ran into trouble with Diana and me, doing her ironing after dark. Because she had a tendency to leave mundane things to the last minute, she was often trying to iron outfits for that evening after sunset. Now, no matter how often I asked our landlord to fix it, the power supply to our house was only sufficient to run the lights or to use the iron. Not both. If you tried to iron with even one light on, then the circuit breaker cut in. Fortunately, it was a circuit breaker, where you just had to get the torch; go outside; find the switch and throw it. Replacing fuses would have been far more inconvenient. But it did happen more than once.

Later the landlord would provide two additional beds. Both the same as mine, no mattress, I got the first CivPol member who went to Dili to visit the markets and purchase three foam mattresses. Also, after four blockages, the owner did have a plumber come and rebuild our two footprint toilets and the associated pipes for the first time.

By now I was feeling pretty good with myself. It had been a good day all round, then Alessandro arrived at Bad Manor. There had been trouble in Liquicia. The Militia had attacked UN personnel and as a result all UN in Liquicia had been evacuated to Dili. A directive had been issued for no movement of UN personnel until further notice. I drove to the headquarters immediately to inform everyone arrangements for the following day were cancelled and we were temporarily in 'lock down'. For the first time I tried the emergency contact number for Ari. It worked. Within ten minutes I was speaking directly to him and requesting he pass a message through the Polri radio network to the Hatolia teams about the lockdown.

When I tried to get information from him on what had happened at Liquicia, he said that he knew nothing about Liquicia. After I pressed him on a potential security threat to UN personnel in Ermera from the Militia, he agreed to double the security at our headquarters building and to have a mobile team patrol the houses where UN personnel were living.

I followed my conversation with Ari with a telephone call to the UN Joint Operations Centre in Dili. All I managed to confirm was there had been an evacuation of UN personnel from Liquicia. Beyond that, information was scarce. Until things could be sorted out the next day they claimed to be just as much in the dark as we were. I passed this information to Alessandro and then called it quits for the night.

With tomorrow's work cancelled, the team decided to have a little party. In addition to the usual few bottles of Bintang someone produced a bottle of Bundaberg OP Rum. In the early stages of the night one of the Kiwis asked me, 'Why are you Aussies being so nice to us?'

It was a question I had also been asked by a Kiwi soldier in Mozambique. My answer was the same, 'Back home it may be the Wallabies versus the All Blacks. But once you get to a place like this that gets put away. For looking after each other there is only one thing that counts, we are ANZACs.'

He understood my answer. This matter was never raised again.

As the night wore on many a joke was told, including one from Jose, in Spanglish with lots of actions. Even though we did not understand much of what he said there was so much laughter there were tears in my eyes. There was even a brief game of rugby on the veranda between would-be Wallabies and would-be All Blacks. The party went on for some time, but well before it finished, I headed off to the stretcher. In the morning I was out of bed well before everyone else. My head was fine and believe it or not breakfast was sweet potato wedges, cold again.

I got to the office well before Brett called in at 7.30a.m. I told him about Liquicia. Once again, the teams had to re-arrange their plans for the day. But at least they had plenty of work that could be done within Hatolia without the need to travel further afield.

My next priority was to get more on Liquicia. Phone calls to various people in Dili elicited a variety of replies that included a number of different versions of events. Some of the scenarios were compatible with each other, but in most cases, they could not have been talking about the same incident. The only consistent points were an armed Militia group had threatened UN personnel and forced their evacuation to the beach area where they were picked up by helicopter and flown to Dili. Local Indonesian authorities appeared to have lost control of the Militia and they posed a real threat to the lives of UN employees. The Liquicia incident reinforced my opinion that the Militia groups were extremely undisciplined. Even though they were supposed to be under Indonesian control, I already had suspicions they would not always follow Indonesian orders or meet Indonesian expectations.

Allessandro and I discussed Liquicia and decided to use the postponement of travel for me to meet local Indonesian authorities, beginning with Constantino Soares, the Bupati of Ermera. Bupati is an elected position with some similarity to a Mayor in Australia.

This meeting began with local coffee, light snacks and general conversation. The Bupati had a good command of the English language and, if you listened carefully to his words, he knew that although he was the Ermera District's most senior elected official, he had little power or authority. From his perspective the real power in the district was with Lieutenant Colonel Gultom, Polri commander, and Senor Claudio, the most senior public servant. It would not be long before I would meet Senior Claudio.

Whenever we tried to turn the conversation towards a substantial discussion about security, the Bupati immediately manoeuvred it to a much less political subject such as the quality of the local coffee. I agreed I liked it. Primarily I am a tea drinker, but I was finding the local coffee to be very palatable and it did not taste at all rubbery.

From there we drove to the Indonesian Army base where I met Lieutenant Colonel Nurr, the battalion commander. Again, there was coffee. However, the conversation here was far more probing. He recognised my service ribbons and politely enquired about how and when I went from the Australian Army to the Australian Federal Police. He was definitely probing to ascertain if I really was a police officer, or a soldier sent to the mission wearing police uniform, or possibly an intelligence operative. I openly gave him a brief truthful resume of my life story. I am not sure whether he believed me or not, but I had been truthful with him.

Allessandro became involved in conversation with other officers and I had a much closer discussion with Nurr. He mentioned previous conversations he had had with other Australian Vietnam veterans and likened East Timor to Vietnam. He told me his frustrations matched theirs. Frustration because, as in Vietnam, success in the field was negated by influences outside the control of the ordinary soldiers. It was very upsetting to him that the loss of so many friends and subordinates in East Timor might, in the longer term, be for no reason. Some of the points mentioned started me thinking that Indonesia had probably lost many more soldiers in East Timor than had been publicly acknowledged. Later conversations with others would reinforce my opinion. Though brief, the meeting had been worthwhile.

From the Indonesian Army base, Allessandro returned to our base and I went to take possession of my new home. Another surprise awaited. The building I was directed to was the administrative centre for the district. The man I met was Senor Claudio, the Assistant Governor appointed as the administrative head of the Ermera District. Senor Claudio, for I never heard anyone refer to him in any other way, was an East Timorese who had been appointed to the position by the Indonesian authorities. Another 'get to know you' session followed, of course with coffee.

The meeting with Senor Claudio had a very different tone to earlier meetings. For the entire meeting I felt as if an attempt was being made to con me. So, before I left, I paid the full rent for the coming month, even though he indicated this was not absolutely necessary. My gut feeling told me if I let him do me a favour, he would soon expect something in return. I was not prepared to fall into that trap. In the following days, discussions with others convinced me Senor Claudio held the real political power in Ermera. Later still I would get enough information to be personally satisfied he was the 'behind the scenes' controller of all Militia in Ermera.

Now happy, and with key in hand, I moved my possessions from the grand heights of Bad Manor to my own place on the flatlands. I now lived immediately behind the local telephone exchange.

Now I had a place to live, I settled back into work; more calls to Dili, trying to get more details on the Liquicia incident and arrange final Japanese encephalitis injections for Antonio and Jose. The injections were something all UN personnel had to have. Getting results on both proved to be difficult, it was late afternoon before I had answer to all my questions.

Staff at the Dili headquarters were now satisfied the Liquicia problem was localised and all other districts could now resume normal activities. Now it was a matter of getting everyone together to put into place steps for the next day's activities. This would include Antonio and Jose going to Dili for their injections.

In the middle of getting everything together for the next day, a UNV brought a local to me. He came from one of the nearby villages and had a complaint about Militia intimidation and violence which had occurred two nights ago. At first, he reported seeing horrendous violence including murder and a large number of seriously injured people. But as I questioned him a little deeper it came out, he had not actually seen or heard anything. The troubles had occurred in a village near his and someone from a third village had visited him that day and told him the story. But this second person had not been at the incident either. He had been told the story by a person from another village. I thanked him for bringing the information to me and gave him an undertaking that I would have CivPol visit the village and would make Polri fully aware of the situation.

My approach to this report of violence and intimidation was to advise Captain Ari and see whether he and his officers would conduct a meaningful investigation while launching my own investigation with CivPol officers. Ari seemed surprised and claimed not to have heard anything from the named village. However, he took notes and promised to have an answer within two days. After he left, I briefed Paul Morris and Wayne Corbett on the incident and gave them the job of visiting the village the next day, without a Polri escort. A start had to be made somewhere and this may as well be it.

CHAPTER 9

A time of Firsts

At 6pm that night the girls and I moved into our new home. More furniture, including proper beds for the girls, was now high on my list of things to do. Once settled, Diana suggested we go to the restaurant for dinner. This was the first I heard of a restaurant in Gleno, but it had to be better than Vanda's cooking. We drove down to Headquarters and then walked fifty metres up one of the side streets to the eating establishment. While food was served it could not be called a restaurant. It was a house that had become the place where new arrivals were first accommodated, like the Dili Hotel but without rip-off prices. There were two 'bedrooms', one for males and one for females. The floors of each room were just about covered with foam mattresses. There was only one 'bathroom'. But for the boys already being in Bad Manor this would have been my initial place of residence in Gleno. As good entrepreneurs they had also seen the financial possibilities of providing food. Because of this, from then on, I referred to it as the Guest House.

The cooking and eating areas were an L-shaped room. In one part of the L all the cooking was done on kerosene cookers placed on the floor. Against the wall in the other part of the L was the table where they placed the dishes of food as it was cooked and around the wall where a number of the ubiquitous pink plastic chairs to sit on. In the corner was a small fridge with soft drink and Bintang. You paid your money, the equivalent of about $2 Aussie, picked up a bowl and spoon, then served yourself. You could eat as much as you liked for the one price. To get your food hot you had to arrive just after it was put on the table or wait until all that had gone, and another lot was put out. As long as people were in the room the food kept coming. Drinks were extra but still very cheap. Shortly after this we found out the Guest House was owned by the family of someone we were told was a Polri Sergeant.

Paul and Don had already nicknamed him 'James Bond'. The nickname was generated on a sound basis. James, with his motorbike, was almost a constant companion to the UN in Gleno, always hanging around UN people or locations. He dressed in Polri uniform with sergeant's rank insignia, but he was very rarely seen at the police station. The only times I saw him there he was speaking with the Polri Intelligence Officer. With that in mind, we were careful what we said when in the Guest House. 'James' was most likely a member of an Indonesian intelligence organisation whose job appeared to be to maintain surveillance and report on all UN personnel.

Guest House cooking and dining areas (and overleaf).

Even here there was no peace. I received a call on the portable radio that was now a permanent attachment. It was turning out to be as big a nuisance as the mobile phone back home. This call was from Gleno headquarters and it got me out of the Guest House before I had really satisfied my hunger. An Indonesian soldier had walked into one of the houses occupied by some volunteers. The emergency contact worked again and soon Ari and I were at the house. Apart from the soldier walking in and looking around nothing had been done. No threats were made. No physical contact occurred, and nothing was taken. But it was likely to have been an attempt to intimidate. Ari now had this to follow up on as well. I decided I would also tell Baldev. It would give him a good reason to have a meeting with Lieutenant Colonel Nurr.

Before he left, Ari told me he had been going to come and see me anyhow. The Bupati wanted to invite me to visit one of the local villages with him tomorrow. I readily accepted the invitation.

First meeting with Militia

On the drive home I had to go through Gleno's biggest intersection. As I approached, I could see a group of about six men around a fire. Before I reached them, I realised they were members of the local Militia and I could see they were armed. The only thought that went through my mind was here was my first, and maybe only, chance to get to meet junior level Militia members. I had already formed the opinion I should try and meet at least some of these people. So, I stopped the vehicle. Got out. Walked over to their small camp. All of them picked up their weapons. Homemade firearms. Poorly carved wooden stocks. Water pipe barrels. No triggers. Later I found out the fuses were put into the side of the barrel and struck on match boxes to fire the weapons. It was a very hit and miss system because you could not always get the weapon aimed before it went off. Locally they were known as Racatan.

John and me with local 'handmade' weapons. (see overleaf also)

I kept my hands in full view and in the best Indonesian I could muster I tried to say, 'Hello'.

On later reflection I am pretty sure I wished them a good morning. But it did not seem to matter. The fact I tried to speak in Indonesian elicited a response. I did not understand it all but knew enough to recognise it as a return greeting. A couple of them had a smattering of English and I managed to introduce myself. Something must have got through because I am pretty sure what each of them said back was their names. I tried to ask them what they were doing. But I got no reply to this. Either my language skills were insufficient, or they were unwilling to give me the information. So, I indicated to them in words and actions that I would visit again on other nights. Then turned. Walked away. Got back in the vehicle. And drove home. My hands were shaking, just a bit. But I had pulled off my first meeting with a Militia roadblock and walked away from it.

This was the first of a number of times I would drop in on these roadblocks. The next time I was also met with raised weapons, but from then on, they continued with what they were doing while I walked in. On an average of one out of every two visits at least one of the Militia present, had a reasonable command of the English language and exchanges of information were possible. I made sure I avoided the topic of politics.

When I combined the information from these short visits with information from other sources, I developed my own understanding of the four major groups who made up the members of the Militia units in Ermera.

- There were those who were genuine in their desire to remain within Indonesia. Individuals may have had different reasons, but they all had the belief they were better off staying as part of Indonesia;
- There were some whose extended families lived on both sides of the border with West Timor. In general, this group wanted independence for Timor and believed if East Timor gained independence by itself then the two sides of Timor would be forever separated;
- There were criminals who were just taking advantage

of a situation which allowed then to carry out their activities with complete impunity; and

- By far the largest group were those who had joined because it was the easy thing to do, either because they made a choice to join or they gave in to pressure to join. Once you became a member you and your family were safe.

First Night in the new home.

I felt pretty good. It had been a day of progress. It had been a long day, but only the first of many. Finally, at 10.30 p.m. I arrived home and, believe me, went straight to bed.

After the best night's sleep since leaving home I got up at 5.45 a.m. I immediately lit up the small Trangio white spirit stove and heated some water to have a warm shower (wash). Pure bliss. From the backpack food stocks came cereal, well muesli. Reasonable milk was created by mixing a little from a tube of condensed milk with water. Along with a good strong mug of Nerida tea it was the best breakfast so far. Once finished I got into uniform, put some water on to heat for the girls and gave them their early morning get up call.

Both complained about the noise from the portable radio during the night. Because there was not enough staff to man the base radio 24 hours a day, I had decided to just put the portable by my pillow each night. Even though it had been sitting right next to my ear I must say I heard nothing.

'Did anyone call 'Base 3' or 'Uniform 60', I asked.

'Base 3' was the radio call sign for our Headquarters and 'Uniform 60' was my personal call sign.

'No, but it was so loud it kept us awake in our room', was the reply.

'That's why I didn't hear it. No one was calling me or Base 3'.

From previous service, both Army and Police, I had developed the ability to tune out things I didn't want to hear. On a number of later occasions there would be a middle of the night call to Uniform 60. On every occasion my brain woke me, and I answered the call.

But the girls were not happy listening to radio traffic all night. Their replies do not belong in print. But, if they wanted to share this house, it is something they will have to get used to. I headed off to Headquarters leaving them to their own devices to get ready for the day ahead.

First Village Meeting

I skipped the normal morning work routine today and went straight to Allessandro. There was a shortage of interpreters and today I definitely wanted one with me. It didn't take much to convince him. When I told him of the invite from the Bupati I think he would have liked to come along, but he already had other commitments.

I arrived at the Bupati's compound at five minutes to eight. The Bupati's car, two Polri vehicles and a Polri motor bike were there and ready. The Bupati came out of his office exactly at 8 a.m. With the convoy now complete we drove out of town. The lead Polri vehicle had its lights and sirens activated. Just a little pretentious, I thought.

The trip to the village of Talimoro took us just over an hour. The road was easier than the Hatolia Road because the mountains were not as high. The village elders were waiting for our arrival. As we got out of the vehicles, I saw Ari and a Polri Lieutenant Colonel get out of the second Polri car. Following the usual start to these events everyone had to meet and shake hands with the village elders. Then before we entered the meeting room Ari introduced me to the Police Commander for Ermera, Lieutenant Colonel Doctor Erry Gultom, my Polri counterpart.

Brimob in escort vehicle.

There was no time for any discussion as we were whisked into the building where the meeting would be held. At the far end was a head table set with three chairs. We walked down the centre aisle past the villagers who occupied every chair that filled the rest of the room. The large windows on both sides had no glass and were full of people standing outside. The place was so crowded I believe everyone who lived within walking distance had turned up to hear or participate.

The Bupati took the centre chair with Gultom to his left and me to his right. A chair was provided for the interpreter immediately to my right rear. The meeting was opened with a political speech by the Bupati, in Indonesian, about the forthcoming Popular Consultation. From the translation I was happy with the unbiased explanation he gave of the intended process. But, as expected, in the end he spoke of his strong personal preference for the autonomy option. Gultom's speech was a real surprise. He professionally explained what Polri would do in providing security for the ballot. There was no politics in his speech.

Then it was my turn. It would have been nice to have advanced warning. At least they left me till last which gave me time to think about what to say. In simple terms, I explained the UN involvement in the process. Like Gultom, I carefully avoided using words supporting either of the positions that would appear on the ballot paper.

A question and answer session followed with the initial questions directed to me. The prime concern was a rumour the UN would leave immediately after the ballot. I explained a number of times no matter what the ballot result the UN had a continuing role and would stay. I emphasized the electoral workers would leave because their job would be complete. But everyone else, including CivPol, would be remaining for the second phase of the mission. To my surprise, Gultom supported me. This was a question which would come up time and time again.

As I left the meeting, I felt a sense of accomplishment. A good start had been made in developing a relationship with the villagers. Gultom and I had met and tested each other in an unexpected and complex environment where first impressions were important. My initial impression of him was of a professional police officer. I was looking forward to a meeting between just the two of us.

On the drive back the interpreter gave me a little more information about the village, the Bupati and Gultom. From this I deduced that Gultom was the real source of my invitation to the meeting. A complex man. As we entered Gleno the leading Polri vehicle activated its lights and sirens again. They were left on until Gultom's vehicle pulled into the police compound.

I arrived back at Headquarters to another surprise. Four new CivPol had arrived. From Pakistan were Superintendents Ashraf and Robin, and from Malaysia Warrant Officers Ali and Ruslan. Others were already looking after them, including feeding them and finding temporary accommodation. They asked me to deliver the initial briefing to the newcomers; amazing how quickly one becomes an expert in this place! One of the things I told them was that in allocating duties I would try and keep at least two members of each nationality together. There was discussion on the two sub-districts still to have CivPol allocated. As a result, Ashraf and Robin were allocated to teams to be based in Letefoho with Ali and Ruslan destined for Fatobolo. Ali and Ruslan's language skills were an additional benefit for the teams. Interpreters would not be required for the teams they were allocated to.

We had hardly finished our discussions when there was another urgent request for help on the radio. This time it was not from one of our groups based in Ermera, but a group who were coming over the mountains to Ermera with armed Militia in pursuit. From their call sign I thought they were a UNAMET communications team from Dili. As a guess I presumed they had been establishing radio relay sites in the mountains and ran into a bit of trouble. The rest of the afternoon was now spent on the radio, and telephone to Dili, guiding the errant team to safety. While there was not a great deal we could do, the fact I kept in contact with them provided a degree of moral support. After a while they reported the Militia did not appear to be behind them anymore. I still was not certain who they were, and Dili was just as confused. There were not supposed to be any communications people in that area, but it was definitely a communications team call sign they were using to identify themselves. Eventually we guided them into a safe arrival in Hatolia. Brett Swan, with the help of John Tanti, took over before sending them on their way to Gleno.

Now it was time for my normal end of day activities. First debriefing CivPol members on their activities, including the patrol members who followed up on yesterday's report of Militia violence. Phil Hunter and Max Knoth also gave a report on their first visit to Atsabe. They had not had sufficient time to arrange things as it took over three hours to drive there with a drive back of the same duration. With the teams they had made a start and should be able to get everything sorted out well before the start of voter registration.

This was followed by the daily management and planning meeting for tomorrow. During the meeting Baldev informed us of his discussions regarding the soldier who had walked into the UN house the night before. Lieutenant Colonel Nurr had given a personal guarantee that it would not happen again. Activities for the next day were confirmed and outlines for the three days following were tentatively agreed to.

At the end I just managed to allocate all the CivPol tasks before Captain Ari arrived for our daily meeting. As promised, he had some answers on my question about the alleged Militia violence. Yes, there had been trouble in the nominated village on the stated night. It had started as an argument about politics between two individuals. One, who just happened to be the pro-independence supporter, had been beaten up by a few pro-autonomy supporters. The only injuries were bruises. Ari had not found out if the pro-autonomy people were Militia or not. The report Ari had obtained coincided very closely with the report I had received from the CivPol who went to the village. The main difference being the CivPol patrol was told that it was definitely Militia who started the argument and did the beating.

This verification of who had provoked and perpetrated the violence now established two things for me. Ari had followed up on my question and come back with an answer that was very close to the truth. Whenever possible I would continue to have CivPol conduct investigations into complaints made to us as well as report the matters to Polri. Generally, future responses from Ari were always similar to the information gathered by CivPol. I didn't know why at the time, but I sensed Gultom was the driving force behind this cooperation.

The second thing I learnt was the propensity for the local population to exaggerate. The exaggeration on this occasion was later matched or bettered in almost every report of Militia violence. Only once would I receive a firsthand account of an attack, every other time the story had been told through a number of people before finally getting to us. The more people involved, the greater the final exaggeration. Even though frustrating, we continued to follow up as there was always some basis to the report. However, not all reports were related to political activities, there were occasions where they were purely day to day criminal matters and therefore out of even my extended protective mandate.

Before Ari left, I told him about the incident of the UN team being chased out of Bobinaro by the Militia and asked him to follow up for me. He undertook to try, but indicated an answer would take some time, if it came at all, because it occurred in another district. He would have to speak to Gultom who would have to personally send the request through Dili. Finally, I finished the daily routine of meetings and reports by reporting to the CivPol duty officer in the Dili Joint Operations Centre (JOC).

It was almost dark when the harassed UNAMET 'communications' team arrived in Gleno. It turned out they were not a communications team at all. It was Dave Savage and his electoral team from Maliana.

'Boss I've never been so happy to see someone in my life', were Dave's first words.

He quickly told me the story. Briefly they had left Maliana to conduct an education program in a nearby village. Before reaching their intended destination, they had run into a Militia roadblock and had just gone straight through it, seemingly without problem. But suddenly there was a change and the Militia were in vehicles and following them. So, Dave put his foot down, lost the Militia and ended up in Gleno. From his expression and his voice, it had obviously been a traumatic trip.

While comparing the work with Mozambique, I put my arm around his shoulder and said, 'Already I'm not sure if I've been here for 5 days or five months.' (The full story of this incident is in Dave's book *Dancing with the Devil*)

I suggested he use the satellite telephone (satphone)and call home. He jumped at the chance. The AFP had provided one satellite phone for each district for reporting emergency situations, but for some unknown reason from Gleno it would not connect to any number in Dili. In addition, each AFP member was allowed ten minutes phone time each week to call home.

As I was walking Dave out to the telephone pole beside Headquarters I said, 'And we are really going to earn this one.'

Then I pointed out the area, about one square metre in size, where the satphone would work. Everywhere else around the headquarters building was a dead zone as far as it was concerned.

At 7.45 p.m. we called it quits and I took Dave to the Guest House for dinner. He claimed it was the best meal since his arrival in East Timor. With hunger sated, we headed home for a warm shower and a good night's sleep. I noted in my diary that night '*Going to have to go to point form* [rather than narrative entries], *just not enough time in the day*'.

Morning. It seems strange, but the roosters were not as loud down in the valley. Or is it I am getting used to them? No more complaints from the girls about the radio noise.

Dave wanted to make an early start as it was a long trip to

Maliana via Dili. So, breakfast was a 6.45a.m. cup of tea at Headquarters. I gave him the letter I had finished last night so he could get it into the mail for Australia. Contact with home was problematic in Ermera.

After waving Dave and his team off, there was a little time before my first meeting. I started putting together the information I had already gathered. I was looking for the small clues that either linked events together or indicated larger security challenges which would impact on future planning for the preparation and conduct of the ballot. I only got so far before there was another radio call for assistance.

This call was from one of the UN helicopters trying to land. The assigned landing zone was covered with children. I drove a short distance to the football field (soccer) that doubled as our helicopter landing zone (LZ). It was easy to see and hear the helicopter, a Super Puma, circling the town. On arrival I saw the field covered with what I was sure were hundreds of children, although that may be a slight exaggeration on my part. Other adults arrived, including a number of Polri, and with a lot of effort from everyone we created enough open space for the pilot to land safely. I was not expecting what happened next. The pilot shut the engine down. With the rotors stopped there was nowhere near enough of us to control the kids as they closed in around the aircraft. They did not touch anything, just got as close as they could.

The pilots had shut down because they would be waiting for their passengers, technicians from UN communications, who they were flying around all districts updating base radio equipment, including better aerials. One of the crew, two UN people and Polri stayed to protect the helicopter. The rest of the chopper crew headed to the local markets. I took the technicians to Headquarters with a specific request to improve the communications with Hatolia. I then left them to it and went to my first appointment, briefing yesterday's new arrivals, both CivPol and volunteers. Their entire morning would be spent being briefed by different UN people.

The technicians finished their work. Before I drove them back to the landing zone, I called Brett and John at Hatolia. I was delighted because the new communications set up enabled direct contact between Gleno and all parts of Hatolia village, including their house and the registration site. Communications are an important safety measure that reduces risk and enable quicker responses in emergencies.

Somehow, we managed to clear the children off the landing zone again. The crew started up and the chopper lifted off. Any control we thought we had over the children immediately ended. It was like a flash flood as they poured onto the field and underneath the lifting chopper. We watched as they were blown over by the down draft from the blades. Blown over and rolling along in the wind. And laughing! Laughing and having fun! This was definitely the best game in town, and they made the most of it. It was to be repeated every time the helicopters came to Gleno. And every time I worried there would be a loss of power and the chopper would come down on top of them. But there was nothing any of us could do, and definitely not enough to physically stop them. It did not take many days for us to realise somehow the children always knew the helicopter was on its way long before we did. With this knowledge we quickly identified the mass movement of children towards the landing zone as the indicator we would be needed to clear the space because a chopper was coming.

Immediately after the helicopter lifted off the children's attention had switched to us as we walked to our cars. Each of them wanted to hold, or at least touch, one of the UN people. I tried to count the number hanging onto me as I walked off the field. Twenty was as good a number as any. Finally, I extricated myself and got into the vehicle. I immediately did a check of all my pockets. On previous missions if that many children had got that close then my pockets would have been rifled. In fact, I would have been lucky not have lost my pants as well. This time nothing was taken. And nothing disappeared on the many future visits of the helicopters. The children were poor but honest.

Just after lunch another convoy arrived from Dili. New people were arriving very quickly now. There were more UNV and new CivPol. Three Lieutenant Colonels from Thailand, including the Thai contingent Commander, Somchai 'Sam' Ratanaarpa, with Nitaya Bongkot, the only female officer posted to Ermera, and Natsakon 'Nat' Ajjanasupatn; and three Police Officers from the USA, Tommy Kinsella, Randy Martinak and Jim France.

Sam; Randy

First off, I shouted them lunch at the Guest House. During the meal Sam approached me requesting I find a position for Nitaya, who was the only female CivPol officer deployed to Ermera, at my headquarters. I agreed at the time but was to find out later he had not consulted her. After lunch I gave them the standard briefing including discussion on deployments to fill vacancies that existed. We settled on Sam and Nat joining Phil and Max in Atsabe; Nitaya and Jim staying in Gleno in the role of CivPol duty officers, including communications; Randy joining a Gleno-based team; and Tommy volunteered to join Brett and John in Hatolia, he claimed working with Aussies was the same as with Americans. At the time everyone seemed satisfied. However, shortly after Nitaya approached me and strongly requested I place her in a team. To keep Sam out of possible trouble I told her I had selected her for the duty officer role because of her high standard of English. This was partly true and also essential for the position, but I think she knew Sam had spoken with me. After further discussion, and just a little pressure from her, I agreed to put her in a team as soon as a suitable replacement arrived for the duty officer role. She was a very determined lady.

During this time all the patrols were getting reports of, or experiencing, increased Militia activity in every village they visited. Dili Headquarters warned of a threatened Militia attack against an unspecified UN location. It was a general threat with no specified place or time but the number of sources of the threat raised concerns. The residents of Bad Manor volunteered to carry out an all-night watch. To them it made sense. There were enough of them in the house for the shifts to be short; and, the Bad Manor was in the ideal position to look over the whole town. It made perfect sense, so I accepted their offer. For a few days we were on increased alert 24/7, if it was actually possible to be on a higher state of alert.

The rest of the afternoon and into the early evening I spent at meetings. It was 7.30 p.m. when I finished the daily meeting with Ari. He still had no information on the Maliana incident, but he had something on every other matter from the previous day. When asked about the increased Militia activity he agreed Polri had also noted it. He could not, or would not, provide any further information.

Diana and Saku arrived at Headquarters just as Ari was leaving. So, we headed off to the Guest House for dinner. Shortly after we got home there was a power failure. Not just a small one but the whole town. With the current Militia threat my heart rate went up. The Bad Manor boys called on the radio to reassure everyone they were watching. This settled my mind a little. But I turned the volume up on the portable radio. Just in case. I kept writing my letter by candlelight. The two girls were chatting about Saku's phone call home. She had told her family about the 'father figure' she was living with.

She turned to me, 'I was really looking for a mother figure, but you'll do.'

At least it was good to be wanted. Finally, we heard the town generator kick in and the power was back on. As good a time as any to end another day.

Next morning, I was at the helicopter landing zone by 7.30am to greet the CivPol Chief of Staff who was dropping in for a visit. While waiting I asked a couple of the Polri NCOs to get a message to all the kids about the hazards of the landing zone. I explained what could happen and the simple way of reducing the risk. Somehow, we managed to get the message across to them that when the helicopter was arriving no children were to go onto the landing zone until we said it was 'OK'. Later helicopter arrivals showed that part of the message got through. Every attempt we made to change their behaviour on the departures was completely ignored. When the chopper lifted off the tsunami of kids always poured out into the downdraft.

The Chief of Staff's visit was a personal check on how we were progressing. More on how the different components were getting on with each other than anything else. Ermera was working reasonably well. I was happy with the cooperation and relationship I had with Allessandro, Baldev and Samulcai; the different nationalities within CivPol were working together without problems; all CivPol appeared to have an acceptable relationship with the DEOs in the teams; and then there was our Political Affairs Officer. Well, perfection was something that could not be expected. After a CivPol briefing from me, Allessandro gave him an overall management briefing. As he left, he gave his opinion that we were a little further ahead in preparations than other districts. My only thought was, there is still a lot to do.

Once he was gone it was time to get the teams up and about. Today was market day. A busy one for Polri as people flooded in to either buy or sell. So, few escorts were available for movement of UN personnel. It was time to move autonomously. The locations selected for patrols had been carefully chosen and were reasonably close. For the second time, I dispatched unescorted teams. Just in case there was Militia intimidation or other misadventures, I had a small quick reaction reserve of CivPol on standby near vehicles. They were not needed that day.

About this time, I submitted my first request to Dili to be allocated some helicopter time for reconnaissance purposes. I expected to get a more comprehensive understanding of the district by viewing it from the air. I was told they would think about it. Regularly I updated my request, but never got the flight.

CHAPTER 10

Establishing Relationships

Meanwhile it was time for my first one-on-one meeting with my counterpart, Lieutenant Colonel Doctor Erry Gultom. Captain Ari was there to interpret. I was determined to make this a good start to our relationship. I knew showing respect would be essential so when I entered his office the first thing I did was salute. Ari then made the formal introductions and the first cup of the obligatory coffee was served. Brewed differently than previous locations and tasting even better. This was followed by our first cigarette together accompanied by polite questions on family and background. Just 'getting to know you' stuff. Discussion of our joint participation in the recent village meeting proved to be an excellent way of moving from the polite conversation to more serious issues. After a while we found ourselves relying on Ari less and less. Gultom was speaking in Indonesian, but I could understand most of what he said. I was speaking in English and generally he could understand me. Although I have to say he had more trouble understanding me when I tried to use my limited Indonesian. Perhaps it was my accent. However, he acknowledged his appreciation of my efforts.

I considered this initial meeting a success. He had accepted my decision to send patrols without escort but nominated areas where there should always be an escort. These areas just happened to coincide with those I considered to have the most active Militia. As we concluded the meeting Gultom suggested we not have a fixed meeting regime, such as the once a week suggested by Dili, instead we should meet only when necessary. Although I was certain he wanted to avoid meetings, I agreed. I was already confident enough to believe that anytime I requested a meeting, I would get it. I was not to know I would test this expectation that very afternoon.

The tempo of the day increased suddenly about the same time as I arrived back at headquarters. A message from Dili Headquarters arrived directing the commencement of the registration process on Tuesday 13 July, 35 days away. So little time. So much to do. Joint planning started there and then. Just when we thought we were finished; Dili threw in a variation. UN personnel had moved back into Liquicia after the recent Militia attack but had not been able to reach one area in the mountains close to the Ermera border. Therefore, they had allocated the area to us. UNVs for the extra team would be sent later. Unfortunately, there would be no additional CivPol. I would just have to find a way of putting a member with the team. This also meant I had to reduce CivPol strength at Gleno Headquarters, so Nitaya would get her request.

With the initial UN news, I had already decided to ask for another meeting with Gultom. The news on Liquicia just added to the urgency so I decided to push for it that afternoon. I called Ari. He made the arrangements while we were still on the phone. Gultom was available right now. This was the first of many meetings where we got together and got on with the job. It was almost a pleasure working with him. The only area of competition seemed to be which of us could smoke the most cigarettes and/or drink the most coffee.

There were even times when I felt sorry for the non-smoking Captain Ari. On this occasion we had little trouble in reaching broad agreement on the support of registration processes in Ermera. Further joint meetings would be held once the detail was worked out by both sides. Liquicia was a different problem. I could tell he wasn't happy this new area had been added. He would either have to get the area reallocated to him or arrange for Polri, in his words preferably Brimob, from Liquicia to take over the escort at the district border. He was not happy with either option. But considered the second as the most likely outcome. Again, a productive meeting. I left with a feeling I had been working with a professional. He seemed determined to carry out his allocated role to the best of his ability.

Now another meeting with more detailed planning between the ensemble of UN component groups — electoral, police, security, administrative, political and military liaison. The leading components were Electoral and CivPol with advice from the Security Officer (SO), administrators (FSA)and the MLOs. There was a little, not so helpful pro support for the independence side, advice from our Political Officer, Helen. Allessandro then briefed all who were at Headquarters. This was followed by more detailed briefings to the members of each component. First was to the UNV. I followed this with a private briefing of the CivPol. Paul volunteered to be the CivPol officer with the Leorema team, something I appreciated very much. I informed Nitaya she was now a member of the Railaco Leten team. Her face lit up. Now I was wondering how I was going to explain to Sam one of his subordinates was going into the field against his advice.

By the time we finished briefings it was well after dark and too late to cook at home. So, to the Guest House again for dinner. Once more a meal was interrupted by an urgent radio call. Plans had to change because Ian Martin, the Special Representative of the Secretary General (SRSG) and the most senior UN person in UNAMET, was going to arrive at 7.40am the next morning. I thought, poor Captain Ari he will be sorry the day he took on this job. Before I could do more than think about special security arrangements, Ari was there. I almost believed in telepathy. But no, he had a problem this time. Two Australian CivPol were camped by the river at Manussi and Polri were concerned for their safety. Did I know who they were or why they were there? A check quickly revealed they were not from Ermera District. As the location was almost on the joint border for three districts, I contacted Dili and left the problem with them. At least for the night. It was time for my first nip from the bottle of single malt in the bag, yes, the bag had even had one bottle of a good single malt, and then a good night's sleep.

Introducing Seco

The day after taking over the house I had interviewed and employed Seco as our house boy. He was a strong local lad about 16 or 17 years of age. His father, Nicolai, was the janitor and maintenance man at UN Headquarters, Gleno. Seco's tasks were to keep the house clean, wash any dishes that happened to have been used; wash our clothes, although there were indications, he subcontracted this task to ladies in the town, and, polish my boots. I had two pair of boots so that I could wear them day on and day off, standard procedure for drying them in a tropical climate.

The agreement I reached with Seco was I would leave the house key in the door when I left each morning and he would lock up and bring it to Headquarters when he finished work. This morning I saw another example of Timorese honesty. Seco arrived early and handed me my Mozambique coin. While the coin itself is almost worthless, in fact about 1/20000th of a dollar, Seco could not have known this. I had a strong sentimental attachment to the coin and if I was caught without it by another member of that contingent it could prove expensive for me as I would have to 'shout' all present former ONUMOZ members a drink of their choice. Therefore, I normally kept mine with me all the time, tied up in the corner of a handkerchief and in my pants pocket. Yesterday morning I had forgotten to remove it when I put the pants out for washing. Seco found it and returned it. He was turning out to be a very good employee.

From the beginning he kept the house and our clothes very clean and was doing a reasonable job polishing my boots. The only complaints I had related to the boots. There always seemed to be wet polish on the laces, and this got onto my hands as I put the boots on. That and the tins of polish were used up very quickly. A few weeks later, on a rare occasion when I went to the house for lunch, I found out why. In essence both problems were my fault. How could I possibly have expected someone who had never owned a pair of shoes, or even seen polish, to know how to clean them properly? In his attempts to do the job properly and get the shine to match what it was before he started, he just kept rubbing on more and more polish. No one had ever shown him how to put it on and then brush it off to get a shine. So, I gave him a short lesson on polishing boots. Both boot polishing problems immediately went away.

The only other issue I had in these very early days was a desire to have my uniforms more highly pressed after the wash. Seco was getting a pretty good standard just putting creases in the local fashion, with his hands. Even so, I knew an iron would do a better job. It was only a few days later I would find the time to visit the local markets and make a number of purchases, including an electric iron. Other items purchased were two kerosene cooking stoves, some pots and pans, a plastic bin for additional water storage and two large plastic bowls for showering. The shopping in the markets had its own surprise. This was the first place I had ever been where no one wanted US dollars, which was what Mission Subsistence Allowance (MSA) was paid in. Indonesian currency was the only acceptable tender. There were not even any black-market money changers. So, there was a regular need for someone going to Dili to visit the bank and convert the US dollars from those who wanted it, into local currency.

Once I got the iron back home, I showed Seco how to use it. I have to say he learnt quickly, and my uniforms looked much better, at least at the start of the day. Later, after he left with most of his family on the first evacuation convoy to Dili in early September, Seco 'went to the forest' which is a term the locals used when someone left their village to link up with Falantil guerrillas. As I think of it now, he was probably a member of Falantil all along and part of their security plan for us. The last I heard of him was in 2006 when he was a member of Bishop Belo's staff.

CHAPTER 11

THE NEXT STEPS

With the Mozambique coin safely tucked into the pants pocket I headed off to Headquarters in anticipation of Ian Martin's visit. I wasn't quite as clean as usual because today there had been no water through the system. With the cistern being low, a shower was replaced with the bare minimum of body wiping with a wet cloth.

The Super Puma helicopter arrived on time not only with Ian Martin, but his entire senior management team including Alan Mills, the UN Commissioner of Police. Thankfully, every component head from the Ermera district was present with their vehicles so we had sufficient transport to get the VIP group to Gleno HQ.

Ian Martin told us he and his team were visiting to be given first-hand reports on the security situation and to present their ideas for the registration phase. With Allessandro leading off, each component leader gave their impression of the security situation in Ermera. In essence, each identified the potential for violence, but there was disagreement about who was thought to be controlling the Militia. I had deliberately waited till the last because this was my first chance to hear some of the opinions and ideas of others on this important issue. Amongst information that came out was a suggestion the second in command of the TNI battalion was directing the Militia in Ermera District. The MLOs suggested on Militia matters he reported directly to someone in Dili and not to, or through, Lieutenant Colonel Nurr. When it came to my turn, I gave them my opinion that the Militia had instructions to intimidate local and UN personnel, interrupt the electoral process if possible, encourage a pro-autonomy vote but not to injure international persons. While this did not surprise many who were there, my follow-up point about the role of Indonesian authorities in Militia violence did. Plainly put, I told them in my opinion Polri in Ermera would do everything they could to assist getting the ballot process completed and protect UN internationals. But, and it was a big BUT, the Militia are so ill-disciplined with many having their own agenda, there was a strong possibility they could, and probably would, ignore Indonesian orders. I stated my belief that with the help of Polri, we could hold the Ermera Militia in check and conduct the ballot successfully.

With our input completed, Ian and his staff briefed us on voter registration. It would commence on time and would be run in 5-day blocks. There would be four full days of registration followed by a half day. On the afternoon of the fifth day teams would consolidate the information gathered so far, get that information to their district headquarters where it would be further consolidated and forwarded to Dili. From Dili it would be sent to the Australian Electoral Commission (AEC) in Australia. The AEC had the responsibility of turning this into site by site electoral rolls and other materials needed for the ultimate conduct of the Popular Consultation.

This 5-day block process would be carried out four times. However, at the end of the second 5-day period there would be another visit from Dili senior management to assess the security situation. If the security situation did not improve, the decision had already been taken to postpone the second half of registration, and the remainder of the process, including the vote. It would only be recommenced when security improved.

As everyone was getting ready to move to the landing zone,

Alan Mills reminded me, he would probably have to replace me with one of the incoming South American contingent commanders.

Briefings done, the senior management team got back in the helicopter and were on their way to the next district.

When Allessandro and I got back to Headquarters, the teams, who should have already been out on the road, were waiting expectantly. They had every right to be just as curious as we had been at the start of the day. Between the two of us we gave them a full run-down on the meeting before cracking the whips and sending them on their way. Not long after this Brett and John arrived in from Hatolia. They claimed that without an escort the trip took them only 45 minutes. I would not have liked to have been sitting in that vehicle!

I gathered all of the CivPol who were still in Gleno, including Phil and Max, so they could get first-hand information on the situation at sub district level. Brett described the roadblocks set up just at the edge of Hatolia every morning. Six Militia armed with homemade weapons and machetes used a small tree trunk as a barrier across the road. John tested the nature of the roadblock by getting out of his car and putting the barrier aside and driving through. Since then, the Militia group had remained on station but had not put the barrier across the road.

More ominously, the afternoon after John had first driven through the vehicle check point, and just about every afternoon afterwards, the local Militia leader had ridden back and forward past the UN house with a sports rifle across the handlebars of his motorbike, the barrel always pointed at the house. This was an obvious attempt to intimidate. Brett had spoken with the local Polri Sergeant who had shrugged his shoulders and said there was nothing he could do. I put this on the top of the list to discuss with Ari when we next met.

The most pressing security situation was a report that west of Hatolia at a place called Sare there were 4,500 Internally Displaced Persons (IDPs) doing it tough. The Militia had driven this group from Bobinaro and Liquicia so they could not register for the Popular Consultation. Reportedly, the Militia were forcibly holding them at that location. A CivPol patrol had discovered well-manned Militia roadblocks in the area. Later CivPol patrols, comprised of Australian, New Zealand and US police, took the risk and pushed through these roadblocks to reach Sare and the IDPs.

The tactic of isolating large groups of IDP from the registration process was direct defiance of UN agreements with Indonesia. Allessandro and I decided to establish a small permanent registration site in Sare. US CivPol Officer, Tommy Kinsella, became part of this electoral team. In the entire period leading up to the Popular Consultation he, along with Brett Swann and John Tanti, were to regularly patrol into the border area of Liquicia in response to reports of violence being committed against the population. On some of these patrols they took steps to release persons who had been taken hostage by the Militia. On others they brought back persons who had been injured/wounded in a Militia attack. Arrangements would then be made to have the person/s taken, by road, to hospital in Dili.

At the meeting John Tanti put forward a request, because of the heat, to wear shorts instead of the long uniform pants. I explained to him, and everyone else, the Dili directive, shorts were not to be worn, adding, ''I will give you advance warning whenever I am coming to visit.'

John started to ask the same question again but before he could complete it a sudden elbow to the solar plexus from another interrupted his words. They all understood the import of my message about warnings before visits.

Phil and Max gave us an update on their visits so far to Atsabe, including a description of their future house with the 22 steps to the front door, and their plans for the move in two days' time. Phil was still having a little internal team trouble over who should have the key to the vehicle. While the senior UNV was happy for the CivPol to drive the vehicles, once back in base, he wanted the keys because he considered himself personally responsible. Phil did not want me to take this key matter any further at the moment, just to be aware of the tension.

Atsabe House

Max also raised the issue of escorts. From what they had seen so far, they were pretty sure Atsabe Polri did not have any vehicles to provide any of the escorts they were going to need.

I told them my decision, 'I accept the responsibility of Polri travelling in UN vehicles, but you are to make sure their weapons are placed out of sight on the floor of the vehicles while you are travelling.'

Everyone seemed happy with the solution. I also passed on the serious consideration I was giving to authorising travel without escort including the discussion I had already had with Gultom. I had already implemented, after reaching agreement with Gultom, travel to and from Dili without seeking approval or having an escort. In addition, between meetings I was broadening my experience by doing a bit of unescorted patrol work of my own. I was now very close to making the final decision to extend the 'no escort' policy to almost all our operations.

Before Brett and John headed off back to Hatolia we all went up to Bad Manor where half of the rations and water in the unauthorized storeroom was split between the Hatolia and Atsabe teams. The rest would be split between the other sub-districts as they were deployed. I also made a mental note to have any CivPol going to Dili include a visit to the UN warehouse. The target would be to get as much rations and water as they could without signing for it. These we would continue to quietly distribute among the sub-district teams to build up contingency stocks. That afternoon I joined other component commanders to brief more newly arrived UNV.

Following this briefing I debriefed CivPol officers as they returned from patrol. Paul and Crazy had been to Leorema, our added village from Liquicia District. They had no trouble getting to the village and had not only received a very warm welcome, but a mini festival had been put on by the local population, I had heard some of it when Paul called on the UN radio. A lot more reconnaissance needed to be done to find more ways in and out of the village. Robin and Ashraf had been to Letefoho, which was about halfway to Atsabe and would be able to deploy in a couple of days. Ali and Ruslan had been out beyond Ermera village. This area was set up last and therefore it was the furthest behind in preparations. Because of the travel time from Gleno they were still to get to the furthest villages in their area. Therefore, in the interim, they had arranged temporary accommodation in Ermera Village itself, which would become the permanent sub district base.

With just about everything done for the day, including telephoning an update to Dili, I was waiting for the generator mechanics to finish so that I could get the report typed. At 6.45 p.m., as I watched them continue their struggle with the infernal machine, I decided a mere written report could wait, at least until tomorrow.

At home I tried the first test of our new stoves. They worked but with a lot of black smoke, so they had to be used outside. I later found Seco had purchased petrol to fill them instead of kerosene. His rationale was, petrol was cheaper and he didn't want to waste our money. Once we got onto kerosene, they worked much better, the pots did not get as black and the wicks lasted longer. Tonight, was tinned Irish stew and Aussie rice for dinner and afterwards one nip of single malt before I climbed under the mosquito net and had a good night's sleep.

CHAPTER 12

First Political Meeting

I now had a new early morning routine. Yesterday I had found a small bakery in the local markets only five minutes' walk from the house. So, I got up a little earlier than usual and straight after a shower, the water had run for about 20 minutes this morning so we were about 50 percent full, and shave, I did the short walk and bought some of the buns. They were only small and did have a slight kerosene taste, but they were bread and toasted nicely on our new stove, although I made a note to get a longer fork to protect my fingers from the heat. Later I would find the local 'petrol station' received a supply of fresh buns from Dili each evening, and these had no taste of kerosene.

Captain Ari called very early in the morning. Amongst other things he was after any information I had been able to get on the two Aussie CivPol who had been by the river. Unfortunately, there was still nothing I could tell him, but I made a mental note to apply some pressure and get information from Dili before our next meeting. My thought process was if I couldn't, or perhaps from his perspective wouldn't, answer questions like this then why should he go to the trouble of finding answers to my questions. Co-operation needed to go both ways.

The main matter he wanted to bring up was to check if I was aware of a political meeting being held at the UN office that day. I knew a meeting with at least some of the political parties was planned by the electoral component but did not have exact details. Ari informed me Gultom had found out about the meeting and was aware representatives from both pro-independence and pro-autonomy parties would be present. Gultom felt both he and I should also be present, if for no other reason than to ensure the meeting remained just that, a meeting, and did not degenerate into violence. I immediately saw the value in this and told Ari I would re-arrange my priorities for the day.

What a meeting! It went for hours. There was argument back and forth. There were threats thrown around. Accusations were dragged out both by pro-independence and pro-autonomy representatives. Accusations which could have derailed the whole process, but it was in this area that Gultom and I had our major impact. Between us we had an answer, gathered by previous CivPol and/or Polri patrols, for every accusation. The effect of our input was to calm the meeting sufficiently for the electoral and political components to get agreement on topics, procedures and dispute resolving processes for future meetings.

Meeting of political groups at UN HQ Gleno.

Now we were into the early afternoon, so I shouted Gultom a cup of our coffee, nowhere near as good as his, as we sat outside the UN building and had a well-deserved cigarette, or three. We agreed there was a need for both of us to be at all meetings of the political groups to input information with the idea of easing tensions. Both of us could see potential problems if they made decisions without our input and guidance, at least on security and implementation aspects.

As Gultom left I realised we had been meeting for just over 4 hours. A long meeting indeed. After he was gone, I rang Dili Headquarters again making sure they had received the written daily report (called the Situation Report shortened to acronym Sitrep) and again asking for an answer on the two CivPol camping in an isolated location. It seems my 'hurry up' message earlier in the day had the desired impact because they had an answer for me. From my position the best part of the answer was the two officers in question were not from Ermera. The later meeting with Ari went very well for both of us.

I took the opportunity to use the satellite phone and call Margaret, my wife, that evening. Apart from just wanting to say, 'Hello', I wanted her to pass on to Max and Phil's wives they would have the phone the next day and Brett and John would get it the day after. This was the only way we had of giving the wives advance notice of when their partners would have access to satellite telephone, so important for morale both at home and in Timor, and to hell with the ten minute per person per week allocation. Every time I knew someone would be going to the sub-districts or they were coming to Headquarters I called Margaret and gave her advance notice to pass on to the families. Much like the Mozambique mission, Margaret was being a great help by looking after the wives of the Australian police who were with me.

Another different day in UNAMET was almost over when I

arrived at Bad Manor. I had been invited to join them and some others for dinner. Bad luck for me the others arrived much earlier and by the time I got there all the food had been eaten. So, I went back to the Guest House.

CHAPTER 13

GETTING THE TEAMS IN PLACE.

Next morning, I was down at HQ early with the aim of getting the teams deploying to Atsabe away on time. It turned out to be a good move as added pressure from me was definitely needed. Even with that the teams did not get away anywhere near on time.

At the designated time the four CivPol, two Thais and two Aussies, the locally employed staff and the Polri escort were there and ready to go. But there was no sign of any DEOs. They, with all sets of vehicle keys and one of the vehicles, were missing. Sam coordinated the search by Phil, Max and Nat. After an hour they finally rounded up all eight DEOs, some even had their luggage with them. A couple had not even begun to pack. It became obvious they really did not want to move to Atsabe. With a lot of coercion, and an offer of help, they were persuaded to get ready and join the others.

Once this was underway the senior DEOs handed over the keys to the vehicles. Sam and the crew found none of them had been refuelled. That was when all present DEOs, whether from the Atsabe teams or not, they got their first example of me as an angry CivPol Commander. Refuelling of vehicles took a lot of time because the only fuel point in the town stored the diesel in 44-gallon drums. There was no pump you could pull up to and put the nozzle in and just fill up. You had to wait while fuel was pumped by hand from a drum into a five-litre plastic container which was then poured into the vehicle. This process was repeated until the tank was full. As there was only one worker at the service station only one vehicle could be done at a time. You were not allowed to assist with the refuelling. That was the reason the policy had been implemented, but obviously not obeyed, for vehicles to be refuelled at the end of each day.

The CivPol and local drivers headed off to refuel the vehicles. I kept a close eye on the DEOs. I was allowing no one to slip away. Once the vehicles were back it was everyone on board and I got them on their way about 10.30am. In normal times it would take one vehicle three hours to get to Atsabe, but travelling in convoy always takes longer, in this case an extra hour. The escort had to turn around and come back to Gleno. I hoped this delayed departure would not cause problems with the escorts for future convoys. Two more were planned for the next day.

Refuelling Gleno Style

Once that convoy was out of the way I needed to get away from HQ and cool my head down. So, I decided to patrol the streets of Gleno. I got one of the interpreters to come along with me as there might just be an opportunity to speak with some of the locals, or even better more of the Militia. As I headed down towards the TNI base I remembered Paul had left earlier for Leorema. Yesterday he had given me very good instructions on how to get there, so I decided today was the day to go through Militia territory without an escort.

The first part of the trip was on the road to Dili and then you turned left onto a dirt track and started climbing into the mountains. Now if Paul's directions had not been so good, I am not sure where I would have ended up, because there was a multitude of track options. For one brief moment I thought I had made a wrong turn, but all of a sudden, I was out in the open and right on top of a real razorback ridge. To the north I could see all the way to the ocean and to the south Gleno itself. In both directions the view was magnificent. The top of the razor back ridge itself varied between 15 and 30 metres in width with a track down the centre capable of taking one vehicle. On both sides grass was growing to about one metre high with the odd flattened spot to assist with vehicles travelling in opposite directions passing each other. Every so often there was a small dwelling, with thatched roof, perched on the very edge of the ridge. While I was on the ridge line the track was amazingly straight but before too long it was back on the mountain and the winding roads resumed.

I arrived in Leorema and stopped. Before I could get out of the vehicle I was completely surrounded by locals. Welcomes in other areas had been warm but this was extraordinary. While Paul was introducing me to the village elders' others had started to prepare a meal. This was something that had not occurred so far, but I would see it more and more in the coming weeks. Almost every time I arrived in a village, food would be prepared. Depending on the time of day it would be morning tea, lunch or afternoon tea. Later I tried varying my arrival times hoping they would not go to this trouble. I was singularly unsuccessful; it was something they insisted on doing.

On this visit I was given solid information by the village elders on their concerns about the local Militia. They had very good grounds for their concern as the Militia came from Liquicia. Lead by Guteres they were arguably the most violent group in East Timor.

After lunch I was taken for a walk around the village which was typical of everywhere I had seen so far, with one small exception. Between two of the largest buildings there was a small gambling operation being conducted. You could almost say it was a small outdoor casino. I watched for a short while. The games they were playing were completely unfamiliar to me, so I declined an offer to participate. Each time I was to come back to this village the gambling den was always in full swing.

Just after we started our return trip, I heard one of the Letefoho teams report that there was a house on fire at their present location. Jim France, the operator at Base 3, said he would pass the information on to Polri. I asked the interpreter with me what they did for a house fire. His answer was pretty blunt, nothing. It was too dangerous to try and put out a fire, so you let it burn until it went out. What you did do was make sure if sparks reached other buildings they were quickly put out. The villagers would then help rebuild the burnt house.

A little further along the track Base 3 called me. Jim told me two more CivPol had arrived. They were from Brazil and one was Lt Col Amorin. Memories of Mozambique flooded back. Could this possibly be the former Major Amorin de Sousa who I had the privilege to serve with in Beira as part of ONUMOZ. No, coincidences like that are just too good to be true. When I arrived back at HQ, I found they do happen as this was the same Amorin from Mozambique. There were man hugs before we got away for a short time and brought each other up to date on mutual friends and what we had been doing ourselves. I explained to him we did not have the luxury of numbers here that we had in Mozambique. I explained the roles we were performing and what I was aiming for if/when current numbers improved. He informed me he was the Brazilian Contingent Commander and his offsider in Ermera was Captain Delmer. That gave me three contingent commanders working for me.

Then it was back to work. The teams being deployed to the sub districts of Letefoho and Fatu Besse were all in the conference room. I followed Electoral, Security, the Doc and the FSA in briefing them. As I stepped in front of them, I could almost see in their eyes memories of this morning's events.

At the very end I made it simple, 'Two convoys will be leaving here no later than 8 a.m. tomorrow morning. Anyone who is not ready and in the vehicle at that time will not be going. I will personally take everyone who is late to Dili where I have arranged for them to be put on the first flight out of the mission. All vehicles will be fully fuelled tonight. Are there any questions?'

There were none.

With the briefings finished we held the regular afternoon meeting. A short meeting because with everything just having been put into place there was not much to discuss. We would need more information from Dili and a lot of feedback from the teams before we started to firm up our plans.

But you could almost bet on it, before the meeting finished there was a radio call for help. This time from the CivPol located in Maubessi, a sub district of Suai. They were concerned as they could not contact their district HQ and a patrol they were expecting was now well overdue. I became the relay point between Maubessi and Dili, with Dili being a relay point back to Suai. It took a while, and I fitted in the daily meeting with Ari between radio and/or telephone calls. Finally, at 7.40 p.m. everything had been resolved, the missing patrol had been located and was safe. I had agreed for us to act as a radio relay for Maubessi until better communications were established for them.

That night the Guest House was full of Aussies and Kiwis but there was plenty of food for me before I headed off home. Seco had ironed my uniforms and they looked considerably better than the old finger pressing way. He had put two nails in the wall of my bedroom that were just perfect for hanging my newly ironed uniforms on the wire coat hangers he had obtained. The housemates were still out, this time having dinner with the MLOs. I managed to write a bit in the diary and some more in the latest letter before the eyes got a bit heavy and I went to bed.

Monday 12 July and at 7 a.m. I was at work. I probably could not keep my promise of putting people on a plane if they did not turn up on time for the convoy, but I was still determined to get them away as early as possible. As it turned out I needn't have worried. My statement had its effect and the first convoy left 20 minutes early with the second rolling with one minute to spare. Although other problems would hold up convoys in the future, never again would it be because the UN personnel were not ready.

By the end of that afternoon, Monday 12 July 1999, the UN in Ermera had established an ongoing presence in all of its sub districts. As further personnel arrived, they would be placed into current teams or additional teams would be created to meet identified needs.

The afternoon started with a planning meeting between me and the MLOs This was followed by being at the helipad at 2 p.m. to welcome an MLO group from Dili, including Brigadier General Rezaqul Haider (Bangladesh) the Senior MLO for the mission. Baldev and I gave a briefing at our HQ and then returned to the helipad for the usual fun and games with the children.

All this took time and the daily Sitrep to HQ Dili was a little late, they even telephoned to remind me, and there was still the

Electoral meeting to be held. The meeting was successfully over, the verbal Sitrep had been given over the phone and the written version completed so that it could be faxed in, when the secure fax machine worked that is. More often than not it was taken to Dili the next day, with the helicopter crew picking it up on the days they visited.

In their short stay today the helicopter crews told me each week some of them went to Darwin for a two-day break. If I had letters pre-addressed and stamped, they would post them in Darwin. This promised to be a much quicker system than through the UN. From then on, I kept the current letter with me all the time, adding when possible, and sealing the envelope whenever a chopper arrived. I passed this offer on to the others and kept their letters in the glove box. This was another much-appreciated bit of assistance from the helicopter crews.

CHAPTER 14

PRE-REGISTRATION PERIOD

Planning in Ermera was for the creation of 21 Electoral Teams. The sub districts had now been established and staffed:

- Fatubesse — two teams
  (based in the village of Ermera itself);
- Letefoho — three teams;
- Hatolia — three teams;
- Atsabe — four teams; and
- Based in Gleno — nine teams.

For the teams based in Gleno there were still shortages of personnel, both DEO and CivPol, and vehicles. In addition, I was trying very hard to get additional vehicles just for CivPol. Both would be resolved in time. Personnel would continue to arrive until after the start of registration and additional vehicles would be delivered.

Each of the teams was responsible for a Polling Site. However, in almost all locations, there would be more than one Polling Station at the site. Information had been provided by the AEC that, on the day of voting, a Polling Station could readily handle 600 people and, if pushed, the maximum number of persons it was estimated could be processed was 800. So, as the numbers of people registering at each site increased so the number of Polling Stations within those sites increased. As an example, once the final numbers were in, the Polling Site in Gleno needed a total of seven Polling Stations to handle the number of people registered at that location. Each additional Polling Station created a need for an additional three or four local staff. Recruitment and training of these people commenced at this time.

With the reluctant agreement of Gultom, with exceptions for a few locations, I had done away with the need for the teams to have a Polri escort when travelling. One proviso I placed on the teams was whenever they planned to go into a new area, they would fully brief me with the details so I could discuss it with Gultom. This worked very well from then on.

On the majority of days each of the teams would visit either their selected polling site or a feeder village in the morning. While there they would provide information to the local population on the processes put in place for voter registration. The teams mostly returned to their base about lunch time.

I had instructed the CivPol to conduct vehicle patrols, preferably with at least two members in each, whenever possible. The instructions included approval for short one-man morning patrols while their team conducted education sessions. As all sub-districts had more than one team two member patrols were possible when the teams remained in their base and/or in the afternoons after returning from education visits. In Gleno, due to not all teams being involved in education each day, it was relatively easy to arrange to have at least one CivPol crew available every day for patrol or other activities. On most days there were at least five CivPol patrols out and about in various parts of the district.

From the very commencement of the work in Ermera information was regularly being received on the threats and intimidation being carried out by pro-autonomy forces against the local population. The general theme pushed by the Militia was there was no purpose in voting in the upcoming ballot as nothing would change.

Shortly after CivPol commenced accompanying DEOs on the educational visits, rumours, and, in a few cases, actual letters, threatening the lives of UN personnel started arriving at the Gleno Headquarters. As per usual the rumours came second or third hand. We were informed the Militia had visited a village and told the locals UN personnel would be killed if they came to, or back to, the village.

The letters we received were always typed and never signed and there was a variety of delivery methods. One just appeared on a desk by the entry door and another was delivered by a local child who said he did not know the person who gave it to him. A third came from a village chief who said he had been visited during the night by masked Militia and they ordered him to get the note to us, or else. Other information came in from the Sub District bases.

How they arrived really was not the issue, the attempt to intimidate UN personnel was clearly there and needed to be addressed. After the first threat I presented the next District Management Team meeting with a policy and plan to actively patrol immediately into each and every area connected with these threats. Although there was some apprehension by the civilian personnel, I received strong support from the MLOs and the Security Officer. The policy was accepted, and implementation was left to Baldev and me.

Implementation commenced immediately. From that day on whenever one of these threats was received the next day one or more of the following would patrol into the village concerned; Myself, the MLOs and/or CivPol Patrols. On rare occasions the initial patrol was just one of these. More often than not it was a combination of two of the three. On some occasions all groups arrived together for the first visit and then came back separately at different times during the day. On a few occasions there was only one patrol available for the initial visit, but that visit was always made. Follow-up occurred by at least one group on the following day and, if at all possible, on further days. The fact CivPol and the MLOs, both groups unarmed, had ignored the threats with impunity was not lost on the volunteer DEOs.

In the case where there had been no previous educational visit to the village by an Electoral Team, arrangements were quickly put into place for the first visit to occur. Meanwhile CivPol and MLOs would continue to call in to these locations whenever they were nearby.

I could go into a description of one or more of these visits, but there is really not much to tell. On every occasion there were no problems, apart from the odd flat tire. Most of the roads were very rough and the tyres had been on the vehicles sitting in a warehouse for two years before the vehicles were purchased by the UN. If the Militia were there, they stayed out of site of the UN people. In reality the highlight of every such patrol was the warm reception all UN personnel received from the villagers. This prompt response, and the commitment we kept to ongoing visits to those villages, helped to build public confidence.

If there was one issue that may have caused a problem it was the fact I did not, at the time, inform Gultom of the threats nor of the patrols and we did not request, nor take, Polri escorts. That would have defeated the process. During later discussions I am sure Gultom knew what we were doing and was keeping a distant eye on us. In fact, one of the earliest ones was the second time he became angry with me, the first had been when I went to Leorema by myself. On this second occasion everyone else was fully committed for the next day so I decided to do the patrol by myself. That afternoon Gultom had some harsh words for me. I accepted them and we moved on. I think those occasions actually reinforced our relationship.

In addition, I tasked all CivPol members with the responsibility of building a good knowledge of the geography in their area and developing at least one alternate route for use should an evacuation be necessary. In some areas finding an alternative was very difficult, but they kept looking. In others they developed more than two options.

I followed my own rules and did as much patrolling as possible with the view to 'knowing' the district like the back of my hand. A significant difficulty was the lack of topographical maps. We had only one in the district, and it was permanently attached to the wall in the CivPol office. I almost said my office, but as already described that little room was far more than that. Individuals, including myself, had other 'maps', more tourist brochures we had brought with us due to preliminary warning that availability of maps would be an issue. They were of some help. Over time I built up four different options for withdrawing from Gleno by vehicle, two options for helicopter evacuation and, as I will explain later, an option out of left field.

It took only a short time driving myself to realise 100% of your concentration was required to survive on the narrow, winding, mountainous roads of Ermera. A stretch of 200 metres without a bend was a novelty and most roads were so narrow only one vehicle could be on there at a time. At various intervals along the roads there were short areas which allowed one vehicle to pull off to the side to allow the vehicle travelling in the opposite direction to pass. On most occasions when you met a vehicle going in the opposite direction one had to reverse back to the passing point. Generally, it was the one who had the least distance to go, but when on steeper sections it was nearly always the one that was travelling uphill who got to do a bit of downhill reversing.

Because driving was not what I wanted to concentrate on, and after asking a few questions on skill levels, I selected one of the locally employed staff, Celestino Soares, to be my driver. He was a distant relative of the Bupati.

Initially at the end of each day I got him to drive to his home. I would leave him there and drive back down the hill to my residence. I became aware he was not happy about this, but he would not tell me why. Eventually one of the interpreters told me in their society it was not proper for someone of my status to do this. So, we changed the pattern, drove to my residence and he walked up the hill from there to his home. He was always waiting by the vehicle for me the next morning. He remained my driver, and became my friend, until the day of the ballot when he was planning to take his family to vote. I never saw him after that day. About two weeks after I arrived in Darwin, I was informed he was among the UN locally employed staff who had been killed after our evacuation.

Some of these patrols I did on my own, much to the displeasure of my counterpart; others I did with a Brimob escort, always under the direct commander of 2Lt Audi. On one of the earlier patrols I was driving behind the Brimob vehicle when a number of gunshots rang out. The Brimob vehicle stopped. The following actions by the squad were as good as I had seen from an Australian infantry section in a similar situation. With one minor change. As I got out of my vehicle two of them came straight back to my vehicle and positioned me against the side of the vehicle with them between me and any other threat that may have developed. They made sure I did not do what I wanted to, join the sweep by Audi and the rest of his men. Once Audi was satisfied it was safe to proceed, we loaded up and continued on our way.

On other occasions I went with Allessandro to visit the sub districts; and there were a number of occasions when Gultom and I went in convoy to visit different villages. Trips with Gultom always involved sirens and flashing lights as we entered or left a built-up area. In those villages it was interesting to watch Gultom at work. He was definitely utilising a 'hearts and minds' approach to the locals. I could not help but think, if Indonesian officials had used that approach in the late 1970's then this mission would never have been necessary.

About this time, I decided it was time to make another visit to the Letefoho area. I had the perfect excuse as the CivPol member for their third team, Delmer from Brazil, and new DEOs needed to be transported to that location. Diana was coming along to give new instructions to the DEOs. Once again there was the age-old problem of getting everyone ready at the right time. These DEOs had not been present when my law had been laid down. They received a quick introduction. We got away only 20 minutes late, which for East Timor was not too bad. Just a short way down the road, and not quite out of town, we were called back. Another local driver had just arrived from Dili and had been allocated to the Letefoho teams. Finally, 40 minutes late now, we were underway on a trip of 22 kilometres, mostly uphill, that was to take us 58 minutes. The scenery was magnificent and now, with my own driver, I could enjoy it. During the trip we came across road work gangs in two locations. Everything being done by hand. Pounding a compound of dirt and rocks into the ruts and, in doing so, smoothing out the road. Amazingly, this kept the roads open.

On arrival in Letefoho we discovered the teams had changed their housing arrangements not long after my first visit. They were now in an idyllic spot in a brand-new building, owned by the church, at the top of a ridge line. Their accommodation was far better than anyone in Ermera and probably all other UN people in East Timor. To top it off the church was providing it free of charge. The view from the front veranda was spectacular, I could just imagine the place as a future tourist hotel. There was one problem, for the teams and the locals; food was in short supply. Even with their own shortages the locals still fed the UN personnel whenever they could. The team still appreciated the ration packs and bottled drinking water we had managed to acquire. This was just another bit of logistical planning I would have to try and continue, one way or another.

As was happening whenever I arrived in a village, and even with the food shortage, the people insisted we stay and have a meal with them. Even those who had very little always wanted to share with us.

While we were there Sam drove in from Atsabe, an hour or so further down the road, and we discussed the issues they were facing. In general, they had the same problems as everywhere else but, because of the extra travel time involved to get anywhere, they were understandably feeling a bit isolated, unsafe and left out.

Back to Gleno where I found there was a bit of internal politicking going on within the Electoral component. Allessandro, a good administrator, was not so good at managing or leading people. I had seen similar in previous missions. Over the next day or so I diplomatically spoke to a number of the volunteers and was able to convince them to get this job done we had to all work together. Problem suppressed, but not solved.

Just to show not every night was a jaunt to the guest house, this night was one of a number where I dived into the non-perishable supplies I had brought with me. On this occasion dinner, prepared by me for the three of us, was a tin of Thai Style Tuna, beans and rice with a packet pumpkin soup added for flavouring.

CHAPTER 15

Discovering who was in control

Not long after dinner Ari called around to the house. He really had a bee in his bonnet over a report Paul had submitted. Gultom had directed him to approach me. The two of us spent some time discussing everything in the report. Eventually we agreed that the facts stated in the report were probably correct, however, the 'tone' of the report showed some bias against the pro-autonomy case. I undertook to raise it with Paul. Finally, just after 10 p.m., Ari was satisfied and left. Time to get a bit of shut eye.

The following morning Ari was back at Headquarters. This time we examined all of the reports I had provided to Polri. In each instance we compared the information CivPol had obtained to that of Polri. As in the past we agreed on the facts but had difficulty in agreeing on who was 'the cause' in each instance and who was in control of Militia intimidation and violent acts. However, during the process we identified different people were providing information to each of us. In our case locals, mostly victims of intimidation and violence. Typically, the Militia did not speak with UN personnel except to try and intimidate them. For his part, Ari got the majority of his information from the Militia, with just some coming from the local population. In simple terms, locals did not trust Polri, who they believed were connected to the Militia, and trusted UN personnel to maintain their confidences. Locals were very apprehensive about complaining to Polri on anything about the Militia, fearing the information would be passed to the Militia and there would be reprisals.

We both agreed variations in perceptions or memories from participants were a normal part of police investigations. The situation that existed in East Timor made it difficult, if not impossible for either of us to get the objective truth, everything was personal perspectives. Therefore, we would continue with our established process of sharing and corroborating information. If further disagreement occurred, then we would gather more information and conduct further discussions.

Electoral staff from Dili Headquarters flew in later in the afternoon. As usual, local children let us know the helicopter was not far away long before we heard it, or the pilot called us on radio. For the children the coming and going of helicopters was still the 'best fun in town'.

After landing, and a lot of 'Hello Mister' greetings, we got everyone to our Headquarters for a meeting that went until 5 p.m. This was a follow-up to the earlier visit by Ian Martin and his Senior Management Team. We discussed the processes and time frames for the registration of the population in detail, the start had now been put back by three days. The 20-day period would still be divided into five-day phases of people being registered with the collected information being sent, through Dili, to Australia at the end of each five days. The security situation, perilous to say the least, was still considered one of the major challenges. They confirmed the initial direction, if security did not improve by the end of day 10 the next phase of voter registration would be postponed until the Indonesian authorities properly addressed the security issue. The UN Senior Management Team wanted evidence it was going to be safe for the people and all UN personnel, both international and locally employed staff. In effect all they did was repeat instructions provided on the previous visit.

Meeting over and the visitors loaded up onto the helicopter. With the usual children's game, they departed just short of 6 p.m.

I decided to do something a little different tonight and went home, showered, well washed, and put on civilian clothes for the first time. I had brought two pairs of wash and wear slacks and two short sleeved shirts with me. Then I went to the Guest House for dinner.

Well I had paid for and almost got my meal when Letefoho team was after me on the radio, even though in civvies I still had that infernal machine with me. It was 6.45 p.m. and one of their teams had not returned to their base. So, the short walk to HQ and just on an hour staying in touch with Letefoho and providing information to Dili. Just after 7.30 p.m. their missing team turned up, in the long run it was just a case of having a bit of difficulty changing a flat tyre and having forgotten to turn the radio on in the vehicle. So, they did not hear the calls from Base 3 or the sub district.

Thursday 15 July 1999, one day to go before the start of registration. Did the muesli and milk trick for breakfast this morning. Not exactly like home but an acceptable variation. The first radio call came in at 6.45 a.m. The first sub district teams were on their way to Gleno for their final briefing and to pick up the registration documentation. Once again much of the morning was spent with electoral personnel helping them with planning and organisation. Phil, John and Max were among those who came in, and they were all wearing long pants.

I managed to slip out to see the landlord, Senor Claudio, to try and get something done about the toilet blocking up, again. This time he was at his house where he was having a meeting with a number of other locals. Some I recognised immediately as being leaders of different Militia groups in the area. Anyhow he left that meeting, we had a coffee in a different room, and he undertook to have the plumbing fixed. He agreed I would not have to pay the next month's rent until the plumbing was working properly.

My attempt to get a less sensitive circuit breaker for the electrical system did not get as good a result; essentially, he said that was the best that could be supplied. Later I found out all his guests were leaders of the different subgroups of Militia in the district. So, while I had intended this to be more a 'domestic' visit it had turned out to be a good intelligence gathering opportunity.

That morning Don and the two Kiwis went to Dili. Trips by different persons to Dili had been occurring three or four times a week since our arrival. Regularly there was a need to go to Dili; sometimes to pick up recently arrived staff; sometimes to attend meetings; sometimes for repairs or service to vehicles; sometimes logistics; sometimes just for repair of tyres; and sometimes just because volunteers wanted to go. Who actually went varied with the reason; sometimes UNV's; sometimes, MLOs; sometimes full time UN personnel; sometimes CivPol; and often, a combination. Whenever the CivPol went they had unofficial instructions to visit the UN store and obtain, without signing, as much bottled water and ration packs as they could. On this occasion they were after water and rations but the primary reason for the trip was the repair or replacement of some absolutely essential items, a number of our portable radios were not working.

I gave Don a roll of film to be dropped off for development. One week later another group would pick up the prints and negatives for me. The prints were all black and the negatives completely clear. I decided I would keep all other roles of film until I got back to Australia. (Unfortunately, they were all left in my vehicle when I was evacuated and never seen again.)

Just as an aside, in one of the earlier trips to Dili someone had found a bakery shop had opened up. Included in what they baked, and sold, were donuts. That first group brought some back. Whenever I was aware of anyone going to Dili, I always gave them some cash to purchase me a few fresh donuts. No good getting too many they would just go stale, but always got enough to share around at least a bit.

Late in the morning Captain Ari arrived with an issue. When registration commenced Polri would not be able to provide security at all the sites. They would only be where Polri already had a presence. Gultom was obviously expecting me to want to see him about this as Ari said if I was not happy about this Gultom was prepared to see me immediately. Obviously, I went. Not that it did me much good. Gultom informed me that he had been directed not to 'thin out' his people any further than they already were, and he was definitely not to send security with the Leorema Team. Raising my voice with him might have made me feel a little better, but it made no difference. He had his orders and was not prepared to ignore them. As part of trying to push the issue I reminded him that the Indonesian Government had agreed the Polri would provide security for all UN personnel. Again, it made no difference. So just prior to walking out I told him it would not make any difference, all the teams would be going to their registration sites tomorrow. Captain Ari left the room just in front of me. Gultom called me back and quickly told me he did not think Liquicia Polri would be providing security in Leorema either. This raised some concern in me, but I could get no more from him. One thing I was glad of, the CivPol in the Leorema team was Paul Morris, it would be hard to find anyone better to handle whatever may occur.

On return to HQ I informed Alessandro and the rest of the management team. They agreed, registration was going ahead.

This was just not to be my day as at lunch time, while I was helping sort out some of the teams, Diana asked if she could borrow my car to go back to the house. She had a UN licence so no worries. Well I should have been worried because she was back in the office very quickly. Seems she had not realised someone had opened the passenger's door and as she was reversing out of the parking area the door had swung open and came in contact with a power pole, the only power pole in front of the building. The vehicle was still drivable, but it would have to go to Dili for repair as the door could not be properly closed.

These things are sent to try us but, as it turned out, it could not have happened on a better day. When the group arrived back from Dili, they not only had some extra UNV's but also three extra vehicles, all for CivPol. One of them was silver in colour, so in keeping with my earlier decision to be as visible as possible, this became my vehicle. The second I allocated to Atsabe, because of the four teams in that location; for the third the facts indicating it should go to Hatolia rather than Letefoho were -

- the larger area they had to cover;
- one team was based at a separate location (SARE); and
- the rougher nature of the ground they drove on, resulting in them getting three times as many punctures as everywhere else combined.

My original vehicle, when it returned from Dili, would be based in Gleno.

The boys also brought back a goodly supply of rations and water. We made sure enough got out to the subdistricts to last them for the next five days and kept enough so we could resupply when they came in on day 5 of registration. Don informed me he had been forewarned at the store getting rations and water without signing would be very difficult, if not impossible, in the future. It had been good while it lasted.

Before he returned to Letefoho Superintendent Robin asked if he could speak with me. It seems I have been causing him a little angst. Robin explained to me in his police force the junior officer is always expected to work harder than his superior. His problem was he was trying to work harder than he saw/heard me doing, and to quote him 'there was not enough hours in the day'.

I explained to him I had a completely different philosophy; I did not expect anyone to work harder than I was prepared to. If they matched or exceeded me, I was very appreciative. I also told him I was very satisfied with what he was already doing. He appeared a little confused at the concept but happy I did not expect him to do more.

With all this done I thought that was enough for one day. But no, one of the UNV's wanted to change how everything would be done by 'his' team. Personally, I thought hanging, drawing and quartering him might be the appropriate solution. However, he accepted the original process after I had a long chat with him. He was an Australian who was causing Allessandro, some of the other UN people and some locals a bit of heartache. This was because of his insistence on wearing ' Warwick Capper' style tight shorts in a colour which was best described as looking like well-tanned skin. Complaints had been made by other UN people and some of the local village elders. To be quite honest I considered his shorts, and him, offensive. A number of days later Allessandro would give up trying and ask me to convince him to wear more appropriate clothing. I had another long discussion with him after which I arranged for him to visit the markets and purchase some new trousers/shorts. That problem was now solved.

Another call from Dili, they expected us to meet 14 VIPs who would be flying in by helicopter at 10.45 a.m. tomorrow, the first day of registration, transport them to our HQ and brief them. They did not inform us who the VIPs would be. With registration started I knew we would only have 6 people available at HQ, and not enough vehicles to transport that many people, I strongly argued against the visit. In the first phone call my arguments were ignored. However, a short while later Dili called back and said they had cancelled the visit.

Tomorrow is Day One of registration. A few days later than first planned, but it was happening.

CHAPTER 16

REGISTRATION PERIOD COMMENCED 16 JULY 1999

To get to their registration sites in time to set up and open at 7.30 a.m. some teams would have to start their journeys at 6 a.m. with all intended to be underway by 7 a.m. On top of this I expected some would be very late arriving back to their base after the day's work. To give them the best support possible I decided for the registration period the HQ radio would have to be manned from 6 a.m. to 10 p.m. I intended to provide Jim France (USA) with some assistance by identifying a second person for this duty. On day one there was not enough personnel to do this so every second day I did the 6 a.m. start with Jim coming in by 8.30 a.m. On all days Jim stayed till 6 p.m. Most evenings there were things going on in HQ which meant someone was there to cover for him. Quite often it was me while I finalised reports. Diana also helped out; she had become a very good radio operator. For later in the night I was still putting the portable radio on the pillow.

For the whole registration period CivPol were 100% committed to the teams, therefore following up on issues that came to notice would be very difficult if not impossible.

The interpreter shortage was still a problem, one which would never be overcome. However, every team managed to find a way to get the job done. The Malay CivPol helped, many of the local employees also had some English and there was help from other locals. Sheer determination to get the job done meant we managed.

On Day One all teams had departed District or Sub District locations before 7 a.m. and arrived at their registration sites, at the very latest at 8 a.m., without problem. One team reported driving by a Militia group who looked like they were about to set up a roadblock. In every area the teams were greeted by large groups of people already there waiting to register. In some locations there were more people than the teams thought they could process in one day. It took some of them a bit of time to convince the people that it did not all have to happen today; the teams would be there for the next twenty days.

Registration sites Ermera and Homboe (overleaf also)

Registration Humboe Village, Saku and Yoda

As I listened to the reports coming in, I knew I just had to go and see at least one of the locations myself. So, I drove the short distance to the Gleno site, the local school. I had a walk around amongst a much larger number of people than I had expected. All seemed very happy and most wanted to shake hands. Then I went into the building and watched the process for a short time. Everything seemed to be going exceptionally well. As I walked back to the vehicle, I had a feeling of euphoria, this might just work.

Just as I got into the vehicle an old man, dressed in the traditional costume of a Timorese warrior, came up and stood by the driver's door. When I opened the door to see what he wanted he gave me an almost perfect Australian army salute. So, I got out of the car and returned his salute. He took hold of my hand and started shaking it; and shaking it; and talking, in Tetum; he did not want to let go. I could not understand him, and he could not understand me. Celestino, who was helping out in the Gleno site that day, came across and interpreted for us. The old gentleman had worked with the Australian Commandos in World War II. In my diary I wrote *'The look on his face really took me over the top'*. This was going to be a very worthwhile mission. As I got back into the vehicle, I was glad I was wearing sunglasses. They hid the emotion that might just have been showing in my eyes.

I visited Rob Mills at the Railaco site. Instead of just sitting around as 'security' he was helping out with the registration process and appeared to be having the time of his life. This was something the CivPol were going to voluntarily do at all our registration centres. There were a lot of very happy people there, with lots of hand shaking with the adults and high 5's with the kids for me.

Then back to HQ in Gleno.

2 P.M 16 July 1999
Leorema | Paul Morris

The Leorema Team had established itself in the village by 7 a.m. with a large crowd already present and eager to be registered. About 2 p.m. in the afternoon one of the DEOs advised District HQ by radio there was a large band of Militia approaching the village, many of the people had left the area and he was seeking permission to abandon the registration site. At that time Paul Morris had already driven to where the Militia were located to gather and provide accurate information. When he got back to the village, he advised the local people were attempting to prevent the Militia reaching the registration centre and he believed if the team remained, they had a chance of success. He also stated if the team left, he did not believe they would ever be able to return.

For the next hour and a half Paul provided continuous information by radio on the development of the situation in Leorema. Quite often while he was transmitting the sounds of gunfire could be clearly heard (over the radio). During the radio conversations he not only provided information but, in answer to my questions, stated if it became necessary, he would evacuate with the team. The DEOs, that night, and the village elders, on a later visit by me, informed me for this entire period Paul had stood in the middle of an open area in the centre of the village and had refused to be moved.

Throughout the entire incident I had an open telephone line to the JOC in Dili. While they said they would do whatever they could, in reality, all they could do was notify Indonesian authorities. It was a lesson worth having and something that would have to be taken into account in all future planning.

This open display of courage by Paul and his willingness to expose himself to danger had a profound effect on the local population and the DEOs. After half an hour the people began to return to the registration site. About 3.30 p.m. he reported there were more people there than at the beginning of the day. Over the radio the sounds of these people had completely replaced the earlier gunfire and by 4.30 p.m. the Militia had completely departed the vicinity.

At least until the announcement of the result of the Popular consultation, this was to be the last occasion where the Militia made any serious attempt to enter this village. I just had a feeling Falantil may have had a presence, perhaps even a significant presence, in the area and played a part in the withdrawal of the Militia. Even so I doubt they would have made their presence known if it wasn't for the actions of Paul Morris on the day. His courage instigated the response of whoever resisted the Militia. It also guaranteed the continued success of the Popular Consultation in the area.

Following is my diary entry for that evening -

'- numbers coming in, nearly all good — planned tomorrow with Ari- being very co-operative. Teams coming in all smiles — this is working. Made sure everyone was home and safe then finished'.

Paul Morris

From Dili information arrived of an incident in Suai where Militia had tried to take over a village *'and got their butts kicked'* to quote the duty officer's words.

Finally, home to find the plumbing had been fixed, again. A good day all round.

Day two and everything got off to a good start except in Atsabe where there was now no room in one vehicle for the Polri escort. Phil solved the problem. He reported arranging for him to travel to the site by local bus.

Later that morning Alessandro and I went together and visited the sites in Letefoho (Ashraf, Robin and Delmer), Estada (Amorin) and Humboe (Saku as the only DEO in the team but Antonio was being of great assistance). All the registration sites were doing really well. The friendly interaction with the children at the registration sites was something none of us will ever forget. 'Hello mister' continued to be the greeting to all from the UN, females and males alike; and they all wanted to touch you and specially to hold your hand. Many of them were also developing a reasonable understanding of English. In Humboe one local told me he had heard '*the commandos who cannot be beaten would come back*'. Perhaps this was just a foretelling of the deployment of INTERFET in response to events yet to occur.

Late in the day and back at HQ in time for the meeting with Ari. He had only one problem. A UN Media Team had come into Ermera, neither Alessandro nor I knew they were coming, and had managed to 'slip' their escorts. The escort leader was a Brimob officer from Dili and he was not very happy. We managed to convince them the media team was from Dili HQ and we in Ermera had not been informed they were going to visit.

The extra bit that convinced him was my statement, 'Do you think Allessandro and I would have left Gleno HQ if we knew a media team was arriving?'

The rest of the meeting went very well and everything for the next day was put into place. In a later call to JOC Dili I was informed that over their lunch break, when the escort went elsewhere, the media team decided they had enough and so had returned to Dili without informing the escort. Gultom and Ari appreciated this information when I passed it on to them.

Day Three was something different again. After getting all the teams into place, the Political Officer, Helen, advised that with the Bupati she had arranged a trip to the mountains for me and the MLOs. She said it was to be a meeting with the leaders of a local political party, CNRT.

It was a long, round about trip to a place very high in the mountains. Afterwards Baldev and I agreed there was one intersection we went through on three occasions and a couple of other spots we saw twice. From the point where we passed through Ermera Village I regularly saw armed individuals at a number of what could be best described as strategic points. During the trip we were slightly concerned they might be Militia. However, when we arrived at our destination and after being introduced to the leaders of the Ermera based Falantil units we were informed the armed persons had been 'freedom fighter' sentries. It was a good meeting, lasting three and a half hours, with both sides feeling each other out and relationships being established that would be of great assistance in the future. Most of the Falantil leaders there had a good command of the English language.

First meeting with Falantil. Sean Fox, me and Bupati.

For a short period, I was virtually alone with one of the leaders. He gave me a very good description of where the CivPol had been over the past weeks. Without him actually saying it I gathered Falantil had people at least attempting to watch over us.

During the meeting there were a number of occasions where Helen was caught out by Baldev providing inaccurate translations. She continues to be overly biased towards the pro-independence cause and very naive in accepting everything they tell her. My impression of the Bupati's participation was that he was there as a politician trying to keep one foot in each camp.

The trip home was much more direct and took less than a quarter the time. I believe on the outward trip they were uncertain of us so were trying to conceal their location as much as possible. By the end of the meeting they were satisfied any information we obtained would be for the UN and would not be passed on to others. By the same token I believe they understood we would not be passing information back to them. This was of course with the one probable exception, Helen. Both Baldev and I were able to convince them we were going to be professionally impartial. Later the two of us would also agree to be careful about passing information we received from Polri or TNI to Helen.

That night at the Guest House, Helen was regaling people with stories about the day. From what she was saying I almost believed the two of us had been at two different locations and had met with completely different groups of people.

Day four and everything started well till a call from Humboe. Armed TNI in uniform were walking around the registration site. With no one else available to respond I headed off immediately. By the time I got there, my quickest trip ever, they had left. This was one I would pass on to the MLOs to raise with Lt Col Nurr. Seeing I was out that way I called in to the registration sites where Don and Wayne were working. It was very similar to my visits on day one. The exception being slightly smaller numbers but still enough to keep the team busy. As with the other sites Don and Wayne were helping out with the registration processes.

The rest of the day went very well until the evening. As I

arrived at Bad Manor for dinner, Phil was on the radio insisting I read a report he had prepared which should have arrived at Gleno HQ by now. So, it was, forget dinner, and head down to HQ. The report stated Phil had been told by the local Polri there would be no escorts on the next day. In as coded a way as possible I discussed the situation with Phil by radio. By the time we finished it was too late to make any changes for the next day, which was to be a half day anyway, so I told Phil to leave early for the trip to Gleno with the work they had already done.

First up the next morning I raised the Atsabe situation with Ari who claimed complete surprise but undertook to speak with Gultom when he got back from a senior officers meeting in Dili.

At Allessandro's request I spent the rest of the morning escorting a recently arrived group of Portuguese Electoral Observers to the following registration sites.

Fatubolo — where there were about 500 persons waiting to register and, because it was so much higher in the mountains, the temperature was much lower and the UN people where all wearing jackets.

Potete — 'Wayne's World', where the locals had us sit down to coffee and some very good local cakes.

Ermera — 'Don's party', a choir of six local children were there to greet us with song.

Humboe — Saku and Antonio, so well organised with a committed village chief.

Gleno — where the numbers were still much higher than elsewhere.

Back at HQ and I got together with Phil and Max. They were very concerned about safety for their teams. This was partly because of the long travel time for any sort of assistance to arrive. I fully understood their concerns. But there was also a job that had to be done. After a number of discussions, it was finally agreed the Atsabe teams would at least attempt to go to their registration sites the next day even if they had no escorts. For the time being this decision would just be between us, the Ermera UN management team, and them, the Atsabe teams. During one of the discussions between me, Phil and Max I told them about some of the things that had been mentioned in my meeting with Falantil. It may not have been much, but it was something indicating that support may not be as far away as they thought.

During the afternoon I tried to ignore the cacophony of noise HQ had become. With at least some representatives of every team in the building there was a lot going on. The building really was not big enough for everything that was trying to be done, leading to noise and more noise.

A little later it was time to slip away with CivPol from the sub district teams and share out the water and rations we had squirreled away. Once this was all done, I manned our base radio until all teams had returned to their sub district bases. A late finish was a good excuse to not consider cooking the evening meal. Off to the Guest House it was and then home for a shower, well good wash, and bed. The girls were still at HQ doing electoral paperwork.

First five days — General Comment

During this initial registration period a number of reports were received about Militia roadblocks being established. From the reports it appeared they were designed to prevent people from outlying villages getting to the registration centres. As all CivPol were fully committed to the registration process, there was no team that could be deployed just to examine this issue. The few vehicles that POLRI had were also committed to providing security at some of the registration centres, therefore Captain Ari informed me they could not take on this role.

To meet this new 'threat' I suggested to the CivPol they consider the following, because of the potential danger I was not prepared to make it an order. After establishing the team at a registration site, all CivPol officers should consider making the occasional, short distance, one-man patrol or patrols on the roads leading to their sites.

To do this they had to negotiate with their DEOs, because as an electoral mission the leader of each team was technically the senior electoral person. Many of them were very concerned about their personal security if the unarmed CivPol were not physically present. However, in most instances they agreed and the CivPol individuals patrolled, for short distances, on the roads leading to their registration sites. Regularly they reported coming across roadblocks. In some cases, they just remained at the roadblock in a monitoring role to ensure no person was prevented from passing. At other times they physically dismantled the roadblocks. Both situations obviously created high levels of animosity from the Militia. In almost every instance, threats were made to, and ignored by, the CivPol officers.

A few of these roadblocks would continue during the next five days. But from my perspective the direct result of the CivPol actions at the roadblocks was a significant reduction in daylight attempts by Militia to prevent access to the registration sites and intimidation of people going to register during the second period of registration.

Start of the Second Five Days

Wednesday 21 July and I was at HQ at 5.45 a.m. ready for the first teams to depart for the registration sites. There were no escorts in Atsabe, and I instructed them to go without them, but to be very careful and be prepared to alter plans if required. As it turned out all the Atsabe teams reached their registration sites without incident.

Baldev and I talked this over that morning, and it was our impression this unavailability of escorts was a different attempt to interrupt the registration process. Threats had not worked so they were trying something else. If either had worked everything we had done so far would have been wasted.

All through the last few days there had been concerns about security. I decided that today was another one where I could try and set the example. So, it was on patrol again, without notifying Polri. With Celestino helping at the Gleno site that day I drove myself.

First off, a visit to Leorema. As before it was a drive that, in other circumstances, would be a real tourist attraction. Three kilometres of the drive were right along the very peak of a razor-back ridge, spectacular views to both sides. On arrival I was surprised to find a Brimob member there for security, and even more surprised when he saluted me as I got out of the vehicle. This was the first I knew security had been provided in the village.

To top it off all the people in the area broke into loud applause. Paul was in the registration centre helping the DEOs with registration. He came out with me and introduced me to the village chief who insisted I stay for lunch. While they were getting it ready, I wandered around the village to the 'casino' area. The same patch of dirt between two houses. There were three games under way; low stakes, medium stakes and high stakes. I was still not sure what the actual game was being played, but it did involve three dice. Once again, I politely declined an offer to join in. After lunch I was introduced to some more local elders who claimed to have assisted Australian Commandos in WW II.

From there I drove off to the village of Railaco Leten. Only a few locals were present when I arrived. The DEOs informed me they had already registered more than 70% of the overall total they were expecting from that area. There had been large numbers in the initial days and now it had tapered off. Each morning there were still a number of people waiting for them to arrive but generally in the afternoon it was quiet.

Nitaya was taking a report from a representative of a nearby village. He was saying the people had been told not to go to the registration site and also not to vote. He did not mention what threat had been made if they ignored Militia instructions. He also told her the villagers had decided if the UN people could ignore the threats, then so would they. When she had finished getting the information Nitaya showed me the new TNI post that had been established in the village only the day before. This information I would take back to Baldev.

Nitaya

Just before departing Nitaya told me of the alternate route she had found to get out of the village if it became necessary. She did say the road was very dusty, but easily passable in high range four-wheel drive and, she added, the village where the latest threats had been made was also on this road. This made my choice of route back very simple. I could drive on this 'road', which would also get me to another registration site, the main village of Railaco and, at the same time, show a presence in another village.

The hills and ridgeline I drove along could almost have been somewhere in Australia. Tall gum trees everywhere and bull dust, real thick bulldust, to drive through, even when you got off the actual track. Different to everywhere else in Ermera.

After stopping briefly in each of the two villages on this track I continued to Railaco where I arrived late in the day. Registration was pretty well finished with the team getting the days documentation together. However, there were still crowds of people, including the children, all dressed in their Sunday finery. There had been a First Communion service in the village that day. Before I could get away there was some hand shaking, and more than a few high-fives with the children, before I was on my way to Gleno.

Once back there, I got one of the drivers to go and wash the car, dust was absolutely everywhere. Then it was time to check the reports. Everyone was back safe and sound. There had been no trouble on that day.

I had planned to cook at home and have an early night. But before I could even get out of the office Ari called to arrange a meeting with Gultom who wanted a meeting to discuss security. He did start it with a mild rebuke to me for my travels that day without telling him, and for not taking an escort. It was the mildest rebuke he had given me so far. In the end, and after considerable back and forth, he gave an undertaking that security would be provided for all electoral teams operating in the district.

CHAPTER 17

FIRST VISIT TO DILI — THIS TIME FOR MEETINGS

The following day all the teams were in the registration locations without any troubles. Once they were established it was time for me to head off for my first trip to Dili. Allan Mills, Commissioner of UN Police, had called a meeting of all CivPol district commanders. The original arrangements were for all, including me, to be picked up by helicopter. The instructions had included we should arrange with a contingent member based in Dili for accommodation as we would be staying overnight. Rob Hunter had contacted me before I got around to making arrangements and told me he had a stretcher at his place that I was welcome to.

Unfortunately, 24 hours before the helicopter was due to pick me up, I was informed I would have to drive to Dili. This was my first drive all the way back to Dili. After spending a number of weeks driving around the mountains of Ermera I now considered the road to Dili as relatively straight and definitely not narrow. I arrived by the set time, but others were missing. The start time was put back as there were some problems with tasking the helicopters and some district commanders coming in by air would not arrive till 4.30 p.m.

This gave me my first chance to be taken to 'the bakery'. What an eye opener. The shop could have been in any mall in Australia. Not only were there the donuts but a wide variety of other breads and finger food items. My future purchase requests for patrols going to Dili would be a bit more expansive. Lunch was definitely different that day.

After lunch it was back to the JOC where we spent the afternoon putting pins into their large-scale map, with team radio call signs, showing every registration/polling site. It was a pleasure to be working with such a large scale, topographical map.

Finally, the meeting got under way with a reduced agenda. The only items covered during the afternoon were the additional paperwork items we would all be required to complete. Just what we all needed, more red tape. At least most of it was not a daily requirement. Some was weekly, one was monthly and a few for other times. One good thing about the late start was the meeting had to finish early. In fact, after not much more than half an hour.

Then it was back to Rob's place where I had a shower, from a real shower. A very pleasant experience even if there was only cold water. The house also had the ultimate in luxury, a real, sit down toilet.

In the evening there was a function at the Commissioner's residence. A social get together to give us time to get to know each other. There was a strong possibility we would have to depend on each other in the not too distant future.

Finger food was the order of the day, obviously from the Bakery, and it was accompanied by VB beer and some Sake, provided by the two Japanese Police officers who were attached to Dili HQ. During the evening the Commissioner pulled me aside and informed me that I would not be replaced as the CivPol commander in Ermera. It appears he had spoken with Allessandro and the national contingent commanders who were working in the district and they all wanted me to stay in the job. It was very good to get that acknowledgement. Before I left the party, I also had a good conversation with the Suai district commander. Our careers and skill sets were very similar even though we came from two very different nations, Russia and Australia.

I snuck away from that party a bit earlier than most. A bit of sleep was what I needed even though it was just a stretcher. The next morning, I woke feeling better than I had since arrival. Although back in Gleno I was able to ignore the radio on my pillow, my brain was obviously listening for it. The two nights in Dili there was no radio on the pillow. In the morning I had another shower followed by breakfast of Wheat Bix with UHT milk. Neither item available in Gleno. Rob had been a very good host.

The whole morning meeting was just CivPol. But nothing new came out of it. Primarily each district commander gave a report on what they were doing. There were significant differences in approach to the circumstances with only the Dili district having sufficient personnel to establish a full CivPol team for investigations or other tasks. All other districts had just enough police to work with the electoral teams. Some others had unsuccessfully tried to pry some of the police away for other tasks but had eventually given up. As a general statement nothing new came out of the meeting; no central concept of operations; no forward planning.

The afternoon meeting was very different. This time all our Polri counterparts were present. Unfortunately, they all sat behind a table on one side of the room and we sat behind another on the other side. There were some very important issues raised, primarily over co-operation and security, and a few accusations thrown around. Not much was actually resolved other than for a working group to be established comprising people from the UN Police HQ and Polri Headquarters who would develop processes to resolve the identified problems. In the long run this group never met.

As usual at the close of a meeting the chairman asked was there any other items to discuss. I had one idea that made sense to me so I suggested at the next meeting the seating should be re-arranged so the police from each district were sitting together rather than all UN in one place and all Polri in another. The response was interesting. With some, both Polri and UN, it went down like a lead balloon; but others, again both Polri (including Gultom) and UN, supported me. Perhaps it had something to do with the 'relationships' already established or not established.

That night there was another party. This time hosted by the Kapolda, Alan Mill's counterpart, at his home. There were traffic police and security on the roads leading to, and right around, the building. Lots of light wands and whistles. Any vehicle that did not have a UNAMET or Polri number plate had to wait or was redirected. I lost count of the number of times I was saluted by the Polri personnel.

The tables were set up outside and there was a band playing on a small stage with a painted map of East Timor as the backdrop. It was a good get together. The food was very good, at least to me it was, and it was served at the table by female Polri members. There was more than enough of the local beer being handed around, although our counterparts did not appear to be drinking as much as some of the UN people. Maybe there was a reason behind this. There were other women present, I think all of them where Polri officers in plain clothes. During the meal they sat at separate tables to the men. The band, which included some good singers, played throughout the meal.

After the meal came the traditional karaoke, something very popular throughout south east Asia. A number of the Indonesians were dancing while the early performers were on. After his turn at singing, Kapolda came to me and said it was my turn. Now I had drunk nowhere near enough for me to get up and sing, so, I told him I would dance instead. He arranged for one of the policewomen to come over and with some good old rock and roll being played I managed to get the two of us through a bit of old-fashioned rockabilly dancing. This really tickled the fancy of Kapolda, and I saw him talking with Allan Mills. Later I would find out that, amongst other things, Allan had informed him I was a Vietnam vet. Well there was a lot more dancing after that with many of the UN joining in. By the time the night came to an end it had proven to be a far better ground breaker between the two groups than the earlier meeting. Before he left Gultom spoke with me and said we would have to have one in Gleno. I had to agree.

As we were departing Kapolda found me again. He threw his arm around my shoulder and told me he liked the way I did things and he was going to have me transferred to Dili.

My reply was simple 'I would rather you didn't.'

He said, 'why'.

Instead of answering directly I posed a question to him -'would you prefer to be where you have your own command, or have a job in someone else's headquarters?'

His response was a hearty laugh and a big slap on my back. As a post note I did not get transferred to Dili.

One of the Swedish police officers had driven me to the dinner. On the way back to Rob's place he became slightly geographically embarrassed. But, after a bit of a tour of the streets of Dili, we did arrive there, and I had my second excellent night's sleep.

The next morning was the start of week five. Had it really been that short a time? It seemed like a lifetime had passed since I arrived in East Timor. Before I left the house, I had another real shower, then off to the JOC and collected all mail for Ermera. With that done it was time for a little bit of shopping; a frypan, some Nescafe for the Americans; a few other odds and ends that individuals had requested; before the final stop at the Bakery; treats on me for everyone and spring rolls for dinner that night.

Once the food was safely put away it was time for the best part of the morning, the road heading back to Ermera. Firstly, was another drive along the very photogenic coastline heading towards Liquicia until you reached that left-hand turn. It was still the best part of Dili; the first hill on the way out of town. Once again, I could feel the temperature and, more importantly, the humidity drop. I was almost 'home'. Strange how quickly a place can become home.

Back in Ermera and in the first instance it appeared I had not been missed all that much. All the registration processes had occurred as they were supposed to and there had been no issues of threats or attempted intimidation being reported to Gleno. However, there was a problem with the radios. For an 'old soldier' who had a bit of signals training it was relatively easy to establish the problem was in the radio repeaters, which were in the mountain top base stations and the responsibility of the communications unit in Dili. A quick telephone call to the JOC and three hours later everything had been fixed as far as they could at the time. Unfortunately, we still had more 'black spots' with no radio communications that I was happy with. Then there was the daily Situation Report. Somehow Jim had forgotten to do it while I was away. After feeling so good it was disappointing to have been let down over something so simple.

Shortly after contacting JOC about the radios I had my first meeting with a group of the East Timorese university students. While at the Dili meeting others had spoken about student groups already operating in their districts. In some areas they had been very active. Their stated aim was to assist the UN in educating the people. Those at the meeting who had experience with the students stated the students real aim was to actively promote the independence cause, which was their right. The problem was they included in their activities events or provocations which appeared to be specifically designed to antagonise pro-autonomy groups into some form of physical reaction. At the conference another District CivPol Commander had stated his opinion the students deliberately provoked pro-autonomy groups when they were near international media or UN personnel. When the reaction came the students ran to the media or UN. Another had stated he believed at least some of them were looking to be martyrs.

On this, my first meeting with the students, they had a complaint about threats they had received from a Militia group. So, for the first time, I got to fill out one of the new forms. I informed them I would follow up with Polri on their complaint. Before they left, I politely mentioned to them, for the first time, how unhappy I would be if their actions resulted in any of the UN personnel being exposed to unnecessary danger.

At my evening meeting with Ari I raised their complaints. He already had a counter complaint for me about the actions of the students. When we considered both reports it was obviously the same incident and to be quite honest there was enough information to satisfy me that blame could be attributed to both sides. Looks like the students may become a bit of a problem for me as well.

That evening I went for a walk up to the Bad Manor to collect the satphone. I called Marg. Our son Leigh was with her so a short chat with both. Followed this up with a late evening 50-minute walk around town. Including two short stops at some Militia posts. No threats to me at either, I think they may be getting used to me just dropping in.

The next morning, after all registration sites had been established without a problem, I dropped round to the Polri HQ for an early morning meeting with Gultom. He suggested it was time for the two of us to visit a few more villages. So, in convoy with the sirens blaring and lights flashing on the escort vehicle, off we went. First to Letefoho; then Estabe and finally to Homboe.

At each location I continued to be very interested in watching Gultom's interaction with the locals. He handed out cigarettes and asked about their problems, without ever raising the political situation. When asked he always stated Polri would provide security on polling day.

At Homboe the village chief invited us to have lunch with him. As the registration site was very quiet Saku and Antonio joined us. The villagers had laid on a small feast, it appears information had been passed along the 'grapevine' and they were expecting us to arrive around lunch time. Amazing how, with no telephones, the message could get so quickly between villages.

During lunch Gultom spent some time speaking with Antonio and Saku. While he was doing this the village chief and I had a conversation. This was not the first time we had met, and I think now he was really prepared to trust me. We spoke about the planned forthcoming events and he surprised me when he said he knew about the UN intention to defer the final registration and vote if security did not improve. Then he very bluntly put it to me that if the UN decided to postpone the registration and/or the vote then it would never be held.

His comment was 'the people will trust you once; but not a second time'.

This solidified and reinforced comments and hints made to me on earlier days in other villages and the information a number of CivPol had received from people in their local villages. I was glad someone had finally given it to me as it really was.

From Homboe it is a relatively short drive back to Gleno where there was plenty of time to do the daily paperwork. When I had almost finished someone yelled out that the kids were heading to the sports ground, our helipad. So even without hearing anything I got into the vehicle and as I got the motor started received a radio call from the helicopter. They were only five minutes out. Once again, the best show in town. This time it was a quick visit, touch down, hand over mail and some supplies, one DEO returned from a medical trip; and a team from Dili HQ to ask about security.

There was a quick meeting on the helipad. Essentially, we told them security was no better than at the start of registration. If anything, a little worse. Having said that, I added my opinion, reinforced by what the Homboe village chief had told me, do not stop now because the people will never trust you again. Later I was to find out they were given exactly the same message in every district. The meeting had been so quick the helicopter did not power down. Once again immediately after it left the ground the kids were out in the downwash. There was nothing the UN people or Polri could do to stop it. It was just too much fun for the children.

When the teams had come in earlier that day Phil had left behind a couple of reports.

Atsabe Sub District Lassaun Village
Max Knoth

Lassaun village was the most southerly located registration site in Ermera. It was one hour's drive from Atsabe, and four to five hours drive from Regional HQ. Max Knoth was the CivPol allocated to the Electoral Team for that village.

Late in the second five-day period the Militia made one further open attempt to prevent the registration process. A roadblock was established in the early morning to prevent the team from reaching the village. Max Knoth was driving the UN vehicle that morning. On seeing the roadblock, manned by armed Militia, he stopped the vehicle and then in full view of the Militia he informed Regional HQ, by radio, that he would be driving through the roadblock. He carried this out even though the Militia fired some shots in the air.

This was the last roadblock known to have been established in Ermera prior to the completion of voting in the Popular Consultation.

A day or so later a written note was received at Regional HQ from Atsabe detailing how the Militia were going to use a sniper to kill Max and other members of that Electoral Team. Over the radio the information was discussed with Max. He stated he had a plan that should succeed in overcoming the threat. Without him giving any of the details, there was a high probability of a radio intercept and his plan getting back to the Militia, I agreed to let him try it out the next day.

In the morning, immediately on arrival at the registration site, Max confronted the local Militia leader and in a heated discussion issued a challenge, a challenge to an arm wrestle. Failure to accept the challenge would have been a considerable loss of face for the Militia leader. Max won that bout and then expanded the challenge to all other members of the Militia, who, one by one, he defeated; this was followed by a challenge to all soldiers of the TNI unit and then the POLRI members in the village. A total of around sixty individuals. Max won every bout. From that day on there were no attempts to disrupt the process in the village, at least not that Max let me find out about.

Afterwards Max got representatives of all factions together and arranged for the previous confrontations to be replaced by late afternoon volleyball games where people from every faction were required to participate. He stipulated each team had to be a mixture of individuals from every group.

Lauana Village | Phil Hunter

As Militia intimidation decreased in this village it was replaced by direct action from soldiers of the nearby TNI post. The Electoral

Team members were very concerned for their personal safety and the CivPol officer allocated to the team was unable to calm their fears. Eventually there was a day when they declined to travel to the registration centre. Phil Hunter arranged to change assignments with this CivPol officer. The next day he led the team back to the village. The intimidation attempts continued from the TNI personnel. Daily, Phil confronted these issues and after a few days they ceased their activities, thus allowing the completion of registration at that village. I had informed Baldev of the incidents and he had taken it to Nurr.

That night there was a radio call from one of the DEOs from Hatolia stating they had a major problem. This call would never have been received if the relay links had not been re-established less than 48 hours before. This time trouble was coming from the local TNI unit. Posturing and threatening at this stage, but it could get worse. When I asked where the CivPol were he said they had gone to solve the problem. I contacted Baldev and he immediately made contact with his counterpart while I spoke with Ari. Ari obviously immediately contacted Gultom and he arrived at our HQ within 10 minutes. He issued directives to the Polri unit in Hatolia and Nurr advised Baldev that he had ordered the Hatolia personnel to get back to their base. I was told the potential problem had been resolved very quickly. At least our counterparts had made an attempt. I could not help believing it was at least in part due to the respectful working relationship Baldev and I had established with them. Apart from notifying Dili, which was done, there was nothing else I could do but listen to the radio overnight.

This matter reinforced my opinion that situations could very easily arise where individuals and/or groups of pro-autonomy in Ermera would ignore directions from a higher authority. Security was still a major concern.

CHAPTER 18

Second Ten Days of Registration

I slept in the next morning till 6.05 a.m. But the first thought was to check with Hatolia. Brett knew nothing of a radio call being made to Gleno HQ. Later he would explain how he, with John and the local Polri, had resolved the situation. Seems that one of the DEOs had called in without informing Brett or John. While Brett appreciated the efforts of Gultom and Nurr he was not sure of how much impact they had in actual rectification of the situation. This morning everything was 'normal' in Hatolia, if there is any such state.

Once the teams were in place, I was intending to take another trip to Dili. Two new CivPol had arrived and I was the only person available to pick them up. I mentioned this to Ari at our morning get-together. It should be called a meeting but 'get-together' better describes what it had become. This agitated him somewhat and he asked me not to leave until he had spoken with Gultom. Next thing you know he was back with 2Lt Audi and a vehicle with a mounted Brimob section to be my escort. This was the first time in some weeks Polri had considered this necessary. As they had a far better intelligence collection system than the UN, I accepted the escort and we drove to Dili. I never did find out why they thought an escort was needed that day.

I had sent a message ahead I would collect the two from Senegal from the Hotel Dili, yes this was still being used by new arrivals, at 10 a.m. Neither were present when I arrived. I was not impressed. Someone mentioned they might have gone for a run along the beach. As I still wanted to discuss some communications matters with HQ, I left a message I would be back shortly, and they would need to be ready.

I had a 'warm' discussion, only called warm because no one actually yelled at anyone else, with the leader of the UN Communications Unit where I made certain he knew of my concerns about the radio reception black spots in Ermera. Even though, much the same as everywhere, it would be very difficult to physically respond to problems in those areas. The people had a need to at least be able to call for assistance or give information on what had occurred. Being able to communicate was a definite benefit for morale. Although no guarantees were given, he undertook to try. I could ask no more.

Back to the Dili Hotel and the two new CivPol were ready and waiting. Later I was to find my initial poor perception of these two would prove to be wrong. One of them, Superintendent Mbaye Diouf, was the contingent commander of the Senegalese Police Contingent. The second was his staff officer, Warrant Officer Robert. Earlier I described the stature of Max and Phil well, beside Robert, they were small. Once loaded up we headed first to the bakery, for supplies, and then back to Polri HQ to collect the escort. Another delay because we were a bit later than expected. Audi and his team had already been sent back to Ermera. While I offered to go without escort the Polri Duty officer insisted I wait for him to arrange one. The delay was not all that long before we were again heading to that first hill out of town. Because there were only CivPol involved I was able to give them a considerable part of the regular briefing while we travelled.

For the first time I had more CivPol than the bare minimum to cover the electoral teams. After a brief discussion with Allessandro I replaced Amorin in the electoral team with Mbaye and appointed Amorin as my second in command. I also replaced

Rob Mills in his team with Robert. Rob now picked up the dual role of assisting Jim on the radio and being the lead, and only permanent, member of the investigations team I had always wanted. Later that afternoon the new members met their teams and the other CivPol.

It was about this time the third MLO arrived to join Baldev Sing and Sean Fox. This was Yuri, I never heard any other name for him, and he said he was an officer in the Russian navy. He had volunteered for service in Bosnia and had ended up in East Timor. He did not like the tropical climate or the mountains. I never saw any badges of rank on Yuri's uniforms, but he was very friendly, did the job and Baldev was happy with him.

That night there was another long meeting, this one made necessary by the actions of the students. Present were the leaders of each element of UNAMET in Ermera, Gultom, the Bupati, student representatives and a new group, the Indonesian Task Force. The Task Force was the organisation Indonesia had established to be their observers during the polling process. Every one of them I met was well educated, said they were Javanese and looked like they had military training. The meeting eventually finished just before 9.30 p.m.

Once again, I was not filled with any confidence the students would follow through on their promises, even though they said they would comply with the decisions reached. After the meeting I spoke with Gultom and he had the same impression as me. We were both sure the students were going to cause us a bit of trouble.

27th of July was one of those days. Stuck in the office spending time working out everything for the new administrative 'stuff' that had come out of the conference. Better to figure out the best way to comply with the new requirements now so that mistakes, which would require extra work to fix, were not made later. In the afternoon I did manage to slip away for a short period. Went to a house where some of the Brimob platoon where billeted as I had heard one of them was an acceptable cutter of hair. I would have said barber, but the final result dictated the use of different terminology. At least it was now short again. That night I was paged to Bad Manor as Margaret was calling from Australia.

The next morning was complete pandemonium amongst the DEOs. Someone, Allessandro and I never did find out who, had made some re-assignments within the teams. Apparently without consultation and definitely without passing on the information about the changes being made. Some were there arguing; some had left with their team before they knew of the changes; some had just ignored them and gone off with their original team; others had accepted and headed off with their new team, included in this final group were some who had already left for Atsabe. Now there were some CivPol with local employed staff who were waiting for their team, but no DEOs to go with them. Finally, after a few hours of effort most of the mess was sorted out. All teams now had personnel, although for now some only had one DEO, and were at the registration centres. Everyone was put back to where they had been and there was now just a little more work to do to get the few who had gone to Atsabe back to their original teams. My suspicion was one of the original Atsabe team DEOs had promulgated the changes, but there was no proof.

This convinced me now was the time for me to put all of the information I had been gathering into formalised plans for all UN personnel in Ermera. Once done the problem would be to have it accepted by the management team.

I came up with my own concept of operations which revolved around the following points -

- I knew immediately after the final day of registration the DEOs would be coming into Gleno for five or more days. To maintain a physical presence, it was essential for the immediate return of CivPol to all sub-districts; this included the Gleno based CivPol to visit all their locations;

- there would be a minimum of a two-person CivPol team available every day to conduct investigations;
- A roster would be prepared to allow all CivPol members in Ermera at least 24 hours where they were off duty and could get away from the area;
- plans had to be prepared for -
- the day of voting;
- the withdrawal of the UN volunteers after the ballot day;
- CivPol patrols and return to sub-districts from the day after voting.
- a concept of operations for CivPol after the vote with special consideration to the day when the result would be declared.

It was now time to clear my head and reduce my frustration level and the best way to do that was to get out on patrol. From now on much more of my time would have to be spent gathering further information and preparing plans.

In the afternoon I again visited the registration sites in Fatubolo, very high in the mountains and even during the day much cooler than Gleno. The teams had found it to be far too cold at night and that was the reason they made their base in Ermera Village, just on forty minutes' drive from the two registration sites.

Travelling back, I was on a very steep downhill, rough and narrow section of a mountain road. Perhaps dirt mountain goat track would be a better description. I came across a Suzuki minibus going uphill. While most of the road was definitely only one vehicle at a time, I had just passed what I will call for now, a parking bay. So, I reversed the 50 or so metres and got out of the way. Now I did describe the vehicle as a bus. However, all the passengers were walking up the steep uphill section; two were carrying large rocks; which they threw behind the back wheels every time the wheels lost traction; about every 40 metres or so; then all the passengers would get behind and push until the bus was moving forward again; the rocks would be picked up and the process repeated. It took them just on 20 minutes to cover the 150 metres to get from below me to far enough past for me to drive on. I hope the passengers had a subsidised fare for the efforts.

That day was the start of another period when the water was not turned on for Gleno. So, a proper wash was out of the question. A couple of days later I would be out the back of the house one morning when I heard water running.

I yelled out 'YES.'

A female voice from inside the bathroom replied, 'No, sorry it is just me.'

Also, no mail had arrived, and it would be another four days before any reached us. Just my mentioning it here shows how important mail from home was. We never found out the reason for mail being held up, it may have been there were no flights from Darwin during that period.

The morning of the 29th was to be an early start for a patrol to Hatolia and SARE. I wanted to go on this one as I was still concerned about the recent incidents in Hatolia and knew the best way to get accurate information was directly from the people involved. Another reason for this trip was to take additional UN personnel to help out with the registration at SARE. With their being somewhere in the vicinity of 4,000 people in the area it had become obvious there was insufficient time for the process to be completed by the one team allocated the job. At Homboe, due to the work of a highly efficient team effort combined with a committed and organised village chief, there were very few people still to be registered. After conversations with Allessandro it was decided we could, for the time being, reduce the UN personnel in that team. Antonio, with one of the local staff and support from the village chief, was certain that he could complete the process in that village. Saku, with another local staff member, agreed to working for the final 8 days of registration in SARE.

Representatives of the Indonesian Task Force had approached Allessandro and requested they be allowed to follow me to Hatolia and SARE and I could not see any reason why we should say no. Gultom also considered it essential Brimob escort me on this trip. So, at 8.30a.m. everyone was ready to go except Saku. Forty-five minutes later we were underway. Brimob ute in front, 2Lt Audi and the driver in the cab and 8 men seated in the back, me with the UN personnel immediately behind with the Indonesian Task Force people in a third vehicle, the only two-wheel drive vehicle in the convoy. As usual while leaving town the Brimob vehicle had sirens blaring and lights flashing.

The back of the Brimob ute had two rows of seats, back to back, down the centre of the tray. Once we had left town, they all cocked their weapons, two men closest to the cabin stood and faced forward resting their weapons on the cabin roof and the two rear mostly adopted a position so they could watch the opposite side behind the vehicle. As usual they gave a professional and reassuring impression. The thing that really amazed me was they were able to hang on, maintain their positions and at least give an appearance of vigilance while travelling over those roads. Even inside the UN vehicle with seat belts on you were bounced around a lot.

One hour and forty minutes later we had completed the 32-kilometre trip. There were no problems on this trip, although the condition of the road had deteriorated even more since my last visit. To this day I do not know, and have difficulty accepting, how Brett and John managed to complete the trip in less than an hour.

Brett, John and Tommy met me there. The Indonesian TF members took the short walk to the nearby registration site and my Brimob escort went to the local Polri station. Brett and John explained in much more detail the recent problem and the steps they had put in place with Polri to prevent and/or manage any future problem. They convinced me that, at least for the rest of the registration period, security for the UN personnel and the people coming to register was guaranteed. After this they both had the opportunity to call home on the Satphone. With the return of the Task Force people it was time to continue on to SARE.

This trip was a little different as we spent much of the time driving in a riverbed. Very rocky and it was easy to see why the Hatolia teams were getting more punctures than anywhere else. While most of the riverbed was dry there was still a little water flowing in the centre. Following the Brimob vehicle our speed was a bit higher than I would have chosen. For one short period we even had a 'bow wave' coming off the front of the vehicle. From the brief look as we arrived, I could see in the wet season SARE would be an island in the middle of a very wide river. We were now in the dry season and it was very hot and dusty. The actual topography of the location placed it about 100 metres closer to sea level than Gleno with a corresponding higher average temperature. Not a very comfortable place to live.

In part we had planned our arrival to be after the normal midday mealtime so that they would not feel obliged to feed us. It was worth a try. However, as soon as we arrived the village chief took over insisting we had to stay for a meal. I tried to explain it really was not necessary. It made no difference as he said preparation had commenced shortly before our arrival as they knew we would be coming. If we didn't eat the food, it would be wasted. While I doubted the 'wasted' statement it was impolite and impossible to refuse.

While the meal was being prepared Tommy showed me around. Their house was part of a compound which included the registration site and a house occupied by a Brimob Section. By local standards it was very good accommodation. Some years before, it had been constructed for a non-government organisation working in the area. Although no one remembers what the letters S A R E stood for, they had eventually just run the letters into a word, and it became the name of the compound and the small local village just outside it. All around was a large area of temporary accommodation housing somewhere in the vicinity of 4,000 internally displaced persons. These people had been chased out of villages in the neighbouring districts of Liquicia and Bobinaro. Hopefully, after the conduct of the ballot, they would be able to return as the majority of the temporary accommodation was in the riverbed and would have to be abandoned in the wet season. There was nowhere near enough space for that number of people to live in the combined facilities of the compound and village. The bit of land that would be above water was just too small.

Once again, we had a very good lunch. It will never cease to amaze me that these people, who have so little, insist on preparing a meal every time I turn up; and it is always good food with plenty to eat, although not a great deal of variety.

After lunch Audi took me over to meet the sergeant of the local Brimob team. They had been sent from Dili as a result of Brett's earlier report of finding this large group of people who otherwise were unknown to the authorities or to the UN. Just another benefit of active patrolling. While I was doing this Saku was talking with the DEOs. Before I left, she told me they had not had a full understanding of the requirements and this was part of their slow registration process. Before I left, she told me she was sure they could now get it completed in time.

Eventually it was time to leave. After talking with Audi, we decided to take the 'easier' route home. Audi said it was a bit longer but much better road and no mountains. We headed off back into the riverbed, continuing to travel down river. Once again with the Brimob vehicle leading as we were now off the edge of any map I had or had seen. I was completely dependent on his local knowledge and navigating skills. The riverbed had what could be called a vehicle track going along it. Every now and then you crossed the shallow water; occasionally drove in the water for short distances; but always there were lots of rocks; but no punctures, yet. We came to a point where the track branched into two; Audi decided to take the right-hand track and the rest of us followed. A couple of kilometres later the track climbed the riverbank. Whoops, slightly geographically embarrassed. Once out of the river there was no track, it just stopped at the top of the bank, and we could find no track going on any further. We retraced our steps and took the left track. A short distance later we were out of the riverbed and driving on a makeshift track through very long grass. Every now and then we came across small creeks that had to be crossed; no problems in a four-wheel-drive. As I followed Brimob out of one of these creek crossings I looked in the rear-view mirror and saw the third vehicle stuck. It was not going anywhere. I attracted Audi's attention by blowing my horn and we all went back to the creek. No tow ropes in any vehicle so there was a lot of pushing and shoving before we finally got the task force vehicle onto solid ground. We were now in Liquicia district. A bit further on we came across an abandoned village. Audi told me the people who had lived in this village were probably some of the IDPs in SARE.

A little further along, and after being geographically embarrassed one more time, I noticed the 3rd vehicle was not behind us again. We stopped, waited five minutes, then drove back to find them. They were in another abandoned village and this time had a flat tyre and no tools to fix it. Once again, the Brimob team fixed it for them. While they were changing the tyre, using the Brimob spare, I wandered around the village. Many of the homes had been burnt but I did find one old man. Audi spoke with him and told me the old man had just refused to leave the home he had lived in since birth when the rest of the villagers had decided to flee. Ever since the rest had left, no one had come to cause him any trouble and he had all the food that had been left behind. Audi undertook to advise Liquicia authorities about this old man.

Once the tyre was changed Audi laid down the law to the Task Force members. Basically, if you stop or break down again, we will not be stopping to help. Off we set. Through a couple more abandoned villages, all with at least some homes that had been burnt, and finally reaching the main road between Dili and West Timor. We had travelled so far west we were now very close to the border with West Timor. When we looked around the Task Force vehicle was nowhere to be seen. Audi was as good as his word and it was straight onto the sealed road heading for Dili. It was a fast drive right along the ocean front until we got to what was now a right turn and the first hill on the way back to Gleno. It had been a very interesting day and I decided I would never use the alternate route again, although I knew this was one of the options Brett was considering. The next time we were face-to-face I was going to suggest he do a full reconnaissance so that they knew exactly where they would go if the situation got bad enough.

The following day, Friday 30 July, was the next half day of registration. That afternoon all teams came in bringing the electoral roll data they had gathered in the past 4 days. The CivPol all brought with them incident reports (Increps) on the new forms. That meant tomorrow I would be summarising them all onto the new 'covering report'. Just a bit more administrative BS to keep people in Dili HQ occupied.

Phil, Brett and Tommy with Brimob checking alternate evacuation route Hatolia and Atsabe. (It was not until we were back in Australia, they showed me this photo.)

Keeping Dili happy meant on the following day I did little else than consolidate all of the reports from the sub districts and then translate it all into a format which fitted the new forms. All just to create statistics. Fortunately, it was a quiet day with nothing to distract me from completing the task and then get it all onto a late arriving helicopter. This meant I would not be bothered the next day by JOC chasing me up to get the documentation to them as soon as possible which would mean, if they had not gone by helicopter, I would have wasted a day just driving to and from Dili to hand in the forms.

So, on the 1st of August I was free and clear of paperwork with a plan in mind to not only visit Atsabe, but to travel further and see Max at his registration site. I had this discussed with Gultom the previous evening and he had arranged an escort for me. When I told Allessandro of my plans he asked me to take Diana with me as there were some additional information and new instructions that had to be passed to the DEOs. Helen overheard the conversation and said she would be coming along as well, although her vehicle had been taken to Dili for service and she would need a lift. Because our HQ was so small keeping anything from anyone was well-nigh impossible and Baldev called out from his office the MLOs would come along and Helen could travel with them. With this larger group came the usual problem of getting everyone together to get underway at the established time. As it turned out the biggest delay was the new instructions for the DEOs being put into a written form they would understand.

Because the original plan was that I would meet the escort at Polri HQ, I told the others to meet me there. Gultom heard about me waiting outside and invited me to his house, which was inside the Polri compound, for coffee and to introduce me to his wife. This was a slightly different get together, purely social with no talk of work. His wife's command of the English language was almost good enough for her to be an interpreter.

Eventually we all got underway; Brimob leading with the lights and sirens on until we were out of the Gleno town limits. Because of the late start we did not stop at the registration sites on the way, so it took the convoy a bit under three hours to reach Atsabe. As with the other registration sites we did not stop in Atsabe because I really wanted to get to Max's registration site for the first time, another hour down the road.

After the usual bumping and bouncing over very rough roads, we arrived. The village was on the side of a ridge with magnificent views. I have been on volleyball courts in many places, but none of them had the views that could be seen from in front of the registration site. This was where Max had persons from all the different groups turn up each afternoon to play volleyball in mixed group teams.

Once again word had reached the location before we did, and on arrival we were met by a small group that included the village chief, TNI Sergeant, Polri Sergeant and a leader of the local pro-autonomy faction, read Militia leader. There was no animosity from anyone in this group and it seemed a genuinely warm greeting. Max's efforts appeared to have paid off. My work was finished fairly quickly but getting away would take a little longer. Eventually I would have to put my foot down to the others and say sorry, but it is time to leave. Diana and Helen, particularly Helen, stated they had not been able to do everything they wanted to. Bringing people from the different components of Gleno HQ proved to be a problem. Each wanted the same amount of access to the team and the locals and there was just not enough time for everyone to do everything they wanted.

On the road again and back to Atsabe where the DEOs and Sam had arranged a late lunch for us. It became a working lunch where some of what needed to be done was completed. After lunch Diana was with the DEOs passing on the essential information and instructing them to pass it on to the other two teams because, although we would call in on the way back to Dili, there would not be time for her to repeat the process at those locations. Baldev and I agreed that as soon as Diana was finished, we would leave. This information was given to Helen and she said she would go and speak with the village elders. We told her we would call on the radio when we were ready to go and, after waiting no longer than five minutes, would leave. Baldev went and visited the TNI unit while Sam gave me a short tour of the village. Diana finished, MLOs, me and escort ready; Helen running late; we started to drive off; Helen appeared just in time.

On the way back to Gleno we stopped at the other two

registration sites that were working out of Atsabe. Both had issues, mainly security, they wanted to raise. In my diary at the time I wrote *'more in the mind of the staff than real'*. Later events would show I had underestimated the potential problems in one of these locations.

Finally arrived back home late in the evening. Brimob were a very unhappy lot. I apologised to Audi and we agreed we would never do it again. The different requirements of each component meant no one was satisfied because no one had time to achieve their objective for the day. That day taught me going with all the different UN components at the same time was a mistake, one I would not make again.

The following day was another where I had trouble getting out of the office because of meetings and administrative matters. Firstly, I had a meeting with Gultom where we discussed the agenda for another of those large group, political meetings that was to follow. We came to agreement on just about everything in a very short time.

This was the next of those meetings between the two political groups with the UN people trying to act as mediator. On this occasion there were additional players; representatives from the Indonesian Task Force; a group of Portuguese observers, representing the Government of Portugal; and, the current local administration, but not Senor Claudio. While Gultom and I were on the 'same page' it did not help that the local political groups were not the only ones with different agendas. The different UN groups had not discussed the agenda beforehand and there were some differences between them on the preferred outcome. Most were at least displaying professional impartiality, but as usual one was in total support of every argument that came from the independence side. As can be expected the meeting dragged on far longer than it really needed to. After a lot of backwards and forwards between the different parties, at the end of the meeting the processes agreed to were much as the earlier agreements between Gultom and I.

In the afternoon I finally got out of the office after being contacted by Dili and told I had to personally meet the helicopter. They did not tell me why. Turned out to be more administration, although good administration this time. So, accompanied by the local children, I met the helicopter. On board was a Finance Officer from Dili with the MSA payments for all of the CivPol in Ermera. Initially I thought this might be a quick process. I soon realised otherwise when the helicopter crew shut down the engines and said they were going to the marketplace to do a bit of shopping. With the Finance Officer, I had to separately count and sign for the payment going to each individual. Only after I was satisfied with the money for each individual did he say I also had to do an overall count and check everything against a master roll that suddenly appeared from his briefcase. It could have all been done at the same time but that is the UN. Finally, they were gone, and it was back to our base to wait for the CivPol members to return from the day's work and get them to sign for their MSA.

On the way back to the office I called into the house as a couple of days before I had again complained to Senior Claudio about the plumbing problem with the toilet. It was continually getting blocked and we had to go to HQ when we needed to go. The good news was the plumber was back. He explained how he was replacing all of the pipes from the house to the main drain with larger pipes. He said it would be finished that afternoon but should be left overnight to fully set. But tomorrow morning should be fine.

From there it was back to HQ and a bit more of the new paperwork. I had earlier discussed with Amorin we would split that part of the role between the two of us. It would have been very unfair of me to land it all onto him. While doing this one of the student organisers turned up. He had a letter he wanted to hand deliver to Helen. She was not there so we had a short meeting of our own. Recently Dili had provided us with information on additional incidents in other districts where the students had created further circumstances resulting in unnecessary danger for UN personnel. So, this time I was a little more forceful in advising him of how to conduct their activities in Ermera. I carefully explained the anger I would feel if he put any of my people in danger. Without saying much, he decided he would leave and see Helen on another day.

By the end of the afternoon I had all the necessary paperwork up to date, had written a letter home and was paying the CivPol as they arrived back from daily tasks. The last was definitely a pleasant part of the day. When Rob Mills arrived back, he showed me a letter he had written home. At the time it was an excellent description of the situation. He told me he had shown it to others, and he was about to make copies so they could send it home as well. I got him to add me to the list for a copy and as I still have the copy, I now fully reproduce it -

Dear —,
Hello here is another cheat's letter from the frontline of modern peacemaking! Life here has been very busy with the registration process nearly finished and the prospect of a few days off hopefully in the near future. We are all hoping to go to Bali for a week but that is a distant unobtainable dream. Two days in Dili is the reality. Dodging bullets and Militias in the night compared to supping piss on a golden beach seems to be the choice preferred by our hosts here.

None the less we are all looking forward to the first days off since setting foot here. I managed to complete 928 registration cards while I worked at the registration centre in Railaco, the bird finger bled on the first day, so I have applied for a purple heart for shedding blood in a war zone! After 11 days of that I had a job change to a 4-man roster at Ermera HQ. Working 1 day on the radio and 3 days out on patrol around the region including admin trips to Dili for theft and repairs. Theft is not so easy now that everything is now established and there are security guards to check what comes and goes. And if you are going to sign a bogus name remember to take the name badge off first.

The guy in charge of the store is an emaciated pommy alcoholic, who is always at breaking point almost a cross between the stress level of Basil Faulty and the frustration level of Wyle E Coyote. The first encounter with this fella came on the first night hear when our gear failed to appear. Volunteers were despatched to retrieve said items (never volunteer for anything) from the airport. On our arrival we were met by this man who was at breaking point on seeing how much gear each of us had imported into the country. After a few threats he calmed down and said he was only joking with us. It makes trips to Dili fun especially seeing him.

There is more character here like that now that the mission is established the best way to deal with them is to give them humour. Not to let them win. Most of them consider you as an invader in their little part of the world, forgetting that we were actually here while they were wanking themselves in a hotel room somewhere in Australia. There is a saying the UN exists despite itself in some cases that is true but as long as you ride it and don't let it bother or stress there is no problem.

We are still happy at the bad manor. Our new cook is great; she cooks food, cleans our clothes, and keeps the place clean. All the qualities treasured in a good employee and sadly lacking in our ex one who we had to give the D.C.M. Her standards faded into obscurity as did her mental state, rising at 4.00am to chop wood some days not cooking on others had us knocking on the doctor's door for blood pressure pills and cyanide paste. It was a cruel tale of bad luck her father died on the day we sacked her, he actually died that day and we sacked her when she got back from the funeral! She took it well, along with a month's pay free.

Ermera is still the best posting in the country compared with some we live in relative luxury with our fridge, TV, and huge outdoor couch. These features are the envy of all the Kiwi boys. It was been quiet not too much to report, feel free to write. We had a party at the Portuguese house last weekend which would have been a whole lot better had the next day been a day off instead of being another Troy Dann adventure. The beer here is like a bullet, it has no friends once it leaves the barrel, or neck of the bottle in case of a Bintang. The worst hangovers to be had in the world by far come in green bottles in crates of 16 costing 140.000 rupiah! the hangover is like nothing else previously experienced. It is resistant to berrocca and Panadol, like and introduced noxious pest inured to cyanide. Everyone knows you have one and no one cares like owning a Skoda. Fresh air is the only gas that gets to the root of it, hanging the head out of the land rover window in the morning seems to work. In the tropical environment everything takes longer to heal like cuts, blisters, this also applies to the cranial residue of a good night out unfortunately!

That's about it really till next time take care.

That evening word came through Falantil would be taking their people to Fatubolo on 3 August to register as voters. I arranged a meeting with Gultom and he assured me there would be Polri there to ensure they would be able to do so without interference.

As a little insurance policy, I had Rob and Jim head up to that registration site for the day. Their stated reason for going was to take the MSA payments for the CivPol. I would have gone myself but I had already committed to going the other way, to Letefoho, where I would pay the MSA to those located there and meet a representative from Atsabe who would collect theirs.

Rob 'Fingers' Mills.

It was one of the few days where I was able to get an interpreter to be with me for the whole day. This meant at each of the villages I was able to speak directly with members of the local Polri unit. Although their words did not reveal anything but full conformity with Gultom's official line, their limited equipment, body language and general demeanour was such that I was far from convinced of their ability, or willingness, to protect UN personnel if it became necessary. This was good additional information that would be part of my future considerations.

One of the villages visited that day was Homboe. Even with Saku helping out in SARE it was still one of the most organised and prepared registration sites in Ermera. When we arrived at the village, the chief introduced me to his father, the former village chief. As a young man his father had been a guide for the Australian commandos during World War II. This time I had an interpreter and we had a good conversation over coffee with cake. The best part of the conversation was there was no mention of politics.

When I got back to HQ there was a local waiting for me who wanted to report being beaten up by the Militia. For the first time I was getting the story from the actual victim. He said that he was walking from his village to the Gleno market when he came across a Militia roadblock. At the road block the Militia where asking everyone how they were going to vote.

He said his answer to them was 'Independence'.

He told me immediately after he said 'independence 'they had beaten him with their fists and told him he had to vote for autonomy. He continued by saying he did not bother to reply, and they let him go. A quick examination showed all he had was a few minor bruises. When pushed to name his assailants he stated he did not know the people and would not be able to identify them. Every effort I made to get a name or names met with the same response, even though I was sure he did know the person/s who had beaten him.

In trying to get a better understanding I asked him why, when they asked him, he had not just said I am going to vote autonomy. His answer took me a little by surprise. He told me he knew he would get a beating, but it would not be too bad. However, if he told them he was going to vote autonomy and then actually voted for independence then, after the ballot, they would kill him. I pressed him on how they would know who he voted for and all he kept saying was 'they would know'.

With the former Village Chief of Humboe.

On a later day, just after the finish of the registration period, I would be in a school room at another village speaking with the teacher and village council. I noticed at the top of the blackboard were three names, underneath each other, with a large number of chalk marks next to each of them. I asked the teacher what they were for. He told they were from the Indonesian election held earlier that year. With a bit of prompting he explained the names were those of the local candidates. The election officials were in the room when the voter entered; the voter told the election officials who they wanted to vote for, and the election officials then put a mark next to the nominated name. Later they counted the total numbers and advised the central organisation of the results at that site.

It was just like the cartoons. A big light up in my head. While this was not the way it was done in the major centres it was how the smaller villages conducted voting. The people in these areas did not know how a secret ballot was conducted. They probably didn't know such a thing existed. To me this information was so important I informed Allessandro as soon as I returned to Gleno. In addition, just in case he did not report it to Dili, I included it in my daily report. It was a simple matter from there to include it in the training being conducted for the DEOs and Local Staff so they could include it in the education sessions they were conducting in the villages.

The last few days of registration were a little hectic with almost constant changes going on. A lot of this centred around the timing of visitors to Ermera. While registration had to keep going there was a need to accommodate various VIPs. But plans kept changing, in military terms it was a real 'great coats on, great coats off' period. In these final days of registration Allessandro made another visit to Hatolia without me this time, and yes, he went in the Land Cruiser. When he returned, I had another accident report to complete.

Not only were there changes to our daily plans but HQ Dili advised the registration period had been extended by two days. Apparently, some districts still had a lot of people to register. Amongst our DEOs this just brought on moans of displeasure, because they had completed their task and were looking forward to a couple of days off. At SARE they accepted it without complaint. While they believed by working a few extra hours a day they could have completed everything on time, the extra time made it a little easier. In the end they completed their registrations on the first extra day.

To add to my workload CivPol Jose Pena came back to the office with some fake registration cards, photocopies of our originals, that had been handed to him at the Gleno registration site. The voters were given these cards at the time of registration and would be required to present them when they came to vote. These ones were obvious photocopies of an original. My guess was an attempt would be made to have additional votes cast for one side or the other. Fortunately, they were done by an amateur and very easy to detect.

I immediately took these to Gultom whose first statement was there were not many photocopiers in Ermera, and he should be able to find out who had done it. In short order, the next day actually, the culprit had been tracked down. The Bupati had arranged for the photocopies to be made. He had a very good excuse. He was going to have his people use them as examples in an education process he was organising before the ballot. It sounded like a good story. In the existing political situation, there was not much we could do about it. But the matter had been resolved; UN Dili had been informed; all UN staff were now aware of the fakes and how easy it was to detect them; and the Bupati knew that we knew. As an aside both Polri and TNI were extremely embarrassed and concerned they might be implicated.

Following up on this, Captain Ari arrived at my home late in the evening to discuss how this would be reported to UN HQ in Dili. It was difficult to establish exactly what his concern was. I showed him a copy of my written report, which was phrased in very diplomatic language, and he went away satisfied. The report to Dili had been part of normal reporting but I had also intended it to be circulated to all districts as a warning of possible attempts to have an illegal impact on the final result.

One of the VIPS who dropped in on the last day of registration was Mick Keelty, an Assistant Commissioner in the AFP. After

Dili advised me that morning, I arranged for Rob and Jim to go the registration sites and relieve Don Barnby and Paul Morris so that they could meet with him. Late in the afternoon he arrived by UN helicopter, the AFP Doctor was with him. This time it was a Huey rather than the usual Super Puma. There would not be so much fun for the kids today as the down draft from a Huey is not strong enough to blow them around. We drove to Bad Manor and sat on the verandah answering their questions as best we could over a couple of beers. When they left, I gave Mr Keelty a letter to my wife and asked him to post it when they got back to Australia.

The Assistant Commissioner took my letter back to Australia but instead of posting it thought it would be good if he personally delivered it to Margaret. So, after work one day he went around to our home and rang the doorbell. Margaret got a shock. As the wife of a former soldier who had served in war zones the unannounced visit of a senior officer in uniform meant only one thing. Fortunately, Mr Keelty was quick to explain why he was there. Just another thing the AFP needed to learn.

During these last couple of days, I took a bit of time to put together an 'essential logistics' roster which covered 'dot point 4' of my concept. The first day after registration finished it was important as many villages as possible in the district receive a visit from a CivPol patrol. To this end everyone was rostered on a patrol that day. However, the day after that a roster covering a 20-day period commenced. On day one of the roster two CivPol would be given a task to complete in Dili. For each pair the task varied. Some were vehicle related, for example tyres, other logistics related and the odd occasional medical matter. In all instances their instructions were to remain in Dili, or somewhere else they chose to visit, for the next day to ensure the task was properly completed. On the third day they were required to be back in Gleno by 3 p.m. On the morning of the third day the next pair would head to Dili with their task to complete, and so on. There was just enough time between the end of registration and the period immediately before voting day for all my CivPol personnel to get this very short, but well earned, break. When the people going to Dili came from a sub-district the roster included provision for their area to be covered by others while they were away. I entitled this my 'Essential Logistics Roster'.

Visit of Assistance Commissioner Keelty with Dr Czoban

A further complication arose when the JOC advised me they would be transferring Nitaya from Ermera to Dili HQ to become the officer in charge of CivPol Personnel. I told Nitaya this when she arrived back from the last day of registration and she 'hit the roof'. After asking my permission, she rang Dili. It was very interesting listening to one end of the conversation, and I was glad it was not me trying to reason with her. Eventually she got them to agree to one more day before she had to report to Dili, and they would allow her to return to Gleno on the day before the vote as she wanted to be at her polling site on voting day.

After she hung up, she looked at me and asked if I minded the arrangements she had just made. I had no objection; in fact, I was happy. While covering for her during the intervening period would pose no difficulty, polling day would have been a different matter. Her determination resolved one potential problem before it occurred.

The next day Nitaya took one of the vehicles and went out to Railaco Leten with what she considered her excess clothing and food. She left them with the villagers and promised them she would be back.

We were now at the end of the registration period. In the final few hectic days stories had come in of a re-commencement of night-time intimidation in a number of villages by Militia, this time with TNI support. No CivPol personnel had been available to respond to these incidents at the time but I kept a list of all locations and they were all scheduled for a visit or visits from the very commencement of the next phase.

CHAPTER 19

Immediate Post Registration

On 7 August 1999 all Electoral Teams, including CivPol members, where brought into Regional Headquarters for a debrief. The DEOs remained at headquarters for a further 5 days to allow them some rest and to be trained for their roles in the next phase of the overall process.

When I met with the incoming CivPol I found we now had a couple of 'mascots'. Max Knoth had visited a cock fighting session, a popular and legal activity in East Timor, and after a lot of persuasion had placed a bet. He deliberately put his money on the smallest and scrawniest rooster there. Who would have guessed it, that rooster won? The owner was so pleased someone else had bet on his rooster he gave the animal to Max. The rooster now had a name, Bruce. Meanwhile, in Hatolia, Saku had purchased a piglet and then given it to John as a joke, if not as a bit of an insult. John turned the whole situation around, cleaned up the piglet, named it Sally and we had another mascot for the CivPol.

Now it was time to get back to work. With the four additional vehicles and a bit of negotiation with some of the more amenable DEO team leaders I was in a position to implement my plans. On 8 August CivPol from the sub-districts returned to their bases and the Gleno based CivPol commenced patrolling. The instruction to all was- be innovative in conducting your patrols and continue doing it up until 28 August, two days before the ballot was to be conducted.

Our mascots — Max with 'Bruce' and Rob with John's piglet, Sally.

The following day the 'essential logistics' roster came into effect and the first pair headed for Dili.

In every location when the CivPol arrived back they were informed pro-autonomy forces had visited immediately after the UN team's departure. The people had been told UNAMET had left and would not be returning. The prompt return of CivPol challenged the credibility of the pro-autonomy propaganda and significantly reduced any adverse effect it may have had on the people's willingness to continue participating in the process.

As part of their training I had a session with all the DEOs where I informed them of my intention to have the CivPol work separately to the teams during the next phase. Many expressed concerns they would not have CivPol with them during the education visits. Even though CivPol were unarmed the DEOs felt much safer when they had a uniform person with them. This was discussed and in the end an agreement was reached. Each evening they would inform me where they would be the next day. I would then assess the security issues and either allocate a CivPol to be with them or make sure CivPol patrols called in at different times during the day. This they accepted. One of them came to me after the session and asked if I knew that the DEOs were calling me 'Uncle Geoff'. I had not heard it before then but considered it something I should tuck into the back of my mind as it could come in useful.

If for no other reason this patrolling was conducted to directly counteract the new phase of reported attempts at intimidation by Militia. The reports coming in included comment that TNI were now providing additional support to the Militia. Although exactly what constituted this support was never stated, my presumption was a physical presence of at least some TNI personnel with the Militia.

Don and Jose on Patrol

As before, each day patrols were conducted to the area or areas where intimidation had occurred. First preference was given to localities where the information indicated the highest threat level had been presented. But I still ensured that everywhere the Militia had appeared was visited by UN patrols.

In the early days of this period the availability of interpreters to accompany CivPol was a significant benefit. Their language skills meant inquiries were able to not only get more information but for that information to be more accurate. While the UN mandate did not give any authority to conduct investigations, it did include a requirement to secure the ballot. The CivPol continued to use my definition of this part of the mandate to conducted inquiries into intimidation on the basis it threatened the ballot process and provided information essential when advising Polri. The presence of the interpreters increased the effectiveness of this task providing me with firmer ground when I discussed the incidents with Gultom or Ari.

While some patrol tasks were established by me in Gleno, I gave the sub-districts the responsibility of developing their own patrol plan. They had the immediate knowledge of their local area necessary to identify where UN visibility would be the most effective. Further, them preparing the plan and no information being passed by radio meant no possibility of radio interception and therefore no forewarning reaching Militia that a visit was about to take place. At times, due to acceptable connecting tracks, Hatolia and Atsabe worked together. For one part of the day there would be a number of one vehicle patrols with two police in each; at other times of the day, these one-vehicle patrols would meet up with one or two others and conduct a patrol in much greater strength. A similar process occurred with the Gleno based CivPol, on occasion also linking in with Letefoho and Fatubesse teams as well.

While the prime target areas where the villages intimidation had occurred, my aim was still to visit every village in the district. On two occasions patrols located villages formerly unknown to local authorities. Each of these two villages was near a border with other districts and neither appeared on any map. However, when CivPol arrived and spoke with the villagers they found everyone eligible to vote had registered in one or another of the registration sites. They just preferred to keep their village locations to themselves. Understandable.

Late that afternoon it rained. I mean really heavy, tropical rain. I went home; put my swimmers on; grabbed the soap; stood under the water running off the roof and had a real shower. At the same time, I became the entertainment for the local children. They thought it was hilarious. Even some of their mothers stopped to watch as well. Lucky, I had brought the swimmers with me.

9 August started with a bit of a nightmare. A large group of the DEOs had been told they could go to Dili for the day. However, they could not find enough vehicles to take them all. When I looked there were seven vehicles in the parking area. More than enough for everyone if the keys had been available. Some

individual DEO team leaders still considered the vehicles their personal property and kept the keys secured away from anyone else. My persuasive skills were again the order of the day and before too long there were enough vehicles, with keys, to convey all who had been informed they could go to Dili.

This was followed by the next major meeting between the two sides, again hosted by the UN. This was the first occasion when Gultom and I had not had the opportunity to discuss the agenda beforehand. The meeting started and dragged on and on and on. A couple of times I felt myself falling asleep. Nearly three hours into the meeting and Gultom got up, said nothing and walked out. I followed him out and spoke with him. He said that we had heard exactly the same things on more than one occasion. Neither group had changed their opinion and he doubted they ever would no matter what we said.

He then explained it does not matter if we reach an agreement here because the people in the meeting, from both sides, are not the real leaders of either group. Therefore, the real leaders would not feel themselves bound by any agreement coming out of the meeting. I thought the real leader of the pro-independence group in Ermera was in the meeting, but I may have been misinformed on that. I was certain the real leader of the pro-autonomy faction was not there. Senior Claudio had not attended any of the meetings.

After a short break and a couple of cigarettes each, Gultom and I returned to the meeting. No progress had been made in our absence and none was made in the next hour or so. Just arguments and accusations going backwards between the two groups. Then a fax message arrived from Dili. It was a copy of an agreement, a Code of Conduct, signed that morning by the two most senior representatives of each side in East Timor and witnessed by the UN SRSG.

The terms of the 'Code of Conduct' had been agreed to in Dili. Those terms were read out to everyone at the meeting. That stopped both groups in their tracks and they all agreed to abide by it. They did not have much choice. The meeting finished. I thought at the time, it will be interesting to see if they actually do what they agreed to. As history recorded the agreement lasted till polling day. After that everything changed. It was 2.45 p.m. when the meeting finished, it had started just before 10 a.m.

There was an outdoor basketball court at the Bupati's office compound. I had taken a leaf out of Max's play book and arranged a game for that afternoon between the UN and the local Indonesian authorities. We had agreed on two halves of ten minutes and ten minutes between the halves. The UN team was a mixture from every component, some knew how to play others had no idea. The main strength of the Indonesian team came from three of the Task Force people, all almost my height and they seemed to know a bit about the game. About 300 spectators had turned up and their support was roughly even between the two teams. I must admit throughout the game there was more laughter than cheering. For those interested in statistics, UNAMET 12 defeated Gleno Administration/Polri 10. My personal statistics scored the first and last field goals; one steal; three blocked shots; two fouls; and a lot of rebounds. The best cheer/laugh came when I walked off at half time and lit a cigarette.

After the game

At the end of game, we agreed there would be a game held each afternoon with no preset teams for anyone who was available. On most days leading up to the ballot a game was held. I had time to join in on only two occasions. On one of those I was in a team with two of the Task Force members.

The Bupati was holding a party that evening. Along with senior locals, both East Timorese and Indonesians, he invited all the senior UN people. After the basketball there had been a bit of work, mainly administrative stuff, before I headed back home to shower and then have a rare change into civilian clothes. My initial packing had included two pairs of slacks, two short sleeved shirts and one pair of slip on shoes. When I got home, I found three other UNV's had been invited around to use our 'shower'. So, I just had to sit for a little while and wait.

Eventually I washed, got dressed and went next door to the MLO's house. Even though it was only a five-minute walk to the Bupati's home Baldev had offered to drive me to the party. We arrived, on time, just after dark. Very quickly I realised arriving on time was not really the done thing. The most 'junior' invitees were expected to arrive on time. As the importance of the individual increased so did the time before you arrived. We were quite a bit early in our arrival.

As we walked up the drive, I saw a large number of the ubiquitous plastic chairs lined up in three rows on one side of the driveway. An army tent, without the sides, was set up over these chairs. A few people were already in those chairs and there were others on a few chairs in other places. On the verandah of the house was a number of large cane lounge chairs with cushions. Baldev and I had a brief discussion and decided the cane lounges would be much more comfortable than the plastic chairs, so we took a seat there. Although we were the only people in those chairs at the time it turned out to be the correct move. Those chairs were intended for the very senior VIPs attending the party and, apparently, we were included in that group.

Shortly after Baldev and I had chosen our own seats the ushers for the evening appeared. They met everyone from then on and there was a definite hierarchy to where they seated people. It appeared the more important you were the closer you were to the verandah. There was one exception to this, all the women were directed to go inside the house. The looks on the faces of a few of the UN ladies was priceless, a couple even tried to flaunt the local customs, but gave in before too long. In the meantime, there we sat, no drinks, no nibbles. Just us, the other VIPs and the Bupati, chatting and smoking.

Once the Bupati was satisfied all the important guests were there, obvious because all of the cane lounges were occupied, he stood up and invited the VIPs to come and get some food. What a table, taking only one spoon full of each dish completely filled my plate before I reached the end of the table. There I was handed a bottle of beer. Now I have had warm beer before in many places but this one was beyond warm, it was HOT. Food was excellent, the beer not so. Once us VIPs had our food those in the front row of the seats were invited to get theirs. After them the women came and got theirs, before going back into the house; finally, the remaining guests got to eat. While we were eating dinner, a band started playing. The sound system was woeful and the singer, while enthusiastic, was not much better. Not long after deserts were brought to us in our seats. Having already eaten more than my stomach had become used to I politely declined the desert. At this time the ladies came out of the house and joined the rest of us.

With the band still playing in the background I got myself a second hot beer and started mingling. Two of the TNI Military Liaison Officers took me aside and explained that, as the senior visiting officer, it was my responsibility to start the dancing for the evening by inviting our host's wife to dance. I put the beer down and went over to the Bupati's wife and requested the pleasure of a dance with her. That got the next part of the evening off to a flying start. For the next hour or so I was almost continuously on the dance floor, well actually it was the concrete driveway, but dance floor will do. After the first dance there was obviously no inhibition or social restriction on who danced with who; nor who asked who to dance. The majority of my dances were with ladies who approached me. One of the early ones had apparently been to the party in Dili and wanted me to teach her the 'rock and roll' I had done there. So, the rest of my time there was attempting a version of 'rockabilly' dancing with various ladies.

Dancing with Bupati's wife

About 11.15 p.m. I was just about worn out, so I told Baldev I was going to walk home, after all it was only five minutes or so walk, and downhill at that. I made my farewells to the Bupati and his wife and was making my way to the front gate when the Gleno power system decided it was time for a total blackout. Everyone stopped and looked up. The sky was magnificent. I have never seen so many stars and the milky way was clearly visible. Almost took my breath away. The guests just ignored the blackout and kept chatting, although now most conversations were about the spectacular skies.

It did not take long and the power was back on. My personal opinion was one of the towns folk had turned the generator off in an attempt to silence the band at the Bupati's party. Even after I arrived home it was loud. But not loud enough to stop me falling asleep.

CHAPTER 20

OFFICIAL OPENING OF FALANTIL CANTONMENT SITE

The next morning there was the usual problems amongst the DEOs over vehicles to go to Dili for the day. This time I left it to them to sort out amongst themselves.

Allessandro approached me about going on a trip to the 'forest'. There were people coming from Dili and he had received a request for a senior member from Ermera UN to accompany them. It meant getting out and about, so of course I would go.

While I waited for the Dili group to arrive Diana asked my assistance. They were preparing a plan for the return of the DEOs to their sub-districts the following Thursday. For someone with planning experience it was not a difficult job. But that type of experience was still very short in Gleno. Although Diana was learning very quickly.

The entourage from Dili arrived. Brigadier General Rezaqul Haider, Senior MLO for all of East Timor, was back in Ermera and the senior person in this group. There were also a couple of high-ranking UN politicos, a few hangers on, some of the Portuguese observers, two vehicles with Indonesians from the HQ of their Task Force and three vehicles full of various media.

When the guide vehicle from a local pro-independence group turned up it was time to head off. Led by the pro-independence vehicle were nine UN vehicles, two Indonesian vehicles and the three media cars. This was another of those drives that went around in a few circles to try and keep us a little confused as to exactly where we were and how we got to the final destination. One thing that was easy for me to recognise, we were climbing to the highest mountain in the district. For all but the media vehicles, the three of which were all two-wheel drive, there was no difficulty in getting to our destination. Somehow the media managed to arrive not too far behind the rest of us. I think they got a lot of help from Falantil members who, like my previous visits, were watching over us throughout the whole trip.

It was now I found out this was part of the recent agreement reached in Dili and the visit was for the announcement of the official cantonment of Falantil Para-military personnel. In a clearing, just outside the main camp, Falantil had set up a parking area for all the vehicles. At the other side there was a boom gate manned by two persons armed with modern weapons. The small hut beside the gate was the guard house. There was no fence or wall on either side of the boom gate. While we were waiting for the media to get in position, the Brigadiers ADC instructed everyone on the order of precedence for us walking into the camp. The Brigadier would be first, followed by me, then the ADC, the senior UN personnel and finally the Indonesian party. The media were to make their own arrangements, not get in the way, but make sure they got good coverage of the Brigadier.

As we approached the gate the sentry called out the guard. Just like an Australian Army base the guard lined up and presented arms, they had a wide variety of weapons including some being the local homemade variety.

The boom was lifted, and we walked through. That was the signal for an enormous chant to go up ... VIVA ...VIVA ... VIVA ... over and over again. It was accompanied by whistling and cheering. In those first moments the topography of the top of this mountain prevented us from seeing who was chanting. This mountain top was not your standard tabletop or a single peak.

Instead of that it was similar to a tabletop but with a lot of hillocks, the best word I could find to describe them, spread over what otherwise would have been a large tabletop mountain. I am sure it had been volcanic sometime in its past.

As we walked through a gap between the first two hillocks there were the people. Thousands of them. Every one of them chanting or cheering. Goosebumps standing up all over me. What an experience. Touching hands on both sides as we walked through lines and lines of people. High fives with the younger ones. These were not the Paramilitary of Falantil but anyone who could get there for this day. Because of the hillocks it was impossible to see all of them at once. They covered each one of them. To my mind at least half of Ermera was there. Definitely no less than 20,000 people. The chant and the noise went on ... VIVA...VIVA...VIVA.

Then the gap between the two lines of people opened. Waiting for us was one of the female elders of the area with four children. The children were all holding a number of the local handmade scarfs, known as 'tais'. As each of us approached the elderly lady took a scarf from a child and hung them around our necks. I felt extremely privileged.

The two lines closed in again and we moved on a bit further. A short while later they opened out again. This time there was a group of village chiefs waiting for us, all dressed in traditional costume. I knew all of these chiefs, some only by sight and others almost to the point where I could call them friend. The eldest of the chiefs made a speech. While we could not understand what he was saying the emotion he was putting into it was obvious. Some of the locals in ear shot were crying. When he finished the speech, he presented the Brigadier with a traditional sword. It was now time to move on a bit further.

Again, we were passing between the crowds of people. While

there was not a lot of room, they always left enough room for us to easily pass. There were no barricades to prevent them getting closer, just well-behaved people.

The crowd parted again, and we were looking onto a large clearing. In the centre of the clearing a guard of honour were standing in parade formation. The Brigadier had been a little ahead of me, but I managed to arrive in time to stand near him as we returned their salute. Some of the weapons they had were only pieces of wood carved to look like rifles.

Behind the guard was the centre of their camp. A number of huts constructed out of bamboo with orange plastic being the primary roofing material. There were the usual pink plastic chairs but also some other seating constructed from bamboo. If you looked closely you could still see sap. There was a place in the centre where tables and chairs had been set up. Here, with the Brigadier, I got to be at the head table. There were speeches from a number of people, including the UN, followed by food. The food was more part of the formality than an actual meal.

Once the formalities finished one of the Portuguese observers came over and said 'Geoff this is one of those days that a man will always remember'.

I could only agree with him. The emotion in that place was so strong that you could not help but be affected by it.

While chatting with one of the Falantil commanders I saw a lad wearing an Australian flag T shirt. I just had to get my photo taken with him. When I went and asked him if that would be okay, he answered in perfect English. We had a short chat. The photo was taken and then he offered to interpret for me if I wanted to walk around and meet the people. There was no way I was going to miss that opportunity. The two of us wandered around and I got to meet and talk with a lot of people. Some of them had been guests at the Bupati's party the night before. Interesting.

There were others who I recognised as being from the UN's locally employed staff; more military aged men than I had seen anywhere in Ermera; and, some individuals I knew to be part of Militia groups. The latter were perhaps 'conscripts' in the Militia. Or were they spying?

Before we left my young interpreter insisted I go with him to the top of one of the hillocks. He told me I would understand why when I got there. It was a relatively short climb, but we still had to find our way through the crowds of people, with the many handshakes that went with it. When I reached the top and looked out, I knew why he took me there. Not only was it a magnificent view but I knew exactly where we were. In the distance I could see Gleno and the riverbed. This was just the information I needed to add another alternative to my planning. But I would have to have a serious discussion with Falantil leadership, without the presence of others, beforehand.

After a day I will never forget it was time to leave. As I had been driving up to the camp, I had a cassette in the vehicle's player. Just as we arrived 'We Are the Champions' had just started and then stopped as I turned the vehicle off. When I got back to the vehicle and started the engine the music started again. What a perfect fit. I was now certain I knew which way the vote would go. But only if we could make sure it went ahead.

The next day arrived with a few problems. Firstly, it was very hard to get back to normal after the last two days. Secondly paperwork. There was two days of administrative stuff had to be completed on top of the normal everyday stuff. Finally, there was my counterpart. Gultom was very unhappy he had not been informed about my visit to the Falantil cantonment. Over some coffee with a few cigarettes I managed to convince him I had only found out about the trip on the morning and it wasn't until the convoy arrived from Dili that I knew anything about the reason for the trip. I did not describe what I had seen nor the emotional effect of the day.

Official opening of Falantil cantonment.

CHAPTER 21

Education Period

Most of 11 August was spent with a CivPol member from Dili HQ. He had been sent because someone thought it was time to get me thinking about planning for the next stages, the campaign period, polling day and afterwards. He was very surprised when I presented everything I had already done. Apparently having a concept of operations was something they had not considered. The major achievement which surprised him was I had managed to extract the CivPol from the Electoral teams until polling day. This had not occurred in any other district. The current patrol plan met with his approval. However, I cannot say it was all my way, there was additional information from him, particularly with regard to helicopter tasking, I could and would incorporate into my plans. As part of this meeting, I again requested a helicopter tasking for me to do an aerial reconnaissance of the district. Once our meeting was over, he headed off to call in on another district.

Thursday 12 August was another of those meeting days. This time it was to be the first meeting of the Regional Campaign Committee. This was a new committee established under the Code of Conduct. After the first hour I got up, walked outside and screamed. When I returned the meeting continued for almost another hour. The whole meeting was spent arguing over whether the pro-independence party, CNRT, would be allowed to establish an office. The major issue causing disagreement between the two parties was where the CNRT office could be located. By the end of the meeting nothing had been decided. No other agenda items were considered and both sides left very unhappy.

I was not exactly happy either. Somehow, I had been appointed as chairman of this committee and it was supposed to meet every day. In the long run it met now and then. More often than not, one or both parties just failed to appear. Not once did either of them notify they would not be attending and there was never a later explanation or apology. The first meeting was the only long one. From then on, they were short and based around attempts at political point scoring. The two groups were so diametrically opposed to each other I doubted these meetings would ever achieve anything.

Immediately after the meeting Allessandro cornered me and allocated another task to me for the day. The Australian Consulate in Dili had arranged with him to bring another VIP to meet with me. Turned out it was a senior member from New Zealand Department of Foreign Affairs and a couple of supporters. They wanted to talk about Wayne Corbett and Rob Mills, my Kiwi police. Why he wanted to meet with me first I never did figure out, perhaps it was just Allessandro avoiding certain situations. I am sure Allessandro gave them a bit of a warning about my dislike of meetings as they came bearing a gift, a slab of VB beer. I took them to Bad Manor, where we left the beer. While we waited for the troops to return from patrol there was a long discussion about the overall mission situation and, in particular, the work being done by my two Kiwis. Had someone told me before their arrival I could have changed that day's arrangements so Rob and Wayne were available when they first arrived. In the long run they enjoyed some of the camaraderie in Bad Manor with time for productive conversations with Rob and Wayne plus some of the other CivPol.

Just as I was ready to leave the VIPs with their countrymen

Antonio arrived home and immediately informed me Saku had told him he was to go with her tomorrow when she went out to conduct an education session in Homboe. Apparently, she thought he could be her interpreter, as he is fluent in Portuguese. There were some things she had not taken into account. Firstly, Antonio was not part of the Electoral Component. Secondly, most of the people she was going to see did not speak Portuguese. Finally, Antonio already had a task from me for the next day. I think Antonio was very happy when I told him he was not available as an interpreter for her. Shortly after Saku and I had words. Later that evening she apologised.

The following evening both my house mates were out at a housewarming party. In fact, now at night they were out more than they were in. I prepared myself a very hot curry with bully beef. Not long after that Wayne Corbett and Don Barnby called in. They wanted my approval to do some civil assistance road works the next day. Naturally I asked what they were intending to do, I know enough to be careful about approving requests like this. They explained there was a track from Wayne's registration site down to a point on the riverbed which was very close to Gleno. However, at the moment there was one sharp drop off on the track too steep and high even for 4-wheel drive vehicles. If they could smooth it out, and they believed they could, then both Wayne and Don would have another evacuation route from their registration sites. As an additional advantage, and the public reason for undertaking the task, the people of the village would be able to get carts down to the river to collect water. The next point completely won the argument. They had already purchased, with their own money, picks and shovels for them to do the work. After this explanation the benefit to us and the local community was obvious. They also asked could Paul Morris and Rob Mills go with them to assist. They knew me very well. Permission was granted.

CivPol roadwork's creating an alternate route.

On the following day, while the four road workers were out doing their thing, I received more reports of pro-autonomy groups visiting villages and telling the people that UNAMET had left and there would be no vote. Amorin and three others were dispatched to follow up. By the end of the day they had tracked it down and showed a presence in an area not normally covered by Ermera CivPol. While the reports had come from Ermera villages this was a typical East Timor report, they were passing on what they had heard second or third hand. The actual incidents had occurred in a couple of villages in Liquicia. As in the past the visit by Ermera CivPol, for however brief a period, put paid to a bit of propaganda.

The Australian Consulate was on the telephone again. This time directly to me. They wanted to arrange a visit to Ermera for Mr Tim Fischer, former Deputy Prime Minister of Australia, and a group of others who would be in East Timor as part of the International Electoral Observer group. I asked exactly what they were looking for. Mr Fischer was looking for a meeting with a senior politician, in our case the Bupati, who was not based in Dili, and a meeting with UN people in one of the outlying districts. Because there was a reasonable road between Dili and Ermera they thought we would be the best place to visit. Not a problem, this was something I was sure I could organise even though it would be during the campaign period.

Their suggested order was a meeting with the Bupati about 10 a.m. followed by a meeting with the UN management team in Gleno. I told them 10 a.m. would be a good starting time but strongly suggested we reverse the meeting order and have the meeting with UN personnel first. When they queried my reason, I had a simple answer. With the Bupati as the second meeting I expected we would arrive at his place around midday and I was absolutely certain he would love to show off Ermera by putting on a very good lunch. From everyone's perspective food in Ermera is always a high priority. With a bit of laughter my suggested change was agreed to.

Then he had a second request. Was there any way I could arrange the meeting without Helen finding out or being there? She was known even beyond Ermera. I would do my best. So, in the coming days I locked in the visit with the Bupati and managed to inform the UN personnel who should be at the meeting without Helen finding out. Later the Consulate would call and ask me to change the date. However, the new date they wanted was the last day of the campaigning period. I told them I was pretty sure the Bupati would not be available that day, still I would try, but it would cost them.

He was obviously expecting that as he said, 'I already plan to bring a slab of VB'.

My answer may have surprised him when I told him I could now get VB in the local market for the equivalent of $17 a slab, so what would really go down well would be a reasonable bottle of Australian red.

The withdrawal of the CivPol from the electoral teams meant

even though the 'logistics roster' for CivPol had commenced, there were personnel available for patrols every day. Not only were there sufficient police to patrol all areas of Ermera, we were in a position to also react to any incident/s brought to our attention. Over the next few days all areas in Ermera were actively patrolled.

One other really good aspect about these few days was no meetings. No one turned up for any of the Regional Campaign Committee meetings. I managed to get out and about myself every day. In the three days I not only visited every sub-district in Ermera but also added to our efforts in the Liquicia border areas. One day I gave Celestino the day off and Amorin came with me. On this day one of the village chiefs was very concerned about the future and really pushed us about UNAMET staying after polling day. When we queried where he had got the information UNAMET would be leaving it turned out it had come from the DEOs. They had told him when polling day was over, they would be leaving. He had extrapolated that to being UNAMET would be leaving. Their statement was true. But only the volunteers would be leaving. UN employees, MLOs' and CivPol would be remaining. I realised it was very important to change the message everyone in UNAMET was giving. Yes, the Electoral side would be leaving. All other groups would be staying regardless of the outcome of the poll. This was an issue that had come up before and would continue to be raised.

On one of these days, early afternoon of 15 August, I was called back to HQ for a meeting. This meeting was about something completely different to all prior meetings. We had to plan for the 'as soon as we could possibly arrange it' movement of 250 members of Falantil from Maliana to the Ermera cantonment site. This was due to an agreement reached elsewhere. We never did find out if it was from Maliana itself or something from Dili. This was a meeting worth being held. With a bit of smart thinking we decided that it should take place on 17 August, Indonesian Independance day. We knew there was a major event being planned in Gleno and all pro-autonomy groups were expected to be in attendance. Although we did not know as a certainty, we were pretty sure an equivalent event would also be conducted in Maliana. With just a bit of organisation one day would be enough time for them to get from one place to the other, especially as there would be no chance of them running into Indonesian or Militia groups. Once the decision was made Sean Fox was tasked to co-ordinate the movement as Baldev and I were committed as guests for the national day functions being be held in Gleno. I gave Sean the authority to call on any of the CivPol he required to get this job done.

Early in the evening of 16 August Militia groups from all over Ermera began arriving in Gleno. I fully expected by the morning of the 17th they would all be here, thus removing a possible obstacle to the movement of the Maliana Falantil.

The senior UN personnel in Gleno had previously been invited to a celebration of the integration of East Timor into Indonesia. On that occasion we had politely declined the invitation as it may have been perceived as siding with the pro-autonomy groups. However, Indonesia's Independence Day had no connection with the circumstances in East Timor and therefore our attendance was considered to be diplomatically appropriate.

The principal celebrations were to be held on the football field adjacent to the school, which also doubled as our helicopter landing zone. I ironed the pair of black civilian slacks I had brought with me; got out the black police tie; put Collinol on top of the well-polished boots; and, got dressed for the day. The photograph shows that I scrubbed up to a standard more than sufficient for the occasion. The senior UN people were all seated in the front row as VIPs.

The program was very long, many speeches; a march past with Polri, TNI and Militia groups, presentations from school groups; some music; and about two thirds of the way through a UN helicopter landed. We had no warning the helicopter was coming and to say it was a bit embarrassing, was an understatement. A major reason we were caught by surprise was, for the first time, none of us at the event had portable radios with us. We were able to get the helicopter to promptly depart and the event was back under way with very little loss of time. As an aside, since the arrangement I had made with the helicopter crews about mail, this was the first time the helicopter arrived in Gleno and it departed without taking a letter from me. The events at the field were followed by a late buffet luncheon before the celebrations broke up into smaller groups.

As far as the UN personnel were concerned it was time to get a bit more work done. The particular task I had was to finalise a plan requested by CivPol HQ Dili for the period immediately after the end of the polling period. The major issues they wanted identified were the number of police I required and the equipment I wanted and needed for them to be operationally effective. The submission was finalised and submitted through the secure fax that evening. In the meantime, the movement of Falantil from Maliana to Ermera went ahead without any incident. The only report Baldev and I heard was much later that afternoon when Sean told us the task was complete.

After completing the submission and other administrative paperwork it was time to return to the football field for the end of day ceremony. The guard of honour for the flag lowering ceremony was provided by children from the district who were all dressed in white.

Later that evening there was another reception at the Bupati's house. Once again sitting around for an hour, smoking, while waiting for everyone to arrive. However, just as the meal was served, we received reports of problems in two locations, Letefoho and on the road leading to Leorema, Liquicia.

Indonesian Independence Day. a: Nur, Baldev, Me, Gultom. b: Allessandro, Amorin, me Ari and others. c: pose with the ladies.

Gultom and I both left the reception and headed to his communications room. I provided him with the information I was receiving on the radio and he issued orders to Polri in Letefoho and passed information to Polri in Liquicia. I also had the information we had received on the Liquicia incident passed to UN HQ Dili. In less than one hour from the first report to me CivPol in Letefoho radioed informing us that Polri had resolved the situation to their satisfaction.

With regard to Liquicia all we could do was accept the undertaking of Polri in the district to attend and resolve the situation. A patrol to the Liquicia area the next day would ascertain the Militia had been persuaded to leave the area before the arrival of Polri. How I was never sure, but I believe a Falantil group may have again had a bit to do with it.

Gultom and I returned to the reception. Food was still available, although cold, and the beer was just as hot as the previous occasion. Again, a bit of dancing. Because of my temporary absence someone else had danced with the Bupati's wife, although dancing with the lady definitely was not an onerous task.

During the evening I was approached by the leader of a

pro-autonomy organisation; at least this was how he was recognised on his name tag. Actually he was the leader of a Militia group. In this approach he accused the UN of lying about the number of police deployed to Ermera. He said the information coming to him showed there were far more UN police than we had told him and, if we could lie about that, perhaps we were also lying about being unarmed. My first thought was here was the excuse they had been looking for to openly attack CivPol. However, even before I could respond, Gultom was beside me speaking with this individual. When they finished, and the Militia leader stormed off, Gultom told me not to worry as he had resolved the matter. Just a little later one of the children told me Gultom had said there were no extra UN police in Ermera, and he was keeping an exact count of them. He also said he knew they were completely unarmed. It was interesting that one of the children would think to pass this information on to me.

Before I called it a night, I was persuaded by some of the older school children, all senior high school students, to teach them some rock-a-billy dancing. Of course, I was also expected to join in.

With the exception of the helicopter arrival, it had been a very good day for the UN. Falantil had been relocated, good diplomatic relations had been maintained with Indonesian authorities, Polri had provided an appropriate response to an incident, and Gultom had stood up for me.

Early the following morning we had to be at the LZ to meet a helicopter bringing in all of the ballot boxes for Ermera. With help from some Polri, a few of our local drivers, Samulcia and some CivPol were unloaded and transported to our HQ.

On arrival at HQ I was met by some of the DEOs based in Hatolia. They were complaining John Tanti had left without them the previous day and they now needed someone to take them to Hatolia. Unfortunately for them someone else had seen them the previous day and told me, in front of them, they had been hiding in the Guest House just watching while John waited for some time for them, before he eventually drove off. Once he left, they had come out of the Guest House complaining about being left behind. Caught. Anyhow I told them to sit and wait we would get them to Hatolia when we had transport available, which was going to be the following day.

Dancing with student, Rock a Billy.

There was another meeting of the campaign committee. Not much came out of it, although one thing was interesting. This was the only occasion when neither group, nor any individual, accused any other group or individual of wrongdoing. They did everything they could to convince me they were getting on with each other and were determined to get the process done. As later meetings would show, for whatever reason, it was only an impression they were trying to make.

After that it was off to Homboe for a training session on 'how a secret voting system' works. As he had not previously been to a public education session, and because Saku and Diana are good friends, Allessandro came along with Diana. Saku had again co-opted Antonio to be with her without checking either him or me to see if he had other duties. This time I let it slide, till later in the day.

The program was in two parts, a talk by one of the UN personnel, with assistance from an interpreter, followed by a 'play' put on by a group of teenagers. One of these was playing the part of CivPol and Saku had persuaded me to loan him one of my shirts. The play was very good, covered the message excellently and, at times, was very amusing. The best thing was it really showed how they would be able to vote without anyone knowing who they were voting for. Afterwards there was another social session with the villagers. Allessandro and the others were with the current village chief, but his father managed to get me away from them. One of the interpreters came with us and our lunch time conversation was enlightening. He gave me additional understanding of the local history and, given the information they had received that morning, his opinion on how the vote would go. His opinion would turn out to be very accurate.

Before heading back to HQ, I took a 'wrong' turn and ended up at the Falantil cantonment camp where I had a good sit down and chat. I wanted to put my third evacuation option to them. If all other options were not possible, we could leave our HQ, drive into the riverbed, go up river, instead of down, and after just on 2 kilometres later we would be level with the cantonment. At that point we could leave the vehicles and climb the mountain. Everyone present acknowledged if this became necessary then we were all probably in a lot of trouble. However, the concept received a very warm reception. One stated they already knew the skill sets of most of the CivPol and could see us being of value to them if the situation deteriorated to that level.

The education play.

Later one took me to their cache of modern weapons, primarily M16's. What I saw was a far greater number of modern weapons than I expected. My immediate thought was the weapons being carried by the two guard groups on the day of official cantonment were a ruse. This individual was sure they would be more than willing to share the weapons with us and fight side by side if the situation demanded.

While with this individual he told me of the group within the Militia they were most concerned about. Apparently, about two years before, this group of 60 persons had been members of Falantil. They had been sent to punish a particular village for co-operating with TNI. As part of this they had killed 19 people in the village. Even within Falantil this had been considered excessive. However, while Indonesian authorities had been trying to apprehend them, they had been protected by Falantil and other locals. Shortly after the Militia units were set up the entire group saw this as an opportunity and had defected to the Militia. There were still about 40 of them in Ermera and the rest had returned to Militia units in their home districts. Their defection had forced Falantil to make a lot of changes and for some individuals to leave their homes and 'go to the forest'.

Meanwhile they wanted more information, primarily how many would be coming with me if I had to implement the last-ditch evacuation plan. My answer was the 23 CivPol, the three MLOs and maybe four civilians. I was working on the principle the volunteers would have been evacuated before the situation got serious enough to warrant this action.

A question caught me by surprise — 'Where would the rest go?'

It took a while to convince him that there were no 'rest'. As with the earlier discussion with the Militia the CivPol patrolling techniques had convinced Falantil our numbers had been tripled. When I explained what we were doing he expressed surprise that so few had been able to cover so much ground. It made me really proud of the efforts made by them all.

I am not sure how the UN would have reacted if they were informed of this arrangement. Really, I was sure that publicly they would be very unhappy. Privately individuals were likely to have a different perspective.

In our discussion I explained the need to make sure knowledge of this agreement was kept amongst the few of us at the meeting. They understood the need for secrecy as well as I did. Not only would the UN have an opinion, but it could have an influence on the conduct of the Popular Consultation. While I considered it would be highly unlikely it would be needed, secrecy was essential. For myself it was reassuring to have the arrangement in place.

Meeting at Cantonment.

Before I left that afternoon, I was informed of some of the options they were considering, depending on what happened. One point they made very clear to me was any threat to their food supplies would result in them taking offensive action of some sort. They also had a few options they were considering. The primary option was the complete opposite to what I knew Lt Col Nurr was expecting.

Back at HQ and there was a management group security and safety meeting, except once again there were a lot of hangers on that insisted on being part of the meeting. So, it dragged on into the early evening and achieved very little. Finally, it was over, and I thought I would be able to type up the daily report. Unfortunately, quite a few of the CivPol were around the computer. Mbaye was dictating and Robert typing their reports on a number of matters they had attended during the day and the others were waiting to do the same. For a number of reasons, I did not want to claim the privilege of rank to get immediate use of the computer. First, I had to include at least a reference to their reports in mine and, second, the fact they were doing so much work meant they were intensely motivated and needed to be supported, not challenged. Life would have been a bit easier with additional equipment, at least one more computer.

On 19 August Don was tasked with taking the allocated ballot boxes to Hatolia, so he took the DEO's who had been left behind along with him. There was another short meeting of the Campaign Committee. It was becoming more and more obvious they were only meeting because the Code of Conduct said they had to. As Gultom's participation was never in the Code of Conduct he took the opportunity to remain away.

I left that meeting and went straight to Gultom's office. We had arranged to have a discussion that morning about ongoing security. Letefoho was turning out to be a problem area for both of us. The problems were being created by two brothers; Miguel Babo, the local Militia leader; and, Father Domingos, Babo's brother, the local priest. They were on opposite sides of the political fence and were constantly baiting each other. Gultom and I agreed to split the responsibility of talking with the individuals to try and calm them down. It is obvious who would be talking to who. Neither of us would be completely successful, but the talks we had with the respective individuals did get them to tone down their rhetoric a little.

That afternoon I was getting my second haircut, this time

a scissors and comb job from one of the local drivers. For ten minutes or so this became the local entertainment as a crowd gathered around to watch, offer advice and laugh. It was good for everyone to relax a little.

Ari was with me for our evening get-together, still exchanging information every day, when one of the university students turned up. His nose was obviously broken and there were a few other visible bruises. He said that he had been beaten up by Militia in Atsabe and had caught a bus to Gleno to report it. Ari took the details and told him how to get to the local doctor in Gleno. I told him I would have CivPol follow up on the Polri investigation instigated by Ari.

As it turned out I didn't have to start anything. CivPol in Atsabe had already investigated this incident and their report arrived just after the student left to go to the doctor. Apparently two of the DEOs had been nearby when, in their words, this student had begun deliberately antagonising some of the local Militia in the local cafe. When the Militia got up and started to approach the student, he had run towards the DEOs. Unfortunately for the student he had tripped and fallen, which is where they believe he got the broken nose. While on the ground the Militia had reached him and given him a few kicks to the upper body before they just walked off. The DEOs had put him on the local bus and told him to report the matter in Gleno. When the CivPol patrol arrived back in Atsabe the DEOs had described to them the incident in detail. A prompt report was prepared and sent to me. I immediately passed this information on to a very grateful Captain Ari. At the same time, I was very unhappy the university students were again up to their idiotic, unnecessary, attention seeking tricks.

The following day, 20 August, I had set down as a full day in the office. As far as I was concerned, I had only one task for the day. I had now gathered enough information, noted down with the odd comment and option, to have the plan for polling day sketched out. Today was the day I was going to turn that into a written Operational Order for the polling period that would apply to, and task, all UN personnel in Ermera. I was also including tasks for Polri, though I knew implementation would require careful discussions and negotiations with Gultom. During the day there were a few interruptions but by 5 p.m. I had produced what I considered an acceptable plan capable of getting the job done with the available UN resources. However, I already knew Polri would have a problem with what I envisaged them doing. They simply did not have the number of vehicles required to undertake everything I had included in the plan.

Firstly, I had to get the plan approved by Allessandro, as the overall UN Co-ordinator for Ermera. Initially I printed only one hard copy. The soft copy was on a floppy disc so that changes could be made if, and as I expected when, they became necessary. At this time the broad implementation phases are -

- Physical security of voting materials at our Gleno HQ;
- **10 a.m. 29 August** — conduct briefing for all DEOs and CivPol at Gleno HQ, distribute ballot materials to teams, sub districts to return with Polri escorts to their bases;
- **4 a.m. 30 August** — Polri escorted convoys to depart all locations to the Polling Sites, most convoys would have multiple teams, progressively dropping teams with Polri security as they reached each polling site;
- **7 a.m. 30 August** — Polling Sites to open and conduct the Popular Consultation;
- **4.30 p.m. 30 August** — voting should be complete, complete paperwork and commence return of convoys to their base, in reverse order to the morning;

- **31 August** — pickup of ballot boxes by helicopter, 4 locations;
    - sub district teams in Ermera Village to return to Gleno by 8 a.m;
    - despatch first convoy to Dili with the UNVs (DEOs) who had been based in Gleno;
    - -Hatolia sub district teams to return to Gleno by road;
    - Atsabe sub district teams to return to Glen by road picking up Letefoho teams on the way;
    - CivPol patrols to be conducted out of Gleno;
- **1 September** - remaining UNVs (DEOs) to be taken to Dili in convoy;
    - CivPol teams to return to sub districts; and
    - CivPol to commence patrolling.

CHAPTER 22

Campaign Period

The next day started with a quick morning visit to Dili with Amorin for a meeting called to discuss what would happen in the immediate post ballot period. HQ CivPol Personnel unit wanted to inform us of the intent to create additional districts and the subsequent re-deployment of people this necessitated. In addition, there were other re-deployment plans for some individuals to meet a perceived higher demand in particular locations. For example, Maliana was to receive a significant increase which included both Phil Hunter and Max Knoth from Ermera. There were others in Ermera who were going to be moved to other locations. I immediately realised this would cause angst with those nominated to move from Gleno.

Aside from the meeting itself, Amorin and I were informed there was a proposal to split the Dili district into two before the ballot day. The Commission asked who I would recommend out of Amorin and Sam to be the new district commander. I informed him I had no trouble in recommending either of them for the role but releasing Amorin would require less internal re-organisation in the District.

Back from Dili before lunch, via the bakery, then it was the usual things. Incidents being reported, follow up, paperwork and the Campaign Committee. Although on this day, as was continuing to happen, both sides of the political divide were obvious by their complete absence at the scheduled time. Only the UN mediators were present. So, no meeting.

This evening had a difference. The sound of sirens, not just one but many, continuously blaring away. A quick walk to the corner and I could see a number of trucks, minibuses and other vehicles driving around and around on the streets of Gleno. All vehicles had flags or placards displaying the pro-autonomy cause. I don't know where they got the sirens from, but at least four of the vehicles had sirens blaring. This was the start of the formal campaigning for the Popular Consultation. They went around and around for thirty or so minutes before all heading to the sports field. Then it was a PA system blaring out one speech after another. I walked down to observe. I recognised all those who spoke while I was watching, every speaker was Timorese. As all the speeches were in Indonesian, I only gathered the general gist of what they were saying. But they appeared to be in accordance with the code of conduct. The Bupati was introduced and then delivered the longest speech of the evening. Once he finished there were a couple of shorter ones from people who had been there before. I figured the event was just about over so I walked back home. By the time I got there the vehicles were driving around the town for one last time, again with those sirens blaring. One thought occurred to me; Senior Claudio had not made an appearance at the rally.

The campaign period was now well and truly underway.

Not long after the rally concluded Ari contacted me and asked if he could have two CivPol to be independent witnesses while Polri investigators interviewed two people. After a couple of quick calls on the radio Antonio Cubel and Jose Pena took on this task. They later informed me those being interviewed were two of the university students. A far as they could ascertain the interviews had been fairly conducted and the two students were released before the CivPol left.

22 August and after the usual Campaign Committee meeting,

junior representatives from both sides turned up this time but were very happy to finish quickly, it was time to hit the road again. This time to Letefoho to brief the CivPol there and Phil, who would come up from Atsabe so he could pass the information on to the others when he got back. The two topics were an overview of my plan for polling day and the proposed redeployment of people after polling day. Not much reaction about my overview but a lot of unhappy people about the proposed redeployment.

Travelling to Letefoho I had my ABBA cassette in the vehicle's player. It was one of two cassettes I had put in my luggage. The other was a combination of Tina Turner and Cher. The locals preferred ABBA but when I had a Brimob escort they much preferred Tina Turner and occasionally requested I wind down the window and turn the volume up loud enough for them to hear. This drive was different. There were a lot more people on the sides of the road. They were waving, cheering and giving us the V sign. They knew it was getting close. It was on this drive I really listened to the ABBA song, Fernando, for the first time. On that day the refrain of the song became my life's theme -

There was something in the air that night
The stars were bright, Fernando
They were shining there for you and me
For liberty, Fernando
Though I never thought that we could lose
There's no regret
If I had to do the same again
I would, my friend, Fernando
If I had to do the same again
I would, my friend, Fernando

Driving back was just as good. Paul was in Leorema and every now and then had his press to talk switch held down on his radio so we could all hear what was going on. No one could help but be moved by the happy sounds coming over the air. No matter how professionally impartial I had managed to remain, deep down I had a personal preference.

When I arrived back it was time to put the Operational Order to its first test. I took it to Allessandro and presented it as my option for how we should run polling day. There was one part in particular I was concerned about. The first point under the heading Command and Control stated I would be the commander of all UN personnel in Ermera for the two-day period. I had expected a bit of an argument from him about that.

After reading the whole document Allessandro's complete enthusiasm caught me by surprise. He wanted to immediately take it to Dili and show them how advanced our planning was in Ermera. I had to pour a little verbal cold water onto him when I explained the plan included Polri providing more convoy escorts than they had vehicles. Before he could take it to Dili, I needed to negotiate the details with Gultom. I added I was hopeful he would find a way to provide the escorts I asked for. If not, then amendments would be necessary and some of the convoys would be larger and have an earlier start than the 4 a.m. of the current plan. Allessandro said he would wait. Because he had not brought up the 'command' issue I raised it with him.

His comment was 'I was wondering how to raise this very thing with you?' He was more than happy to hand over the responsibility. That resolved that concern. Only Gultom to go.

Amorin had also arrived back from his first visit to Aileu. Although an early move had not been formalised as yet, in our own discussions we had agreed he should visit as soon as possible. In fact, it was one of the easier places to get to from Gleno. I had driven there when checking it out as an alternate vehicle evacuation route should one be required. It was now included in my planning as vehicle evacuation option number three out of my four route options. The roads between Gleno and Aileu were the best in the area. Amorin informed me of the arrangements made so far. If the change was implemented both he and the CivPol already in the location were ready for an immediate transition.

There was also a small parcel from home waiting for me. Inside the parcel was a cassette Margaret had prepared with most of my favourite songs on it. I thought there were two of my favourites missing, 'We Gotta Get Out of this Place' by the Animals and 'Green, Green Grass of Home' by Tom Jones. When I telephoned Margaret on a later day, she asked how I enjoyed the cassette. I said I really liked it but raised the issue of the two songs. She told me she thought I would mention them being missing but her reasoning for leaving them out was she did not think it would be appropriate for me to be driving around with those songs blaring out. Clever lady.

The parcel also contained an envelope with instructions, in bold printing, written on it — 'DO NOT OPEN IN UNIFORM'. Of course, I was not going to wait until I got back to the house to change before opening the envelope. Mistake. Scattered through the letter was a reasonable quantity of 'glitter'. So, for the next few days I was 'glittering'. It took two washes to get it all out of my uniform and there were bits in my hair and on my skin for longer than I thought they would hang around. Everyone thought it was hilarious. I justified it to myself as being another little morale boost for all the UN people as they got to forget other things and smile about my predicament. Even Gultom had a little laugh.

When I walked out the front door of the house the next morning there was one beautiful, deep pink bloom on the rose bush that somehow managed to survive amongst the rocks in my front yard. This was something I had not expected to see and definitely brightened the start to the day.

But the prime task for that day was to take the Operational

Order to Gultom. With Captain Ari we sat and discussed it for over three hours, with numerous cups of coffee and many, many cigarettes. As expected Gultom did not have enough vehicles to meet the requirements of the plan. However, he was very happy there was a plan and if I gave him 24 hours to consider it, he would have a definite answer the following day.

Back at our HQ and Dili was on the line to inform me there may be additional helicopters with Polri escorts available for the delivery of the actual ballot papers. With the extra helicopters the ballot papers would be delivered to all districts on the one day, the day before the vote. This had little effect on my plan, except to reduce the number of days where physical security would be required on the ballot materials.

Meanwhile Amorin was working on his own plan for Aileu.

That evening the Portuguese observers had invited Amorin and I around for dinner. I had a bottle of Penfolds Shiraz Margaret had sent me, so I took it along. Their house was one of the best in the town and I decided to make arrangements to move there when they left after the vote. The food was excellent and they had a very good cook, who added Piripiri sauce to give it the final touch. This brought back memories to both Amorin and I of our previous mission in Mozambique. There was just enough wine in the bottle for all of us to have one very enjoyable glass. What a great taste.

A local arrived at the front door when we were at the coffee and cigarette stage. He had with him some pro-autonomy pamphlets. When translated they had a very anti UNAMET slant. He told us that they had been thrown from a Polri 'car' driving around the town. This was something I had to follow up. So, a few more questions to him. Turned out it was a friend who had found the pamphlets and given them to him. Once again, the whispers of East Timor. The following day one of the teams would contact this friend, who had still more of the pamphlets, and find out he had found them lying on the road. He claimed to have made no mention of Polri but had said they must have been thrown from a vehicle because of where he found them. This saved a potential embarrassing meeting with Gultom. Although a couple of days later I did pass on the information to him, including the incorrect attempt to implicate Polri.

Tuesday 24 August, I had to look up a calendar to see what day it was. Dates are easy but the days of the week just flow one into another, there is nothing to differentiate one from another. This morning's campaign committee turned out to be a very easy task. Pro-independence had a limited representation (CNRT) but no pro-autonomy. There was an attempt at some political point scoring by the CNRT representatives but none of it was worth taking any further.

Then the important part of the day. Visit Gultom to discuss some previous incidents and, more importantly, the plan. The various reports we had both received from our people on the incidents were factually very close. Once again where they differed was who had caused the incident. Not much more either of us could do about it other than send reports to our respective Dili headquarters. Although on this occasion Gultom made a comment that some circumstances existed where he was not happy about not being allowed to arrest members of the Militia.

Then the plan, well operational order actually. Straight away Gultom stated we, yes, he used the term we, would be implementing the plan in its totality as it covered polling day. He informed me that overnight he had resolved his vehicle shortage by arranging the 'hire' of enough trucks for him to attach a Polri escort to every one of the proposed convoys. While I was a bit uncertain, he had 'hired' the vehicles, this definitely was a move I appreciated.

His next request caught me a little off guard. Could he borrow the Operational Order for another night to convert the parts relating to polling day into his plan for Polri on that day; and would I mind if he then submitted it as his plan to Polri HQ Dili? There was no way I could have said no. Although I must admit to some concern about where the information could end up.

When I arrived home that afternoon there was a second bud on the rose.

CivPol members were now primarily involved in monitoring the campaign process. This was instigated to ensure as much fairness as possible for all parties. There were occasions when the CivPol, including Australians, placed themselves between pro- independence campaigners and pro-autonomy groups who were seeking to disrupt their legitimate activities.

Mid-morning on 25 August, with the exception of Jim France manning the Base Radio, I was the only CivPol not committed to monitoring a political rally. One of the senior pro-independence people came to me with a report concerning an armed robbery of a pro-independence supporter that had taken place less than an hour before. While he was telling me his story Ari arrived for our usual morning discussion. As the alleged victim was still at the location where the robbery occurred, and it was only half an hour drive away, Ari suggested we both go out and investigate. When we got there the alleged victim gave his version of what happened. We also spoke with witnesses, one was the primary victim's driver, two others had seen the actual incident and then there were the ones who always turn up after the event and want to give their version.

There was no doubt he had been ambushed and robbed of a significant amount of money by an armed group of men. Most likely that armed group had been pro-autonomy Militia. The question I needed answered was, is this a politically motivated offence? From the initial story by the victim and his driver they, and the money they had been carrying, had nothing to do with either political group or with politics in any way. From other witnesses the victim was not exactly an upstanding member of the local community and the money was probably obtained by nefarious means. Ari and I discussed the information we had gathered and were in full agreement. A criminal offence had been committed, but all the evidence pointed to it having nothing to do with the conduct of the Popular Consultation. Therefore, the matter was one for Polri attention with no further UN action required.

When we advised the victim of this, he appeared satisfied. But, and in East Timor there is nearly always a but, the pro-independence leader who had followed us to the location immediately stepped in and started to give another reason why the matter was politically related. It was easy to tell him how his statement was wrong; that just lead to another statement just as easy to dismiss; and then another. He kept making up stories until finally we convinced him no matter what story he made up, we were convinced of the facts and this matter belonged purely with Polri.

Back to Gleno where another pro-independence representative was waiting. This time to complain about one of their people being beaten as part of a Polri interrogation. The one mistake he made was to pick one of the interrogations where Gultom had requested I have a CivPol present. As per the earlier incident after I explained how I knew no beating had taken place during the interrogation the story changed; changed again; and again; till finally he gave up and left. This was a constant issue from both sides. All reports or information from either side had to be checked. Exaggeration and straight out lying was the order of the day.

26 August, Margaret and my wedding anniversary. Not the first one where I was away on an overseas mission. In the morning I rang, and we had our one conversation on this mission which was just about us. Short though it was, it helped.

But back to work. First information from Dili on the secure system; the second Australian contingent would be arriving in late September and by the 25th would have completed the changeover and we would be flown out; Amorin was to move to Aileu as soon as possible; I would be getting a replacement for Amorin, eventually; and a helicopter would arrive that afternoon with all our ballot papers and materials for Ermera. Looks like they never got those additional helicopters after all.

First job. Arrange security at the LZ, Polri and CivPol. Relatively easy to accomplish.

Second job was to discuss with Gultom and Audi about twenty-four hours a day armed Brimob security at our HQ. Just being in the building over the road would not be sufficient.

Third job. Monitor the campaign rallies taking place in the town that morning. Both political groups had rallies going on. The pro-autonomy rally was larger than usual as immediately following the Gleno portion they were driving to Dili for the main event. All we had to do was see them out of Gleno, hopefully without incident. Polri, including Brimob, did a very good job of staying between the two groups. There was a lot of objectionable verbal interchange but no violence. The pro-autonomy drove off to Dili and the pro-independence dissipated almost immediately after. Job done.

Fourth job. I now needed to create a night-time roster for security inside our HQ as additional protection for the ballot papers, even if we were unarmed. Well at least I was being kept occupied.

The campaign period also saw the return of East Timorese university students to the District. They continued their false claim of being neutral and only intending to assist UNAMET. Ari was providing me with reports on the students' activities. It was obvious they were still trying to elicit a violent response from pro-autonomy groups, preferably with international media or UN people nearby. As if there was not enough danger already this additional potential for injury was more than I wanted.

In Ermera we had already had minor incidents, including in Atsabe with Max Knoth, and shortly after there was a another, this time in Ermera village, with Don Barnby. So, I went and found the leader of the students and had another conversation with him. In no uncertain terms I gave him my opinion of the irresponsible and unnecessary nature of their actions. I also told him to make sure that if they did create an incident, they were not to put UN personnel in danger by running to them.

The day after our talk the individual himself was involved in an incident, this time in Gleno. While no UN person saw how or where the incident started, his reaction to the Militia response was to run straight to our HQ. There were five-armed Militia hot on his heels. I was standing out the front of the building having a cigarette break. As he went to run past me my forearm went out and caught him high on the chest, in football terms I got him with a 'short arm' tackle. His upper body stopped, his feet kept moving and he ended up flat on his back on the ground. The Militia stopped, laughed and walked away. I then verbally dissuaded him and his group from continuing with this tactic anywhere in Ermera. After that discussion, with one minor exception, there was no further incident in Ermera involving the students until polling day. In other districts there were a number of more serious incidents involving UN personnel when students were chased by pro-autonomy groups.

I had received information on a particular incident in another district where two CivPol, Christopher MEAGHER (Australia) and Rangi MANIAPOTO (NZ), had been involved in a violent confrontation with Militia.

Following is the report of Chris Meagher on that incident. *At 1000hrs on Thursday the 5th of August 1999 Ainaro UNAMET personnel were invited to attend a meeting of fifty (50) university students conducted at a marquee erected by the students in the township of Ainaro. This marquee was set up on the main entrance road to Ainaro from the direction of Cassa. The marquee is located approximately 400 metres south of the town square and 25 metres north of the entrance to the Ainaro registration post which is clearly marked with the UNAMET sign. The students invited us to explain the registration and consultation process to them.*

This meeting was being addressed by MEAGHER and THOMAS. MANIAPOTO was standing next to the U.N. vehicle parked next to Marquee. At approximately 11.20am a group of approximately 20 men came to the front of the marquee which was backed onto the roadway. They approached from the rear of the seated students. They were all dressed in civilian clothing and seem to be led by an elder male wearing a khaki vest with an Indonesian flag over the breast. He began shouting in Tetum and waving his arms in a gesture that we interpreted to mean 'Get out.' Other males then began to yell as well

At the time the shouting began the main body of seated students ran forward to where MEAGHER and THOMAS were standing. As a result of this both MEAGHER and THOMAS were trapped in the front of the house to which the marquee was attached. The attacking mob then began to turn over the plastic seating and then began hurling large chunks of concrete directly at UNAMET personnel. As MEAGHER picked up a chair to defend himself a large chunk of concrete shattered the plastic back of the chair. MEAGHER held this chair in front of his body. He was then hit by another large piece of concrete in the left shoulder that came from the other direction.

MANIAPOTO then picked up a coffee table and both CivPol members began to fight their way out of the marquee toward the street using the shattered chair and the coffee table. None of the attacking crowd were hit by these items as they began to flee in opposite directions on the roadway. THOMAS managed to get to a position of safety near a U.N. vehicle as CivPol began to exit the marquee. During this process both CivPol personnel were under constant attack from thrown missiles. During this entire process both CivPol member were shouting clearly and loudly in English 'Back Off!!'

The mob were clearly under the direction of the previous mentioned elderly male who on retreating clearly pointed at both CivPol members and appeared to be making verbal threat against us. MEAGHER pursued this male at a safe distance and demanded his name in Bahia. The response to this was more missiles throwing which did not come near the CivPol member. The male then retreated to a safe distance shouting at CivPol continually. MANIAPOTO pursued another group in the opposite direction, at a safe distance, on the roadway, with the same results.

Polri were alerted of the situation and arrived at the scene within 4-6 minutes. They were alerted by a Polri intelligence Officer who was seated within the student body. Both CivPol members pointed out to the attending Polri the main players in this attack who were still visible to CivPol. Polri were slow to act even on the insistence of CivPol that these persons were to be arrested. CivPol then found themselves trying to calm the students who emerged from the house and were attempting to attack another unidentified male who was near the student body. This was quickly calmed, and the situation was restored to some state of normality.

We have sought Polri assistance re the identification of the male leader. To this point a satisfactory result has not been obtained.

In brief summary this was a vicious and swift attack which appeared to be well organised. The entire attack lasted no more than 4-5 minutes. At no time were any firearms seen by CivPol in the hands of the attackers. Given the situation of UNAMET being backed into a house front by this mob if firearms had been produced the situation would have resulted in at least 10-15 fatalities including UNAMET.

MEAGHER sustained a slight injury to his left shoulder as a result of being hit by the concrete, otherwise no other UNAMET personnel were injured. No students were injured but the marquee/house suffered some damage as a result of the attack.

The New Zealand Government subsequently recognised the bravery displayed in the incident by Rangi MANIAPOTO.

Our troubles were not restricted to the students.

The morning of the 27th started so calmly. A campaign committee meeting where I was the only one to turn up. A very boring political rally in town with very few voters turning up. An unnecessary meeting with Samulcia to re-discuss security matters already agreed. A quick trip to the Falantil camp for the CNRT flag raising. Fortunately, the trip to Falantil was now very quick, by East Timor standards, as they had shown me the most direct route. I no longer had to go around in a variety of circles, nor did I need an escort.

After lunch everything changed. Problems were cropping up just about everywhere. The first was in Leorema and I was by far the closest CivPol, so my job. That one was just about resolved by the time I got there. Someone had been in the village taking photos of the people. No one knew who he was or where he had gone.

Meanwhile another incident started up in Letefoho. This was another occasion when two of my earlier decisions were proven to be correct. With Celestino driving I was able to concentrate on the issues and because I had driven all over the district more than once I had an understanding of what they were facing. For Letefoho I contacted Ari by radio, and he undertook to despatch Polri investigators.

Before I was back on the main road Brett Swan contacted me from Hatolia to tell me they were about to follow up on a report of a kidnapping. Based on Brett's initial report to me this appeared to be a relatively minor incident. Later, when I got the full story from them, it became obvious it was far more than a minor incident. The three CivPol members willingly went into a location where they had no communications with me, or anyone else, and took on a large armed Militia group with nothing but their negotiating skills and bravado.

The story of that event is best told by one of them —
27 August 1999 Acelou: Brett Swan, John Tanti and Tommy Kinsella

On 27 August 1999, in company with Brett SWAN and American Police officer, Tom KINSELLA, I attended to an incident in which two people had been shot by Besi Meraputi Militia within the district of Liquicia. Following observation of the victims and crime scene, we returned to a base camp in Acelou/ Sare in order to prepare reports relating to the incident.

Whilst preparing our reports, villagers from the nearby town of Acelou came to our residence / office and told us that the Militia were campaigning in the town and were intimidating villagers there. On this basis, we attended the town and were immediately conscious of the danger involved in our being there because it was a very tense situation in which about one hundred armed Militia members were in the company of military, police and the local governor (cemat). Whilst maintaining an obvious observation point, we were informed by a local villager that the Militia had taken a person by force from his home and had stabbed him. Given this, a search commenced for the victim in order to render first aid (experience had taught me to carry a medical kit for first instance aid to knife wounds and gunshots).

Whilst patrolling the village which essentially consisted of a dirt track going through the middle of two rows of thatched huts, we observed that there was a heavily armed Militia presence both in the centre of the town and again at the far eastern side of the village. During this extensive search for the victim, we were met with hostility, intimidation and verbal threats from the Militia. On reaching the far eastern side of the village we exited our vehicle to speak with the group who were gathered there. Upon approaching we observed that one of the men in the group was tied up by his hands and he was being interrogated by the Militia on the edge of the cliff.

It was made apparent to us that this was the alleged victim who had not yet been attacked. It was later made clear to us that his fate was to be shot and thrown over the cliff after the interrogation had finished.

At that point we began negotiations with the Militia leader to secure the man's release. Discussions with the Militia proved fruitless and they were insistent that the man was their prisoner and that we did not have the right or power to remove him. At some time in the negotiations the Militia adopted a very hostile attitude to the UN civilian police and threatened us with harm if we did not leave. About the same time, one of the Militia men had called out for more Militia members to attend. It was clear that they were preparing to attack us. At this time there were approximately 25 Militia members involved in this confrontation.

Tom KINSELLA (US CivPol) and Brett SWAN continued to negotiate but the Militia chief grew agitated and angry at our representations and he handled a homemade firearm which was essentially a triple barrel shotgun in pistol form in a bid to intimidate and remove us from the area.

At this point in time, I attempted to keep the rest of the Militia members at bay by standing between the main group and the growing number of Militia members who were approaching the scene. I could see a mass of Militia members approaching (about 100 men) and I informed Brett that we urgently needed to extract the victim and depart the area.

As the situation grew more serious, we knew we could not resolve the situation by negotiation. Tom and Brett were negotiating by telling the Militia that we would take the man, (whose only crime was to be wearing the colours of the independence movement) to the local police so that they could investigate and allow the administration of justice to take its course.

At this the Militia chief told us in strong terms to get lost and mind our own business. He started to walk away from the place, towards the edge of the cliff. At this time, he was stopped by Tom and Brett, Tom took the rope from the chief's hands forcefully and he instantly ran to my vehicle and the open car door that I had prepared for him.

This action stirred the Militia into a frenzy, Brett returned to my vehicle and Tom went to his. Just prior to their return the Militia members who by this stage numbered in excess of one hundred were shaking their fists, pointing their firearms at us and some were attempting to ignite their charges. Others shook their machetes at us. During the negotiation period, these men, and their ice cold looks of hatred were standing no more that centimetres from my face. They seemed to be stopped by my barrier (hands outstretched), mostly because they were waiting for direction from their leaders who were at the time locked in discussion with Brett and Tom.

We were able to escape with their hostage in our custody.

A debriefing was held later in the day regarding the earlier incident and it was revealed that during the Militia campaign in the village, the victims house was stormed because it was known that he was an independence activist. On their entry he was in a hiding spot within the premises. The Militia told the victim's family that they were going to take his wife, who was in the premises and kill her if he did not surrender himself to them. He immediately came from his hiding place upon which he was beaten, tied up and paraded through the village during the campaign as an act of intimidation. It was clear that the Militia were showing that they were going to kill persons who were not for the Militia.

The victim stated that our arrival at the scene was extremely timely as the Militia leader was discussing where he was going to dump the body before the interrogation (the cliff face decided upon) and just seconds prior to our arrival, he had decided on this course and death was imminent.

This Militia activity was doubly dangerous because our rescue and knowledge of the incident demonstrated that the local police chief, cemat (governor) and the team of police present (about twenty officers) were all complicit in the intimidation and killing that was occurring within our district. We had in effect witnessed serious criminal offences and were able to identify all offenders within the whole chain of command spanning both the local government and the police.

The faces of the cemat, the Militia and the attending police on our arrival were stone cold and very hostile, it later became apparent that the reason for the complete about turn by these people was that they had been caught out in their conduct.

In a chance meeting with one of the Militia chiefs a few days after this incident, we were told that our conduct was not impartial and that one of us would be killed for our actions. Other specific threats were levelled at our interpreter and we were in fear of his and our own safety.

There is no doubt the three CivPol involved had completely disregarded the immediate threat to their own safety and through their courageous actions saved the life of that person.

By evening I thought all the day's matters had been resolved and I was heading to the Guest House when Allessandro caught up with me. With him were a few of the university students. They wanted to complain about how they had been treated earlier that afternoon in Letefoho. I had already been briefed by Robin and Ashraf (CivPol in Letefoho) and Ari had provided me information on what Polri had done. Once they finished their complaint, I told them what the CivPol and Polri had passed on to me about the incident. Their version was nothing like either police version, which although not exactly the same, were in agreement on the basic facts. All of a sudden from the student's perspective it became a different problem. When that did not get the response they wanted from me, it became another problem. The same old story. If you don't get what you want, make it up to try and reinforce your position. It did not take long before Allessandro realised what they were doing and brought the discussion to a quick end.

Once the students left Allessandro wanted to talk about plans for the next week. Again, something we had already been over in detail. Forty-five wasted minutes later he conceded there was nothing else that he could think of that needed attention. Time would show the most correct part of that statement was the words 'he (or I) could think of'. In the very near future all CivPol in Ermera would have to prove their adaptability.

After I left Allessandro I met Randy in the Guest House. He briefed me on a matter that he had attended to, and resolved, in Mirtutu that day. Another good job done. He told me he had not called it in by radio at the time because it appeared there were already enough other issues going on to keep me occupied. If another reminder the situation was warming up and security was becoming a far more important issue was needed, this was it. Mirtutu had been one of our quietest villages.

28 August and first up in the morning I made the final amendments to the operational order for polling day. This was followed by a pre-arranged meeting with Ari and Audi where we went over the whole plan in detail. They guaranteed Polri would be ready to carry out all tasks in the order. One concern at least temporarily addressed.

Due to my misfortune at being made the Chair of the Campaign Committee I was then required at the Bupati's office for the meeting. Only a few there and it was dragging on over nothing. Because I had another commitment, I told them I would be leaving, if they wanted to continue, they could, but I doubted they would agree on anything.

Time to get back to our HQ to meet the group of Australian VIPs who were in East Timor as International Electoral Observers. This group was led by the former Deputy Prime Minister, Mr Tim Fischer, and included Marise Payne and Laurie Brereton, both members of the Australian Parliament. The initial part of our briefing was in the CivPol office, because the wall in the office had our only topographical map. It was a tight fit. After that we went to the meeting room where they were briefed by almost all members of the district management team. I had followed instructions and Helen did not know in advance of the visit. However, somehow, she found out and turned up in the middle of the briefings. Immediately she tried to take over the whole meeting. I managed to persuade her to wait until the rest had spoken and then she would have the opportunity to speak. When she spoke her open bias to pro-independence was obvious. At the end of her talk she offered to take the entire party to the Falantil cantonment. In the following discussion Mr Fischer stated he still wanted to meet with the Bupati so the group split in two; half came with me to the Bupati and the rest went with Helen.

The initial part of our meeting with the Bupati was in his office. There he gave a very good presentation on the economic and administrative challenges, needs and capabilities of Ermera. Politics were completely excluded from his presentation. Pushing economics was his primary theme, in particular the coffee crops. Later, back in Australia, Mr Fischer would pass this information on to people who arranged the importation of East Timor coffee.

Once that was finished everyone was invited to the Bupati's home for lunch. I had presumed correctly. I was also glad Helen had taken half the party to Falantil because it was a far larger group than I was told to expect.

Gultom was present at the lunch. The food was excellent. Five courses and definitely the best meal I had had in East Timor. After lunch we were sitting around having a general discussion. Mr Fischer asked Gultom a question. Gultom's reply was surprising. His entire reply was a series of comments on how well I had performed my duties. I was actually becoming embarrassed. Then, saved by our radios. Both Gultom's and mine were calling for us at the same time. Another issue in Letefoho. The visitors saw in real time what both of us had said about the co-operation existing between the two of us. This time it was relatively minor and the response from both Polri and CivPol resolved the incident so quickly our program for the visitors did not need to be disrupted.

With the post lunch discussion finished all loaded into vehicles and drove the short distance to the Gleno polling site. No sooner had we arrived and there was another incident this time with the potential of being much bigger. Again, the two of us being side by side allowed for instant co-ordination of a joint response. For East Timor the most amazing part of the response was the speed at which they arrived. A Polri group were on the scene in two minutes and the CivPol patrol were only one minute behind them. That prompt response resulted in the incident being closed down before it became violent. While this response time was amazing, it could never have happened if the patrols were not out and about in the first place.

After that it was back to Gleno HQ to get the visitors off on their journey back to Dili. Before leaving, Mr. Fischer handed to me two bottles of Penfolds bin 128, a much-appreciated gesture. Immediately after they drove off, two of their party came wandering into HQ. Somehow, they had been left behind. A very quick drive to catch up with their small convoy to get them back on board just before the last bridge out of Gleno.

As we were getting back again to HQ Rob Hunter arrived from Dili. He had Nitaya, they had kept their promise she was back for polling day, and a new Aussie CivPol, Peter Watt, with him. Peter had been brought in early from the proposed second contingent and was allocated to Ermera as a replacement for Amorin. Rob had also brought with him a good supply of goodies from the bakery. Also arriving while I had been involved with the VIP visit were two additional MLOs for Ermera including an Australian, Captain Dan Grogan.

While getting the daily Sitrep ready Don Barnby came in and reported another incident -

28 August 1999 Ermera Village Don Barnby and Wayne Corbett

Don Barnby was on patrol with Wayne Corbett (NZ CivPol) when they received information that an armed man was threatening the DEOs at the Ermera Village registration site. The two CivPol were close by and quickly attended placing themselves between the man and the DEOs until POLRI arrived shortly after. He was disarmed and taken away by Polri.

This day was my final meeting with Gultom before polling day and he showed me a one-page document one of his men had brought back from a meeting of the Militia leaders. While it was written in Indonesian, I could clearly see that it was a list of names. Some I could read, the rest Ari translated.

On the top of the list was Gultom himself;
then his wife;
then me;
4 to 8 were the Falantil leaders;
9 was Helen;
10 to 15 were prominent independence leaders;
16 was any Australian CivPol;
17 was any local employed by the UN;
18 any other CivPol;
19 any Australian; and
20 any other UN person.

Gultom told me the police officer who had been part of the Militia meetings informed him this was the priority list for assassination when the time came. Apparently, they were very angry with Gultom because they did not believe he was doing enough to support them. His wife was on the list just because she was his wife. This was information well worth knowing, but not much could be done about it.

The 'campaigning period' had been our most volatile to that time. Whenever we knew that a campaign event would be held, we had either a CivPol team or the MLOs present as observers. They were not there to monitor the content of the campaigning but, by their presence, to deter violence from one side or the other. Tensions were at their greatest during this period and there was more than one occasion when violence would definitely have occurred but for the presence of the UN personnel.

It was towards the end of this period I noticed a change in Brimob personnel. Some of the familiar faces were gone and new ones were present. When I passed this information to the JOC I was told this was being seen across all districts. The Duty Officer stated some thought the Brimob were being replaced by trained TNI soldiers. Others had said they were Kopassus. I watched our Brimob on parade one morning. These were not trained TNI or Kopassus. They were hardly more than 18 years of age and were having difficulty in the most basic of drill movements. 2Lt Audi and his NCOs were trying very hard to get some basic training into them. There was obviously a reason for this change, and I was not too happy with what I thought it was. There was no way I could see this group defending us from an attack.

CHAPTER 23

Polling Period

All UN Staff were in Gleno HQ by early on the morning of the 29 August. Some had come in the previous night; others arrived that morning. Once all were there my main task was to brief them on the plan for the following two days. My briefing to the UN volunteers was very specific. This was the plan of 'Uncle Geoff' which had to be followed to the letter, no deviation was allowed unless CivPol told them otherwise. The briefing included a change in team leadership. On polling day CivPol would be the team leader in every team and I would be in overall command. There was not one objection raised to this change.

Once that briefing was over it was time for an additional briefing with all the CivPol and MLOs. I explained to them the plan was only good if everything went well. I reminded them of the preparation work they had already put in and, should unforeseen events occur, they had to be ready for change. Change may be instigated by me or, if they saw a necessity, by themselves. We were all hoping change would not be necessary.

After the briefings the sub-districts collected their polling materials and prepared to travel back to their bases. By midday all had departed, with escorts. I definitely wanted all travel with the ballot papers completed in daylight hours. CivPol now had the responsibility of securing those materials until handover to the DEOs at the polling sites the following morning. The materials included a flat pack, cardboard polling booth from the AEC for each polling station. With each of these was a pencil, to mark the ballot paper, and a six-inch nail. Punching a hole in the ballot paper was just as acceptable as putting a pencil cross or tick.

Final briefing for CivPol and MLOs.

Each Gleno based team had a specific spot in the HQ building to gather and place their materials. They would need to load up very quickly in the morning.

The arrival of Peter Watt allowed me to allocate two CivPol at the Gleno polling site, purely due to the far greater number of voters expected there. Jose was very happy to have this extra assistance. Rob Mills had the role, with one of the DEOs, to run a polling centre in the local prison. This was not expected to take much time and once all prisoners had voted I had him pencilled in as the emergency reserve. He was to spend some of his time, both before and after the prison, at the Gleno site.

With Jim France and Rob Mills I stayed at our HQ building that night as security for the Gleno ballot materials. The plan called for a 4 a.m. start so we intended to get to bed early. The three of us climbed under our mosquito nets around 8.30 p.m. I don't think any of us had managed to fall asleep before the telephone rang at 9.10 p.m. All three tried to get out and it was Jim's more expensive zippered mosquito net which enabled him to be first. It was a lady ringing from Spain to wish us all very well for the next day. We later found out she telephoned every district and gave them the same good wishes.

That had our brains fully ticking again so it was on the front steps for a chat. Nicolai turned up with some hot water for another cup of coffee, so why not. A little later we decided it was time to try again for a bit of sleep.

At 11.22 p.m., and still I had not managed to fall asleep, Phil Hunter radioed from Atsabe. In the background I could hear automatic gun fire. Phil reported the gunfire was coming from two directions and going over the top of their house, with some rounds hitting the roof. Initially I was on the portable radio sitting on my pillow. But I was quickly out of bed and onto the main radio with the telephone close at hand. As soon as I got into the office, I telephoned the JOC Dili. As expected, there was nothing, they could do about it apart from contact Polri and TNI in Dili. I contacted Ari by radio to inform him, but he could already hear it on his radio, and he was contacting Gultom. All I could do was stay on the radio, give them moral support and report everything to the JOC. For three hours I stayed on that radio. Reports from Phil and the sound of automatic gunfire continued sporadically for the whole time. I asked Phil a number of times if he could see the people who were shooting at them. His answer was always no, from the sounds they seemed to be firing from two positions well away from their building. At 2am Jim came over and told me he would man the radio and I should get some sleep. I got onto the stretcher, but sleep would not come. The Atsabe teams also had no sleep that night.

The three of us in HQ were out of bed around 3.20am as the Electoral Teams began arriving and making a racket as they loaded the ballot materials and boxes into their vehicles. Atsabe had been quiet for the past hour.

The plan called for all convoys to depart their base at 4.00am, the one exception being the Gleno polling site team who only had a five-minute drive. Precisely at 4.00am on 30 August 1999 all convoys reported departing their base locations for the polling sites, with Polri security. There were twenty-one polling sites that corresponded with the former registration sites. Once again excluding Gleno, each Team only had one unarmed CivPol officer with it.

Polri escort on hired truck passing local 'bus'.

It was then a matter of wait. For those at HQ the hardest part of all. Well before we expected any of the teams to have arrived at their polling site they started calling in on the radios. Everywhere they were seeing people on the road walking towards the polling places.

Don was the first to arrive. He not only reported a great crowd of people already there, but he held down the press to talk switch and we head singing. There was a children's choir waiting for team to arrive.

Gradually every team started reporting in. At every location the people were already there, in large numbers. The cheers we heard over the radio had the whole of our HQ cheering as well. The Gleno team, who only had a five-minute drive, decided they were not going to wait any longer. They wanted to be part of this, NOW.

Don at Ermera Village polling day

They asked and I said 'Go'.

It did not take long to hear the cheering from that location as well, and this time we did not need the radio.

The people had turned out in vast numbers to cast their vote.

Just after 8.30am US CivPol Officer Martinak called in from the village of Mirtutu. An intoxicated Militia man had approached the polling site armed with a pistol. Martinak had disarmed the individual and handed him with his weapon to Polri.

At 9 a.m., I had had enough of waiting. I got into my vehicle and drove to the Gleno polling site. This site was in a school grounds with each of the seven classrooms, in a rough square, being used as a polling station. When I arrived, there were a large number of people waiting at each room. The total number of people justified my decision to add an additional CivPol to that location. One person would never have managed the early surge of that crowd.

Gleno polling site.

Lauana Polling site.

In the open centre of the school I noticed Capt Ari with one of the local Militia leaders. I walked over to them and the Militia leader was very agitated about the presence of the university students. They were talking with the people waiting in line. He said they were telling the people to vote for independence. In my opinion he was probably correct, but it was something I would easily solve. I spoke with the student leader, confirmed from him all the students had already voted and persuaded him to take them away from the area. It wasn't too hard to convince him. I don't think he wanted another run in with my arm. More importantly I asked him did he really think all these people would be here at this time of the morning if they were not voting for independence. When he heard that his eyes lit up and I am sure he realised the truth of what I had just said. He and the students departed immediately.

About this time Gultom also arrived and then we went through a period where the Militia leader just kept coming up with one complaint after another. Some we checked by having him walk through the polling stations with Capt Ari and one of the CivPol. That resolved the second round of his complaints. But, typical of East Timor, that did not stop him. As fast as we countered his complaints, he invented a new one. Eventually Gultom told him to go away. Surprisingly he did, without any complaint Gultom and I returned to our relative headquarters and Rob Mills headed off to the gaol.

The rest of the morning was quiet. Updates coming from all polling sites were positive. At all sites more than half those registered had already voted. At a few sites more than 90% had already cast their vote. It was too good to last.

12.02 p.m.   Gleno: Peter Watt and Jose Pena

I was out the front of the Gleno HQ when I heard gunshots coming from the direction of the Gleno Polling Site. My immediate reaction was to get in my vehicle and drive there. Unfortunately, Samulcai had borrowed it to go home for lunch. I went straight inside to get the keys for another vehicle, but there were none there. Jim France and I were the only people in our HQ. Jim informed me Peter Watt had just radioed in the Gleno site being attacked by Militia. I told Jim to report the matter to Dili and made a radio call for anyone nearby to get back and hand over their vehicle to me.

The exact timing of 12.02 p.m. was from Peter Watt, the HQ radio log recorded his first call as coming in at 12.10 p.m.

Peter later provided me with the following description of the incident —

At 12.02pm around 50 Militia armed with modern revolvers, large stones, machetes and handmade guns attacked the Polling site in Gleno. Shots were fired at voters and into the buildings. I approached who I believed was the leader of the Militia in the midst of the attack, asking him to call off the rampaging Militia attack. He looked straight through me as if in a daze to offer no response. His eyes were blood red, probably from crazy dog, a drug administered to the attacking Militia to deaden their emotions to the carnage they were inflicting and fuel their aggression.

Coincidentally, the American Ambassador, who had arrived only a minute or two before and witnessed this violent assault, was immediately pushed back into his vehicle by his security detail and sped off away from the polling site.

To this day, this scene is still vivid in my mind. I noticed Militia throwing stones and shooting into a building. I believed there were people trapped inside through everyone else except the Militia and Polri had fled. I ran to the room and stood at the doorway. This prevented any entry by the Militia.

The Polri were already there but instead of managing the Militia, it appeared that they only added to the chaos, firing their service revolvers aimlessly into the air and having little impact on controlling the Militia who were continuing to run riot.

Samulcai arrived at the polling site. He quickly reversed the UN-badged Land Rover to stop about fifteen metres from where I guarded the doorway. I was then grabbed from behind by a team of Polri, who also led the trapped people away from the polling room and dragged me from the door and to Samulcai's car. Jose was already in the car. A number of Militias surrounded and blocked the UN vehicle. At this time, a Militiaman walked up to the back-seat window where I was seated and pulled out a police service revolver tapping the window and pointing the barrel to my head. As I contended with this Militia not to engage the trigger, Samulcai gunned the UN vehicle, dodging the surrounding Militia to speed away and drive directly to the main police station.

Later the DEOs and some of the local staff from the Gleno Polling Site gave me additional information about Peter Watt's efforts. Not only were they certain he had saved their lives, but also that he had saved the ballots and thus the overall integrity of the process. They told me they had seen shots continuing to be fired and rocks thrown at the building while Peter stood in the doorway. One of the rocks had struck Peter and pistol rounds were hitting the wall immediately beside him, between chest and head height. More than one informed me Peter had put himself in a great deal of danger to personally ensure the six ballot boxes located in the other rooms were properly sealed. At the same time Electoral people also informed that, apart from a small number who had gone to join Falantil, all of the local staff from Gleno were at our Headquarters. After what seemed an eternity, I got my hands on a vehicle. To this day I do not remember if it was mine or another one someone had brought back. I do not know how long Peter felt this incident had been underway, but I am sure that it seemed like hours. In fact, by checking the radio log, I was in the vehicle and on my way to the polling site at 12.17 p.m.

That drive was the quickest I had ever travelled in East Timor. As I arrived there was a Polri team blocking the road so I could not drive into the school grounds. I got out of the vehicle intending to walk, well run, straight in. Four Polri surrounded me as soon as I got out of the vehicle and prevented me from moving. The sergeant told me his commander was in the school and he had left this team with the express instruction to protect me when I arrived and not let me into the school grounds until they received further orders...

Again, it felt like I was waiting forever, it was actually only a short while before the sergeant indicated to me that we could enter. His team of four went with me. One on either side, one in front and one behind. They remained with me until we reached Gultom. I could not help but think, because of our difference in height, there was no protection for my head.

I could see a large group of the Militia, in plain view, just outside the school square. Two remained inside and Gultom was standing with them. When I arrived, he informed me they were the leaders of this group. I had never seen these individuals in Ermera.

In the background I saw another person I had not previously seen. A tall very well-dressed Indonesian with obvious military characteristics. After I arrived, he just stood back watching. A large group of them were armed, but I saw no homemade weapons this time, Militia were hanging around just behind this individual. They remained just outside the school square.

These Militia leaders came up with a new set of complaints. Once again Gultom and I went through a very long negotiation process similar to the much simpler one earlier that morning.

As we were approaching the end of these negotiations a UN helicopter landed. A variety of senior representatives from both the UN and Indonesian authorities were on board. The first task they wanted to undertake was to check the ballot boxes to make sure they had been properly sealed. I went with one of them and we checked every ballot box, all were properly sealed. If they had not been then the UN Electoral representative on the helicopter said he had a different set of seals to put on them. With those different seals they would not have been counted as part of the overall Popular Consultation process.

Further negotiations were conducted between the UN HQ people and the Militia leaders, with Gultom and I having a bit of input. It did not take all that long for an agreement to be reached. The polling site would re-open at 2 p.m. staffed entirely by international personnel and using only one room. The one room idea came from me, after a word with Peter, for a number of reasons. The first being there was only one of the seven that could be properly secured; the second was the limited number of people we had to staff the site; and the third was most of the people registered had already voted, one site could handle the remainder. Also, by agreement, the staff were instructed not to give any verbal instructions to the people when they came in to vote, just hand over the ballot paper. If necessary, the site could stay open for an extra 2 hours.

A significant proportion of the people had already voted and, when I arrived, there were some others who were still at the site, close to where Peter Watt had stood in the doorway. Others had scattered, but people were already returning while the negotiations were underway. By the time the site re-opened at 2 p.m. the majority of those who had not already voted had returned. A total of 3,960 people were registered to vote at this site.

On a later day Allessandro would telephone me from Dili and inform me the figures in the tally room showed all but eighteen of them had voted. In addition, he provided information that throughout Ermera only thirty registered voters did not show up. He had also spoken with a representative of one family, with eleven voters, who had taken a seriously ill senior family member to Dili hospital the day before and had not as yet returned. For this vote there were no provisions for voting other than on the day and at the site where you were registered. He also told me, when checked, the ballot box that had broken in the dry riverbed was only two ballot papers short of the number that should have been there.

Once Gleno was up and running again Gultom and I went to his HQ and stood immediately outside his base radio room. From then until much later in the afternoon we were constantly co-ordinating our responses to the reports coming in on both radio systems. That cooperation played a significant part in the final success of that day.

From 2.45p.m., reports were being passed from various polling sites of heavy Militia activity directed at the polling sites and the UN staff. Particular threats were being made against the locally employed persons who were staffing the polling stations. By 3.30p.m., 14 of the 21 polling sites were under direct and immediate Militia threat. Although, due to radio aerials being deliberately damaged by Militia, I would not know about some of them until later in the evening.

The following incidents directly involved AFP members. There were similar actions by the majority of CivPol in the district that day.

Poteete and Ermera Villages:Don Barnby

A large Militia force established a roadblock between the polling sites at Poetete and Ermera Villages. This would prevent the Poetete team with its POLRI escort from travelling to Ermera, collecting the Ermera Team and then going to Regional Headquarters. The roadblock was within site of the Ermera polling station. Don Barnby left the building, stood on one of the tables in the school yard to properly observe and report on this roadblock. In doing this he was fully visible to the Militia at the roadblock. Despite repeated requests from POLRI and threats from the Militia he remained in full view and provided ongoing reports on Militia activity.

> ***In Don Barnby's words***
> *the incident at Ermera on Polling Day with the truckload of Militia that were blocking the intersection that Crazy had to pass through on his way back to Gleno was 'up close and personal', I recall that I was having quite a 'long chat' with the Militia head at the time with the barrel of his automatic inches from my face and attempting to persuade Polri to do their job!! I was also having a 3way conversation on the radio with Crazy, Jim France and Sandra whilst trying to resolve the impasse.*

This enabled me to pass information directly to Gultom, who arranged for additional POLRI resources to go to the scene and remove the roadblock. Immediately the roadblock was removed Don informed both me and the Poetete Team. This allowed a quick and safe return of both teams to the Regional Headquarters. Without his presence and reports it is likely this would not have occurred without loss of life, particularly local employees, and probable loss of ballots.

BoboiLeten (Atsabe sub village): Phil Hunter

BoboiLeten is a village between Lauana Village and Atsabe. At 3.30 p.m. a report was received the Militia were preventing any departure from this location. The UN staff making radio transmissions from the area were hysterical. On occasion gun shots could be heard in the background. They managed to pass the information that most of the ballot boxes had been loaded into the vehicle, but the staff were still in the building. Militia were around the vehicle and had massed in the enclosed area at the front of the building. POLRI had withdrawn and could not be seen.

The original plan called for the Electoral Team at Lauana to travel to BoboiLeten at 4.30 p.m. with the additional POLRI escort, collect the Boboi Leten Team and then travel to Atsabe.

On receiving the initial report from Boboi Leten I contacted Phil Hunter. He informed me everyone on their electoral roll had voted. There was no need for them to remain where they were, so I directed an immediate load up and departure from his location.

Following are Phil's words on the incident:
The Lauana voting centre was closed and local staff departed for their homes. All ballots and associated paraphernalia were loaded into one UN vehicle. The second UN vehicle consisting of Mr. Brew, Mr. GOLPAR and Mr. MAIA prepared to depart for BoboiLeten. The convoy departed Lauana with the Brimob/Polri escort.

BoboiLeten is a village situated halfway between Lauana and Atsabe and the local school was the location for people to vote. The intention was for the Lauana convoy to stop at BoboiLeten, collect ballot papers, UN staff and Brimob/Polri then continue onto Atsabe.

As the Lauana convoy approached the school I could see a number of men, carrying firearms, walking towards the school. As the convoy stopped, I saw about twenty to thirty Militia, armed with automatic weapons, in the school yard and around the school building intimidating and taunting U.N. staff. I could also see International UN staff standing around the front of the school and local staff inside the school. Their Brimob/Polri escorts were not assisting, standing about twenty metres from the school building, in company with the CivPol member.

I indicated to the Lauana UN staff to remain in their vehicle and I entered the school yard. The situation was extremely tense, and staff were visibly distressed and confused. I walked the Bob-oiLeten UN staff away from the school and directed them to get inside their UN Land Rover.

One International staff member, Mr. Robert DRAPER (DEO from Africa) brought with him a ballot box. As he approached the UN Land Rover a Militia member knocked the box from his hands and shouted that UNAMET was not neutral. I stepped between the Militia member and assisted the UN worker with the box to the vehicle. I could see that the local UN staff were now running from the school towards the Brimob/Polri truck.

As I assisted with the loading of the ballot box into the rear passenger side of the vehicle, I saw a local staff member walk from the school carrying a box. As this member, Joao Lopes GOMEZ, placed the box into the rear of the Land Rover, I saw another Militia member run at him from behind carrying a long knife. Before I could move to the rear of the vehicle the Militia member stabbed Mr. GOMEZ in the back. I immediately moved to the rear of the vehicle and the Militia member ran away. I saw Mr. GOMEZ slumped over the rear of the vehicle, holding his back and moaning in pain. I saw blood running from the stab wound.

At this point, the Brimob commander ran to the UN vehicle yelling at me to leave. I placed Mr. GOMEZ into the rear of the vehicle. As I began to close the door, the vehicle started and began to move away. I yelled to the driver, the Thai CivPol member, to stop. The vehicle stopped but Mr. GOMEZ had been displaced from the vehicle. Again, I placed Mr. GOMEZ into the rear of the vehicle and closed the door. As I closed the door the vehicle drove out of the school yard to a position next to the Brimob/Polri truck.

As I turned toward my vehicle, I saw another local staff member being beaten by about four or five Militia members. The Brimob commander continued to yell at me to leave the area. As all this was happening the other Militia members were becoming extremely agitated and were yelling death threats to UN staff. I could see that throughout this period all local staff had left the school and were now in the back of the Brimob/Polri truck.

I ran to my vehicle where I saw U.N. DEO, Mr. James BREW. The radio in Mr. BREW's vehicle was inoperable and he had positioned himself to use the radio in my vehicle, if required. I told Mr. BREW to return to his vehicle and we all departed following the Brimob/Polri truck.

Without the valorous action of Phil Hunter, with complete disregard for his own safety, I have no doubt all locally employed UN staff at Boboi Leten would have been killed. As they were witnesses it is highly likely this would have also been the fate of the international staff. The ballots would have been lost. When I spoke with the DEOs from both locations everyone commented Phil was understating the role he played.

Atsabe: Phil Hunter and Max Knoth

The convoy from Boboi Leten travelled the 15 minutes to the CivPol house at Atsabe. Phil Hunter requested by radio for Max Knoth to have a first aid kit available as soon as they arrived. The CivPol house was at the top of exposed steps that led from the car park area. Immediately the convoy arrived automatic gunfire commenced from two directions. This gunfire was going immediately above the heads of the personnel present. Under this gun fire Max Knoth came down to the vehicles and commenced giving first aid to the injured man. Phil again escorted staff one at a time, this time from the vehicles to the house. Polri unloaded the local staff beside the UN vehicles and drove off immediately. Once all the people were in the house Phil returned to the vehicles and the two CivPol members carried the injured person into the CivPol house. One of the DEO's took over the task of providing first aid. Both CivPol members returned to the vehicles a number of times to carry the ballot boxes up the stairs and into the building. Throughout the whole time the automatic gun fire continued immediately over their heads. Either these members, or other staff at the location, provided constant radio reports on what was occurring. In every radio transmission the sounds of gun fire could be heard. While I was receiving the radio reports, I was also on the telephone to JOC Dili. Initially I requested and then I demanded a helicopter to conduct a medical evacuation. All I got was it cannot be done at this time of the day. As it turned out, and despite the first aid efforts, the man died before the helicopter would have arrived.

Following is the description of this event in the words of Phil Hunter:

Monday 30 August

After departing Boboi-Leten for Atsabe, I radioed F/A KNOTH that I would be approximately 15 minutes and that I had a seriously injured staff member in the vehicle. Medical supplies would be needed. I arrived at the CivPol residence with the injured member and I saw F/A KNOTH standing outside the residence, at the top of a flight of approximately 30 stairs, with a medical kit. As the U.N. vehicles stopped heavy automatic gun fire commenced. The injured person was placed in a safe position.

I saw F/A KNOTH talking on the radio. After this, and as the gun fire continued, F/A KNOTH ran down the stairs with the medical kit and commenced first aid on the wounded staff member. After updating Gleno radio base 3, I assisted F/A KNOTH with first aid and we carried the member up the stairs and into the residence. Continued first aid and CPR on the staff member failed to save his life.

F/A KNOTH assisted in ensuring that all U.N. staff were

in the residence. We then retrieved all ballot boxes from U.N. vehicles and locked them in the residence. F/A KNOTH provided food and water to UN staff and acted in a manner which helped calm staff. The Militia set a perimeter around the residence and remained throughout the night.

Both Phil and Max demonstrated valour of the highest order and completely ignored the immediate threat to their personal safety to carry the injured person to the house, secure the ballots and gather all UN staff into one location.

Other Sites

While the situation in Ermera Village was being resolved a radio-call came in from a UN call sign unknown to me. They said they were on the road from Hatolia approaching the junction with the road between Gleno and Ermera. They wanted to know if it was safe to travel to Gleno. I told them to stay at the junction until the convoy from Ermera arrived and then get on the end of that convoy. Don acknowledged he had heard the message. When I finally met this group, they claimed to be UN media who just got caught out in the wrong spot. I still do not know the truth of that statement, but I found out later they had two very senior members of the pro-independence group in their vehicle. When the first convoy finally left Gleno the next evening those two were very carefully hidden under bags in the rear of two of our vehicles.

Shortly after 3 p.m. Fatubolo radioed in that Militia were moving from the adjacent ridge towards the polling site. I asked how many people were left to vote. They told me every registered voter had already voted and when the Militia started to move, they had all left the area. I directed him to get everything loaded into the vehicles, return to Ermera, collect their belongings and then travel to Gleno HQ. The original plan had them returning to Ermera much later and then moving to Gleno early the next morning.

Letefoho reported Militia gathering around their polling sites. At this stage only yelling verbal threats. But they were armed. Once again, all those registered at the sites had voted so they were also directed to leave immediately. I asked them were their bags packed at their accommodation. The answer was yes, so I told them to stop long enough to get them and then drive straight to Gleno. Originally, they had been going to join onto a convoy from Atsabe the next morning.

During this period Gultom was giving complementary orders to the Polri units at those polling sites.

Once all the areas that had been hit were as safe as they could be, I moved back to the UN Gleno HQ. I wanted to be there when the teams arrived.

In the later part of the afternoon we had not heard from the Railaco polling sites. If I thought about them at all it was only that they were doing the right thing and staying off the radio to allow proper attention to the locations where there was trouble.

It was just after dark when Nitaya and her team arrived. The radio aerial on their vehicle had been broken off and they were all visibly shaken. Nitaya quickly briefed me. At her polling site there had been no problem. When the time came to close down and move, they had driven to the Railaco site. There they found the building completely surrounded by Militia. They could see the team's UN vehicle had the radio aerial broken off. She could see Warrant Officer Robert standing in the doorway of the polling site. Armed Militia were standing only a metre or so in front of him. As she was trying to call on the radio one of the Militias broke the aerial off her vehicle. One of their Polri escort called out from the vehicle for them to leave immediately and drive to Gleno to get assistance. The Polri escort followed them.

Gultom arrived very shortly after and told me the Polri escort had gone straight to their HQ and briefed him. He had developed enough of an understanding of me to know that I would immediately set out for Railaco. He had vehicles parked so any UN vehicle I could use was blocked. He told me he was going to resolve the incident and I was to stay right where I was, to leave would be too dangerous. Gultom left in one of the hired trucks with about 10 Polri in the back followed by Lt Audi and a section of Brimob in their vehicle. About 90 minutes later he returned with all UN personnel and the ballot boxes intact.

Shortly after 8 p.m., the last of the Electoral Teams had arrived at their overnight location. This completed the concentration of teams to Gleno and the sub districts of Atsabe and Hatolia. In every case the teams had brought with them all local staff who wanted to remain under the protection of the UN. All ballots were secure, and the integrity of the process had been preserved. One locally employed person, Joao Lopes GOMEZ, had been murdered by direct Militia action. We were later told a second person had also been killed at BoboiLeten, but I was unable to find out his name.

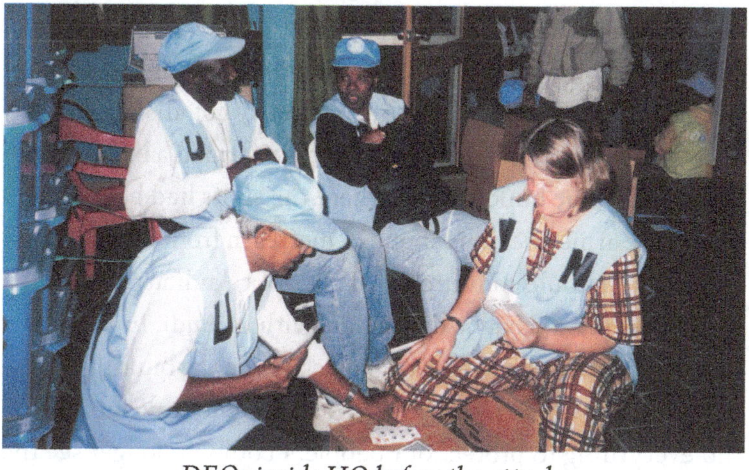

DEOs inside HQ before the attack.

Regional Headquarters — Gleno. P Morris, D Barnby, P Watt, R Mills, W Corbett, R Martinak and J France.

Later in the evening a few of the CivPol and a majority of the UNVs were inside the headquarters building. The UNVs were completing polling administrative processes, something originally intended to be done at their polling sites. Intentions had changed to meet the developing situation. A large number of the locally employed staff, about 95 people, had gathered in the area immediately in front of the HQ building. Every available item, including cardboard boxes, had been stripped from the building to provide them with some level of comfort. The FSA had been pressured to open the ration store and distribute at least some of the food and drinking water. He gave them almost the entire reserve of emergency rations.

I had climbed onto the stretcher intending to get a bit of sleep, regardless of the noise, but never managed to make it as within minutes of my head hitting the pillow gun shots rang out from the front of the building. All CivPol still at headquarters (Australian, New Zealand and USA) immediately rushed out the front of the building, coincidentally breaking the front door in our rush. As we got out of the building further shots were fired and large rocks were thrown towards the local staff and the building. Rocks hit some of the local staff. The CivPol quickly got all of the locally engaged staff into the building and then formed a line between the front of the building and where the shots had been fired. I could see armed persons about 25 metres in front of us.

Before I could move towards them Lt Audi arrived with a BRIMOB team. I had a 'discussion' with Lt Audi. Initially over our security. He wanted us to go back inside the building where we would be safe. I told him we were going to stay outside and do everything to protect our people. I could no longer see the armed group, but I could still hear them. They had backed off but only to a point where they were just behind buildings. Loud verbal threats were still being made. We could also hear other shots being fired nearby.

It was at this time that I lost my cool and yelled at Audi 'if you're unable to do your job then give us your weapons and we will do it for you'. Not exactly in those words as I have not included the expletives.

Obviously, he refused just as I again refused to order my people to go inside the building. For the rest of the night we were outside our HQ protecting our people and watching as homes were set on fire. One home after another. All of them homes of those who had been prominent in the independence movement. The feeling of being impotent is not a good feeling to have.

After sunrise, one of the burnt houses.

BRIMOB provided a thin defensive perimeter around the entire building for the rest of the night. Even with their presence the CivPol also remained outside at the front of the building, occasionally walking around the building. The Brimob personnel were between us and where the Militia were perceived to be, but these were the new 'young' Brimob who were all crouched down behind whatever cover they could find. Had there been further direct attack on us I am certain none would have stayed to assist.

At some stage during the evening Paul and Don suggested I get into one of the vehicles and have a bit of a sleep. I got into the vehicle but like the night before sleep was not easy. I must have dropped off for a short while because when I woke the CivPol had a small fire going to keep warm. For the whole night armed Militia could be seen in the vicinity of the headquarters building, but never quite coming close enough for us to get our hands on them.

Following is an extract from the report by Don Barnby's on this incident -

At approximately 8.30pm that evening, the majority of the locally employed staff (numbering around 190 people) were sleeping and talking in the grounds of the building when the Militia attacked, throwing rocks and shooting weapons. The local staff understandably panicked and rushed inside the building through the single front door, and seven police ran outside and formed a cordon around the HQ. They included the AFP members, 2 NZ Police and 2 US Police officers. Throughout the night the Militia continued to burn buildings in the vicinity and automatic gunfire could be heard. A picket was organised by the above members for the duration of that night, guarding the people inside the building and the ballot boxes. At approximately 3am, I heard the voice of my Electoral officer, Sandra Chestnutt on the Radio. Apparently 8-10 DEO's were in their accommodation which was approx. 150-200 metres from the HQ office. Militia activity was intensifying during the night — and they were concerned for their safety. I took Rob Mills (NZPol) and Randy Martinak (USPOL) and we made our way to their location — gave them an updated Sitrep and took names of all DEOs that were in their accommodation and shortly thereafter, returned to the HQ building. Militia activity had increased, and we had to dodge several Militia patrols on the way back to HQ.

Information was later received that a large group of Militia had travelled from Dili to Ermera late on the day of 29 August. They had supplemented the local Militia in what appeared to be planned attacks across the district from the night of 29 August.

CHAPTER 24

31 August 1999 — The Day After

Very early in the morning Dili JOC advised a helicopter would be arriving at 6 a.m. to collect a Polri Officer before going on to Atsabe. Right on 6 a.m. I drove to the Gleno LZ. I had to approach the LZ very carefully as there were large numbers of Militia on all the roadways around it and I could see them in the nearby buildings. The helicopter had on board a HQ investigation team which included POLRI and TNI representatives. Captain Ari had been nominated by Lt Col Gultom to join the team.

What I saw convinced me to reconsider the original pickup plan for a helicopter to arrive at the main landing zone about 9 a.m. to pick up the ballot boxes. Instructions from Dili were for the ballot boxes, materials and paperwork to be checked against each other before being loaded. The presence of so many armed Militias caused me to re-think that plan. I had already identified and used an alternate LZ in the dry riverbed. This was in a different direction from Regional Headquarters to the primary landing zone. There should be time to load the materials before the Militia could react. The plan was changed. CivPol were briefed. UNAMET HQ was informed by secure radio.

Gleno

Gleno based CivPol and Rob Walker (UK Police)

A convoy of eight UN vehicles full of ballot boxes was drawn up outside Regional HQ and facing in the direction of the primary landing zone. As soon as the helicopter called in the convoy moved off, quickly doing a U turn and going to the dry riverbed. Once there, four CivPol were deployed, one in each direction, to provide an early warning should it become necessary. When the helicopter landed, we started to carry the ballot boxes straight towards it. Much to my displeasure a representative from the Electoral Division got off the helicopter and stopped us, insisting all ballot materials be checked off against each other before they were be loaded on the helicopter.

Shortly after the checking process commenced Peter Watt, who was the CivPol deployed in the direction of Regional Headquarters, called in that Militia were approaching. I looked in his direction and immediately saw the Militia he was referring to. They were coming through the dry rice paddies about 400 metres away. There were 40 to 50 of them and they all appeared armed with traditional weapons. My first thought was to keep them as far away from the ballot boxes as possible. I immediately started walking towards them and called for the CivPol to secure the boxes in the vehicles and form a line between the vehicles and the Militia. They followed my instructions

The Militia began firing the traditional weapons and, every few seconds, I heard gunshots that could only have come from a modern weapon. Shots went in the air, towards the CivPol, towards the helicopter and into the ground around the CivPol. I was one of two CivPol who received minor wounds from the traditional weapons. In my case, we later squeezed out 14 small pellets slightly embedded in my lower right arm. The helicopter was definitely well out of the range of homemade weapons but still a number of rounds went very close, obviously someone was using a modern weapon. The pilot reported he thought a couple of rounds had hit the helicopter and he had to follow procedure and take off.

The CivPol quickly formed a line between the vehicles, with the ballot boxes, and the advancing Militia. We maintained this position and ensured if the Militia wanted to get at the ballot boxes then they would have to go through that CivPol line. The very formation of the line appeared to surprise them, and they hesitated, they appeared to be wondering what to do. A number of times they advanced towards the CivPol line yelling abuse and threats. But the line never backed off and, on each occasion, they went back a bit and started yelling again. On the far side of the riverbed, about 80 metres away, I could see a second group of about 15 persons wearing Militia T shirts and carrying fully automatic weapons. These persons did not move further forward than the edge of the riverbed.

Don Barnby's report included the following words on this incident -

Incident witnessed by DEO's Sandra Chestnutt (AUST) and Inge Borg (Germany). Eight UN Land rovers were lined up on the bank of a dry riverbed (our secondary LZ) waiting for the arrival of the UN helicopter. When the helicopter landed members of the Militia entered the riverbed armed with traditional and automatic weapons and proceeded of fire at the chopper and the UN CivPol. The ballot boxes were stacked on the edge of the riverbed waiting to be loaded on the chopper. The chopper took rounds and lifted off leaving two members (DEO and Rob Walker UK Police) on the ground with the above-named police. One of the ballot boxes split and the aforementioned police managed to recover all except two ballots while being shot at and stoned by Militia. Supt Hazel walked out into the middle of 20-30-armed Militia and attempted to negotiate with them while they were firing weapons indiscriminately around him and the remaining six officers guarding the boxes. All 60 boxes were recovered and returned to Ermera HQ. A short time later still under threat of further Militia attacks the same police managed to load the helicopter at the primary LZ and transport the ballot boxes to Dili

This standoff continued for about 10 minutes before our 'friend' James Bond arrived. I was having a strong discussion with him when a Polri Brimob team arrived. There was a further period of intense negotiation before the Brimob moved between the CivPol and the Militia and then moved the Militia back so that the ballots could be secured in the vehicles and returned to headquarters. Samulcai and our MLOs turned up at the same time.

One of the ballot boxes had been dropped and some of the ballots came out. These were quickly collected, put back in the box and it was resealed. Later we were informed the box was missing two ballots when the counting was done.

Gultom arrived at our HQ almost at the same time we did. This was the first time he expressed his anger towards me in front of others. I did not think it appropriate to respond immediately, deciding an explanation would be better when there was just the two of us. Once he got over his initial burst, he told me he wanted us to take the ballot boxes to the primary LZ. In reply I explained to him the only way I would allow that to happen was if I could go to the LZ, see no Militia there and walk for 200 metres in any direction and find no Militia. He agreed to try and satisfy my demand. He said he would call me when it was done and left.

A short while later he called telling me he had negotiated the Militia off the LZ and Polri personnel were in the process of making sure they were at least 200 metres away. Once they got them away the Polri would remain to ensure our safety. He informed me the Militia had one request. They wanted one of them to be at the helicopter to make sure no pro-independence people were smuggled aboard. I agreed to one representative of the Militia on the basis he was not to be armed.

I then drove to the LZ. Saw there were no Militia in the immediate area. Got out of my vehicle and picked one side to walk into. Went as far as the Polri cordon and saw no Militia. I called the pilot and advised him we would now use the main LZ. He had a very good suggestion. Get the UN people to remove the radio aerials from the vehicles. The vehicles could be backed up, under the rotating helicopter blades, right to the helicopter door where the boxes could be unloaded directly into the cargo bay. Strictly against normal safety protocols. I checked that the people at HQ had heard the pilot and added another instruction. Two extra people would be in the first vehicle to unload that vehicle and stay to unload the rest.

The convoy arrived, parking side by side with the rear of all vehicles towards where the helicopter would land. The Militia representative was there, strange that he was wearing a TNI sergeants' uniform. The helicopter landed and the first vehicle reversed right up to the door. With a short human chain all materials were rapidly loaded into the helicopter. As soon as the ballots were unloaded that vehicle drove off with the second vehicle reversing under the blades as the first left. Then the third vehicle and so on. The only people who got into the helicopter were the Electoral representative from Dili, Rob Walker (UK CivPol who had been her escort) and the Polri member who had been with them. It took less than 4 minutes for the 77 ballot boxes with the materials and documents for each to be loaded and the helicopter to take off.

Rob Walker provided his version of the incident -

Apart from the chopper crew, there were only three of us on the heli, as all of the seats etc, had been stripped out to take the boxes. 1x CivPol (Me), 1x UN Electoral officer (Alisa) & 1x Indonesian Police Officer (who was as much use as a chocolate fireguard!).

As the chopper (understandably) lifted off when fired on, I ended up being left with your guys on the riverbed, with the lads picking up rocks to face off the Militia.

*As things started to go to Rat-Sh*t, I remember standing next to Paul Morris, as the Militia got closer...*

*Morro shouted to the sole Indonesian Police officer from the chopper '**Use your gun...**'*

I took great pleasure in getting Morro to repeat that phrase, when we were safely back in Darwin at a 'Yacht Club' reception, to Amanda Vanstone.

I remember heading off in the Land rovers to the alternate LZ with Morro & your guys and us all getting the boxes into the chopper ASAP & at which point, I hate to say I had to get back on the helicopter & left you to it! We went on to another 4/5 towns later the day, ferrying the boxes back to Dili.

The pilot informed me he was on his way to Hatolia. As the helicopter was a Super Puma, I informed him that the LZ in Hatolia was not big enough to take his machine. If he had attempted to land in their normal LZ nearby houses would have been blown over by his downdraft. He replied, we will not be landing where they expect us; we will re direct your people to a new site as we approach.

Later when I told Gultom why I had changed the LZ site he wanted to know why I did not trust him enough to inform him in advance. I explained I trusted him but both of us knew there were Polri who were connected to the Militia and when he gave instructions for a revised security location the Militia would have also been informed.

That afternoon I was informed the Militia who attacked at the dry riverbed had come from an ambush position prepared for us on the roadway between Regional Headquarters and the primary landing zone. I knew the ambush area they had selected very well. The section of road they had chosen had deep storm water drains on either side. Even 4WD vehicles would not get through them. Senior Claudio's house was at the far end of the ambush site. This also explained how they managed to get to the alternate landing site as quickly as they did. If the ambush had been properly sprung in that location, there would have been no way out. It would have then become a matter of either surrendering the ballots or fighting. I knew the CivPol with me would not have surrendered the ballots. While this information did not come directly from Gultom, I had a strong impression that it was he who made sure it got to me.

Without the courage of the CivPol at the dry riverbed the ballot boxes for the majority of polling sites in Ermera would have fallen into Militia hands. The integrity of the entire Popular Consultation process would have then been in question.

Hatolia

The helicopter then flew to Hatolia where, with directions from the helicopter crew to Brett Swan, a similar process of deception and changing landing zones was put into place. This time there would be no attempt to check the ballot materials. The helicopter landed, the ballots were loaded, and the helicopter took off before the Militia had time to get to the site. I gave the order for the Hatolia teams to use one of their alternate evacuation routes and drive to Dili via Liquicia, with their local staff on board, rather than travel the road from Hatolia to Gleno. Later I found out there was a slight delay before they left. Eventually they arrived in Dili about 6 p.m. after negotiating their way through a number of Militia roadblocks/check points. The three CivPol officers returned to Gleno on 2 September.

The following information was reported by John Tanti on the actions in Hatolia that morning -

UN helicopter attends Hatolia town for the collection of ballots. We knew that the first LZ was going to be a tight squeeze in that the zone was fraught with natural and manmade obstacles given that the terrain was mountainous, and the roads were dominated by the Militia, our options were limited. The mission was further complicated because Militia members had virtually surrounded the LZ (approximately 100 Militia members). A secondary LZ was identified and following a dummy run in the wrong direction (hence sending Militia trucks/members down the wrong way) our small convoy of two land rovers sped to the secondary LZ which was in opposite direction. This dummy run opened a short space in time in which the helicopter landed, a hot extraction of the boxes occurred, (blades still spinning & vehicle backed up to location). Once the Militia trucks descended on the area, the helicopter was again airborne, and the Militia had failed in its mission to take the boxes.

The then frustrated and angry Militia members took into custody four local UN employees. These prisoners were lodged at the Hatolia Police station (further demonstrating the complicity of the police). Brett SWAN and I then began negotiations with the local chief to secure the release of the men so that we could take them to Dili with us. Following heated discussions with the Police chief and local Militia leaders our convoy came to a stop at the local checkpoint which was now the subject of considerable Militia activity. During these discussions, the Militia chief continued to say that the four taken into custody were responsible for the havoc and therefore must stay to face the consequences once the ballot result was publicized. I am convinced that all four would have been publicly killed and their corpses put on display if they had been left in town. (Prior to our arrival, public killings such as intended in this instance, were a key tool used by the Militia in Hatolia to emphasize their wants and demands in gross acts of intimidation.)

Many shots were discharged around our cars and eventually, the district Indonesian Police commander from Gleno was contacted through Commander HAZEL. Commander HAZEL conducted urgent negotiations and secured the relay of a message by the Gleno chief (over UN communications). Commander Hazel ordered the Hatolia Police chief to release the men and allow them to travel to Dili with us. After a tense standoff, the four men were released.

Upon release, the local employees along with the international UN staff and four Australian observers who operated within Hatolia during the consultation were escorted to Dili via the heavily road blocked Liquicia district.

Atsabe

Alan Mills, Phil Hunter and Max Knoth

The situation in Atsabe had not changed. The CivPol house was still surrounded by armed Militia and the normal helicopter pad had Militia all over it. The 6 a.m. helicopter (a Huey call sign UNO 063, crewed by Australians) landed on a very small patch of land immediately behind the CivPol house. The investigation team was not able to leave the house and eventually boarded the helicopter and returned to Dili.

For the remainder of the morning Atsabe continually reported Militia activity that was designed to intimidate them.

Gleno and Atsabe

The planned convoy to take the DEOs, UNVs whose role was now complete, to Dili for repatriation to their home countries, was still sitting outside our HQ. Militia had roadblocks on every road.

I had discussions with JOC Dili and was told a helicopter would be arriving just after midday with a high-level delegation to go to Atsabe. I was also informed Polri HQ had directed Gultom to join this high-level group.

The helicopter, again UNO 063, arrived at Gleno with the high-level delegation, including Commissioner Mills, from Dili. On board was Captain Ari, returning after the first attempt at Atsabe. I was briefed on what they were going to try and do and then tasked to negotiate, with the Militia in Gleno, for the departure of our convoy to Dili. Gultom tasked Ari to assist me in this process.

Commissioner Mill said, 'I thought you told me the Militia was under control?'

My answer to that included the knowledge I now had that a large group of well-armed Militia had arrived from another area of East Timor.

The helicopter departed Gleno and shortly after 1 p.m. landed in Atsabe on the same spot at the rear of the CivPol house.

The following are the words, as usual understated, from a report of Phil Hunter -

Tuesday 31 August — First light.

The Militia perimeter was still present. The Militia stated that they wanted to kill the local staff and that the ballot boxes would not leave the residence. F/A KNOTH remained calm and stated his uncompromising resolve to stay with the local staff and the ballot boxes. About 1300hrs CivPol Commissioner Alan MILLS arrived, via helicopter, with TNI and POLRI Commanders and negotiated the safe release of the local staff and the ballot boxes.

After the local staff and ballot boxes had departed Atsabe, via helicopter, F/A KNOTH in company with other CivPol and 2 Electoral officers drove to Gleno.

The events of the 30th and 31st were extremely dangerous and stressful. Over this two-day period and throughout the entire process, F/A KNOTH acted in an exceedingly professional and uncompromising manner. He displayed tremendous courage and bravery, which had a positive impact on those around him. F/A KNOTH's determination and ability to achieve in a crisis situation significantly contributed to the mission objective in the Atsabe District.

The delegation conducted negotiations with the local Militia. While this was going on the helicopter made a number of trips back to Dili. On these trips they carried almost all the UN personnel, all the locally employed staff and the ballot boxes. Permission for this had been obtained early in the negotiations. A guarantee was also obtained that the remaining international staff, 3 CivPol and 2 DEOs, would be allowed to depart Atsabe after the delegation left.

The helicopter made a final visit to Atsabe late in the afternoon. The delegation boarded taking with them the last ballot box. There was no room for any other person and there was insufficient time for the helicopter to return before dark. Phil Hunter, Max KNOTH, the two Thai Police,Mr. James BREW(Australia), Mr. Rindert LEEGSMA (The Netherlands), the last two both being Atsabe based UNVs, volunteered to remain and drive the vehicles to Gleno.

Shortly after the last helicopter departure Phil Hunter was informed by the local Militia leader that although he had guaranteed their safe departure from Atsabe, this did not include any guarantee the Militia between Atsabe and Gleno would let them through the various villages they occupied. Included in this was the village of BoboiLeten. Phil then entered into further negotiations with the local TNI sergeant and POLRI leader. Eventually the TNI sergeant agreed to accompany the convoy to Gleno and to negotiate the way through the various Militia groups. They left Atsabe about 4.30 p.m.

Gleno

While negotiations had been going on in Atsabe, other negotiations had been taking place in Gleno. At the direction of the Commissioner and with the assistance of Captain Ari I arranged to have direct negotiations with the Militia leaders in the presence of the Bupati at his home. Their body language as they walked in left me with grave doubts as to whether an agreement could be reached for the convoy to depart Gleno. After almost one hour of talking backwards and forwards I realised they had a new concern. They were all worried the UN was going to immediately leave East Timor and leave them to repercussions and revenge from the rest of the population. They were now 'prisoners ' of their own propaganda. It was also obvious they already realised what the outcome of the Popular Consultation was going to be.

By offering to make myself a 'hostage' in any location they determined I got the message across that UNAMET WAS STAYING. Once convinced of this their concern changed. Now they were worried the UN personnel would assist the independence groups to attack them. At this time, I provided examples to them of incidents CivPol had investigated, where at least some of them had direct involvement, which demonstrated our ongoing professional impartiality. Captain Ari strongly supported every example I gave and at least two of the Militia Leaders knew exactly what I was speaking about. This included the one who had been present when I had investigated the armed robbery with Captain

Ari, and he spoke with the others. I gave them an undertaking this professional impartiality would continue.

As part of guaranteeing a continuing presence of CivPol in the district I informed them a prime reason I had so many CivPol in the convoy was to make sure I got the vehicles we would need brought back to Gleno. They readily understood any vehicle without a driver would not return from Dili.

After nearly three hours of negotiations they agreed the convoy could depart. While they requested that they be able to physically see me after the convoy departed, they did not insist I become a hostage.

I was also asked could I make arrangements for some of them to go to villages near the Falantil cantonment and bring their families back to Gleno. I told them I could offer no guarantees other than I would speak to Falantil and if a CivPol escort would help then I would provide that as well. As the meeting broke up their attitude was completely different to when they arrived. Each of them warmly wished me well and shook my hand.

When I returned to HQ with this agreement there was an immediate 'charge' of people to board the vehicles. I checked as there was one person I really wanted to be part of this departure, Helen. I found her, ready to go in her own vehicle. I went up and shook her hand.

She looked surprised and said 'that is the independence handshake'.

I said, 'I know and now I do not have to be impartial.'

In the rest of the vehicles were the majority of DEOs, whose job was now complete: locally employed staff, a variety of international observers, some local families and a CivPol presence. The CivPol presence provided at least a perception of security in the minds of some of the others in the convoy. As I had told the Militia leaders my secondary motive for having so many CivPol driving the vehicles was to have them return, with vehicles, to Gleno for later operations.

A quick briefing for the CivPol who would be going with the convoy and an immediate attempt for the convoy to depart. Before the first vehicle in the convoy had travelled 100 metres it came to a stop. This time there was a TNI vehicle blocking the road. It quickly became apparent I should have somehow had a TNI representative in the negotiations. So, there was a further period where I negotiated with the TNI sergeant who was with that vehicle. In a reasonable timeframe, he agreed to allow the convoy to depart once he had examined each vehicle to make sure there were no independence leaders attempting to escape. With him I walked along the full length of the convoy as he looked into each vehicle. Once we had walked up and down the convoy, he said that he would get his vehicle out of the way and the convoy could depart. What he did not know, and in fact neither did I at the time, was two independence leaders where well hidden amongst the luggage in the rear of two vehicles. This method of hiding was also used on the next two convoys that left, one the next day and another the day after.

The convoy eventually departed Gleno about 5.30 p.m. with 195 persons on board, plus the two carefully hidden pro-independence leaders. The convoy's arrival in Dili about 7.30 p.m. received extensive international media coverage.

About 8 p.m. on 31 August 1999 the small convoy from Atsabe arrived safely in Gleno. They had negotiated a number of Militia roadblocks. I don't think there has ever been a time when I was so glad to see and greet friends.

I had thought of taking them to the Guest House. But it was empty. The family that ran it, and James Bond, were never seen by us again. The following day we found all the shop keepers had left Gleno. Nothing was open.

3 photos of the first convoy.

All personnel were now in the next place of relative safety. All the CivPol had been working in extremely dangerous and tense conditions without a rest or proper meal since 4 a.mm on 30 August, or earlier. In both Dili and Gleno there was still to be further effort required before they would get their first rest.

It was time to telephone Margaret. I was certain she and the families of all the others would be worried. I could now tell her they were all safe and she could pass on the message.

Early in the conversation she said 'Were you scared?'

That gave me pause. I really had not considered it. My answer was 'No, I was too busy and too…angry.'

Left: Phil Hunter in Gleno with repaired front door in the background.
Right: Tommy, Yuri, Jim, Brett and Me

Following is an extract from the Commonwealth of Australia House of Representatives Votes and Proceedings Hansard of Tuesday, 21 September 1999

Mr TIM FISCHER (Farrer) (7.00 p.m.)

The bravery of unarmed people in adding to the integrity of the ballot by dint of sheer courage in extraodinary circumstances had been demonstrated time and time again in the days sinse the ballot, but particularly in a place called Gleno where there were many incidents on polling day. In fact. the polling place had to be closed for one hour when Militia entered and fired their guns into the air.

But it was the next day and overnighte after the polling place closed that the ballot boxes were secured and a CivPol team in the area, lead by Geoffrey Hazel, had to stand guard on those ballot boxes. The collections were to take place by helicopter. Imagine the scene: they decided to switch to a creek bed to load there ballot boxes into the helicopters in order to get the ballot boxes safely away, because at that stage the Militia were after those ballot boxes. They wanted to destroy the integrity of the ballot in the Gleno area.

Suddenly the helicopter landed, but there was a delay in opening the doors and proceeding with the loading. This lead to the disaster where the Militia came running down the creek bed, firing shots and causing the helicopter to lift off and commence a holding pattern some distance away. At this point, the CivPol team led by Geoffrey Hazel and others stood their ground and with no arms whatso ever and surrounded those ballot boxes in distinctly blue colours. It amazed the Militia that the CivPol team did not clear out and allow them to attack those ballot boxes. A critical stand-off occured. The Militia held their guns. They subsequently backed off, the ballot boxes were reloaded into vehicles, taken to a separate landing zone for the helicopters, subsequently loaded and got back to Dili where I saw 850 ballot boxes in the counting compound just near the Dili airport.

Geoffrey Hazel and the many others involved including Paul Morris, Don Barnby, Peter Watt, Wayne Corbett, Rob Mills, Randy Martinet and Jim France, were just part of a huge grouping of volunteers from right around the world who did so famously well and were so courageous in bringing about the result, the ballot, and very clearly the integrity of that ballot.

It was after midnight before the day finally came to an end. My Russian MLO friend, Yuri, told me he was moving in with me. The MLO's house was now a little crowded with five of them living there. Mine was now not so crowded. Saku had left on the convoy and Diana had moved in with Allessandro.

So Yuri and I went back to the house together. He had one of those portable shower buckets with him. So the first thing was heat some water and shower. After I finished I put together a bit of a meal for the two of us while Yuri had his shower. Before sitting down to eat he went into what was now his bedroom and came out with a half bottle of vodka.

' You need this and I 'vont' it.' he said. The bottle was empty when we went to bed.

CHAPTER 25

POST BALLOT

In the days 1 to 3 September CivPol in Gleno, including all the Australians, took two more smaller convoys to Dili. These convoys carried almost all the remaining local staff, all but two of the international civilian staff and other East Timorese who needed or wanted to be taken to a safer place. Included in these were two East Timorese who Mbaye had persuaded Brimob to keep safe and then he quietly slipped them into the rear of two UN vehicles. CivPol continued to be adept at packing the rear of a Land Rover Discovery so a concealed area was created large enough to hide an individual.

The second convoy included both the NZ CivPol; they were due to leave East Timor almost immediately as they were required as part of the security for the upcoming Commonwealth Heads of Government (CHOGM) meeting being held in New Zealand.

Allessandro told me he was going on the third convoy, taking Diana with him, because they wanted to see the counting of ballots. Ballots from all of East Timor were being counted in the one location and the only result to be released would be the final total figure. This was an attempt to conceal how each district, or even village, voted. As soon as this convoy departed Gleno I contacted JOC and requested they keep both Allessandro and Diana in Dili. The fewer civilians I had to worry about the better.

Once they knew Allessandro was not returning the boys from the Bad Manor moved into his house, two houses from me. Everywhere they went they took the 'beer' fridge with them. Gultom had also suggested because of its relative isolation remaining at Bad Manor was not a good idea.

Outside HQ before departure of 2nd convoy with Wayne and Rob.

All we had left now were the CivPol, MLOs, the Security Officer and the Field Service Officer, who was not going anywhere because he had signed for all of the UN equipment in our HQ. After discussion with JOC both Phil Hunter and Max Knoth would return to Ermera instead of the original intention to deploy them elsewhere.

The sound of gun shots and fires being started became a normal occurrence every night. There seemed to be no one around for these shots to be fired at. As far as I was concerned, they were just more attempts at intimidating us. Maybe it was just to wear us down physically because it definitely made sleep difficult. Security threats kept changing so we often slept in different places. From this developed the self-allocated nickname the

'Ermera Turtles', we carried our homes on our back and slept in a different place each night.

All CivPol not involved in the convoys commenced attempting to patrol in and around Gleno. Initially the 'imported' Militia completely blocked all roads and forced the patrols to turn back. Early on the morning of 3 September the 'imported' Militia were no longer visible in our area. Although it would not be long before they, or someone similar, would be back.

CHAPTER 26

The Announcement

Late afternoon of 3 September both Dili HQ and Gultom contacted me. Dili wanted to make sure on the next morning we would be all together with security as this was when the results would be announced. Gultom was even more concerned and directed all UN staff relocate to POLRI Headquarters compound by 5 a.m. the next morning. After brief discussions it was agreed we would all move into Polri HQ before nightfall, no point disturbing our sleep more than it already was by having to get up before dawn. We packed all our belongings and moved into the police compound. The fridge came too. We remained in that location, feeling like hostages, until late in the afternoon of 4 September.

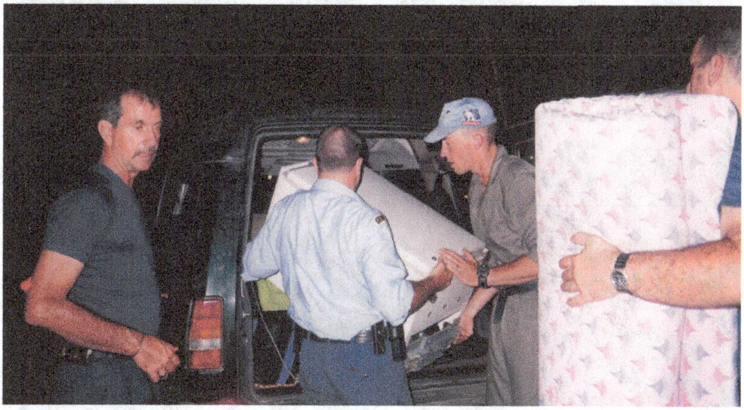

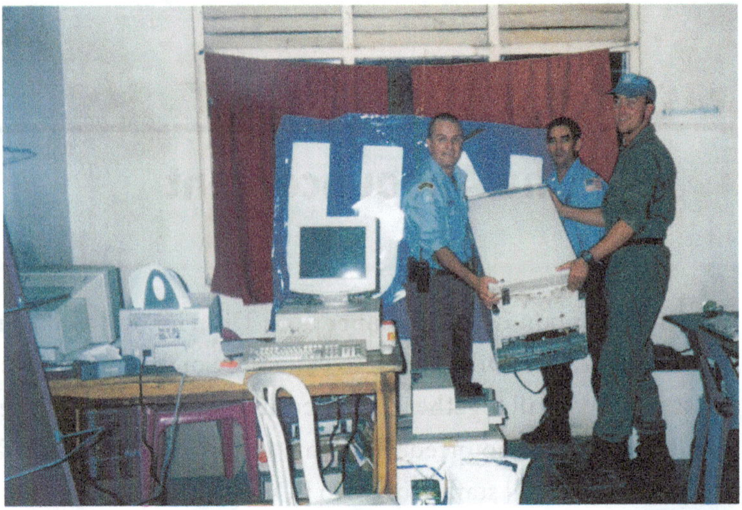

Moving the fridge and hostages in Polri compound.

Final Letter Home — Announcement of Result

At different times during that day I put together the following letter home. The grammar, punctuation and spelling are exactly as they were written at the time -

Well now we wait — it is 9.48am and the results have been announced. We moved into the local police HQ last night — after the information came out the results would be released today. Gultom put me up in his own house — meant I didn't have to sleep on the floor in a room full of snorers. Although somebody got to use the mattress I brought down. Fortunately cooked a good meal last night — and drank the last of the Glen Morange- it lasted well I thought. When I got into his house last night, I turned the radio off — first time in the while time I have been in Gleno. But knew that if anything happened, he and I would be the first two notified. this morning Mrs Gultom cooked nase goreng and omelette for breakfast — a very big meal, but I ate the lot. Now all the UNAMET staff are in a very solid room in the centre of the police compound. There is security all around the compound and Gultom has brought all his people in — but still this is worse than the past days — nothing is happening at the moment but just sitting and waiting is already getting on everyone's nerves — the boys want to get out there and do something — and to be very honest I would be happier doing exactly the same thing.

Now I will try and remember everything that has happened and at least that will fill in a lot of time.

Sunday morning, 29 August, I started work at 6am, it was the last day and there was a lot to do — had an early morning briefing with the boys based in Ermera and then they went off and re-joined their teams. Then the boys from out in the sub regions started arriving — each group to pick up extra vehicles and their ballot papers. Each team had to be briefed and got rolling back to their locations — all were buoyant, confident and looking forward to the events that we were to be part of. The rest of the day was spent at meetings — within UNAMET, a last go over everything, was there anything that we had forgotten; with Gultom — just a final check; with the local authorities — guarantees given for peace on the next day. I slipped home at 6pm, had a hot bath and gathered my sleeping gear, put on a clean uniform. Back to the office at 7pm — staying there overnight as it was a 4am start on the next morning — also we had the ballot papers — there were 3 of us there, with a platoon of Brimob providing external security. Did the final checks with everyone at 8pm — all locked down, safe and ready — climbed into bed, stretcher, myself about 8.45pm — must have just fallen asleep when the phone rang- although this sounds funny it was true — on the line was a 'lady from Spain' just ringing up to wish us the very best and good luck for Polling Day — that was almost unbelievable. Anyhow we got back into bed, after a cigarette and a short chat. Once again just falling asleep when this time the radio went off — it was Phil at Atsabe. There was automatic gunfire near, but not at, their residence. I manned the radio till 2am — when Jim took over — crawled into the cot again, and I do mean crawled — had the stretcher between 2 boxed tables so that I could put the mozzie net up — looked as funny as hell. I think I got back to sleep a bit — but at 3.30am the car doors started slamming — the DEO's were down and getting ready for polling day.

It was early morning of 30 August 1999, a Monday, another moment in history. This day the DEO's were great, on time, keen, doing everything they were told, organised (all except Sako — who was late, just, and I ended up shoving her in the car and saying fix it there — all convoys, 10 of the, hit the road at the right time — the planning had worked- the radio really was going — no rubbish, all good operational stuff — but everyone gave one good luck call. As they arrived at their polling sites, they started calling in the numbers who were waiting- just about everywhere had almost all the voters waiting when they arrived — the people were determined. As it settled down, and they were all calling in that they had opened I drove down to the Gleno polling site- they had just under 4,000 registered voters and at least 3,500 of them were already there — because of the numbers the crowd control was a bit of a nightmare — so I went back to HQ and got 'Fingers' and Peter Watt (an Aussie who had arrived in country only the day before and going to be on loan to me for 3 days, he's still here — now full time). Dropped them off down there and helped a little — it was an amazing feeling, all these people that risked everything to cast their votes — the whole period had been worth it, all the long hours were paying off.

I went back to the office and checked the radio log — everything was going well just about everywhere — then at 9.27am Randy called in — he had just taken a racatan — homemade gun — off one to the people who had turned up, the person and the gun had been taken away by Polri. Then 10.06am a call from Ari — Pro-autonomy had some complaints at Gleno — so I went to the polling site -! st complaint was that the university students were walking up and down the lines and telling people to vote for independence. Well they were doing that, so I hunted them away. Then there were a whole batches of bitches, I checked each one and found no substance — the woman at the ballot box in Site 1 was looking at how the people were voting; there was a man working there — in polling Site 4 the local staff at the door was telling people to vote independence; there was an international staff member at the door in polling Site 6 and a local telling them to vote independence; no international was working at that site — and so it went on. At one stage I even got Ari to go in and check on the report. He came out and said there was no basis to it — I spoke to a number of international observers and they reported no problems.

I decide to go for a short drive, the town was just about empty, everyone was at the polling site. Then I got a call back to the polling site. I arrived about the same time as Gultom — there was a bunch of Militia in the middle of the square and some behind polling sites 6 and 7. When both Gultom and I turned up — they went over all the old complaints and we added the one that the Militia were intimidating people by yelling in the windows of polling sites 6 and 7. After a lot of this we put Polri at the windows of 6 and 7so that they could hear if anything wrong was being said. The Militia moved away — both Gultom and I were satisfied that everything had settled down — we both went back to our respective headquarters — I started to type the report on the morning — never did get to finish that report.

At 12.20pm shorts were fired at the Gleno polling site — well as fast as I got there, and it was fast — Polri had the area under control and they wouldn't let me in, for my own safety — got me back to Polri HQ until they had it fully secured. Went over a little later and was amazed to see that the people had come back and were lining up again to vote — it was very moving — a team flew in from Dili and after a meeting decided to increase Polri security — offered by Polri — change some practices and re-open. It was not the local Militia who had caused the problem — but a group, under the control of Indonesian Army recent arrivals who had travelled from Dili. Later we were to establish that about 200 of the Aithrak Militia had been involved across various parts of Ermera. At Gleno they had fired 40 or so shots in the air from traditional firearms (hand-made, muzzle loading weapons- to fire them you scratch a short fuse against a matchbox — so they take a long time to load, you never know — after striking the matchbox- when or if they are going to fire- and they could explode in the face of the firer). Then they had thrown a lot of rocks through the thin walls of Polling Sites 1 to 5 — one of the DEOs was hit on the arm — the CivPol did a great job — Peter Watt.

After we got this all settled down — station open and operating again — Gultom and I went to his HQ and set up a joint command post — it wasn't long till we were both very, very busy again. At Mirtutu they reported Militia activity, they wanted their man and his gun back — told them to close and get moving (all but 3 voters on the register had turned up and voted — and we knew the 3 were in hospital). In Estado a group of armed Indonesian Army could be seen not too far from the polling site- in Fatubolo there were Militia on the next ridge line — at Bobo Leten there were Militia in the front of the polling site — at RailacoLehu the Militia were gathering as well. Thank God for experience and Sac Pav training. The radio was almost never out of my mouth as we got everything going — moving convoys from all over the place — directing CivPol to order them to forget their paperwork — do it at the office — just get the car and move it- some took a yelling over r the radio from me before they took any notice. A Militia roadblock was set up between the registration/polling sites at Poetete and Ermera. It became a very busy period — the RailacoLehu site couldn't move until the RailacoLeten Team and escort arrived — then the local staff were attacked at Bobo Leten, this was where the man was eventually to die. As the team was driving out, they reported that the Militia were attaching and beating the local people — another person was killed there. (The Polri have now identified and arrested the murderers). Eventually every team was on the way back to their base. I went back to the UNAMET HQ and started checking everyone in — got on the phone and gave the Joint Ops Centre a briefing. It was not what we had expected — then the team from RailacoLeten arrived- the team from RailacoLehu was not with them — they have refused to leave without their local staff — they believed they would have been killed. Gultom took some police and vehicles and went down and got them and the local staff.

Everyone was back in their base — when all the Atsabe teams had arrived back there had been a lot of automatic gunfire around them — both Max and Phil had done an excellent job — I have reports from a DEO about their bravery — in Gleno the decision to stay at HQ or at home changed a few times — some of the internationals were at home others stayed — the local staff were just outside the building -we got whatever we could for them — issued rations for everyone and we started to settle down for the night. Then shots were fired from outside and the local staff and building were stoned. The CivPol poured out of the building. We got al l the local staff inside. The Brimob arrived, actually fairly quickly, and they wanted us to go back inside. There was no way the boys would have obeyed that order — I said we were staying — and if they couldn't do their job, we could take their guns and do it for them — but no matter what no one was getting at our people. (later Lt Audie came and saw me — he said that his respect for the CivPol had gone up so much — no way could he have gotten Indonesian Police to do the same thing). I was proud of my boys — the Aussies, Kiwis and Yanks were great.

While we were standing outside, we saw a couple of houses get burnt by the Militia. it would have been so easy to have stopped them.

(I had a half hour sleep just them — today the 4th that is — then Gultom got back from a meeting and said that the local Militia are getting their families together and leaving for West Timor — other reports, we are still looking after Amorin's group — taken in that might indicate the same — we haven't got our hopes up too high yet — but it just might be happening.)

Anyhow on the night of the 30th, actually early morning on the 31st the boys made me get into a car and have a sleep, around 2am. I woke at 4am and stood around the fire that they had lit. Just CivPol and some of the locals — it was a cool morning.

Then it was back to work — talking to Dili — a helicopter was coming at 6.15am to pick up an investigator from Polri to go to Atsabe with the UN Team to investigate the murder. There were still Militia around our HQ, but they weren't doing anything directly against us. At Atsabe they had the UNAMET residence completely surrounded — and they were not the local Militia.

We moved up to the helipad just after 6am — the Polri were there, but immediately in front of them were 9 or 10 Militia, you could see a lot more in the marketplace which was just over the road. We gave the pilot a warning — he got in and out with only a few gestures. But the looks were enough to convince me that they were going to go for our ballots — a decision had also been made to pick up the Hatolia ballots by helicopter — so they were still on the ground — Atsabe still surrounded.

Decided to change the location for pickup of our ballots — do it in the riverbed — loaded the cars up, faced them towards the normal pad — and had a plan to quickly get to the other area. Chopper called in and we went — chopper landed, we were ready to load immediately but some dipstick electoral wanted to check all the paperwork first — Militia had time to get there- no way were they going to get our ballots. They had the 'traditional' weapons, which they were firing. I do have two new very minor scratches on my arm, will not be worth bragging about — but they expected us to bolt — the fact we went straight at them is something they had never seen before — they kept yelling and threatening and throwing rocks (chopper wisely took off) but wouldn't come close enough to let us get our hands on them — typical bullies. Then Brimob arrived — they had to push them hard to get them to do anything, but they eventually pushed them back. Turns out that this was a smarter move than I thought — I couldn't understand how they had got from one landing zone to the other so quickly — well they weren't at the first landing zone — they were waiting by the road just up from HQ — they were going to block us in at both ends. So, with a now very heavy Brimob escort we went to the normal landing field and loaded up in just under 3 minutes — she didn't want to check the paperwork this time — just get back on the chopper and out of there. It went from us to Hatolia — where the pilot identified a new landing site — again fooled the Militia. I then told Brett, after confirming it with Gultom, to move their convoy through Liquicia to Dili — not to come back to Gleno, at least not yet.

Then, later, we got another chopper into Atsabe — this time it landed right behind their house — picked up the ballots, some DEOs and the local staff — got them all out okay — this was mission accomplished — we had all our ballot papers on the way to Dili.

Then more negotiations — I ended up at a meeting with all the pro-autonomy leaders — they wanted to pass on all their complaints — and very interestingly their fears that UNAMET was leaving — we had a convoy ready to go, with a lot of DEOs, no longer required, and local staff who would be targets for

Militia somehow after nearly 3 hours we convinced them that we would investigate all complaints and the we were not leaving. They agreed the convoy could leave. When we got out, we found out the rest of Atsabe — CivPol and 2 DEOs, driving was on the way in. Then more negotiations about the Dili convoy — finally got it underway at 5.30pm — then informed that Hatolia had arrived safely — great news — then stayed with the radio — convoy got to Dili — Atsabe arrived at 7.30pm — everything had finally come off.

Still very tense — another meeting before we received guarantees for safety — everyone went home at 8.45pm on the 31st of August — from 6am on the 29th it had been a long hard time.

Yuri, the Russian naval military liaison officer, moved in with me that night- he had/has a solar shower. we heated the water on the kero stove and had a hot shower. The dinner — rice and bully beef with a Mongolian lamb sauce. Yuri pulled out a half bottle of vodka and we drank it before going to bed.

I September started at 7.30am — shaved and showered and clean uniform — house boy (Seco) left on yesterday's convoy. Spent all day in meetings — going back and forth — the town still deserted — cigarettes getting low — during the night had heard a lot of firing — more houses burnt — got another, smaller, convoy off to Dili -- it was another long day — the boys on both convoys were stuck in Dili — no UNAMET movement allowed there. Still relatively calm for us here. In the evening two locals came and said their houses were going to be burnt — took to Polri. At 7.30pm Ari advised that we move all people out of the Bad Manor — went up there and told them, spoke to Marg on the phone — boys got out at 10pm — we all went to bed — heavy Brimob security on our houses -

***Today** Just another short break — spoke with Joint Operations Centre — all across East Timor the Militia are getting* *out — went outside and watched them leaving here — then one came into Gultom — wanted fuel for his vehicles to get out — I just think it might be working — I think we have won — I'll just wait a bit more — but we are now getting ready to launch our own patrols.*

I did not sign the preceding letter here, because it was not signed at the time. It was a letter with far more detail of the dangers than I had ever been prepared to send home before. But still not as detailed as it could have been.

As the letter said very soon after the result was announced we observed the local Militia loading their families into vehicles and leaving. A number of hours later we saw the actual Militia members return. Later we were told, while they wanted to go to West Timor, they had been given no choice other than to go back, although their families were allowed though.

CHAPTER 27

Final Days

On the night of 4 September, after a strong suggestion from Gultom for us not to be too spread out, we slept in two locations. Some at Regional HQ and others in the close group of 4 houses that included mine. The Brimob providing security on this night did not include any individuals from the original unit, even the NCOs seem to have now gone. There was a small group of Brimob immediately outside each of the four houses. Militia, two groups of about 20 each, were camped at either end of the short street. It was on this night we noticed Militia camps had also been set up at each end of the roadway in front of our HQ.

Brimob Security at house.

Diary entry -Sunday 5.9.99

Early start — can't remember what time — supposed to be patrolling — went with Baldev& RSO to TNI — agreed to patrol to Hatolia and Ermera — MLO, CivPol, Polri and TNI

— went to Gultom. Also, MLO &CivPol patrol to visit Falantil — Gultom agreed to joint patrol- back to office, Baldev with Peter Watt &Mbaye left for Falantil- patrol left to Polri, Polri wouldn't go to Hatolia — went up to discuss — Gultom asleep & not to be woken — very unusual. Discussed with troops — they went to TNI- now TNI will not go at all — without TNI Polri will not go either. Troops saw truck with 20-25 'MILITIA' armed with semi autos driving into TNI — pointed guns at us. My gut feelings are going haywire — boys need something. Agreed to a 2 vehicle 6-person patrol to Ermera- 4 went. On the way passed 2 utes with 6 or 7 'Militia' in each — they seemed surprised to see UNAMET — with full automatics AKs and M16s — pointed at troops — in Ermera they saw TNI and Militia with autos on all streets — got them to come back rapidly — MLOs called in, answer to Militia request is they have a counter offer — told them to get back ASAP — gut feeling getting worse — call from TNI LO to advise that Militia truck parked outside the base — this is a choke point to Dili — talked with JOC, probably 3 or 4th time today — may require heli evac. Baldev got back — no good news — Falantil running out of food — will not let families go without a meeting — letters for Muspeda and KPS — meeting with all troops — held nothing back — very concerned and frustrated — a week of highs and immediate lows is taking effect — plus helplessness. Decided to give it till tomorrow.

Meeting with Gultom, he looked defeated & worn out — said now had only two roles — secure evacuation of Pro-autonomy& protect UNAMET — Ari packing — while with Gultom UN061 and UN062 called in looking for pad to emergency evac under fire — Dili had been told that we were being overrun — called off, but nearly took the option — arranged meeting with Bupati — eventually left office, after a lot of talk with JOC, at 6.15pm went to Bupati's — he has no answers — offered to help every way he can — both he &Gultom expressed concern that food would run out in 2 weeks at most — very concerned, back home — no security — arranged but very surly, Militia at both ends of street — say they want to be close to us because they have heard Falantil will attack — BRIMOB want to be inside for the same reason — gut feeling getting worse. Then BRIMOB told if attack occurs will have to get in vehicles and go to Polres — boys concerned — looks like set up — more talks to JOC — heli evac considered — loaded cars anyway — Ari called —

That afternoon when all patrols were back at HQ, we had a meeting. It was time to let everyone have their say. Everyone was concerned, some a bit more than others. A few were in favour of immediate evacuation. Our two Malaysian police had moved in with the Brimob.

I asked them 'Would Brimob protect us if there was an attack?'

Their answer was a simple 'No'.

While a few wanted to evacuate immediately the majority were prepared to give it a little longer. In the long run it was Don who finished the discussion when he said 'The boss has kept us safe so far. He will know when it is time to go.'

After that I told them I was constantly evaluating our situation. I reminded them that although it did not appear, we were achieving very much, our mere presence was having a positive effect for the safety of locals.

That evening the Brimob security requested we allow them to sleep in the UN occupied buildings. Their reason for this was they had been told Falantil were going to attack and they were frightened for their safety. These Brimob were very young and obviously did not have the training or experience of the original group. With the exception of 2Lt Audi all the remaining members of the original Brimob had left as escort for a convoy of Polri families going to West Timor. Militia in the street expressed similar concerns. They wanted to be close to UN personnel in case Falantil attacked. This was an excuse used in the past to cover assassinations. The feeling in my gut was getting worse and I was remembering discussions with Falantil leaders. I knew circumstances were changing to a point where there was a high probability of this attack being launched.

At 11.30 p.m. that night, 5 September, Ari rang the phone next door and Samulcia came and got me. Ari was with Gultom and he was translating to make sure there was no misinterpretation of the message. He informed me Gultom had been ordered to withdraw all security for UN personnel at midday on 6 September and not see what happened. Both Baldev and Samulcia were in the room with me and we all agreed there was nothing further to be achieved by remaining. Over the telephone I arranged with Gultom and Ari for security to be provided for our evacuation at 8 a.m. 6 September 1999. I also negotiated with Gultom for a TNI escort to be added to the convoy. He queried my trust of his Polri personnel; I informed him I trusted his people, but convoys escorted by Polri had been attacked in the past, while no convoys with a TNI escort had been attacked. He undertook to arrange for a TNI presence in the escort.

I contacted Dili HQ to inform them of my intention to evacuate. Once we left our HQ there was no way we could communicate with Dili until after we were on the Dili side of the mountains. I requested a helicopter to be overhead as a communications relay platform from when we departed until we regained direct radio contact with Dili. The night duty officer, Paul Gant (USA), informed me the helicopter would be provided. A message was passed to all remaining UN personnel to be ready to evacuate at 8 a.m. in the morning. I don't think anyone had a very good sleep that night.

I awoke at 5 a.m., well I got out of bed as there had not been much sleeping with nearby gunfire rattling away all night. Went to our HQ. Contacted JOC Dili again and informed them if security was okay, we would come by road. I asked about the helicopter as a communications platform. The response this time was not what I expected. The new duty officer was saying it was still being considered but it was unlikely to be provided. They were worried it might be needed to evacuate another district, who up till that time had not had much trouble, but it could happen. Pointing out that we WERE having trouble had little effect. He also insisted, in fact ordered me to bring out all UN vehicles with as much of the UN equipment as could be loaded. This got rid of my intention to leave half the vehicles with Polri and have two persons in each of the evacuation vehicles.

Yuri arrived at HQ and gave me the key to the house. While referring to the parentage of our landlords he told me the house was all locked up and if they wanted to get in, they would have to break the door down. I didn't tell him they probably had a second key. I just kept the key he gave me.

I was told our last interpreter, Ismalio, had 'gone to the forest' during the night after he heard we were evacuating. His family had left on the third convoy to Dili. Before the first convoy departed, he told me he would stay with us until we left because he knew we would have the need for an interpreter. I knew exactly where he had gone.

Paul came over to me and said 'Boss we have not always seen eye to eye, but I could not have done what you did.'

At 8 a.m. on the morning of 6 September all remaining UN personnel were gathered at our HQ. The vehicles had been loaded with everything we could carry, much to the pleasure of our FSA. We were ready to leave there and go to Polri and join up with our escort. There was another phone call, this time the JOC calling to check we were about to depart. I asked when we could expect the helicopter. A further discussion took place, with me getting very heated this time, with the duty officer finally stating he would not authorise the tasking of the helicopter to assist us just in case it was needed elsewhere. I eventually gave up and we drove off to Polri HQ in Gleno. I knew we no longer had any communications with Dili. It looks like we were going to be on our own.

He went to the forest on the last night.

Don, Peter and Samulcai

Gultom met me outside his compound and, I believe, sincerely apologised for not being able to maintain our security in Gleno.

After our farewells I was returning to my vehicle when 2Lt Audi marched over to me, halted, saluted and said 'I have a great ambition to serve with you on a UN mission somewhere else in the world'.

I returned his salute and shook his hand. I am sure both Gultom and Audi had been instrumental in keeping me, and the people with me, alive on more than one occasion.

2Lt Audi with Peter Watt

final convoy and Polri escort

As I turned around to get into my vehicle, I heard a very familiar sound — A 'Huey' helicopter. The last convoy from Gleno was now ready to leave with an unarmed UN helicopter, call sign UNO 063, flying top cover and as a communications platform. The pilot informed me he had flown the whole route from Dili to Gleno and saw no roadblocks or other evidence of Militia activity. The helicopter was piloted by Rob Nivison with 'Buck' Gattlatly as the crewman.

When the convoy left Polri HQ the security was provided by two Polri vehicles, each with about six police on board, and one TNI truck with ten men. As we passed their base at the edge of town the TNI truck turned into the base. We did not see them again, but it was now too late to turn back.

During the trip to Dili there was one period where the helicopter was flying a very strange pattern. It was swooping up and down onto ridges on each side of a narrow pass we had to drive through. Much later, in the Brisbane airport stopover on my final trip home from Darwin to Canberra, Rob Nivison was one of a group of people who were there to say hello. He told me the reason for the swooping. They had sighted two manned machine gun nests, one either side of the road. They distracted the machine gunners while the convoy drove past. At that time, he also told me the flight that morning had not been authorised. Paul Gant had passed my request the night before. The crew decided they would be needed and ignored the later order to stay on the ground.

The same helicopter crew had received praise for their efforts in Atsabe by Phil Hunter -

a) Special recognition should be given to the helicopter pilots and crew who, on the 31st of August, transported a delegation from Dili including, Commissioner Alan MILLS and the Commanders of TNI and POLRI, into Atsabe.

Due to UN staff being held hostage in the CivPol residence we were unable to drive to the designated helicopter landing site. The pilots took it upon themselves to improvise and select an area behind the residence to land. This landing enabled the delegation to negotiate the release of local staff and ballot boxes. Subsequently the helicopters evacuated these staff and boxes.

I firmly believe that if those local staff members and the ballot boxes had remained in Atsabe more local staff and quite possibly International staff would have been killed. The actions of the pilots and helicopter crews significantly contributed in saving lives.

Helicopter UNO063 caption on card sent by crew "Geoff: May this guardian angel watch over you and keep you spirits high."

Between the ballot day and our final evacuation from Gleno food had been an issue. There was none available locally so those who remained were restricted to military ration packs and anything left from what they had brought with them. Our supply had consolidated and evenly divided, each received rations for four days. (Perhaps of interest is Gultom kept me supplied with cigarettes from polling day until we left.) We were very good at managing our supplies and when we arrived in Dili, I still had two days rations.

I wrote shortly after in my diary — *'Gultom was genuinely sorry, I hope he survives, a good mate, a good cop.'*

In Dili there were UN vehicles everywhere. Some were reporting shots being fired at them. We arrived at Dili HQ and were immediately turned around and told to go to the transport compound. Got there, shots were fired towards us and we were told to go back to HQ.

We parked the vehicles in the school grounds next to the UN compound. After we walked into the compound there was no one available to inform us of where we should go and what they wanted us to do.

I eventually got a short meeting with someone where I was informed, as the earliest arrivals, Paul and Don would be on the flight out that day. I was also told there were two other spots available on today's flight for Australian police and I had to nominate the two. I selected Max and John.

With the place being so disorganised and little support forthcoming from anyone at HQ I allocated tasks to three individuals to find accommodation, food and water for our entire group.

Not long after those responsible for the tasks headed off one of the Dili based Aussies, Sean Dunne, turned up with cold beer, enough for half a can each. As a group we were just standing there chatting and having sips of beer. The sound of gunfire, single shot and automatic, was a constant backdrop. John Tanti was on the Satphone calling home.

Max Knot said 'You can relax boss. You got us here safely. Someone else is making all the decisions now'.

CHAPTER 28

Later in other Locations

After my evacuation a number of the Ermera CivPol, including Phil Hunter, Brett Swan, John Tanti and Peter Watt remained at the Dili HQ. With them were CivPol from other districts and MLOs, including those from Ermera. This group went through considerable additional trauma in those final days.

Other members of the 1st AFP contingent to UNAMET were allocated to every region in East Timor. In all areas, from arrival to the final evacuation, going to work each day required a deliberate decision to place yourself in danger. There were constant attempts at intimidation and threats of violence. The efforts of the fifty-two Australian police, along with their colleagues from other nations, played a significant part in the success of the primary function of the mission — to conduct the Popular Consultation.

In those other regions I have been made aware of others whose actions went beyond the day to day efforts. Two Australians, AFP officer, Paul McEwan and an MLO, Captain Paul Scholl, have already been recognised with each being awarded a Bravery Medal. Without any thought for their personal safety they entered a crowd of pro-independence supporters and rescued an Indonesian police officer who would have been killed had they not done so.

After we had evacuated Ermera the CivPol in the town of Baucau came under intense Militia efforts to force them to leave. Reading the reports from Baucau, particularly looking at the dates, it is not beyond the realms of probability the Militia who caused us grief moved to Baucau when we evacuated. The efforts of David Bachi and Gregory Corin manning the UN Baucau HQ while under fire played a significant role in the safe evacuation of UN personnel to the airport. At the airport the courage displayed by Christopher Cooper and Paul McEwan in refusing to board the evacuation aircraft until all the locals with them had also been evacuated undoubtedly saved the lives of those civilians.

CHAPTER 29

Back in Darwin

A pain in the arm woke me. A quick check and I realised it was a nurse taking my blood pressure. I felt refreshed. I felt different, strange even. There was still a drip in my left arm, and when I looked, my getaway bag was still right beside the bed. I had a notion I had told someone to put it right there. When I looked to my left, I saw another person lying in bed. I had a vague recollection I knew him. He was an American whose name was Earl.

The nurse said, 'It's good to see you back with us.'

I answered this with a barrage of questions as I tried to figure out what, when, where, how and why. Typical copper you might say. She did what she could to answer my questions. This was my third morning in Darwin Hospital. I had been a medical evacuee from Dili suffering from dehydration and exhaustion. I was now in no medical danger but needed rest.

My recollection of the previous 3 days was vague at the best. I did remember the inside of an aircraft, Earl embarrassing one of the nurses, and people, lots of people. Dragging the memories back was like trying to look through a thick fog.

I remember having breakfast and then fell asleep again. When I woke later there was a pretty high-powered group standing around the bed. Mick Palmer, the AFP Commissioner, Adrien Whiddett, Deputy Commissioner of the AFP, Sonja Jacob, the AFP Psychologist and Klaus Czoban, the AFP Doctor. What I really needed was a cigarette. So, we went out onto the balcony where Sonja provided one for me. The conversation was mixed.

They wanted to know what had happened and I wanted to know if any of my people were still in Timor. That one they answered. Phil, Brett, Peter and John were still there with a number of other members of the contingent.

Later I found out John had volunteered to give up his spot on the aircraft so that my stretcher and I could be placed on board. Brett and Phil had made sure my main bag had gone with me.

Sonja told me she would get some cigarettes and have them delivered to me. The Doc suggested I put on some pants as the view of me sitting in a hospital gown was not so appealing.

I was trying to give them as much information on the final days when someone shook me and suggested I should go back to bed. I had fallen asleep in the chair.

I woke again later that day. A pack of cigarettes and lighter were sitting beside the bed. So, I got myself out and went to the balcony, taking my drip with me. Returning after the cigarette I noticed a sign on the door which stated all visitors had to check with nursing staff before entering. At the same time one of the nurses came down to make sure I was okay. I asked about the sign. She told me they had to put it up because the two of us needed our rest and more CivPol were turning up to see us than was good for either of us. So, the sign went up. Apparently CivPol ignored it. Therefore, on the previous afternoon one of the nurses had stood guard at the door so no one could just walk in. The Assistant Director of Nursing herself had made this arrangement. Apparently even then they had trouble keeping CivPol out.

Next morning, I felt good. I felt even better straight after breakfast when the drip was removed from my arm. I opened my bag and got out a T shirt and boxer shorts which I quickly exchanged for the hospital gown. Now I felt much more comfortable.

The rest of the day was spent with visitors. It was a rare moment when each of us did not have at least one visitor. Most were CivPol, not only Australians and Americans, many of the other nationalities called in as well. There were even a few of the UNVs who called in to see us.

Two of my visitors were members of the second AFP contingent who had arrived in Darwin to be our replacements. Rod Walker brought in a set of civilian clothes for me. The Commissioner had given him a corporate credit card and told him to make sure all of the first contingent had something to wear. Brett Simpson informed me he had just finished negotiations with the nurses, and he would be back at 6 p.m. to pick me up and take me to a function at the Darwin Yacht Club. Amanda Vanstone, our Commonwealth Government Minister, was hosting a function for all of the first contingent then in Darwin. When he picked me up in the evening, he laid down the law to me. The nurses had very sternly informed him, I MUST be back by 10 p.m.

It was a good function. Gave us all a chance to let our hair down just a little. I vaguely remember offering our assistance to the Minister when the next Australian election was held.

Then Brett was pushing me to leave. 'Remember the deadline' he said.

Eventually we arrived back at the hospital at 10.20 p.m. I figured he would probably be in trouble with the nurses, so I apologised to him for being so difficult to get away from party. He told me he knew I would be hard to move so he hadn't been exactly honest about the curfew time. The actual time I was due back was 10.30p.m. So, we just made it.

Shortly after breakfast on the following day one of the senior nurses came in and told me an Australian TV crew were coming to interview Earl for an American current affairs program and they were moving me to another room for a few hours. I told her I wouldn't mind staying and watching. Apparently, that was not to be allowed. Someone, and she would not say who, was worried the crew would realise I was part of the Australian contingent and want to interview me as well. That was not to be allowed.

So, they moved me across the hall into a smaller room, just one bed, with no external windows. After a few hours, actually I was just guessing at the length of time, but it felt like a few hours, I was getting a bit twitchy and decided it was time to get out of that room. It wasn't claustrophobia but the lack of other people that got to me, along with the need for a cigarette.

When I opened the door, I was immediately met by one of the nurses and taken straight to the balcony. While I had that cigarette, she asked me a lot of questions. Somehow, I must have raised concerns in her because she told me she thought I should speak with a professional about my experiences. She added arrangements would be made for a Psychiatrist to see me that day. I did not think there was anything wrong with me, but nurses are very perceptive, and I was happy to go along with her suggestion.

That evening I was watching the 6 p.m. news. The main story was about the ongoing troubles in Dili and how the UN planned to evacuate all their people the next day. At that moment I knew I would be at the airport when they arrived. Somehow. I watched every news program that evening.

The psychiatrist eventually arrived just after a news broadcast at 10.30 p.m. He asked one question. I started to answer it. I had hardly begun the answer when he stopped me.

He said 'I know what is wrong with you.' He got up and walked out leaving me frustrated and angry.

A nurse came in shortly after with one of those little paper cups they put pills in. She told me this was what the doctor had prescribed for me. I didn't even ask what they were I just informed her I would not be taking the pills and I was going to the airport the next morning.

After another attempt to get me to take the pills she left.

Moments later she was replaced by the Charge Nurse for the ward. Again, I refused to take the pills and added I would do physical harm to that psych if he came near me again. I also told her I would be going to the airport the next day. She let it ride at that.

I woke early next morning and turned the TV on for whatever news I could get. Again, the first item was the UN in Dili. There would be no evacuation that day. The UN people had refused to leave unless all the locals who were now under their protection were evacuated as well. I was proud of them. I was upset with myself. I should have still been there.

Around 10 a.m. the Assistant Director of Nursing called in to see me again. She told me once the Psychiatrist had completed his report I would be discharged. She asked me what had happened the previous evening. So, I told her. She laughed and showed me the notes made by the night nurse. There was a simple statement '*the patient was slightly agitated*'. We both had a bit of a giggle at that.

Just after lunch I was discharged, with a report from the psychiatrist in my possession. Although he did not feel the need to see me again.

Brett Simpson picked me up and drove me to The Callum Bay Apartments. The AFP had booked a number of apartments and/or rooms around the city. All the AFP members coming out of East Timor were put up for 4 or 5 days at AFP expense. This period of time allowed for the conduct of debriefing sessions and for individuals to return to somewhat near normality. The Commissioner himself was running the operational debrief sessions and everyone had an individual debrief session with the AFP Psychologist. In addition, an arrangement had been made for everyone to have a one-hour relaxing massage treatment.

The next morning, I went to one of the Commissioner's debrief sessions. As I had already spoken with him, I sat back and let the others have their say. It was interesting to hear the variations of experience depending on which region the individuals had been in. Also, their experiences over the immediately preceding days in the Dili compound.

I got the one question I really wanted answered in a direct talk with the Commissioner after the group debrief. I was not going to be allowed to immediately return to East Timor. This applied to every member of the 1st Contingent, not just me. He also told me I was booked on a flight home the next afternoon.

I arranged with Sonja to have my psych debrief late that afternoon at the apartment. Sonja bought the pizza and I had purchased a good bottle of red. We sat on the verandah looking out over Callum Bay. While I believed I was perfectly alright the session did go for a long time. Even after she left there was one issue still concerning me. We still had people in East Timor, and I was going home. It did not seem right.

Later I wandered down the street and ran into some other CivPol at a local drinking hole. This was a different type of debrief and one worth having. But it did not help in my major concern. When I went to bed it was still going through my head. Why was I going home?

I woke at 3.30a.m. hungry and with an answer. I would stay in Darwin till everyone was back. Of course, I would have to check with Margaret to make sure she was happy with my decision. I saw that as being more difficult than having to tell the AFP. Decision made I resolved my other problem, hunger, by opening one of the two ration packs in my bag and cooking up a meal. I slept a lot better after that. Later Max Knoth asked if I would give him the second ration pack so that he could give it to his nephew. This was an easy request to meet.

In the morning I rang Margaret and explained to her what I wanted to do.

She said, 'I was surprised when you told me you were coming home so soon.'

She knows me very well. Then came the issue of how do I tell the AFP and cancel the airline ticket. The previous afternoon Sonja had given me her mobile number and I knew she was staying at the same hotel as the Commissioner and the Deputy. So, I rang her. I told her to pass on to the Commissioner I would not be returning home that day but would be staying in Darwin until all of our people were out of East Timor. I added if they were not happy with that then I would take immediate leave and remain in Darwin at my own expense. For a little while she tried to talk me out of it. Didn't work. So, she said she would pass the message on.

Later I caught a taxi to their hotel. Just after I arrived, while I was figuring out how best to get hold of one of the bosses, the Deputy came walking down the stairs. He came straight over to me with a list in his hands. He quickly explained this was the latest withdrawal process for the UN still in Dili. It covered a two-week period with names of some AFP members against each departure. Peter Watt was listed in the final group. The deputy told me if the withdrawal extended out beyond that period the AFP would fly me home and then return me to meet every arrival. He then asked me if this met what I wanted. I thanked him. He checked I had a corporate credit card and told me to use it to hire a car for myself and to stay in the apartment. As people came out, I would get different apartment mates. The final one was Peter Watt.

For the next two weeks I met every flight arriving from Dili and saw off every flight taking people home. One of these homeward bound flights had included Andrew Clarke. His interpreter was also at the airport to see him off. After the flight left, he asked for a lift back to town. On the way he told since being in Darwin his opinion had changed and he now believed in integration. This took me that much by surprise I hit the brakes and pulled over. I looked straight at him.

He smiled and said 'With Australia.'

During this period, I spent some evenings with one or more of the Ermera Turtles. On one such evening Phil Hunter thanked me for the wine. When I gave him a very dazed look, he told me that just before they took me off on the stretcher, I had told him there was a bottle and a half of red in my bag and to make sure they drank it that night. Apparently, they enjoyed it. That same evening someone also told me they had put the key to my car in one of my bags. Thought I might have liked it as a memento. I still have it, with the house key.

On the afternoon of 13 September, I was informed of the decision to fly all remaining personnel out of East Timor the next day. This included all of the local people who were in the UN compound.

14 September 1999 and this morning I dressed in uniform. Full CivPol uniform including the blue beret. I ran into Ray Johnson and he decided to go with me. We drove out to the RAAF base arriving just before the first flight landed. Australia had committed its fleet of RAAF Hercules aircraft to back up the UN aircraft in evacuating everyone from Dili.

As each aircraft landed the RAAF ground crews worked liked demons. Unloading the aircraft, getting the people onto buses, checking and refuelling before each of them took off for a second trip to Dili. I don't think there had ever been a time where aircraft like this had been turned around so quickly.

Buses took the Timorese from each flight past us and onto the camp where they would be staying until arrangements could be made to move them further into Australia. We made sure we were by the road as they were leaving in the buses. They waved. They smiled. I still wished I was back in Dili.

After the first aircraft was on its way back the RAAF movement control people told me the information they got from the pilots was there were too many people to be able to get everyone out in just one day. Then the second aircraft had more people than the first. The third had more than the second. And so on. These crews were packing in as many people as possible. The penultimate flight had more passengers than had ever before been carried on a Hercules C130. They had the last of the East Timorese who had been in the compound. No one was left behind.

The movement control people told us the last flight was in the air. It was carrying all the international personnel. My heart lifted. There had been no reports of any losses. However, there was a change. Because it was full of international staff the flight would be landing at the international terminal so the people could be processed through customs and immigration.

Ray and I got in the hire car and drove around to the international terminal. Ray asked me how I was going to know where they would be coming out. For a little while I thought about it.

I said 'We are in uniform and I am going to meet them at the air bridge.'

I don't know how I am going to do it but if I could get past the Militia, I can overcome that obstacle.

When we arrived at the international terminal it was all paid parking. Except for the hire car areas and I was driving a hire car. Another problem out of the way.

We were walking towards the main terminal entrance when one of the side doors opened and one of the customs people called out 'I think you want to be in here.'

Another problem just disappeared. We were shown upstairs to the arrival room. Directly in front of me were the customs and immigration barriers. On the other side I could see the top of the gangway. Adrien Whiddett, the AFP Deputy Commissioner, was there and I went outside with him to watch the aircraft land and taxi up to the terminal. Back inside and the Deputy told me they are your people, get on the other side of the barriers so you can meet them as they come through the door. Customs and immigration people just opened the gates for me.

I stood there and met every one of them as they came in. Yuri was there along with many others I knew. Then Peter Watt came through the door. We threw our arms around each other.

Peter said 'Boss I just knew you would be here.'

I met everyone else before we headed off.

The next few days were much the same except for one morning. A small group of us had decided it was time to go and see the Timorese who had been on those flights. They were in a secure camp and processing was about to start. There were a couple of potential issues. The major one being there was not supposed to be any unauthorised visitors. I thought, simply put on the uniform again. Another concern we expressed to each other was how would the Timorese receive us? Would they think we had abandoned them? Would they want to have anything to do with us? This was a genuine concern held by all.

On arrival the private security people did not want to let us in. Behind them I saw the Deputy Commissioner of the Northern Territory Police, I had known him when he was an Assistant Commissioner in the AFP. He saw me and came over. There were now no barriers to us going in, seeing whoever we wanted and staying until we decided to leave.

Once inside we were swamped. Every concern we had was gone. They were so pleased to see us, and I believe they were more concerned about us than we had been about them. Amongst those I met was Nicolai, our former janitor at Gleno HQ, who was very surprised to see me. He had been told I had a heart attack in Dili and thought he would never see me again. We had lunch, each of us with people we knew, before leaving in the afternoon. It had been good therapy for all of us.

That was it. Apart from a four-person group now in the Australian Consulate building in Dili all of UNAMET had been withdrawn.

The final debriefs were held and arrangements made for all remaining 1st Contingent AFP personnel to fly home. The Commissioner's group left. I was the last to have a massage and then I paid, with my corporate card for a few more than 52 massages they had been told to bill to the AFP. It seems some of our people had taken a few CivPol from other nations with them. With them all gone there was no way I could tell who and really, I did not care.

It was my turn to go to the airport from the final flights home. The 1st Contingent had left Darwin and the 2nd AFP Contingent was there to take our place, there was now no chance I would be returning to East Timor in the near future.

I made a conscious decision to travel in uniform. I had an aircraft change in Brisbane. Before we landed one of the cabin crew told me I should go to the landside of the airport as there were people waiting there to see me. When we landed, I went down and my son, Leigh, and his partner, Rachel, were there to meet me. Also, there was Irene 'Skip' Menhennit, from the 1st Contingent, and Rob Nivison, the pilot of UNO 063. It was a short but very emotional get together.

On to Canberra and this time Margaret was there to meet me. But she was not alone. There was a good group including the Deputy Commissioner and the Assistant Commissioner for ACT Policing. But no media.

I was asked where the name 'Turtles' come from. I started to explain when Margaret cut in.

She said 'No, it was because you stuck your necks out too... often.'

With the exception of Margaret to me the most important person there was Don Barnby. After welcomes from everyone Don and I went to the baggage carousel to wait for my bags. We stood there, arms around each other's shoulders, saying nothing, tears running down our cheeks. Words were unnecessary. We had been through a lot together. We were alive and home.

CHAPTER 30

My Aftermath

I was home. At least physically I was home, though part of me wanted to be back in Ermera. I was yet to realise the experience had changed me. In fact, I denied I had changed at all, at least to myself. In later reflection I would realise the experience had changed me. I doubt anyone could have gone through those experiences and emerge unchanged. There is no way to avoid it, playing a part in writing history in a violent environment changes you, hopefully for the better.

Now I was having mixed feelings. There was definitely a degree of self-satisfaction, perhaps even pride, in getting the job done. It had been far from easy. Everyone played their part. Security was an issue from beginning to end. I also had some negative feelings.

I was blaming my body for letting me down which led to my medical evacuation while the people I worked with had to remain.

Being honest, I also had a slight concern I had been the cause of the attacks during our final 8 days in Ermera. Were they launched because of the planning I had undertaken? To counter this, I told myself if I hadn't done the planning the attacks would have been successful, and the process compromised. But a little doubt is still there.

After speaking with many of the other members of the contingent I knew some of them had personal issues. Many felt they had let the Timorese down by leaving when they did. In this one area I was absolutely certain I was not affected. With a wonderful group of determined CivPol not only had we got the job done but they had stayed with me for 8 days after the threats became actions and it got really serious. I had only ordered them to evacuate when there was no choice. Staying meant we would have been killed within 24 hours. Of that I have no doubt. Therefore, us leaving made no difference. There was nothing more we could have done.

There were those who came out of this experience with dislike of everything Indonesian. To them all evil in East Timor could be directly worked back in some way to Indonesian authorities. Here is another area where I have a different opinion. I saw good and bad amongst the Indonesians I dealt with. I, like more than a few others, would not be alive now except for help from Indonesians.

Then there were those who saw all East Timorese as noble and brave individuals. Yes, there were some who fitted this idea. However, when you look at the violence which did occur, most of it was done by East Timorese. The Militia did not take much prompting to do what they did. So, there were good and bad amongst them as well.

Both the East Timorese and the Indonesians were just human beings possessed of all the variables and different personality types that goes with being human. I became friends with individuals of both nationalities, and I had enemies in both as well.

In another area I was beginning to understand how Major Harry Smith, D Company 6 RAR commander at the Battle of Long Tan, felt for all those years. While all in UNAMET had done a great job, it is highly doubtful the UNVs, who were absolutely essential to the conduct of the electoral process but completely untrained for response to armed aggression, would have stayed to carry out the process without the presence of, and the example set by, the unarmed CivPol. To my mind recognition was needed. A general recognition for the entire contingent and, more importantly, special recognition for a few who, with courage and valour, had ignored actual and significant risks to their own lives to save others.

In the early days after our withdrawal I was surprised at how little media information was being generated by the AFP. Then INTERFET went in and the Defence Force media took centre stage. From my perspective an opportunity had been missed. There were occasions when a journalist turned up at social gatherings I was having with contingent members. I always answered their questions. Sometimes a report appeared in print. Sometimes it did not.

I made a number of approaches to senior persons in the AFP in an attempt to get the recognition I believed the people had earned. Generally, I was put off with comments like 'we are looking into it'. I had a strong impression recognition was not part of any agenda.

Eventually I offered to gather evidence from the contingent members and present a package to the AFP. I was given the okay to go ahead. After I sent a message to all members, 38 of the 52 provided a written reply. There were a few others who gave a different reason for not wanting to be part of the process. The documents came in a variety of formats including, 'official' AFP report style, email messages and letters. In general, each included evidence from an individual who had witnessed exceptional actions by another or others. I attached these to a draft recommendation I prepared to go to The Australian Honours and Awards Secretariat, Government House for the award of a Group Bravery Citation. Included with those documents were my request that consideration be given to certain persons for individual awards. I forwarded these documents through to AFP headquarters.

In 2001 eight Group Bravery Citations were awarded to the members of the 1st AFP contingent in UNAMET. There was a separate award and citation for each UN District in East Timor. While I have still to give up in getting proper recognition for certain individuals, I am proud of the team I was part of and proud to share this award with them. They are amongst the best Australia has to offer.

How did we do it? I am not exactly sure. However, when you have no actual power, making a request is far more likely to achieve success than making a demand. Offering a suggestion, or a different option is more likely to be accepted than telling someone how it should be done. Showing respect is a good start to having respect shown back to you. Trusting your people generally makes a positive difference in their efforts.

If you ask me now, knowing what would happen, would I do it all again. All you need to do is consider the refrain of 'Fernando' and you will know the answer is simple. Yes.

POSTSCRIPT

I started the book some years ago and stopped as it was not showing the emotion I wanted. It was more like a police report than a story people would want to read. Perhaps I cannot show the necessary emotion in mere words. However, I have not only restarted, but finished. Hopefully, instead of trying to cover a broad history of the entire UNAMET mission I have concentrated on a few of the people who helped make history happen. Along with trying to include the emotions of the time there is also some of the day to day living so that you get an idea of what it was like being a peacekeeper. This story I know from personal involvement, information in my diary, letters home and written documents prepared at the time and provided to me by others. It has been the story of a group of Australian Federal Police officers who joined with other international police (UN CivPol), Military Liaison Officers (MLOs), employees of the United Nations, United Nations Volunteers (UNVs) and the locally employed UN staff who served in the Ermera District. Similar situations and efforts were repeated in all regions of East Timor. In my mind it was one of the most important things I had ever done. The people who worked with me in that troubled place deserved to have their story told.

In the beginning the potential size of the project and my determination to not only get it right but also to make it something that people would want to read, was daunting. Over the following months I sought out and discussed the project with a few others. Their input varied. Some suggested I forget it, definitely no good for 'the career' in the Australian Federal Police because it may impact on Australian-Indonesian diplomatic relations or embarrass individuals. But there were far more who were supportive. Many who had suggestions about what could or should be included. Some of the areas I thought about or came from others were —

To tell how the Australian Government had come of age internationally. An important aspect of this had been the Australian government's ability to negotiate, adapt to, and manage ongoing developments in Indonesia and East Timor. The implementation phase of an international intervention was essentially driven from Australia. Full Australian support played a significant part in UNAMET being established and deployed in a historically short time frame. Later, when the violence commenced after the majority choice for independence was announced, Australia was ready. Two weeks after the announcement all but four members of UNAMET had been evacuated and the deployment of the UN approved and Australian-led International Force East Timor (INTERFET) troops had commenced. Never before has there been an UN-endorsed mission launched only five days after Security Council approval. In fact, regardless of ongoing violence, the Security Council of the United Nations has always taken much longer to approve intervention, never mind having boots on the ground.

Some suggested I write about Portuguese colonisation, particularly those who had served on missions in other former Portuguese colonies. Part of this was the methodical and manipulative means used by the colonial regime to keep the different indigenous groups in a state of almost constant internal conflict. Depending on who you spoke with there were 31 or 33 different dialects of Tetum, the indigenous language. Those who said 31 indicated they did not count two groups who were partly in East Timor, but their greatest numbers were in West Timor. During the Portuguese time whenever a group looked like becoming strong enough to possibly challenge them, a situation would be created which encouraged another group to form a coalition and so return the balance wanted by the colonial masters. This deviousness enabled them to keep control with only a small colonial military force. One result of this is the development of a culture within East Timor which saw violence as the first and primary means to resolve disagreements. Any group finding themselves on the losing side of a matter looked around for a stronger ally to turn the situation around. After Portugal decided to relinquish their control and the first democratic election was held there was one winning and some losing parties. As they had no cultural history of the peaceful change of power in a democratic system the losers followed their tradition and sought assistance of a nearby powerful neighbour. Within Indonesia this request for assistance gave them at least a semblance of legitimacy for the military action they undertook. Indonesian authorities, possibly familiar with similar techniques used by Dutch colonists against them, adopted Portuguese methods of control after their 'military intervention' into East Timor in1975. On the positive side, because alliances could and did change so frequently, forgiveness came quickly, and grudges were rarely held for any length of time.

Over-the-top media reporting of the brutality by the Indonesian authorities was another strongly stressed theme. It cannot be denied Indonesian authorities were involved in the organised violence towards East Timorese deemed to support independence both before and after the vote. There are two matters which should be considered in this; firstly there were Timorese who willingly participated in this violence, and; later investigations, particularly with regard to the post ballot period, established the number of victims involved where nowhere near as many as those presented by the media at the time as 'fact'.

The enmities that had grown during the continuous guerrilla warfare of the preceding 24 years also played a part. Outside of Indonesia there has been little, if any, consideration of the losses suffered by the Indonesian troops involved. During my time in East Timor I had the opportunity to discuss that period with individuals from both sides. The impression I gained was the number of Indonesian victims (military, police and civilian) were far higher than ever acknowledged by Indonesian authorities, if they had acknowledged them at all. One Falantil leader I spoke with pointed out to me the number of modern weapons they had accumulated and told me most of them had been taken from the bodies of Indonesian soldiers. A senior Indonesian Army officer compared their feelings to what he had heard Australian soldiers felt at the end of the Vietnam War.

Danger existed for us in East Timor and it was increased for us by some of our supposed friends in Australia. These included the vociferous claims by some individuals who, seeking short term political gain, presented their perception of the villainy of the Indonesian authorities. In every instance the media grasped, promoted and pushed these interpretations of events. What they all failed to take into account was the Indonesian authorities actively circulated these vitriolic statements as obvious anti-Indonesian sentiment from Australia. Thus, every time I saw, heard, or read any of them I felt the target on my body grow larger and brighter.

Finally, there is the totality of the UNAMET story. Some suggested I make sure it was a 'warts and all' story. Any operation put together as quickly as this one was bound to have some of what some people will refer to as 'warts'. There are others who will have a different opinion on what is or is not a 'wart'. But the important thing is the people involved overcame those issues and a myriad of other problems to get the job done. That story is more important than focusing on 'warts'. Across the whole of the mission more than enough occurred during those few brief months to fill volumes, far more than just one book. I lack the direct and detailed knowledge necessary to properly present the entirety of the mission. But I do know the story of Ermera District.

Another suggestion was to explain the reasons why people, particularly UNVs, volunteered to be part of this mission. I did not know each individual well enough to understand what motivated them but from different discussions the majority would fall into either one of the following categories or, more likely, a combination of a few categories.

Some, including some UNVs, were there for the money. It may seem a little strange for a volunteer to be there for the money as there was no 'salary' as such. However, all received a daily allowance from which they had to make their own accommodation and feeding arrangements. For the UN this was a far more efficient system than creating and operating a complex logistical system to provide everything for those involved. The amount varied from mission to mission and always included allowance for hardship and danger. In the case of UNVs they received an additional percentage above that paid to CivPol and MLOs. So, money was one motivating force for some, from all components. Others had different motivations;

- for some it was seen as a steppingstone to full time employment in the UN;
- similarly, there were those who saw it as being good on their CV for other areas;
- the adventure of it all was also an attraction;
- there were many with a variety of altruistic reasons;
- a few held the hope of meeting a future partner;
- there were those who had the skills sets which they wanted to use in situations where they were needed, that is job satisfaction; and,

- like the French Foreign Legion of old, there were those who just saw it as a means to get away.

There were probably other reasons held by a few individuals. The reason for being there did not matter. Getting the job done was what would be required of everyone.

Somehow, against all odds, we in UNAMET had organised and conducted a popular consultation on the basis of a direct, secret and universal ballot, to ascertain whether the East Timorese people accept the proposed constitutional framework providing for a special autonomy for East Timor within the unity Republic of Indonesia or reject the proposed special autonomy for East Timor, leading to East Timor's separation from Indonesia, in accordance with the General Agreement and to enable the Secretary-General to discharge his responsibility under paragraph 3 of the Security Agreement. In simple terms they completed the UN Mandate.

The people involved where -

- 210 UN employees;
- 271 Civilian Police from 28 nations;
- 50 Military Liaison Officers from 15 nations;
- 422 UN Volunteers from 67 nations; and,
- the locally employed staff; 668 core staff with an additional 401 hired for 20 days voter registration period and a further 3,600 for the five-day period before and after the ballot.

With a turnout of over 98% of registered voters, the people of East Timor told the world what they wanted; by a huge margin they voted for independence.

The full contingent during the pre-deployment training program

Members of the 1st Australian Federal Police Detachment to UNAMET

Commander Anthony Kevin CURTIS

Superintendents

Darryl John GOSSIP
Geoffrey Alan HAZEL
Phillip John HUTSON
Stephen Granado POLDEN

Sergeants

David John BACHI
Donald Richard BARNBY
Shaun Barry BENNETTS
David Richard BOSTON
Neil Roald BURNAGE
Kevin Brett BURRELL
Kendelle Meredith CLARK
Andrew David CLARKE
Christopher COOPER
Gregory James CORIN
Aaron Marcus CRABTREE
Sean DUNN
Andrew Charles EACOTT
Veronica Josephine ELTON
Kate Louise FERRY
Anthony Graham FOWLER
Robert GILLILAND
David Charles HALL
Martin Christopher HESS
Sandra Lee HOFFSCHILDT
Peter Francis HOLDER
Phillip Anthony HUNTER
Robert John HUNTER
Fiona JAMIESON
Raymond Charles JOHNSON
Max William Paul KNOTH
Alan Raymond LELIEVRE
Craig Lovell MANN
Sharon McCARTHY
Paul Alexander McEWAN
Brad Thomas McKEEKING
Christopher William MEAGHER
Paul John MORRIS
Irene Elizabeth MENHENNITT
Paul Christopher MULQUEENEY
Thomas Nicholas O'BRIEN
Terence Robert PARKER
Keith John RANDALL
David Harry SAVAGE
Wayne Thomas SIEVERS
Ian Ross STANDISH
Brett Robert SWAN
John Peter TANTI
Alfred Noel TURKETO
Peter Ian WATT
Ian Francis WHYTE
Brendon Ronald WITHERS.